A Text Book Of

PHARMACEUTICAL ANALYSIS

INSTRUMENTAL METHODS

Volume–II

Dr. A. V. KASTURE

Professor, and Former Head of the
Department of Pharmaceutical Sciences,
Nagpur University,
NAGPUR - 440 010.

Dr. K. R. MAHADIK

Professor, Pharmaceutical Chemistry,
Bharati Vidyapeeth Deemed University,
Poona College of Pharmacy,
Erandwane,
PUNE - 411 038.

Dr. S. G. WADODKAR

Head of the Department of Pharmaceutical Sciences,
Nagpur University,
NAGPUR - 440 010

Dr. H. N. MORE

Professor, Pharmaceutical Chemistry,
Bharati Vidyapeeth College of Pharmacy,
KOLHAPUR - 416 013

NIRALI PRAKASHAN
ADVANCEMENT OF KNOWLEDGE

N1292

Pharmaceutical Analysis - II   **ISBN 978-81-85790-08-4**

Twenty Third Edition : January 2016

© : Authors

Published By :

NIRALI PRAKASHAN

Abhyudaya Pragati, 1312, Shivaji Nagar,
Off J.M. Road, PUNE – 411005
Tel - (020) 25512336/37/39, Fax - (020) 25511379
Email : niralipune@pragationline.com

☞ DISTRIBUTION CENTRES

PUNE

Nirali Prakashan : 119, Budhwar Peth, Jogeshwari Mandir Lane, Pune 411002, Maharashtra
Tel : (020) 2445 2044, 66022708, Fax : (020) 2445 1538
Email : bookorder@pragationline.com, niralilocal@pragationline.com

Nirali Prakashan : S. No. 28/27, Dhyari, Near Pari Company, Pune 411041
Tel : (020) 24690204 Fax : (020) 24690316
Email : dhyari@pragationline.com, bookorder@pragationline.com

MUMBAI

Nirali Prakashan : 385, S.V.P. Road, Rasdhara Co-op. Hsg. Society Ltd.,
Girgaum, Mumbai 400004, Maharashtra
Tel : (022) 2385 6339 / 2386 9976, Fax : (022) 2386 9976
Email : niralimumbai@pragationline.com

☞ DISTRIBUTION BRANCHES

JALGAON

Nirali Prakashan : 34, V. V. Golani Market, Navi Peth, Jalgaon 425001,
Maharashtra, Tel : (0257) 222 0395, Mob : 94234 91860

KOLHAPUR

Nirali Prakashan : New Mahadvar Road, Kedar Plaza, 1st Floor Opp. IDBI Bank
Kolhapur 416 012, Maharashtra. Mob : 9850046155

NAGPUR

Pratibha Book Distributors : Above Maratha Mandir, Shop No. 3, First Floor,
Rani Jhanshi Square, Sitabuldi, Nagpur 440012, Maharashtra
Tel : (0712) 254 7129

DELHI

Nirali Prakashan : 4593/21, Basement, Aggarwal Lane 15, Ansari Road, Daryaganj
Near Times of India Building, New Delhi 110002
Mob : 08505972553

BENGALURU

Pragati Book House : House No. 1, Sanjeevappa Lane, Avenue Road Cross,
Opp. Rice Church, Bengaluru – 560002.
Tel : (080) 64513344, 64513355,Mob : 9880582331, 9845021552
Email:bharatsavla@yahoo.com

CHENNAI

Pragati Books : 9/1, Montieth Road, Behind Taas Mahal, Egmore,
Chennai 600008 Tamil Nadu, Tel : (044) 6518 3535,
Mob : 94440 01782 / 98450 21552 / 98805 82331,
Email : bharatsavla@yahoo.com

niralipune@pragationline.com | www.pragationline.com

Also find us on f www.facebook.com/niralibooks

Preface to the Twenty Third Edition

We express our gratitude to the faculty members and students for their response to the new edition of this book. We are thankful for the suggestions received while revising this book.

General plan of the book remains the same; however some chapters have been revised in the present edition; necessary additions have been made wherever deemed appropriate.

It is hoped that the instant edition will be useful to the teachers and the taught. Suggestions for the improvement of the book will be deeply appreciated.

Authors

Preface to the First Edition

Analytical Chemistry has gained prominence over these years, as this branch has undergone technical innovations and enrichments. Newer instrumental techniques have undoubtedly added immensely to penetrative chemical estimations, not only of the active ingredient but also the quantification of related compounds or impurities in incoming chemicals, drug materials and formulations.

Good manufacturing practices in drug industry demand a zero defective approach in the analytical field. This necessarily means development of reliable, competent, precise, sensitive and selective methods for arriving at a decision to release or reject the incoming drug material and their formulations. The quality control is therefore, the last line of defense for the protection of human health by satisfying the required prerequisites like purity, strength, stability, efficiency and safety of the dosage forms. To study the degradation pattern and drug-drug interactions, the competent analytical methods are necessary.

The purpose of "Pharmaceutical Analysis Vol. II" is to provide the coverage of instrumental methods of analysis. The material presented here is mainly designed for students of Graduate/Postgraduate level in Pharmaceutical sciences and also for the researchers in another field of Pharmaceutical sciences who want to increase their understanding of modern techniques of Pharmaceutical analysis. This book is also useful as reference manual for Quality control chemists, Research and development workers in Pharmaceutical Industry.

Each chapter consists of precise discussion of theory, instrumentation and Pharmaceutical Applications. Unnecessary detailed description is avoided to keep the size of the book. Chapters 2 to 9 are devoted to Chromatographic techniques. Electroanalytical and other miscellaneous techniques have been duly covered. Furthermore, spectroscopic techniques are also presented.

We shall be grateful to all the teachers and students who will be kind enough in pin-pointing mistakes that have escaped our attention. Suggestions for the further improvement will be highly appreciated.

Pune   **Authors**

25.12.95

Contents ...

***

CHAPTER ... 1

INTRODUCTION TO INSTRUMENTAL TECHNIQUES

INTRODUCTION

Logical reasoning to determine the quantity and quality of the ingredients used in a pharmaceutical formulation is **Pharmaceutical analysis**. This involves quantitative and qualitative analysis of a given pharmaceutical. The qualitative analysis gives the information about the quality of the sample while the quantitative analysis reveals the ingredients present in the pharmaceutical product. To achieve this instruments are used to arrive at correct analysis. This chapter focuses on such instrumental techniques.

Analytical methods are generally classified into instrumental and non-instrumental category. In the former, measurement of some physical property is made to determine the contents or composition of a substance, while in non-instrumental, the conventional physico-chemical properties are used to analyze the sample. The non-instrumental methods which are primarily based upon the measurement of mass and/or volume are also called as chemical methods; and include the techniques of volumetric and gravimetric analysis. These even now continue to occupy their place in analytical technique because of simplicity, ease and reproducibility. The instrumental methods of analysis are based upon the measurement of some physical property of substance using instrument to determine its chemical composition. Table 1.1 gives the list of measurement of physical properties and the instrumental method adopted.

Table 1.1: Physical Property and Instrumental Method

Physical Property measured	Instrumental Method adopted
Electrical potential	Potentiometry
Electrical conductance	Conductometry
Quantity of electricity	Coulometry, Electrogravimetry
Electrical current	Polarography, Amperometry, Coulometry
Absorption of radiation	UV, visible, IR spectrophotometry, Atomic absorption spectrophotometry, Nuclear magnetic resonance spectrophotometry.
Emission of radiation	Emission spectroscopy, Flame photometry, Fluorometry, Radiochemical methods.

Physical Property measured	Instrumental Method adopted
Scattering of radiation	Turbidimetry, Nephelometry, Raman spectroscopy.
Refraction of radiation	Refractometry, Interferometry.
Rotation of radiation	Polarimetry, Optical rotatory dispersion, Circular dichroism.
Diffraction of radiation	X-ray diffraction method.
Thermal properties	Thermo Gravimetric Analysis (TGA), Differential Scanning Colorimetry (DSC).
Mass to charge ratio	Mass spectrometry.

Physical property of a substance may be specific or non-specific. In both cases, appropriate measurements are made and their signals converted into units which are used for determination of structure or concentration.

Instruments used in chemical analysis are unique in their function. They do not give direct quantitative data but supplies information which can be converted into a suitable form which correlates with the structure or the content. Thus, it acts as a communicative device.

It consists of the following steps:

1. **Generation of signal:** Signal generator usually gives the signal which is indicative of the component and its concentration. In case of pH meter, the hydrogen ion concentration from the solution acts as a signal generator. In colorimeter, the colour of the solution and the radiation source are the signal generator.

2. **Transformation of signal into measurable form or unit:** The signal generated is converted into a more conveniently measurable unit by use of transducers. In pH meter, the glass calomel electrode converts the signal into electrical potential while in the case of colorimeters, spectrophotometers, the radiant energy is converted into electrical energy with the help of the thermocouples, phototubes, photo multiplier tubes etc.

3. **Amplification of the transducer signal:** Signal processors generally modify the transducer signal to make it more convenient for operation. Generally, it involves amplification of signal. This amplification is many times done electronically to increase the sensitivity.

4. **Readout system:** The transducer and amplified signal is presented as a displacement along the scale or on the chart of the recorder. It involves the

deflection of needle of galvanometer, deflection of light from mirror of the galvanometer, or displacement of meniscus of burette or blackening of photographic phase. It generally converts processed signal into an observable signal.

With the development of instrumentation analysis, electronics has been greatly developed. Modern analytical instruments employ microprocessors, computers, amplifiers, integrated circuits to get a rapid and reproducible signal every time.

It is essential for every instrument that it should give rapid response and the response should be quantitative and proportional to the information it receives. From the generation of signal, its amplification and converting into display signals, etc. a great deal of electronic circuits are involved in instruments. Instrumental methods have their advantages and limitations in analytical field. Considering the pros and cons of an instrument, it is employed in analytical studies.

ADVANTAGES OF INSTRUMENTAL METHODS

(a) A small amount of a sample is needed for analysis.

(b) Determination by instrumental method is considerably fast.

(c) Complex mixture can be analyzed either with or without their separation.

(d) The instrumental method gives reliable and accurate results.

(e) When non-instrumental method is not possible, instrumental method is the only answer to the problem.

LIMITATIONS OF INSTRUMENTAL METHODS

(a) In general, instrumental methods are costly because of cost, maintenance and trained personnel required for their handling.

(b) The sensitivity and accuracy depends upon the type of instrument.

(c) Specialized training for handling instrument is required.

(d) Besides instrumental methods, other methods are recourse for checking results.

(e) In some cases, instrumental method may not be specific.

It is very clear after surveying the development in the field of analysis, that instrumental method of analysis has occupied a prominent place. Every new edition of pharmacopoeia IP, BP or USP and a number of books in analytical chemistry is a testimony to the importance of instrumental methods. British Pharmacopoeia and the USP have introduced the use of IR as one of the tests for identification of compounds. In quantitative analysis, more than fifty percent official compounds are now analyzed by instrumental methods.

Instrumental methods are not only important in pharmaceutical analysis for analyzing basic drugs or chemicals or its formulations but play significant role in other fields also. Various instruments are used as diagnostic tool in medical profession without which diagnosis of disease and its treatment would not have been possible e.g. X-rays, ultrasound, NMR, scanning instruments, laser beam, etc. Furthermore, in clinical analysis of biological fluids, tissue and organ analysis, toxicological and forensic analysis, instruments are widely used.

In pharmaceutical field, instruments are not only used for qualitative and quantitative analysis but they find extensive use in manufacture of various drug formulations from their controlled release and therapeutic value. The role and usefulness of instruments in other areas and fields is endless.

CHAPTER ... 2

CHROMATOGRAPHY

INTRODUCTION

A variety of methods are available for the separation of components from the mixture and to analyse them. There are two methods for analysis:

1. Chemical Methods
2. Physical Methods.

The physical methods include:

(a) Fractional distillation
(b) Extraction
(c) Countercurrent distribution
(d) Fractional precipitation
(e) Crystallization etc.

These methods are effective in separation, purification and identification of many compounds. However, difficulty arises in case of compounds where individual components have similar physical and chemical properties i.e. mixture of liquids having very close boiling points, etc. However, these methods are not satisfactory in biological materials.

Chromatographic methods represent the most useful and powerful technique for these problems. They are used for the separation of components of a complex mixture. Because of the rapidity and effectiveness, chromatography has been used in all the fields e.g. chemistry, biology, medicine, dyes, forensics and clinical studies with advantages over other methods.

A salient advantage of chromatographic methods is that they are relatively 'gentle' and disallow the decomposition of substances. This is important especially for labile substances and substances of biological origin.

Another advantage is that the separations can be carried out on micro or semi-micro scale, i.e. a small quantity of mixture is required for analysis.

Chromatographic techniques are simple, rapid and require simple apparatus. The complex mixtures can be handled with comparative ease.

Chromatographic separation relies on relative movement of two phases, similar to fractional distillation or countercurrent distribution, but in chromatography one phase is stationary phase and the other is mobile. The mobile phase passes over the stationary phase and transports components of the mixture at different speeds in the direction of the flow of mobile phase. The separation of components is a result of the differential affinity of the components for the mobile phase and a stationary phase.

Definition: The term chromatography (Greek Kromatos – colour and Graphos – written) meaning colour writing.

Tswett (1906) defined *Chromatography as the method in which the components of a mixture are separated on an adsorbent column in a flowing system. Recently, the IUPAC has defined Chromatography as "A method used primarily for the separation of the components of a sample, in which the components are distributed between two phases, one of which is stationary while the other mobile. The stationary phase may be a solid or a liquid supported on a solid or a gel, and may be packed in a column, spread as a layer or distributed as a film. The mobile phase may be gaseous or liquid."*

HISTORY

The study of chromatography started in the eighteenth century when Runge studied with great interest the nature of inorganic compounds on filter papers. He separated inorganic salts and observed that inorganic salts travel to different extent producing attractive pattern. In the year 1898, Day in the USA forced crude petroleum through a column of limestone and fuller's earth. He observed that first portion was of light hydrocarbons, followed by hydrocarbons of aromatic nature, unsaturated type, heterocyclic and nitrogen-sulphur containing high molecular weight hydrocarbons.

The Russian botanist, Michael Tswett discovered the chromatographic principle in 1906, he used a glass column of calcium carbonate for separation of chlorophyll pigments from plant by using petroleum ether. The pigments, according to their adsorption patterns, were resolved into various coloured zones; he then separated and estimated them.

Between 1910 and 1930, very little work was published about chromatography. The major development occurred around 1930 when Lederer and co-workers in 1931, separated lutein and xanthenes on a column of calcium carbonate powder. Further developments soon followed when Kuhn, Karrer, and Ruzicka, separated plant carotenes into several components by adsorption chromatography. This helped in resolution of naturally occurring mixture of pigments, sugars, amino acids, proteins, vitamins and hormones. This led to the development of absorption and partition column chromatography for identification, separation, isolation, both on preparative and analytical scale.

In 1935, Adams and Holmes observed some synthetic ion exchange resins capable of exchanging ions and thus ion exchange chromatography came into existence.

Tiselius (1940) and Claesson (1946) studied the properties of solutions in the chromatographic process classified these into three groups based on the principle of separation:

    (a) Frontal analysis   (b) Displacement analysis and
    (c) Elution analysis.

Tiselius was awarded the Nobel Prize for this achievement in the year 1948.

Another broad type of chromatography, involving partition between two liquids was proposed by Martin and Synge in 1941. They used chromatographic column, filled it with silica gel particles with water retained on silica gel and passed chloroform flowing through the column. This system successfully separated the acetylated amino acids according to their partition coefficient.

In 1944, Martin, Consden, Gorden replaced silica gel column by strips of filter paper and developed Paper Chromatography. For this achievement, they were awarded the Nobel Prize in 1952.

Thin layer chromatography though discovered first by Izmailer and Shraiber, was further developed by Stahl and co-workers using silica gel on glass plates. They successfully demonstrated the usefulness of TLC in separation of a wide variety of substances.

Reversed phase paper chromatography was then devised wherein the paper is impregnated with a hydrophobic liquid and aqueous phase (or polar) liquid is used as mobile phase. This technique is used for separation of materials having poor solubility in water.

Amongst the latest and the most effective chromatographic technique is Gas Chromatography. It was introduced by Martin and James in 1952. The components of the mixture migrate at different speeds when carried along by an inert gas which acts as mobile phase. This method is more advantageous than other methods in speed, accuracy, sensitivity and versatility. The instrumentation of gas chromatography followed in the wake; presently this technique is used in routine separation and identification of compounds.

The theoretical aspects of chromatography were first studied by Wilson in 1949, he discussed the quantitative aspects in terms of diffusion, rate of adsorption and isotherm, non-linearity, etc. Glueckauf in 1949, described the column performance in terms of stationary phase, particle size and diffusion. However, it was Van Deemter and co-workers, who in 1956 developed the rate theory to describe the separation process. Giddings in 1963, pointed out that if the efficiencies of gas chromatography were to be achieved in liquid chromatography, and then particle sizes of 2.20 μm were required, this would entail high mobile phase inlet pressure. This led to the discovery of High Pressure (performance) Liquid Chromatography (HPLC).

There has been continuous development in chromatography particularly in techniques, materials and requirement of instrumentation which has resulted in the efficient, reliable and sensitive chromatographic methods in use today. The latest development in chromatography is HPTLC technique.

CLASSIFICATION

In all types of chromatography, separation of the components of a mixture results either by adsorption or partition for the column material. Binding of a compound to the surface of solid phase takes place in adsorption while in partition, a compound gets distributed into two liquid phases. The usual type of chromatography involves movement of liquid phase over stationary phase carrying with it, a solute which has varying degree of affinity for stationary phase. Thus, depending upon two phases, the chromatographic methods are classified as:

I. Partition chromatography:

This involves liquid or gas as mobile phase and another liquid or solid as a stationary phase.

The operations include:

1. Partition column chromatography.
2. Paper chromatography.
3. Thin layer chromatography.
4. Gas-liquid chromatography.
5. High performance liquid chromatography.

II. Adsorption chromatography:

This involves liquid or gas as mobile phase and adsorbent solid as stationary phase. The types under this category include:

1. Adsorption column chromatography
2. Thin layer chromatography
3. Gas-solid chromatography.

Alternatively, chromatographic operations can be classified as follows:

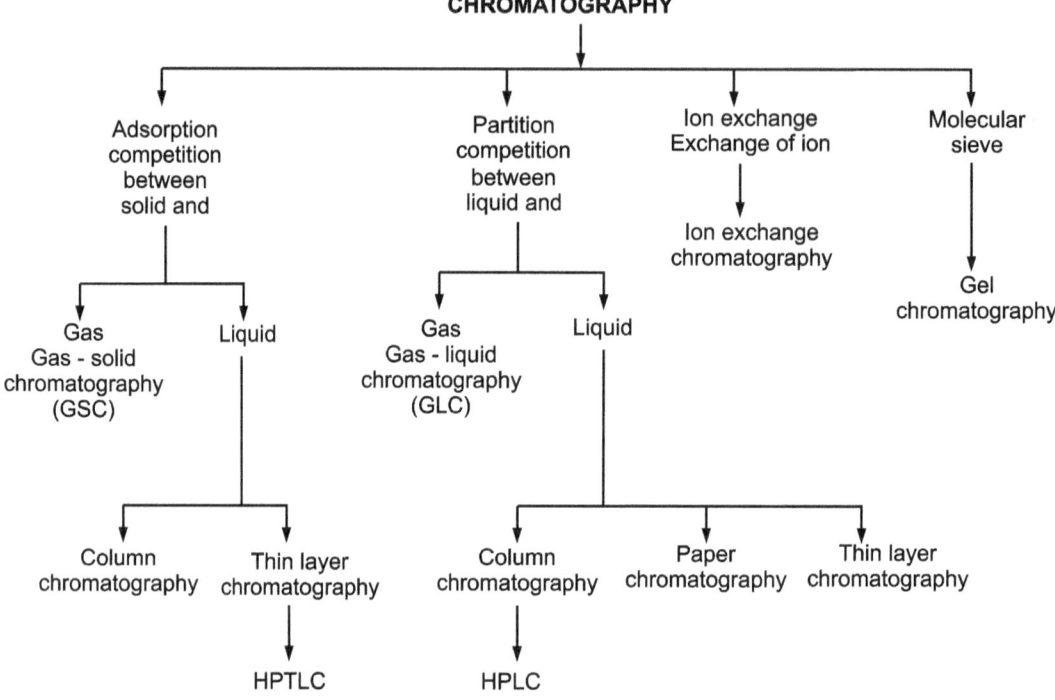

SEPARATION TECHNIQUES

All chromatographic methods are meant to separate two or more components from the mixture, which methods are executed by distribution of components between stationary and mobile phase. Chromatographic separation can be effected by the following techniques:

1. Elution Analysis: It is a very common method used in column chromatography. In this method, a small volume of mixture to be separated is added on the top of column and mobile phase is allowed to flow through column. As mobile phase moves down the column, the mixture introduced on the column gets separated into zones as the components of mixture are adsorbed to the column material to different extent (Fig. 2.1 (a), (b)). On further passage of mobile phase each component of mixture is eluted out as separated component.

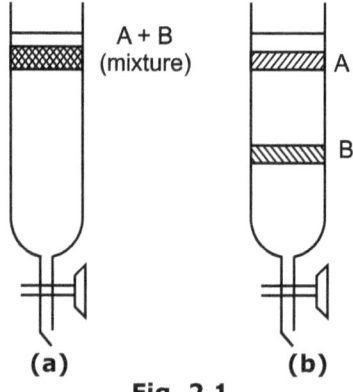

(a)   **(b)**

Fig. 2.1

The graph (Fig. 2.2) shows separated out amount against volume of elute fractions, this is elution analysis.

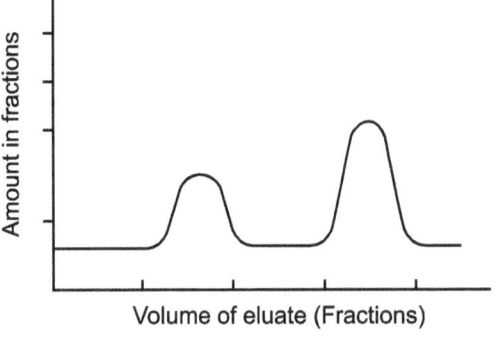

Fig. 2.2

2. Frontal Analysis: In this method, the solution of sample mixture is added continuously on the column. No mobile phase (solvent) is used for development of column.

A mixture containing *A, B* and *C* is added on the column. If component *A* is least adsorbed; component *B* to intermediate extent and component *C* most strongly to the column material, then as the mixture flows through the column, the least adsorbed *A* runs down the column fast; component *B* to intermediate stage and *C* remains at the top of the column. When more sample mixture passes through column, first few fractions of eluate will contain *A*, subsequent fractions will contain *A + B* and the final or the last *A + B + C*. Only partial separation of *A* from *B* and *C* occurs. A complete separation of *A, B* and *C* cannot be achieved unless the fractions are again developed on another column.

A plot of amount of substance against volume of eluate is shown in Fig. 2.3.

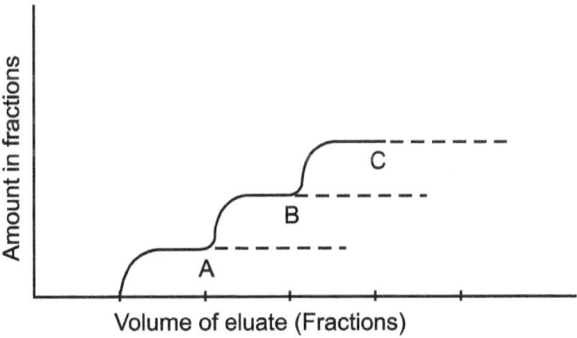

Fig. 2.3

Tiselius developed this technique in 1940.

3. Displacement Analysis: In displacement analysis, a small volume of mixture is added to the column and elution is carried out by a solvent containing a solute which has high absorptivities for column material. The adsorbed constituents of mixture are displaced by the solute from mobile phase. Each solute in the mixture in turn displaces another solute which is less firmly adsorbed. The least adsorbed constituent is pushed out of the column. The substance used in mobile phase is called as displacer; hence, the technique is known as "displacement analysis".

In separation of mixture containing *A, B* and *C* (with *A < B < C* adsorption), if *D* is used as displacer, then the plot of amount of substance against volume of eluate will be as shown in Fig. 2.4.

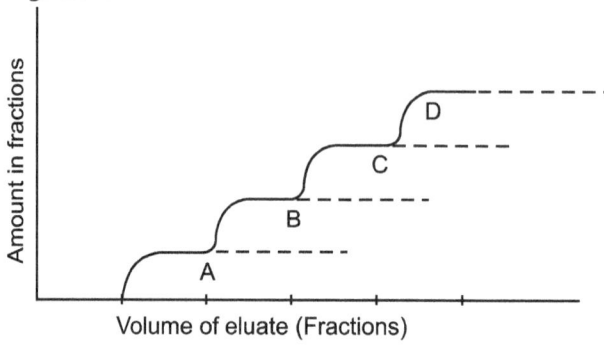

Fig. 2.4

This technique is mainly used in preparative work; hence, not suitable for analysis since there are chances of overlapping forasmuch as zones are not distinctly separated.

CHOICE OF METHOD

The choice of the method is by and large empirical as there is no way of predicting the best procedure for separation, except in some simple cases. It is useful to try simpler techniques as paper or TLC first as they can often provide a useful guide to the type of system to be used for separation. The more sophisticated technique can then be applied or adopted. The following list gives a rough guideline for the choice of method:

1. Substances of similar chemical type.	Partition chromatography.
2. Substances of different chemical type.	Adsorption chromatography.
3. Gases and volatile substances.	Gas chromatography.
4. Ionic and inorganic substances.	Ion exchange chromatography, or column, paper or thin layer chromatography.
5. Ionic from non-ionic substances	Ion exchange or gel chromatography.
6. Biological materials, compounds of high molecular weight.	Gel chromatography, electrophoresis.

In the event of difficult separations, when simpler methods are inadequate, High Performance Liquid Chromatography (HPLC) may provide the results.

CHAPTER ... 3

COLUMN CHROMATOGRAPHY

Chromatography is a technique employed for separation of the components of a mixture by continuous distribution of the components between two phases: mobile and stationary. The mobile phase moves over the stationary phase continuously. When the stationary phase is a solid support of adsorptive nature and mobile phase is liquid or gaseous phase, it is called adsorption chromatography. And when the stationary phase is liquid with the mobile phase as liquid or gaseous, it is called as partition chromatography. When the chromatographic operations are in progress using a column, it is called column chromatography.

There are four types of column chromatography:

1. Adsorption chromatography in which the components of a mixture are selectively adsorbed on the surface of packing column material, i.e. adsorbent.

2. Partition chromatography in which the component is partitioned between the mobile phase and their stationary phase held stationary on inert solid support.

3. Ion exchange chromatography in which the constituent of a sample is selectively retained by exchange resin by replacing ion/s on packing material.

4. Gel chromatography is the method in which the column is packed with a permeable gel which accomplishes separation by sieving or molecular filtration action.

(3. A) ADSORPTION COLUMN CHROMATOGRAPHY

American geologist Day and Russian botanist Tswett are credited with the history of adsorption chromatography. Tswett separated leaf pigments into different coloured bands on calcium carbonate column, while Day achieved fractionation of crude petroleum on limestone. It appears that neither Tswett nor Day was aware of the work of the other pioneers. It was the work of Kuhn and Lederer in 1931 on polygene pigments that renewed interest in chromatography.

Theoretical Principle: The basic principle of adsorption chromatography is adsorption of a component at the solid-liquid interface. For good separation, the component of the mixture should have different degree of affinity for the solid support, i.e. adsorbent and the interaction between adsorbent and component should be reversible. The component which has strong adsorption for column material stays up while that component which has less affinity moves down the column at a faster rate as the eluate passes through the column.

Component of mixture is bound to solid surface by specific interaction between polar groups of molecule on the adsorbing surface. The exterior properties of atoms, ions or molecules of adsorbents differ from the interior. The bonds at the surface layer are perturbed and have higher energy level. This is called surface activity. The attractive forces may be ionic (electrostatic), dipole-dipole, dipole-induced dipole or simple London forces. Thus, the solute from the solution when comes into contact, gets adsorbed on the surface. Usually, the surface loses activity when it is covered by a monolayer of adsorbed species.

Adsorption isotherm, similar to partition coefficient, can be determined for a solute. A plot of equilibrium concentration of species in a solution and that of amount adsorbed is called adsorption isotherm. It can be shown as a graph of amount adsorbed (C_m) *vs.* amount in mobile phase (C_m) at a constant or fixed temperature. Usually, three types of adsorption isotherms are observed.

1. **Linear adsorption isotherm:** It is a linear graph indicating the amount of substance adsorbed per gram of adsorbent proportional to the concentration of solution, i.e. $k = C_s/C_m$.

2. **Convex adsorption isotherm:** This is due to variation in activity of adsorbent and shows that system is not linear.

3. **Concave adsorption isotherm:** In this, the adsorption from strong solution is greater than the weak solutions. The additional reaction that takes on an adsorption enhances overall adsorption process.

For satisfactory separation technique, the linear adsorption isotherm is ideal.

OPERATIONAL TECHNIQUE

Generally, in this technique, the mixture to be separated is taken in a suitable solvent and a small amount of the solution is added to the uniformly packed column with an adsorbent. The sample is allowed to enter the column. A suitable developing solvent is added on the top of the column and the solvent allowed to run down.

During the process, the component with higher adsorption is retained at the top while the one having less adsorption runs down the column. The procedure is continued till the components are successfully separated out. The ease of displacement of the solute molecule will depend on the absorptivities of the solute and polarity of developing solvents. Either the material is separated as bands on the column or eluted out of column.

The practical considerations of a successful technique can be considered as:

1. Columns:

Chromatographic columns can be obtained commercially with spring loaded stopcocks with a sintered glass disc at the bottom. Generally a length to breadth ratio of 5 : 1 or 8 : 1 is good enough for optimal separation. A stopcock fitted to a column is desirable as it allows control of flow rate of solvent. A small plug of glass wool or a porous plate is used at the bottom to support the adsorbent used in the column (Fig. 3.1). In those cases where the substance undergoes oxidation in the presence of air, a flow of neutral gas such as nitrogen is maintained during the operation. The small size columns are only few mm in diameter and few cm in length while large columns are several cm in diameter and correspondingly greater in length.

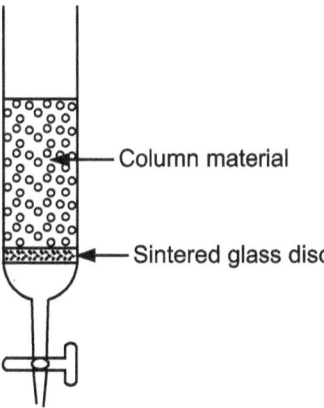

Fig. 3.1

2. Adsorbents:

Many solid organic and inorganic substances are used as adsorbents such as alumina, silica gel, kieselguhr, magnesium oxide, calcium carbonate, calcium phosphate, carbon, starch, sugar, cellulose etc. The selection cannot be made at random as there are various factors which guide their choice. The ideal properties for the adsorbent materials are:

1. There should not be any reaction with the substance to be separated.
2. It should be insoluble with the solution under test and solvents used for elution.
3. It should not catalyze the decomposition of substance.
4. It should be a colourless, uniform in size and shape.
5. Its properties should be uniform and remain so during experimental operations.
6. It should have high mechanical stability.

Adsorbents can be classified according to their activity:

1. Weak adsorbent – Sucrose, Cellulose, Starch, Talc etc.
2. Intermediate adsorbent – Calcium carbonate, Calcium phosphate, Magnesia, Slaked lime, Silica gel etc.
3. Strong adsorbent – Alumina, Fuller's Earth, Charcoal.

The commonly used adsorbents are listed in Table 3.1 below with the types of compounds separated with their aid.

Table 3.1: Adsorbents used in column chromatography

Adsorbent	Used to separate
Alumina, magnesia	Sterols, vitamins, esters, alkaloids
Silica gel	Sterols, amino acids
Carbon	Amino acids, peptides, carbohydrates
Magnesium carbonate	Porphyrins
Magnesium silicate	Alkaloids, esters, glycerides, sterols
Calcium carbonate	Xanthophylls, carotenoid
Aluminium silicate	Sterols
Starch	Enzymes

Alumina is preferred for separation and analytical work, its advantage being that it can be used many times and again by regeneration.

Alumina surface is capable of exhibiting different types of solute-sorbent interaction because of its strong positive fields surrounding the Al^{3+} which allow interaction with easily polarizable molecules, or due to the presence of basic sites (probably O^{2-}) which allow interaction with proton donors. Charcoal and magnesia can be used successfully in chromatography.

3. Preparation of Adsorbents:

Since, adsorbents need activation before use, adsorbents such as alumina and carbon can be activated by heating in vacuum for the loss of water and other adsorbed material. Generally, there is an optimum temperature for activation, e.g. alumina (about 400°C). The period of heating is also important, as long time heating will lose its activity. Three to four hours is usually sufficient. In most cases, heating at 200°C for four hours is safe and desirable for most solids.

If freshly activated solid proves too active for separation, deactivation may be carried out by controlled addition of water. Powdered sugar, sieved and dried in a desiccator has been used for the separation of colouring matters.

4. Developers:

These are the compounds or reagents used for the production of colour for colourless substances. These substances should have less affinity for adsorbents than the components to be separated on column. The general reagents such as hydrogen sulphide, ammonium sulphide, potassium ferricyanide, potassium thiocyanate etc. are used as developers.

5. Solvents:

The success of chromatographic analysis depends upon the solid adsorbent and the solvent mobile phase. Solvent plays an important role. Solvents are used:

1. to transfer the mixture to the column,
2. to effect the process of the development of chromatogram by which the zones are separated to the highest possible extent and,
3. for the complete elution.

The solvent plays an active part in the adsorption process and competes with the sample molecules for active sites on the adsorbent. Thus, the stronger the binding of solvent molecules, greater the amount of time the solute molecules spend in the mobile phase and hence they are eluted faster.

Solvent employed in elution may be single pure solvent or a mixture of solvents or the different solvents at different stages.

The choice of solvent is mainly influenced by the nature and solubility of the mixture. It is always better to choose a solvent of indifferent eluting power so that strongest eluting solvent can be tried at the end. Generally for polar adsorbents such as alumina and silica gel, the strength of adsorption increases with polarity of adsorbate. For carbon, the order is reversed. The sequence of solvents used is in the following sequence:

Petroleum ether	Chloroform
Carbon tetrachloride	Alcohols
Cyclohexane	Pyridine
Carbon disulphide	Acetic acid
Ether	Mixtures of acids or base with water
Acetone	
Benzene	
Organic esters	

The eluting power of the solvent is practically parallel to its dielectric constant. Solvents should satisfy the practical factors such as viscosity, stability, compatibility, solubility and purity. Significant factor is that the solvent should provide maximum separation in minimum time.

6. Packing the columns:

Packing the column uniformly is one of the important ingredients for successful chromatography. This will enable minimizing the distortion of the chromatographic boundaries. For open tubular chromatography, the size of the packing particles should be > 150 μm to obtain acceptable flow rates. Channeling is usually caused by the inclusion of air bubbles during packing.

There are two methods used for packing the columns. They are: (a) Wet Packing and (b) Dry Packing.

(a) Wet packing: (Fig. 3.2) Wet packing is common with adsorbents like alumina, magnesia etc. In this case, the slurry of adsorbent with the solvent is prepared and is poured into the glass column having glass wool or a sintered disc at the lower end; the cotton plug too can be used. The slurry with the solvent is poured until the desired height of column is achieved. When adsorbent settles down, a filter paper disc and washed sand is placed at the top and the solvent is allowed to run down until the liquid level is about 1 cm above the top level of the column. The filter paper and sand prevent the disturbances in column when fresh mobile phase is added. The liquid level should never be below the adsorbent; otherwise cracks will develop rendering the column useless.

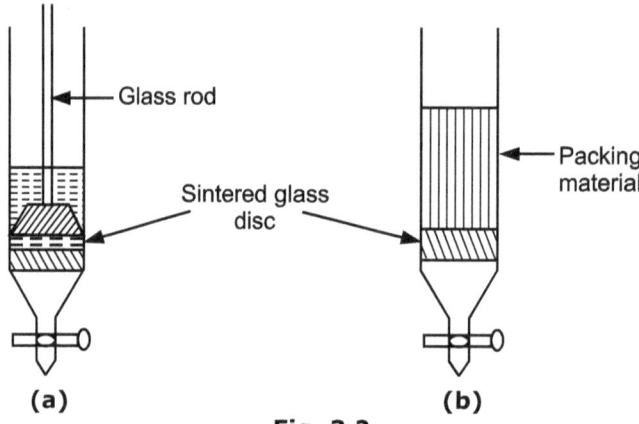

(a)   **(b)**

Fig. 3.2

(b) Dry packing: In this, adsorbent is poured as fine dry powder in column. The column is tapped regularly and carefully during the filling. This is continued until columns of desired height are available. Solvent is added to the column and it is allowed to run down. Air which is trapped in the column is removed by tapping technique (Fig. 3.2 (b)).

7. Application of the sample:

It is important to apply the sample to the top of the column as evenly as possible. Application of the sample can be made by a small pipette whose tip is placed against the column wall just above the surface of the adsorbent (Fig. 3.3). Another method is to use one or two small discs of volatile solvent soaked filter paper. The discs are placed on the top of column.

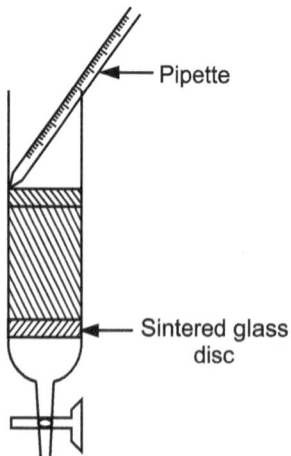

Fig. 3.3

ELUTION PROCEDURES

There are three principle elution procedures commonly employed: (a) isocratic, (b) stepwise elution and (c) gradient elution.

(a) Isocratic elution: In this, a solvent mixture of unvarying composition is allowed to run through the column until separation is complete. The process is terminated when different coloured bands are observed on the column. The contents of the column can now be extruded and the separated constituents extracted by means of suitable solvent. Isolation of the bands is facilitated by the use of transparent nylon tube as the column container. The contents of the column after completion are separated by cutting the tube into sections. An alternative and more commonly used method is to allow the column to run until the separated components can be detected in the column effluent (eluate).

(b) Stepwise or fractional elution: In fractional elution, only one solvent is used; this will result into elution of only some of the components of the mixture. Hence, to remove components which are firmly held, a stronger eluting solvent will be required. Sometimes it becomes necessary to use several different solvents to increase polarity for the successive displacement of different components. This is stepwise elution. The advantage of this technique is that sharper separations are obtained. However, the disadvantage is that a given compound may give rise to more than one peak in the successive steps.

(c) Gradient elution: This technique was first described by Williams and Tiselius which involves the use of a continuously changing eluting medium. The effect of this gradient is to elute successively the more strongly adsorbed substances at the same time to reduce tailing. Thus, the chromatographic bands will become more concentrated and occupy less of the column. Currently, microprocessor controlled solvent delivery modules are available which can generate the required gradient profile for stepwise, linear or isocratic development.

8. Detectors:

For quantitative determination of the dissolved substances in an eluate there are various detectors used: refractometer, colorimeter, spectrophotometer, flame ionization detectors, conductivity detectors etc. The elutes are collected separately. Substances which are colourless in ordinary light but fluoresce strongly in UV light are detected by UV lamps and fluorimeter.

FACTORS AFFECTING COLUMN EFFICIENCY

It is frequently necessary to separate two or more very closely related substances having close chromatographic properties. The various factors which affect the column efficiency are:

1. **Dimensions of the column:** Column efficiency is improved by increasing the length/width ratio of column. Recently length/width ratio of 10 : 1 to

100 : 1 is found to be most satisfactory. For successful separations sample/column packing ratio ranges from 1 : 20 to 1 : 100.

2. **Particle size of column packing:** It is possible to improve the efficiency by decreasing the particle size. This may decrease the flow rate. Particles from 100–200 mesh are generally satisfactory.

3. **Pore diameter of column packing:** Polar adsorbents have been found to have a pore diameter $\leq$ 20 A°. The decrease in average pore diameter from 17–20 A° doesn't impair the efficiency.

4. **Temperature:** The speed of elution increases at high temperature as adsorption is highly reduced. However, column chromatography is preferably carried out at room temperature. Recovery of sample can be increased by decreasing the temperature. Difficultly soluble samples are generally separated at higher temperature.

5. **Quality or Nature of Solvents:** Usually, solvents having low viscosity are chosen for higher efficiency as the rate of flow is inversely proportional to the viscosity. Solvents of proper viscosity, good elution power and good quality are selected.

6. **Packing the column:** The packing of the column should be uniform. It should neither be too firm nor too loose. There should not be air bubbles or cracks in column, otherwise the separation will not take place properly or tailing will occur.

APPLICATIONS

1. **Separation of mixture of geometrical isomers:** The separation of cis/trans isomers is possible by this technique e.g. separation of cis/trans carotenoid is possible on calcium carbonate column and other adsorbents. The separation is mainly based on stearic factors. Isomers whose functional groups can approach the surface of adsorbent more easily are more strongly adsorbed.

2. Determination of amino acids from protein hydrolyzates.

3. Separation of distereomers, racemates and tautomeric mixtures.

4. Separation of 17-ketosteroids.

5. Separation and analysis of binary drugs in combinations.

(3. B) PARTITION COLUMN CHROMATOGRAPHY

In partition column chromatography, the solid adsorbent is replaced by a packing material comprising a support material coated with a stationary phase. The stationary phase should be immiscible or at the most sparingly miscible with mobile phase. In this technique, the solute gets distributed between the two phases, depending on it's partition coefficient.

The solid support used for stationary phase should be inert to the substances to be separated. The coated solid is packed in columns as in adsorption column chromatography. Desirable properties of satisfactory solid support are as follows:

1. The support material must adsorb and retain the stationary phase.
2. It should expose large surface areas to the mobile phase.
3. It should be mechanically stable and easy to pack into the column when loaded with stationary liquid.
4. It must not obstruct the solvent flow.
5. It should be chemically inert and have uniform size and shape. Practically, there is no support which has all these ideal properties, barring exceptions.

Commonly used supports are:

(a) Silica gel (silicic acid).
(b) Diatomaceous earths (Kieselguhr, Celite etc.) and cellulose.
(c) Starch.
(d) Purified sand.
(e) Brick-powder or glass beads may be used to a limited extent.

Silica gel is most commonly used material with water or a buffered aqueous solution as a stationary phase. The amount of liquid held is about 0.6 cm^3/gm of gel. Silica gel used for chromatography is in the form of a fine white powder with a fairly narrow range of uniform particle size.

Diatomaceous earths are available commercially as Kieselguhr, Celite etc. The amount of liquid stationary phase used with these solids is about 0.8 cm^3/gm. Kieselguhr has very little adsorptive capacity and therefore makes an ideal support for partition chromatography.

Cellulose powder is available ready for use and usually requires no further treatment; not even the addition of the stationary phase, since this is acquired from the aqueous solvent.

The mobile phase in partition chromatography may be a liquid or a gas. The partition principle is involved in separation. It is normal to choose a solvent system so that there is a considerable difference between the solvent strength parameters of the mobile and stationary phases e.g. pentane would be the optimum choice as eluent with water as stationary phase. However, solvent stripping, i.e. stripping/washing off the stationary phase from the column may result over a long period of time. This problem can be overcome by pre-saturating the eluent with the stationary phase before it contacts the packing or by placing a pre-column at the chromatographic-column inlet.

Some typical applications and separations effected with partition columns are given below:

Table 3.2: Applications and Separations with Partition Columns

Support	Stationary phase	Mobile phase	Separation
Silica gel or Kieselguhr	Water	Chloroform, butanol	Acetylated amino acid
Silica gel	Aniline	Iso-propanyl/benzene	Alkenes and cycloalkanes
Cellulose	Water	Methanol, butanol, chloroform	Phenols
Starch	Water	Propanyl, hydrochloric acid	Purines
Silica gel	Water (buffered)	Chloroform/butanol	$C_2 - C_8$ fatty acid.

CHAPTER ... 4

THIN LAYER CHROMATOGRAPHY AND HIGH PERFORMANCE THIN LAYER CHROMATOGRAPHY

INTRODUCTION

Thin layer chromatography (TLC) is so widely used that it has become essential technique for analysts and research workers. TLC is a universal analytical technique in chemical analysis for organic and inorganic matter.

In 1938, Izmailov and Shraiber described the basic principle underlying the process and used it for separation of plant extracts. Consden, Gorden and Martin (1944) started using filter papers instead of open column. Attempts were made using adsorption chromatography on impregnated filter paper and later on glass-fiber, paper coated with silicic acid or alumina. It is Stahl (1958) who is mainly credited with bringing out the work on preparing plates and separation of wide variety of compounds.

Thin layer chromatography is a simple and rapid method carried out using thin layer of adsorbents on plates. TLC not only combines the advantages of paper and column chromatography but in certain aspects it is found to be superior to either method. The advantages are:

1. It requires little equipment.
2. It requires less (less than 1 hour) time for separation while in the case of column and paper, it requires several hours or days.
3. It is more sensitive, i.e. separation effects are usually superior to those of other methods.
4. Lower detection limit of analytical sample in TLC is approximately one decimal lower than that in paper chromatography and very small quantities of sample is sufficient for analysis.
5. Spraying with corrosive agents for identification is permissible, which not possible in paper chromatography as cellulose gets destroyed.
6. Individual samples do not get diffused unlike paper chromatography; hence, sensitivity of detection is more.
7. The method is used for adsorption, partition, ion exchange chromatography as there is wide range of adsorbents available.

8. The components which are separated can be recovered easily by scratching the powdery coating of the plate and quantitative separation of spots or zone is possible.

9. It is possible to visualise the components for identification by UV light as the inorganic adsorbent background does not fluoresce.

10. This method can be applied to preparative separation with the aid of thicker layers of adsorbents.

PRINCIPLE OF THIN LAYER CHROMATOGRAPHY

In the classification of chromatographic methods, TLC has been included under both adsorption and partition chromatographs. As various materials of different adsorptive power are used in TLC, the separation of components is not always by adsorptive phenomenon. Separation may result due to adsorption or partition or by both phenomena depending upon the nature of adsorbents used on plates and solvent system used for development.

TECHNIQUE

In thin layer chromatography, the separation is carried on a glass or plastic plate, which is coated with a thin uniform layer of finely divided inert adsorbent such as silica gel or alumina. The plates are activated, the solution of the sample in a volatile solvent is applied by using a capillary tube or a micropipette to a spot keeping 1-2 cm from the bottom of TLC plate. The position of the sample spot is indicated by marking an 'origin line' on the plate with the lead pencil. When the spot has dried the plate is placed vertically in a suitable tank with its lower end immersed in selected mobile phase. The solvent rises by capillary action, resolving the sample mixture into discrete spots. At the end of the run the solvent is allowed to evaporate from the plate and the separated spots are located and identified by various physical and chemical methods.

(A) Adsorbents:

In the beginning of TLC method, only few coating materials were used as adsorbents such as alumina, silica gel, Kieselguhr etc. However, currently, there is a variety of adsorbents which can be selectively utilized. While choosing the adsorbents, factors to be considered are : (a) characteristic of compounds to be separated, (b) solubility of compounds, (c) nature of substance to be separated i.e. acidic, basic, amphoteric, and (d) to see whether compound is liable to react chemically with adsorbent/solvent, or not. Besides, the two general properties that decide its application are particle size and the homogeneity as the adhesion to the support depends upon them. A particle size of 1-25 μm is preferred.

Adsorbents do not generally adhere to the glass plates satisfactorily; hence, binders like gypsum, starch are added. Gypsum (Calcium sulphate) in 10-15% w/w is widely used as binder for the plates.

(I) Inorganic Adsorbents:

Silica gel is prepared by the hydrolysis of sodium silicate to polysilicic acid which on further condensation and polymerization yields silica gel. Binder (10% w/w) is added to complement mechanical strength to the layer and enhance adhesion to the plate. Silica gel G indicates silica gel with a gypsum binder, i.e. calcium sulphate hemi-hydrate. The presence of calcium ions does not affect most of the separations.

Starch is another binder, but it does not allow the use of corrosive locating agents. The silica gel commonly used in TLC studies has a mean particle size of 15 µm with a particle size range of 05–40 µm. The adsorption properties of the silica gel can be modified by incorporating substances such as bases or buffers to prepare coatings with accurately defined pH. Silica gel is most commonly used to separate amino acids, alkaloids, fatty acids, lipids, steroids, essential oils, sugars, terpenoids etc.

Alumina: Alumina (Al_2O_3) is the choice next to silica gel. It often contains sodium carbonate and bicarbonate whose presence affects its adsorptive properties. Alumina can be produced with its Retention factor: acidic, basic or neutral. Neutral alumina is principally used with organic eluent. It is suitable for use with a substance that is either liable or bound to strong alkalis. Acidic alumina is used for separation of neutral or acid materials while basic alumina is used to separate steroids, alkaloids and aromatic, and unsaturated hydrocarbons.

Kieselguhr: Kieselguhr [Diatomaceous earth] has neutral pH. It is available with or without binder. It has less capacity of resolution than alumina and silica gel.

Magnesia: Magnesia (MgO) often replaces alumina. It is too finely divided to allow filtration and can be mixed with filter aid. Active magnesia is obtained by dehydration of the hydroxide.

Magnesium Silicate, Calcium Silicate: These are utilized for separation of sugars and its acetates, phenylosazones. In this, the adsorptive power increases with decreasing water content.

Others: Various other inorganic materials are utilized for TLC such aluminium silicate, bauxite, bentonite, barium sulphate, calcium carbonate, calcium hydroxide, calcium sulphate, dicalcium phosphate, Fuller's earth and zinc carbonate etc.

(II) Organic Adsorbents:

Some organic adsorbents used in TLC are:

(a) Cellulose and its Acetylates: These adsorbents are fibrous and can be used with relative advantages over paper as the flow is more even and there is less diffusion of the dissolved substances. Modified cellulose powders are used to obtain ion exchange separations in TLC and can be used with or without binder.

Cellulose contains adsorbed water which brings separation by partition mechanism. These materials are commonly used for separating hydrophilic substances like amino acids, sugars etc.

(b) Charcoal and Activated Carbon: Charcoal has the specific property of adsorbing strongly aromatic substances. Adsorptive property of activated carbon can be modified by depositing on it a film of a non-electrolyte or a fatty acid.

Others: Similarly other adsorbents such as Dextran gels, ion-exchange resins, polyamides, polyethylene powder, sucrose etc. are used for variety of separations.

Sometimes mixed adsorbents are also used. In such cases, mixture behaves either as one of the two adsorbents and second as a diluent or adsorption is shared between two adsorbents, almost linearly with the percentage composition of the mixture.

(B) Preparation of Chromatoplates:

Glass plates or flexible plates are used for spreading the adsorbent. The size used depends on the type of separation to be carried out, the type of chromatographic tank and spreading apparatus available. The standard sizes are 20 × 5 cm, 20 × 10 cm or 20 × 20 cm. The surface of the plate should be flat and without irregularities. The standard film thickness is 250 µm; thicker layers 0.5-2.00 mm are used for preparative separations.

There are various methods for the application of thin layers of adsorbent on the plates. Suspension or slurry of the coating material is used to give uniform thickness of layer throughout the length of the plate. There are four methods of applying the thin layer of its adsorbent on its support.

- **(a) Pouring:** Slurry of finely divided and homogeneous particle size is poured on a plate and allowed to flow to cover it evenly. To ensure reproducible thickness of layer, exact quantities of adsorbent should be used.
- **(b) Dipping:** This technique can be used for small plates by dipping the two plates at a time, back to back in slurry of adsorbent in chloroform or chloroform-methanol or other volatile solvents. It is the most convenient method for making a number of plates for rapid qualitative separations. But in this case, the exact thickness of layer is not known and evenness of the layer may not be good.
- **(c) Spraying:** This technique is out of vogue.
- **(d) Spreading:** All the above methods fail to give thin and uniform layers. Modern methods utilize the spreading devices for preparation of uniform thin layers on glass plates. Currently, two types of spreaders are used:
1. Moving spreader, (Fig. 4.1) and
2. Mobile spreader

A modified spreader gives the layer thickness from 0.2–02.0 mm.

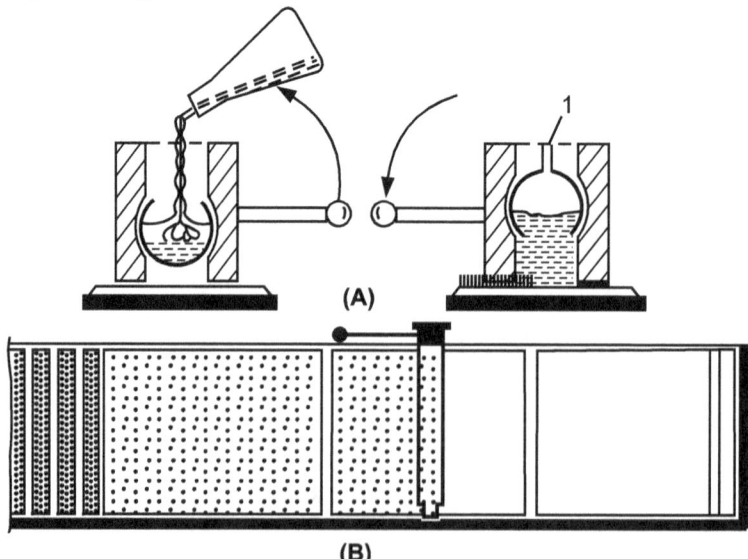

(A)

(B)

Fig. 4.1

Pre-coated plates ready for use of different adsorbents are available in uniform and optimal layer thickness for intended purposes and are abrasive-resistant. They can be sprayed even with corrosive agents.

(C) Activation of Plates:

After spreading, the plates are air-dried for 5-10 minutes; then further dried and activated by heating at about 100°C for 30 minutes. Plates made with volatile organic liquids may not require this further drying. By removing the liquids associated with layer completely, the adsorbent layer is activated. Plates may be kept for short periods in desiccator but long storage is not recommended.

(D) Solvent System:

The choice of the mobile phase depends on the same factors as that of adsorption column, i.e. the nature of substance to be separated and the adsorbent material to be used. It is preferable to use an organic solvent mixture of as much low polarity as possible. Polarity of solvent and substance to be separated plays an important role in selection. Highly polar solvents are generally avoided to minimize adsorption of any components of the solvent mixture. Use of water as a solvent is avoided as it may loosen the adhesion of a layer on a glass plate and give rise to mechanical Retention factor in separation.

A good guide for choosing a solvent system is to consult "eluotrophic series". The suitable mixing gives mobile phases of intermediate eluting power. By and large, it is better to avoid mixture of more than two components for as much as complex mixtures readily undergo phase change with changes in temperature. When mixtures are used, equilibrium is to be taken care of besides the purity of solvents, which is equally important. The following solvents are commonly used:

Petroleum ether	Pyridine
Carbon tetrachloride	Acetone
Trichloroethylene	N-Propanyl
Benzene	Ethanol
Dichloromethane	Methanol
Chloroform	Formamide
Diethyl ether	Water
Diethyl formamide	Glycol
Ethyl acetate	Glycerine

(E) Application of Sample:

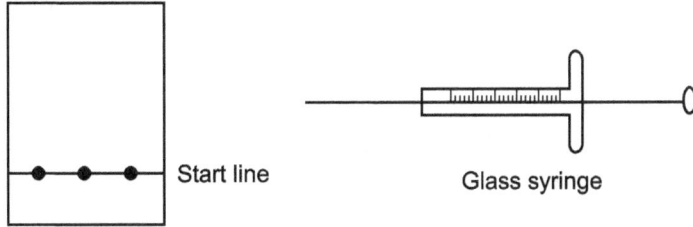

Start line   Glass syringe

Fig. 4.2

The sample solution in a non-polar solvent is applied, which solvent has the tendency to spread out from the starting spot and in turn affect the Retention factor value. The solvent used should be relatively volatile one. The area of application should be kept as small as possible for sharper and greater resolution. For the preparative work, the sample is applied in a narrow band. The pipette, loop or syringe can be used for applying the sample.

Before the sample application, (Fig. 4.2) the starting point and finish line is usually marked. Commercial spotting plates are available for marking the starting line, finish line and for uniformly spacing of spots on the starting line. The spots should be within 2-5 mm in diameter. For the preparative work, sample up to 4 mg is applied on starting line as a streak.

(F) Development Chambers:

The TLC plate is placed vertically in a rectangular chromatography tank or chamber (Fig. 4.3). The type and size of chamber decides the success and Retention factor value. They are classified according to the separation technique used as follows:

(a) Tanks for ascending development.
(b) Tanks for descending development.
(c) Tanks for horizontal development.
(d) Tanks for thin-layer electrophoresis.

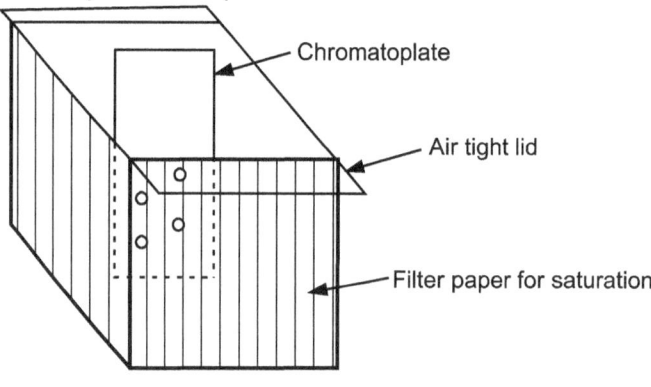

Fig. 4.3

Glass or stainless steel is most suitable for first three methods. Degree of saturation condition of tank atmosphere is one of the very important factors. If the tank is not saturated, solvent will climb up and evaporate, affecting the retention factor value. To ensure saturation, put a sheet of filter paper along the broad side of tank and dipping in the solvent mixture. The development should be carried out at room temperature in diffused daylight. Sunlight should be avoided by covering the chamber with glass plate.

(G) Development of Chromatograms:

Besides ascending method which is common, other methods used are:

(i) Ascending Development: The plates after spotting of the sample are placed in chromatography chamber containing solvent at the bottom. The flow of solvent is from bottom to top [Fig. 4.4 (a)].

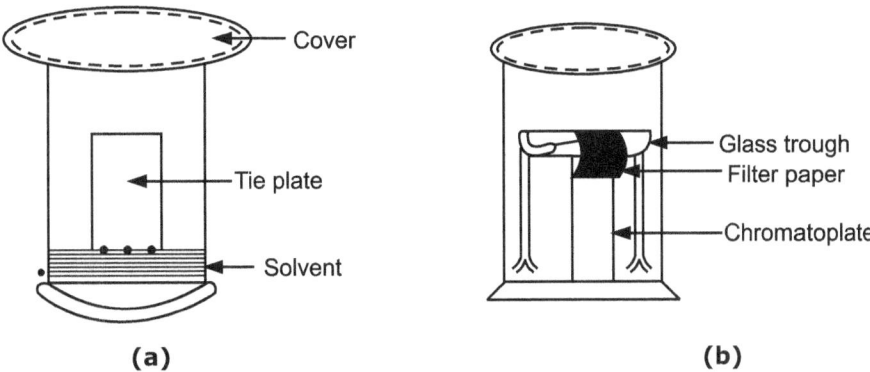

(a)

(b)

Fig. 4.4

(ii) Descending: In this method, flow of the solvent from reservoir to the plate is through a filter paper strip. Solvent moves from top to bottom of the plate as illustrated in [Fig. 4.4.(b)].

(iii)Horizontal Development: In this case, loose and non-sticky layer plates are used with a use of shallow dish with a ground-glass cover. The plate is supported on a T-shaped glass piece and the end of the thin layer plate is pressed against a filter paper strip of same width. This arrangement allows the solvent in the bottom of the dish to be transported up to thin layer film.

(iv)Stepwise and Multiple/Repeated Development: This technique is carried out by developing the chromatogram in a given solvent. It is then removed from the chamber and the solvent is allowed to evaporate. The plate is again developed in the same solvent. This can be repeated a number of times depending upon the separation to be achieved. Thus in this case if the solvent used for first and subsequent runs are the same, it is called 'multiple or repeated' development. But if the solvents used for first and subsequent runs are different then it is called as the 'Stepwise' technique.

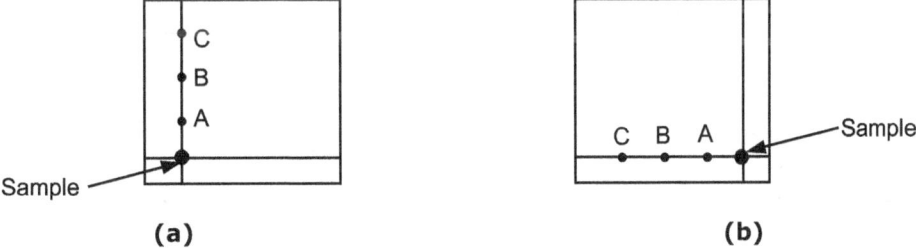

(a)

(b)

Fig. 4.5: Two dimensional developments

(v) Two-Dimensional Development: If the components of the mixture are not completely separated by development in a single direction, it is possible to resolve by developing in second solvent in direction perpendicular to the first development. In this technique, the sample spot is applied at corner of plate. First development is carried out by ascending method in one solvent system. The plate is taken out, solvent allowed to evaporate and second development is carried out in another solvent system by changing the edge of the plate at 90° (Fig. 4.5).

(vi) Preparative TLC: It is an important method for preparative separations. In this method, sample is always applied in bands or streaks and separation is affected by multiple development. After the localization of spot (UV visualization) the band or streak is scrapped out and the resolved sample recovered by extraction with suitable solvent.

(vii) Gradient Elution: Sometimes it is advantageous to change the composition of the solvent continuously during the development and hence specially designed tank is used for gradient elution work.

(viii) Reverse Phase TLC: These chromatoplates are prepared by immersing the adsorbent layer very slowly in 5-10 per cent of paraffin, silicone oil, and undecane in petroleum ether or diethyl ether. After removing the plate and evaporating the solvent, the plate is ready for chromatography. Paraffin and silicon oil provides the permanent impregnation whereas undecane can be removed after development after heating the plate at 120°C.

(H) Location of Spots:

The method of location of colourless substances is similar to those used in paper chromatography. Physical methods include the ultraviolet, fluorescence or radioactive counting. Many a time the whole plate may be made fluorescent at the beginning by inclusion of a suitable dye.

In case of chemical methods, locating agents are applied by spraying and not by dipping. During spraying, care should be taken to prevent disturbing the layers. Concentrated sulphuric acid can be used as locating agent as it produces coloured spots which are visible in daylight as well as UV light. One more locating agent for organic substances is iodine vapour. Plate is exposed to iodine vapours, by placing in closed vessel containing a few iodine crystals. In addition most of the locating agents used for paper for specific compounds are also applicable to TLC.

(I) Evaluation of the Chromatogram:

After locating the spots on plates and marking their position and size, they are evaluated either qualitatively or quantitatively.

(a) Qualitative: In this case, the retention factor value of standard or authentic sample for the same mobile phase is known and is recorded in literature. The retention factor value of the sample is calculated and on comparison of Retention factor values for known and unknown the qualitative identification of sample is made.

(b) Quantitative: The methods for quantitative analysis are as follows:

1. Direct Methods:

(a) Visual Comparison: For a quick semi-quantitative analysis of the amount of components, visual comparison of spot size, intensity of spot or the combination of two with the known standard spots is made.

(b) **Spot Areas and Weight Relationship:** From the area of spot, amount of substance present is calculated. Usually, a linear relationship is found between the spot area and weight of the compound present in it.

(c) **Spot Densitometry:** After development of the chromatogram, the plate is sprayed with specific reagent and colour developed is measured directly in densitometer or spots on photographs or negatives are used in densitometer. This method is applicable for detection of all types of compounds.

(d) **Direct Spectrometry:** Quantitative measurements are obtained by reading the absorption or fluorescence of separated zones directly on TLC plates at wavelength of maximum absorption of substance by chromatogram spectrometer.

(e) **Spectral Reflectance:** The spectral reflectance of dyes adsorbed on adsorbent has been investigated as a quantitative technique for TLC.

2. Indirect Methods:

These involve the separation by TLC, recovery by the quantitative elution and subsequent estimation with suitable method; this is elution technique. In this method, the areas containing the substance after localization are marked and then scooped out with the help of vacuum cleaner without any loss. Then solute from adsorbent is eluted by simple agitation with proper solvent after removing the adsorbent. The eluate is then analyzed by any technique like Colorimetry, Spectrophotometry, Fluorimetry, Radiometry, Flame photometry etc.

APPLICATIONS

The various applications of TLC are as follows:

1. **Purity of sample:** Purity of sample is routinely carried out. For this, direct comparison of the sample and authentic sample is done; if impurity is present, it shows extra spots and this can be detected very easily.

2. **Examination of reactions:** The reaction mixture is examined by TLC to assess whether the reaction is complete or otherwise. This method is also used in checking other separation processes and purification processes like distillation, molecular distillation etc.

3. **Identification of compounds:** TLC is increasingly employed in isolation, purification and identification of various classes of organic compounds. In photochemistry, it is used for identification of natural products like volatile oil (Essential oil), fixed oils, waxes, terpenes, alkaloids, glycosides, steroids etc.

4. **Biochemical analysis:** TLC is extremely useful in separation of biochemical metabolite or constituent from its body fluids, blood plasma, serum, urine etc.

5. **In chemistry:** TLC methodology is increasingly used in chemistry for the separation and identification of compounds which are closely related to each other. It is also used for identification of cations and anions in inorganic chemistry.

6. **In Pharmaceutical industry:** Various pharmacopoeias have adopted TLC technique for detection of impurity in a pharmacopoeial drug or chemical. More than 130 drugs are tested by TLC method for detecting impurity as per BP.

7. Various drugs like hypnotics, sedatives, anticonvulsant tranquillizers, antihistaminic, analgesics, local anaesthetics; steroidal drugs have been tested qualitatively by TLC method.

8. One of the most important applications of TLC is in separation of multicomponent pharmaceutical formulations.

9. In food and cosmetic industry, TLC method is used for separation and identification of colours, preservatives, sweetening agent, and various cosmetic products.

RETENTION FACTOR (R$_f$) VALUES

The difference in rate of movement of the components in chromatography is caused by various factors. It is measured as shown in (Fig. 4.6):

$$\text{Retention factor (R}_f) = \frac{\text{Distance of centre of spot from starting point}}{\text{Distance of solvent front from starting point}}$$

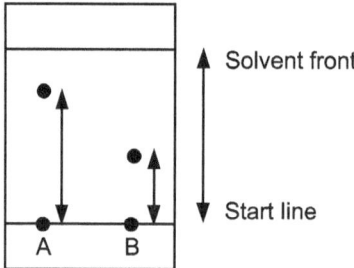

Fig. 4.6

Retention factor value is a constant for each component only under identical experimental conditions. It depends upon several factors:

(a) **Nature of Adsorbent:** Different adsorbents will give different retention factor value for same solvent. Reproducibility is only possible for given adsorbent of constant particle size and binder.

(b) **The Mobile phase:** The purity of solvents and quantity of solvent mixed should be strictly controlled.

(c) **Activity:** Rigorous control on the temperature of activation and the storage conditions of adsorbent.

(d) **Thickness of Layer:** In standard plates approximately 250 µm is preferred thickness of layer. Below 200 µm the retention factor values vary considerably. The layers may be of higher or lower thickness in individual compounds.

(e) **The Temperature:** Generally, separations should be effected at constant temperature to avoid changes in solvent composition.

(f) Equilibration: Equilibrium of chamber used for development is more important in TLC than in paper chromatography; hence, saturation of atmosphere with the solvent vapour is important.

(g) Loading: The best results are obtained with a loading of about 10 µg per spot on 250 µm plate. If loading is more, spreading of spot and tailing may occur.

(h) Dipping zone: Distance of starting point from the solvent surface is also a important factor.

(i) Chromatographic Technique: Depending upon the technique used i.e. ascending, descending, horizontal etc. the Retention factor value will change for the same solvent system.

HIGH PERFORMANCE THIN LAYER CHROMATOGRAPHY

The high Retention factor for thin layer chromatography commonly known as HPTLC is a sophisticated form of thin layer chromatography. It involves the same theoretical principle of thin layer chromatography wherein substances are separated on the basis of their differential migration in a system of two phases on special type of plates. This technique is widely used in many a field both for qualitative and quantitative identification and estimation of constituents in a mixture.

The main and important steps involved in this are as follows:

1. Sample preparation
2. Selection of chromatographic layer
3. Plates
4. Prewashing
5. Conditioning
6. Sample application
7. Preconditioning
8. Mobile phase
9. Chromatographic development
10. Detection of spots
11. Scanning and documentation.

1. Sample preparation:

For normal phase chromatography using Silica gel/Alumina pre-coated plates, solvent generally should be non-polar and volatile type. Since, polar solvents tend to give circular shape at origin. For reversed phase chromatography, usually polar solvents are used for dissolving the sample.

2. Selection of chromatographic layer:

The selection of layer depends on the nature of material to be separated. Commonly used materials are Silica gel 60F, Alumina, Cellulose (micrystalline), PEI impregnated cellulose etc. These materials can be coated on handmade plates with or without binders. Pre-coated plates are commercially available and are commonly used. However, these are costlier than the handmade plates.

3. Plates:

Standard size plates for HPTLC are manufactured by various companies which are most satisfactory.

Handmade plates can be prepared and used. Generally, plates of 20 × 20 cm or 5-7.5 cm size having 100-250 mm adsorbent thickness are used for quantitative analysis. Silica gel $60F_{254}$ having a pore size 6 mm with fluorescent indicator is a coat material. The sorbent layer is fixed to the plates by special glue. The basic difference in TLC and HPTLC plates is particle size of coated materials which is 5-20 μm for TLC and 4-8 μm for HPTLC.

4. Prewashing:

Plates need to be prewashed to remove water vapours or other volatile impurities, which might get trapped in the plates. These give dirty zones and spots on the plates. To avoid this, plates are cleaned by using methanol as solvent by ascending or descending or by dripping continuous mode.

5. Conditioning:

The prewashed plates or plates exposed to humidity and surroundings are need to be activated by placing them in oven at 120°C for 15-20 minutes. This process is known as conditioning; this allows the active centers of coating materials attenuated for better separation of sample material.

6. Sample application:

It is the most important step for obtaining good resolution and results. Application of 1.0–05 μl is most satisfactory for HPTLC application of the sample and standard as a band gives better separation, equal Retention factor values, and less spot broadening. The sample application is carried out by Linomat type applicator on the plates which give uniform, safe and standard results.

7. Preconditioning (Chamber Saturation):

This affects the effective separation of sample. For low polarity mobile phase there is no need of saturation; however, saturation is expedient for highly polar mobile phases. Partial saturation is recommended for mobile phase composition leading to phase separation. For reverse phase chromatography it is essential to saturate the chamber with methanol or polar solvent.

8. Mobile phase:

The selection of appropriate mobile phase is based on the trial and error wherein chemical properties of solute and solvent, solubility of analyte absorbent layer etc. are considered at analyst's discretion. The eluotrophic series of various solvent based on the adsorption energies can be used as a guide for selection of mobile phase composition.

9. Chromatographic development:

Various forms of chromatographic development like ascending, descending, horizontal, continuous, gradient and multidimensional, can be tried. For HPTLC plates, migration distance of 5-6 mm is sufficient. After development, plates are removed from the chamber and dried to remove traces of mobile phase. Common problems encountered during chromatographic development are as follows:

(a) Tailing: This may occur due to the presence of traces of impurities or more than one ionic species of substances under chromatography. This can be reduced by buffering the mobile phase system with acidic (1–2 per cent acetic acid) or basic (ammonia) solution. It keeps the materials to be separated in non-ionic forms. Sometimes, tailing may be due to overloading of sample plates.

(b) Diffusion: This is seen as zones on chromatographic plates. This may arise due to non-uniformity of mobile phase, longitudinal diffusion between mobile phase and stationary phase or due to non-equilibrium of stationary phase.

10. Detection of spots:

Immediately after the development process is complete, the plates are removed from the chamber and dried to remove traces of mobile phase. Generally, detection can be done by iodine vapour in iodine chamber or by visual inspection at 254 nm of ultraviolet region in UV cabinet.

11. Scanning and documentation:

Currently, HPTLC equipments are supplied with computer equipped with data recording and storing devices. The development of HPTLC plates is scanned at selected UV regions wavelength by the instrument and the detected spots are seen on computer in the form of peaks. The scanner converts band into peaks and peak height or area is related to the concentration of the substance on the spot. The peak height and area under the spot (curves) are measured by the instruments and are recorded as per cent on the printer.

Furthermore, the plates carry supplier's name, batch number, chemical code etc. on the edge of the pre-coated plates. This helps in storing the data of individual plates for further use as well as for photo documentation and storage.

Factors Influencing TLC/HPTLC separation are:

1. Type of stationary phase.
2. Layer thickness and binders in the layers.

3.   Mobile phase.

4.   Solvent purity.

5.   Size and shape of developing chamber.

6.   Amount of sample to be spotted.

7.   Chamber saturation.

8.   Size of spot applied.

9.   Solvent level and development level in the chamber.

10. Relative humidity and temperature.

11. Development distance.

12. Mode of development.

✳✳✳

CHAPTER ... 5

PAPER CHROMATOGRAPHY

INTRODUCTION

Cambridge has done it again: this time for Paper Chromatography. Cantabrigians Martin and Synge, Consden and Gorden of the Cambridge School have conferred the current status to this discipline of Chromatography.

Martin and Synge (1941) developed forty-plate complicated apparatus for the separation of acetylated amino acids by partition between water and an immiscible organic solvent.

Afterwards Consden, Gorden and Martin (1944) replaced silica gel with a filter paper by using n-butanol as a mobile phase. Thus, the technique involved is partition as the major mechanism of separation. Paper chromatography is regarded as partition chromatography where stationary phase is water held by adsorption on cellulose molecules which in turn is kept in a fixed position by the fibrous structure of the paper. It was used to separate organic mixtures, but it was quickly adopted for separation of inorganic ions by various workers.

Paper chromatography has a wide and versatile field of applications. It is used in almost all areas to solve the complicated problems in chemistry, biology and biochemistry, etc. It has many advantages:

1. The equipment is very simple and is easily available.
2. It has high efficiency of separation.
3. Separation can be effected on macro, micro or semi-micro scale.
4. Closely related homologues, isotopes, isomers and very labile and reactive substances can be separated readily and satisfactorily.

Thus, paper chromatography is the technique wherein the separation of an unknown substance is accomplished by the flow of solvents on the specially designed chromatographic paper, the solvent goes up by capillary action and the separation is effected by differential migration of the substance due to difference in distribution coefficients.

Theoretical Principle:

The theoretical principle involved in separation by paper chromatography is largely by partition coefficient phenomenon. It is difficult to visualize theoretical plate concept in paper chromatography, it is well known that separation is achieved by successive equilibrations of sample between two phases; one of which moves over the other. The stationary phase is made up of the solvent held by the paper and mobile phase is the irrigating eluent. Both these phases are in contact over a very large interface on filter paper.

In case, water is used as stationary phase, the water cellulose complex concept is involved. The water absorbed in amorphous regions of cellulose is distinct from the bulk of mobile water. The water absorbed may be regarded as chemically bound and not as a liquid; thus various solvent systems containing water or polar solvent act as distinct stationary phase. It is to be noted that cellulose (of Paper) because of its structure can play a dual role of adsorption and partition in paper chromatography. Thus, either partition or adsorption or both may play a major role depending of course on conditions during analysis.

R_f VALUE AND VARIATION

In paper chromatography, the results are represented by R_f value, which represents the movement or migration of solute relative to the solvent front. This indicates position of migrated spots on chromatogram.

The R_f value is calculated as:

$$R_f = \frac{\text{Distance travelled by the solute}}{\text{Distance travelled by the solvent front}}$$

In other words, R indicates the fraction of the solute molecules in a solvent at any specified time. Thus, R_f is a function of partition coefficients and is a constant for a given substance, provided the conditions of chromatographic system are kept constant.

However, for greater reliability, reference standards are used in parallel runs or as internal standards. Sometimes the solvent front runs off the paper (Fig. 5.1) then the position of individual spot is measured relative to position of standard substances (Say x).

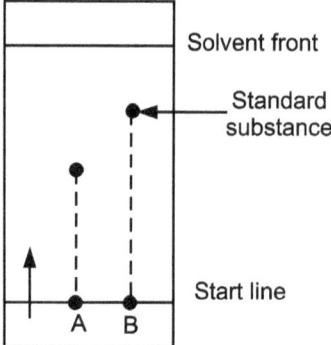

Fig. 5.1

$$Rx = \frac{\text{Distance travelled by substance}}{\text{Distance travelled by std. substance}}$$

It should be noted that R_f value is always less than unity but Rx can be greater than 1.

RF values of two different compounds are different as other physico-chemical constants. R_f values of various compounds are recorded in literature with the mention of solvent system used. It is from the R_f value comparison identification of compounds is possible. The value varies with the solvent used; hence, it is represented with reference to the solvent.

Some of the factors which affect R_f value are:

1. The solvent system and its composition
2. Temperature
3. The quality of the paper
4. Distance through which the solvent runs
5. The quality and nature of solvents used
6. The direction of the fibres of the paper
7. The method of development.

TYPES OF PAPER CHROMATOGRAPHY

Depending upon the migration forces that are involved in separation, paper chromatography is classified into two types:

1. Paper Partition Chromatography:

In standard method of analysis where the paper is utilized as a support with one solvent as mobile phase and other as a stationary phase. The migration of substances is due to differences in partition coefficients.

2. Paper Adsorption Chromatography:

In some cases, the paper to be used is coated or impregnated with adsorbents like silica gel or alumina. Thus, the modified paper is used as an adsorbent and the solvent is allowed to flow over the unknown components. Thus, migration of substances is due to the difference in adsorptive powers of substances to be separated. However, as this technique is not much used, it is only of academic interest.

OPERATIONAL TECHNIQUE

The following points should be taken into account in paper chromatography.

1. Choice of Filter Paper

Chromatography paper is a specially manufactured paper. Whitman filter papers are used extensively. In general, this filter paper contains 98–99 per cent of α-cellulose. The mineral content may vary from 0.07–0.01 per cent. Besides this, β-cellulose, ether soluble matter, ammonia and Lyophillic substances (waxes, fats, etc.) are also present. Chromatographic papers are available in packs of 100 and 500 sheets of 46×57 cm or 58×68 cm and are cut to required size. The rectangular or square papers are cut from the sheet for separation of substances. There are various grades and types of paper available for separation of a sample. The proper choice of paper depends upon the sample and solvent system used. Another important factor that governs the choice of paper is whether the paper is to be used for quantitative, qualitative or preparative chromatographic analysis. The choice of paper is also based on the thickness, flow rate, purity and net strength.

To speed up chromatographic analysis, coarser and faster papers are used, i.e. Whitman paper number 31 is about four times faster than Whitman paper number 1. Slow papers are used rarely but they are important for separation of substances having close R_f value.

2. Modified Filter Papers

For efficient separation of certain substances, specially treated or modified filter papers are used, i.e. buffered or treated papers like Whitman-Phosphate, Whitman-citrate or paper treated with alumina, silicic acid etc. In case of reversed phase chromatography, paper is impregnated in mobile phase (non-polar solvent), dried and then used.

3. Preparation of Paper:

Once the type of paper is decided, it is cut in desired size and shape depending upon the work to be carried out. Generally, rectangular and square shapes are used. After noting the direction of run on paper, start line is marked as shown in Fig. 5.1.

While storing, paper should be kept away from any fume (especially ammonia) and should not be subjected to large changes in humidity.

4. Preparation of Sample:

The mixture to be separated is applied to the paper as a solution. It is important to choose proper solvent for making solution. Generally, a weighed amount of mixture is dissolved in volatile solvent and a minimum volume of concentrated solution is applied on the paper avoiding diffusion of spot. Extracts from soil, biological cells or tissue materials are taken out with the help of some solvent which is directly applied on the paper.

Aqueous biological extracts, urine, neutralized protein hydrolyzates and other solutions which may have to be examined for amino acids and sugars will always contain appreciable amounts of inorganic material. Removal of these is called "desalting" and should always be carried out without affecting organic compounds. Desalting is carried out by electrolytic method, electro-dialysis, ion-exchange membrane, column techniques etc.

No standard procedure for preparation of samples is exemplified, as several factors affect sample volumes of 10–20 μl containing as many μg of substance is spotted.

5. Application of the Sample:

The starting line is marked on the paper with an ordinary pencil some 5 cm from the bottom edge. On the starting line marks are made about 2 cm apart from each other. Micropipette or glass capillary or platinum loop is used for application of sample. The sample may be applied as spots or bands. Generally, size of spot should be as small as possible. Diameter of spot should not exceed 5 mm. The quantity of sample applied to the paper is important rather than volume. When solution is very dilute, it can be concentrated on paper by applying a series of drops to the same spot, allowing each drop to evaporate before applying the next. The micro-syringe is also used for application of sample of proper size. For quantitative work the sample is applied by capillary in the form of narrow strip 5-10 mm long, 25 mm apart or as a single spot at least 10 mm apart. Amount of sample applied to the paper depends on the capacity of solvent. Optimum concentration required for quantitative separation, time required for development etc. vary considerably.

Drying of the spotted chromatogram should be carried out carefully in air. Hot air is not advisable particularly for acid solution as it may cause blackening of paper.

6. Solvents:

A number of solvents can be used in the paper chromatography. The selection of proper solvent depends mainly on nature of substance to be separated. Factors which affect the selection are viscosity, surface tension, polarity etc.

In general, one-phase system is used for development in paper chromatography, avoiding the two-phase system. The solvent should be inexpensive and very pure.

The solvents used in paper chromatography are given in increasing order of polarity as under:

n - Hexane	Ethyl acetate
Cyclohexane	n-butanol
Carbon tetrachloride	n-propanyl
Benzene	Acetone
Toluene	Ethanol
Trichloroethylene	Methanol
Diethyl ether	Water
Chloroform	

If pure solvent is not satisfactory, solvent system of suitable polarity is obtained by trying out mixture of solvents.

Some well-known solvent systems recorded in standard reference books ate:

7. Chromatographic Tank or Chambers:

The chromatographic tanks are made from many materials like glass, plastic or stainless steel. Glass tanks are preferred and are most commonly used. They are available in various sizes depending upon the length and breadth of paper and type of development. The chambers or tanks have a lid with a hole (closed during development) for introducing solvent through it. Equilibrium of chamber with solvent is carried out by using solvent-dipped filter paper.

8. Development of Chromatogram:

For proper development following points are taken into consideration:

1. Sufficient amount of solvent should be present in the chamber.
2. During development, paper should be freely suspended and should be vertical.
3. Large temperature changes and exposure to light should be avoided.
4. The atmosphere of the chamber should be saturated with the solvent's vapours.

The paper is so dipped in the solvent that the spots will not dip completely into the solvent. The solvent will run over the paper by capillary action. It is allowed to run maximum distance not exceeding two-third of total height of paper for better and efficient resolution. After development is complete, paper is taken out of the chamber carefully.

9. Drying of Chromatogram:

The wet chromatogram after development is dried in special cabinet heated electrically with temperature controls. The drying can also be carried out by transferring chromatograms to racks and putting in drying cabinets. They are dried by cold or hot air depending on volatility of solvents. A simple hairdryer is a convenient device to dry chromatograms.

10. Location of Spots:

Once the developed chromatogram is dried, next step is to locate the spots. If the substances are coloured, they are visually detected easily, but for colourless substances, various methods are used:

1. Physical and
2. Chemical methods.

1. **Physical Methods:** Physical methods have the advantage that substances on paper are not converted into other compounds and can be recovered for further studies.

2. **Chemical Methods:** In this, chemical treatment is used to develop a colour. Chromatograms are exposed to vapours or gases of chemicals or sprayed with reagent. The chemicals and reagents so used are called "locating agents".

Various colouring or locating agents are available and used depending upon the chemical nature of substance under examination. For spraying a reagent is sprayed by a glass atomizer (Fig. 5.2).

Physical methods used are observation under UV light, detection of fluorescence and radioisotope (for radioactive compounds) measurements.

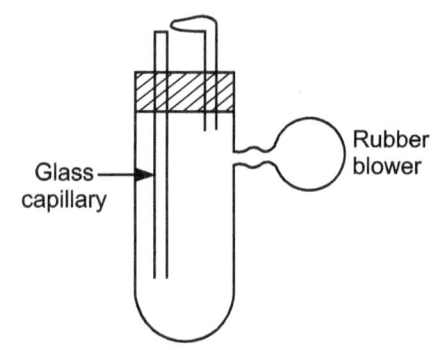

Fig. 5.2

After spraying, the paper is allowed to dry (in air), or heated at specified temperature. The spots developed are marked by pencil; the centres determined and R_f values are calculated.

QUANTITATIVE ANALYSIS

In general, for qualitative analysis the simple measurement of R_f value either by the comparison with the reference substances or with the standard values in literature is done. But for quantitative use the technique requires not only a quantitative separation but also quantitative location and evaluation of the substance present. The quantitative method can be either by estimation of the amount of the substance in the spot on the paper or by removal of the substance from the paper and analysis of the separate fractions by conventional quantitative techniques. All the available methods can be divided into two main groups:

1. Evaluation of substance on the paper directly.
2. Removal of substance from the paper [Elution method].

The proper choice of method depends mainly upon the factors like physical and chemical properties of the compound, composition and capacity of the substance and degree of desired accuracy.

(a) Evaluation of Substance on Paper (Direct measurement methods):

(i) **Visual Comparison of Spots:** In this, a number of chromatograms are run on same sheet with the reference solution containing known amount of substance. Several reference solutions containing different concentrations are needed and the spot is compared for its size and intensity of colour by fluorescence or UV absorbance. The unknown compound is estimated by comparison.

(ii) Measurement of Area of Spot: When the outlines of the spot or zones are well defined, the size of the spot may serve for determining the quantity of substance. Frequently, a linear relationship is obtained between the logarithms of the quantity and area of the spot. The area can be measured with a planimeter or a graph paper.

(iii) Radiotracer Analysis: The radioactive element, which is labelled, is used to locate/determine the quantity of material on the chromatogram. The compound on chromatogram is identified by subjecting to neutron bombardment. The activity and location are measured by passing the paper either in a gas flow counting chamber or a thin window Geiger Muller tube.

(iv) Removal of Substance from the Paper (Elution Method): For quantitative analysis the substance is removed by elution from paper. The simplest procedure is to cut out the appropriate part of filter paper and soak it in optimal amount of the solvent. Extractions may be hastened by shaking or by warming. The eluates so obtained from the chromatogram may be diluted or concentrated and then analysed by any suitable technique.

DEVELOPMENT TECHNIQUES

There are various development methods which can be used in paper chromatography. The proper choice mainly depends upon the class of compounds to be investigated. They are of following types:

(a) Descending Chromatography: The apparatus consists of a well-sealed glass tank of suitable size and shape provided with a trough for the mobile phase in the upper portion. The paper with the sample spotted is inserted in trough containing the mobile phase, the jar itself having been equilibrated with the mobile phase prior to elution [Fig. 5.3 (b)]. Since, the movement of mobile phase is descending, it is referred as descending chromatography. The advantage of this is that the development can be continued even though the solvent runs off at the other end of the paper.

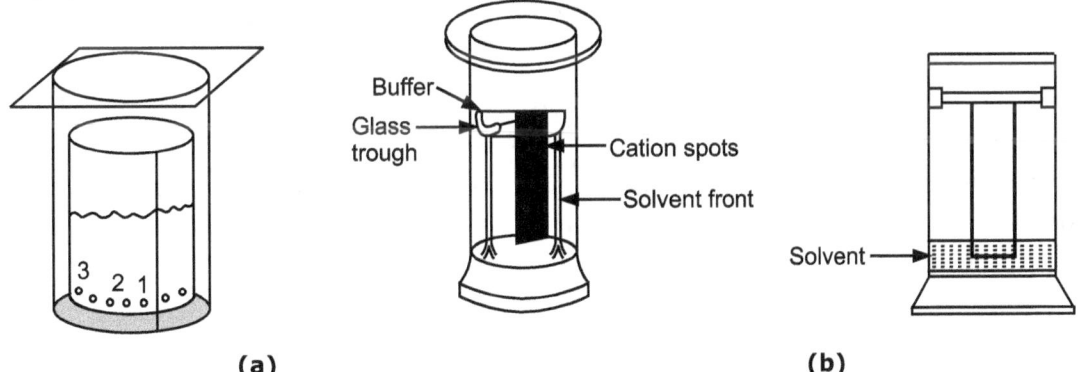

(a)   (b)

Fig. 5.3

(b) Ascending Chromatography: In this case, the solvent stream moves upwards. The mobile phase is placed in suitable container at the bottom of the chamber or in the chamber itself. The samples are applied a few centimeters from the bottom edge of the paper suspended from a hook [Fig. 5.3 (a)]. The paper may be rolled into a cylinder, held together by staples or plastic clips.

(c) Ascending-Descending Chromatography: A hybrid of the above two techniques is called ascending-descending chromatography. Here the upper part of the ascending chromatogram can be folded over a glass to change over into the descending after crossing the glass rod (Fig. 5.4).

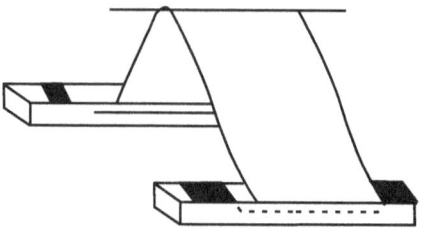

Fig. 5.4

(d) Radial or Disk Chromatography: This is rarely used in extraordinary cases. In this case, a circular piece of paper is taken which has a wick cut parallel to the radius from the edge to the centre. The sample is deposited at the centre of the paper and at the upper end of the wick. The paper is then laid on the edge of a circular disk with the wick dipping into the solvent at the bottom of the dish, as shown in Fig. 5.5.

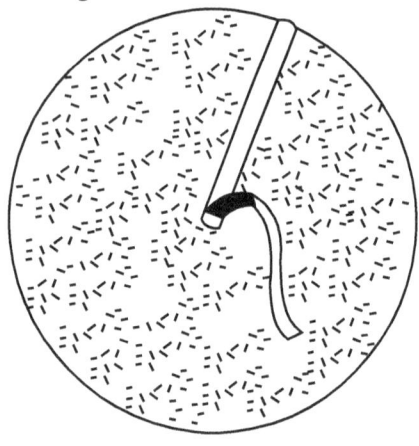
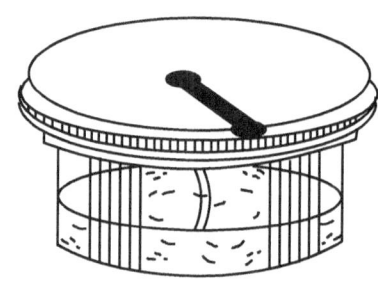

Fig. 5.5

The liquid ascends by the wick and flows radically through the paper. While moving, it carries the compounds with it and thus chromatogram is developed. However, it takes more time for the development.

(e) Multiple Chromatography: This is a technique wherein the irrigation is repeated either in the same direction as in the first run or in the direction perpendicular to the first system.

(f) Two-Dimensional Chromatography: In this method, the paper is cut/square or rectangle. The sample is applied to one of the corners. Using a solvent system first development is carried as per ascending method. The paper is taken out and dried. The second development is performed at the right angle to the direction of the first run using another solvent system. The larger the area of paper, more complete the resolution of complex mixtures.

CHAPTER ... 6

ION EXCHANGE CHROMATOGRAPHY

Ion exchange material is water insoluble solid of complex structure comprising ions capable of exchanging with ions in the surrounding medium in a reversible process. Since, the process involves exchange of ions, the material is called exchanger.

Use of inorganic clays to soften water was recorded long ago. Soils, clays and zeolites (natural and synthetic) are used to soften water. The ion exchange capacity of these materials differs markedly. Zeolite has three dimensional network structure with regular pores through which water can pass. Thus, if water containing calcium or magnesium ions is passed through a bed of zeolite containing sodium ions, exchange takes place and water gets purified.

$$Ca^{2+} + 2\,Na^+\,Z \rightarrow 2Na^+ + Ca^{2+}\,Z \quad \text{where, Z = zeolite}$$

Zeolite type ion exchanger besides being unstable towards acids and bases cannot be used over wide pH range.

Since the synthesis of sulphonic acid and polyamine resins by Adams and Holmes in 1935, a large variety of synthetic resins have been developed. Synthetic resins have larger ion exchange capacity than the resins of natural resources. The synthetic resins are prepared from styrene, Divinyl benzene (DVB), phenolsulphonic acid, phenol-formaldehyde, various amines, etc. (a cross linking agent imparting strength to the polymer by joining the chains of various position).

ION EXCHANGE MATERIALS

Various materials possess varying ion exchange capacity, which can be classified:

(a) Synthetic inorganic ion exchangers:

These materials have a relatively open three-dimensional framework structure with channels and interconnecting cavities e.g. alumina-silicate, TiO_2, ThO_2, zirconium oxide, phosphate etc.

The hydrous oxides of tri- and tetravalent metals are useful as cation exchangers. Besides, phosphate, molybdate, tungstate, vandate etc. of some metals act as cation exchanger materials.

(b) Natural organic ion exchangers:

Coal, paper, cotton and the like can be converted into cation exchange by reaction of sulphonation or phosphorylation. They act as cation exchangers since they carry sulphonic acid or carboxyl groups attached to them. These materials are less uniform in structure and get readily affected by other chemicals.

(c) Synthetic organic ion exchangers:

The synthetic ion exchanger resins are made of cross-linked polymer network to which are attached various functional groups. The nature of functional group determines whether it is a cation exchanger or an anion exchanger. In cation exchanger materials, the acid groups are sulphonic acid, carboxylic acid or phenolic, while in anion exchanger resins the groups are basic as amine, quaternary ammonium, etc. The number and type of functional group is the determiner to ascertain whether the resin is a strong or a weak exchanger.

There are many types of synthetic ion exchangers with different physical and chemical properties. Some are liquid in nature such as long chain water immiscible aliphatic amines which act as anion exchanger or diallyl phosphate of fatty acid as cation exchanger.

SYNTHETIC ION EXCHANGE RESINS

These may be regarded as polymers consisting of three dimensional hydrocarbon networks to which are bonded a large number of electrically charged groups. Originally, the term resin was applied to naturally occurring amorphous solids such as amber, shellac, rosin, copal etc. Many polymeric substances occur in nature such as cellulose, rubber, starch, proteins and resins. Currently, the term resin is used for synthetic polymers which are similar to natural resin in physical properties.

These polymers are cross-linked, show thermosetting properties (polymers which change irreversibly into hard and rigid materials on heating) due to three-dimensional network structure. These synthetic polymers are made from small units of chemicals by polymerization either by addition or condensation reactions.

The ion exchange resin should meet the specified standards:

1. It should have a sufficient degree of cross-linking (approximately 4-8 per cent) for use in chromatography.

2. It should be insoluble in common solvents.

3. It must be chemically stable.

4. It should be sufficiently hydrophilic to permit diffusion of ions through its structure at a constant and finite rate.

5. The swollen resin must be denser than water.

6. It should have desired particle size and shape.

7. It must contain sufficient number of ion exchange groups.

8. The resin should have ability of regeneration and reuse.

9. The resins may exchange cation or anion therefore they are termed as cation or anion exchange resins.

MANUFACTURE OF ION EXCHANGE RESINS

Ion exchange resins are manufactured by different chemical reactions of polymerization, condensation or by addition reactions. Generally, hydrocarbon network is built by polymerization using phenol-formaldehyde or styrene and divinyl benzene as:

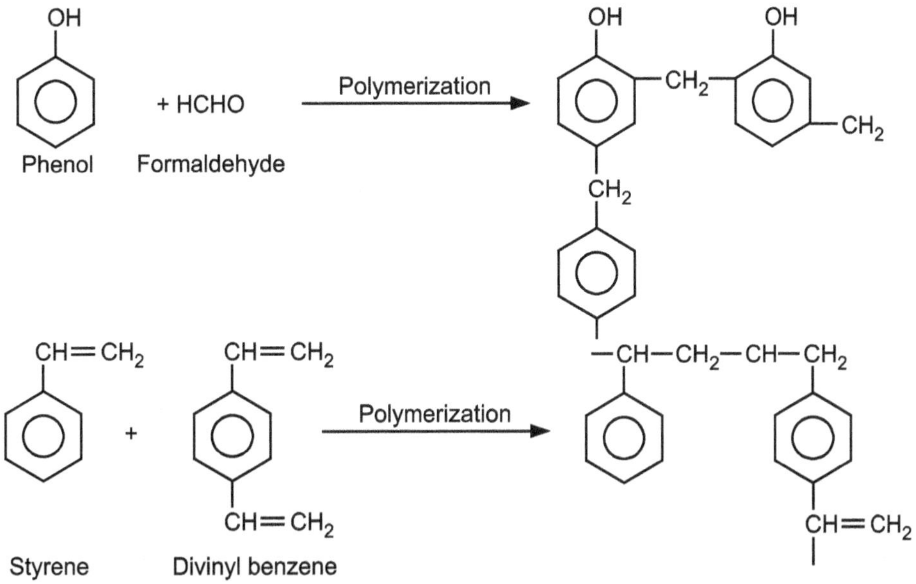

Phenol   Formaldehyde

Styrene   Divinyl benzene

Suitable chemical reactions are now brought about on the polymerized material to convert them into cation exchange or anion exchange resin.

(a) Cation exchange resin: These resins are synthesized by using phenol or substituted phenol and formaldehyde by polymerization as

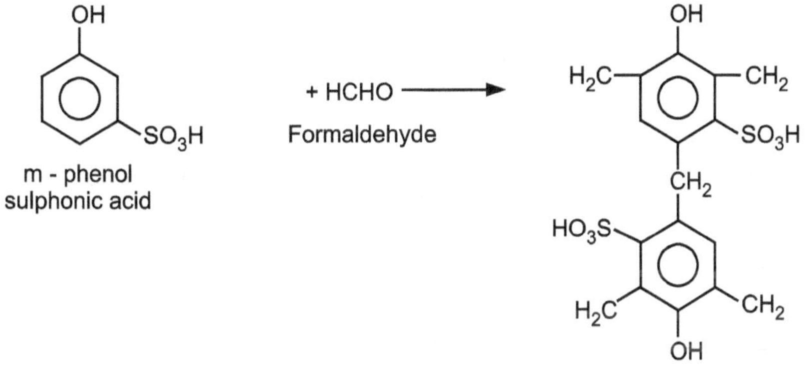

m - phenol
sulphonic acid

or from styrene and Divinyl benzene as

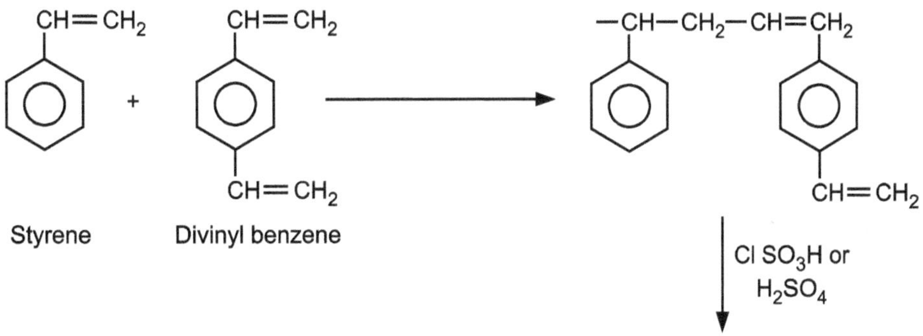

Styrene   Divinyl benzene

A cation exchange resin is a high molecular weight cross linked polymer containing acid groups as sulphonic, carboxylic, phenolic, etc. as an integral part of the resin. A cation exchanger consists of polymeric anion and active cations. But the resin as such is electrically neutral. The resins containing sulphonic group are considered as strongly acidic cation exchange resins. Thus, when the resin is treated with a strong acid (5 per cent HCl), entire sulphonate is converted to acid form (hydrogen form). This resin acts as a strong acid which can be represented as RSO_3^- H^+ where, R represents the resin network. Now if the salt solution is passed through the hydrogen form of resin, the H^+ will be replaced by an equivalent amount of the cation, which in turn gets attached to the resin.

The reaction may be represented as:

$$RSO_3^- \, H^+ + Na^+ \rightleftharpoons RSO_3^- \, Na^+ + H^+$$

From the above equilibrium, it is evident that for equilibrium of sodium ion, one equivalent of hydrogen ion is freed. This equilibrium is mainly dependent upon:

I.   Acid strength of resin.

II.   Concentration of cations in the solution

For a strong cation exchange resin, the exchange affinity for cations depends upon the charge of cations.

Some of the commercially available cation exchange resins are:

Commercial Name	Functional Group
1. Ambulate IR – 100	– OH, – CH_2SO_2OH
IR – 105	
IR – 1019	
2. Ambulate – 200	– SO_3H
3. Ambulate IRC – 50	– COOH
4. Zeolite	– SO_3H
5. SE-cellulose	– C_2H_4 – SO_3H

(b) Anion Exchange Resins: Like cation exchange resins, anion exchange resins are prepared by condensation and polymerization of various aliphatic or aromatic amines with phenol and formaldehyde as

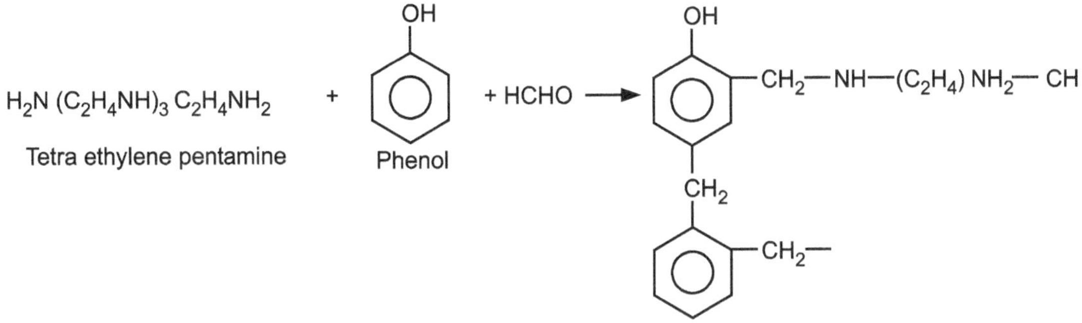

OH
OH
$H_2N(C_2H_4NH)_3C_2H_4NH_2$
Tetra ethylene pentamine
+
Phenol
+ HCHO
CH_2—NH—(C_2H_4) NH_2— CH
CH_2
CH_2—

Alternatively anion exchanger resins are prepared from the transparent beads obtained by the co-polymer of styrene and divinyl benzene. The polymer is treated with epichlorhydrin followed by treatment of trimethylamine.

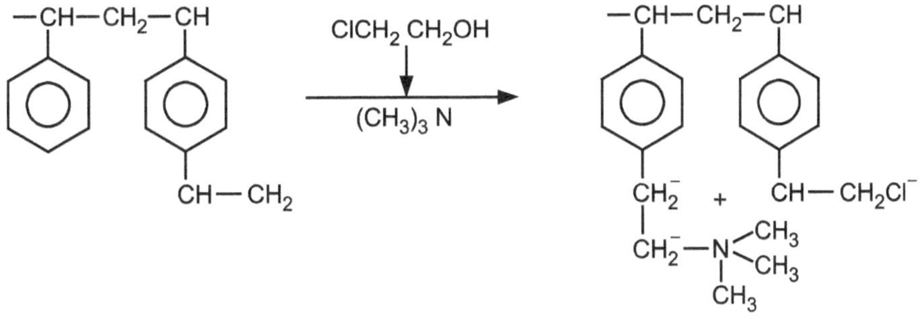

—CH—CH_2—CH
CH—CH_2
$ClCH_2CH_2OH$
$(CH_3)_3N$
—CH—CH_2—CH
CH_2^-
+
CH—CH_2Cl^-
CH_2^-—N
CH_3
CH_3
CH_3

Quaternary ammonium anion exchanger:

An anion exchange resin is a polymer containing an amine or quaternary ammonium groups as integral parts of the resin and an equivalent amount of anions. Anion exchange resin can be denoted by RNH_2. The anion exchange resin when treated with hydrochloric acid, the substituted ammonium cation is obtained as RNH_3Cl^-. When it is treated with solutions of any ionized material, the exchange takes place as:

$$2RNH_3Cl^- + 2H^+ + SO_4^- \rightleftharpoons [RNH_3^+]_2 SO_4^{2-} + 2\,HCl$$

Anion exchange resin thus functions similar to cation exchange resins. Some of the anion exchange resins commercially available are:

Commercial Name	Functional Group
1. Ambulate IRA – 400	– OH
2. Ambulate IRA – 410	Quaternary ammonium
3. Zeolite Pf.IB	Quaternary ammonium – $CH_2N^+(CH_3)_3$
4. De-acidite	– N $(C_2H_5)_2$
5. Dowex A-1	Quaternary ammonium

PHYSICAL PROPERTIES OF ION EXCHANGE RESINS

The ion exchange resins behave as hygroscopic gels, swelling or shrinking reversibly with absorption or desorption of moisture/water. The most important properties of these resins are exchange capacity, density, mechanical strength, particle size, capacity, selectivity, amount of cross linking, swelling, porosity, surface area and chemical resistance.

Cross linking: It affects many properties e.g. swelling and strength of ion exchange resin by its degree of cross linking. As cross linking decreases, swelling increases; it affects the mechanical strength and swelling. Solubility is also greatly affected. If polystyrene is cross linked by incorporation of divinyl benzene, the mechanical strength is imparted to the resin thereby making it insoluble in common solvents.

Swelling: When resin swells, the polymer chain spreads apart forming a narrow passage throughout the resin bed. The weight of swelling of a styrene - DVB co-polymer to toluene can be measured by taking known weight of dry co-polymer in toluene, removing excess of toluene by centrifuging and then weighing the swollen co-polymer. In polar solvents, swelling occurs while in non-polar solvents, contraction occurs. Electrolyte concentration affects the degree of swelling.

Particle size and porosity: Surface area contributes to the rate of exchange. Large surface area and small particle size will increase the rate of ion exchange. Ion exchange resins are stable towards strong acids, strong bases and all organic solvents. Particle size range 50–100 mesh or 100–200 mesh is most commonly employed.

Regeneration: Ion exchange resins after use get deactivated as the replacement of ion takes place. In cation exchange resin, cations from the given solution get attached to the resin and deactivation results. So the cation exchange resins are regenerated by treatment with aqueous acid followed by washing with water. The resin gets converted to H^+ form and can be used for analytical purpose. Similarly, anion exchange resins are regenerated by treatment with sodium hydroxide or sodium carbonate solution followed by washing with water until the washing is neutral. This regenerated ion exchange resin can be reused for the further separation of ions.

MECHANISM OF ION EXCHANGE PROCESS

The ion exchangers behave as a porous network which carries a surplus electric charge distributed over the surface and throughout the pores. The surplus charge is compensated by the ions of opposite charge. When the ionization takes place, they are exchanged with the ions which migrate into the solution. In this process, chemical bonds are not formed but the exchange occurs by the diffusion in two different stages:

1. **Film Diffusion:** Through an extremely thin film there is a diffusion of counter-ions through a surface liquid which surrounds the ion exchanger. It is prominent in dilute solutions and has smaller counter-ions.

2. **Particle Diffusion:** It refers to diffusion of counter-ions within the pores of ion exchanger. It is predominant at high concentration and with large ions. This is increased by exchangers with low degree of cross linking, high exchange capacity, small particle size, and counter-ions with low valency and increasing temperature.

Non-electrolytes and weak electrolytes are usually absorbed by ion exchanger much more strongly than electrolytes. Absorption is enhanced by the formation of complexes between the ionic portions of the exchanger and the non-electrolyte solute. Sorption is decreased when the solute molecule becomes too large to enter the exchanger network. The exchanger then acts as a sieve or filter. In crystal lattice approach, the exchanger acts as a completely dissociated solid in which each ion is surrounded by a fixed number of ions of opposite charge. Since, the ions on the surface are less influenced by attractive forces, the surface ions are readily influenced for other ions, when exchanger is placed in highly polar solvent like water. The ion selectivity will depend on how strongly the surface ion is held by attractive forces within the crystal.

Ion Exchange Equilibrium:

Ion exchange resins contain fixed charge on matrix and counter balanced opposite replaceable charge. The free replaceable charge is readily exchanged with the charge or ion from solution. Thus, in case of cation exchange resin, cation or positive charge on resin is replaced by the positive ion from solution. It can be shown as

$$(Res^-) A^+ + B^+ \text{ (solution)} \rightleftharpoons (Res^-)B^+ + A^+ \text{ (solution)}$$

In running column chromatography, the equilibrium is completely displaced from left to right. If the solution contains several ions of cations like C^+, D^+, E^+ etc. the exchanger shows different affinity for the cations. The extent of one ion exchanged in preference to other ion is of fundamental importance.

The exchange of particular ion is governed by several factors: (a) nature of ion exchange resin, i.e. strong or weak type (b) nature and number of functional groups on resin (c) pH of solution (d) concentration of solution in contact with resin.

It is generally observed that the exchange of higher valent ion on the exchanger with lower valent ion in solution is favoured by increasing the concentration. While dilution favours the exchange of lower valent ion on exchanger for higher valent ion from solution.

Ion Exchange Capacity:

Total ion exchange capacity of resin is dependent upon the total number of ion active groups per unit weight of resin. Greater the number, greater is the capacity of resin. This capacity is usually expressed as milliequivalents per gram of exchanger. The capacities of weak acidic cation exchange or resin also depends on pH. Good values are given about pH 9.0 for weak acidic or pH 5.0 or below for weak basic resins.

OPERATION TECHNIQUE

There are three methods of operation of column for ion exchange chromatography:

1. Displacement analysis
2. Frontal analysis
3. Elution analysis

The basis of all these operations is that the solute has some affinity for the substrate over which it flows. The affinity is due to partition, adsorption or ion exchange properties of the column. The operational procedures in ion exchange chromatography are as follows:

1. **Column:**

   The columns are so designed that any kind of disturbance in the flow of liquid is avoided. All the operations are carried out in the down-flow direction. As the liquid moves down, the ions come in contact with unreacted resin with the result that all the ions are completely exchanged with the resin. The geometry of column depends completely on the separation factor. The separation is improved by increasing the length of the column but the length cannot be increased beyond a critical length. Uneven flow of liquid is possible in case of columns too wide or too narrow in size. Generally, the ratio of 10 : 1 or 100 : 1 of height to diameter is optimal for efficient separation.

2. **Packing the column:**

   The resin is treated with the solvent to achieve equilibrium before packing the column. The slurry of the resin is poured into the column. The solvent which is to be used as an eluent should be used for making the slurry. The slurry is added in several portions allowing the resin to settle down. After packing, the solvent is passed for a certain time to achieve proper flow rate. The level of the solvent is adjusted.

3. **Application of the sample:**

   After packing the column, the solution to be analyzed is added to the top of the column and allowed to pass through the bed of ion exchanger. For this purpose the syringe or pipette is utilized. Some time is allowed so that the ions in solution come in contact with ion exchanger.

4. **Elution:**

   The components of mixture separate and move down the column individually at different rates depending upon the affinity of the ion for ion exchanger. The ions with least attraction will move most rapidly with the solvent. And as they move downwards the distance between them increases. The eluates are collected at different stages. The efficiency of separation increases with increasing column lengths and low flow rates.

5. Analysis of the eluate:

After passing through the ion exchange columns, the eluate is analyzed by various methods such as refractive index, pH, light absorption, etc. The readings are then plotted against the eluate volume to calculate the results.

APPLICATIONS

Ion exchange resins have wide range of applications in many industries.

1. Separation of similar ions:

Ion exchange chromatography is used for separation of similar ions, as different ions undergo exchange reactions to different extents e.g. a mixture of H^+, Na^+, K^+ can be separated by using cation exchange resin. Similarly Cl^-, Br^-, I^- can be separated by passing through basic anion exchanger.

2. Softening of hard water:

By passing hard water through the cation exchanger charged with Na^+, Ca^+, Mg^+ ions from water are retained on the column while Na^+ ions pass into the solution.

3. Complete demineralization of water:

This requires complete removal of ions i.e. cations as well as anions. For this, water is passed through an acidic cation exchanger when metallic cations are exchanged with H^+ ions. The water obtained is then passed through a basic anion exchanger when the anions present in the water are exchanged by OH^- of the exchanger. The H^+ and OH^- ions which pass into the solution combine to form unionized water. Generally, sulphonic acid resin is used as a cation exchanger while strong basic resin is employed as an anion exchanger.

4. Purification of Organic Compounds:

Many natural products extracted in water have been found to contain ions originally present in water. Those ions can be removed by using ion exchange process.

5. Separation of Sugars:

Sugars are first converted to borate complex; the separation of borate complexes of sugar is achieved quantitatively on columns of Dowex. In this, disaccharides can be separated from monosaccharides and individual compounds of hexose pentose from mixture can be resolved.

6. Separation of amino acids:

Ion exchange methods can be used to separate the complex mixture of amino acids obtained by the acid hydrolysis of proteins. The mixture of amino acids is first introduced on a very short column at pH 2 and eluted with 0.35 N sodium citrate buffers at pH 5.25. Acidic and neutral amino acids at first leave the column unseparated; thereafter other amino acids are separated.

7. Purification and recovery of Pharmaceuticals:

The process is used for purification and recovery of antibiotics, vitamins, alkaloids, hormones and other chemicals of pharmaceutical importance during their manufacture.

8. Medicinal importance:

Anionic resins are introduced in the treatment of ulcer while cation exchangers are used to remove Na^+ from body during the treatment of hypertension and oedema. The resins are also used as a diagnostic aid in gastric acidity tests. The resins have been successfully used with other medicinal agent to achieve delayed action dosages.

CHAPTER ... 7

HIGH PERFORMANCE LIQUID CHROMATOGRAPHY

INTRODUCTION

Liquid chromatography though cumbersome has the distinct advantage of operating at low temperatures and is advantageous for separation of proteins, nucleosides which are thermolabile.

In conventional liquid chromatography, a dilute solution of sample is passed through a column packed with solid particles. Thus, liquid is passed through vertical columns under gravitational flow. This is passed with slow speed and especially if the packing granules were small enough to give efficient separation, then the delivery under gravity decreases even up to a few drops per minute.

The obvious way to increase the flow rate and get efficient separation is to force the liquid by a positive displacement pump or by gas pressure. This can be achieved by making certain modifications in columns and using smaller diameter and smaller surface area of column particles with the aid other suitable packing structure. This is HPLC, i.e. High Pressure/Performance Liquid Chromatography. It has several times more resolving power than open column liquid chromatography, HPLC is used for speedy resolution of complex mixtures.

ADVANTAGES OF HPLC

1. It provides a specific, sensitive and precise method for analysis of different complicated samples.

2. There is ease of sample preparation and sample introduction.

3. There is speed of analysis.

4. The analysis by HPLC is specific, accurate and precise.

5. It offers advantage over gas chromatography in analysis of many polar, ionic substances, metabolic products and thermolabile as well as non-volatile substances.

INSTRUMENTATION OF HPLC

A line diagram of HPLC unit is shown in Fig. 7.1. To attain reasonably high flow rates and yet keep particle size of packing very low (3-10 μm), pumping pressures of several hundred atmospheres (2000–8000 psi) are required. Thus, the equipment for HPLC is quite elaborate though simple.

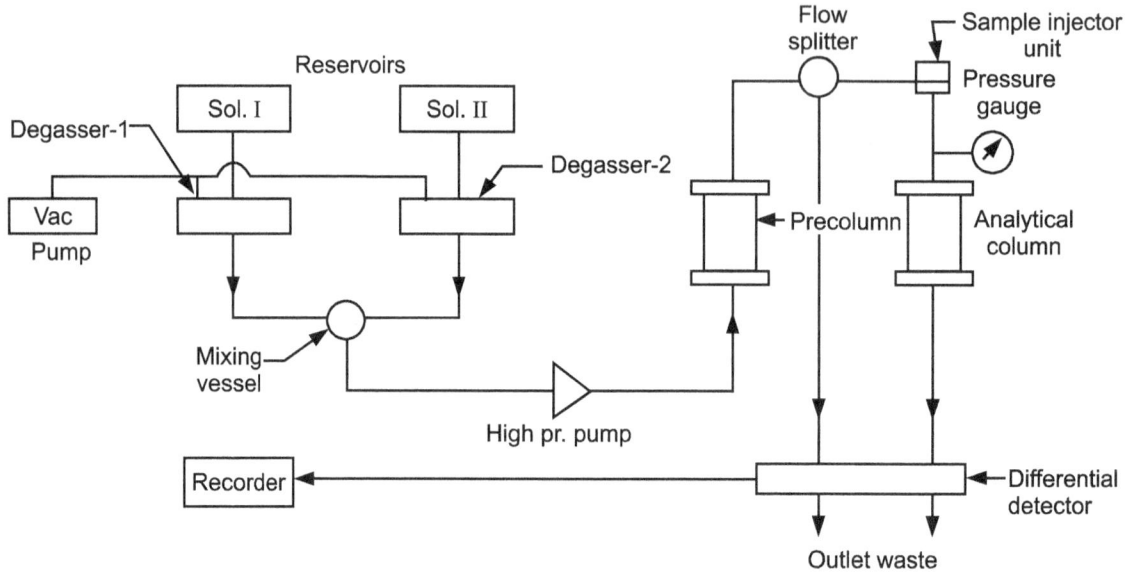

Fig. 7.1

1. Mobile Phase reservoir and solvent treatment systems:

A modern HPLC apparatus is equipped with one or more glass or stainless steel reservoirs, containing 500 ml or more of solvent. The reservoirs are often equipped with a means of removing dissolved gases usually O_2 and N_2 that interfere by forming bubbles in the columns and detector systems. These bubbles cause band spreading; in addition, they interfere with the performance of the detector.

Degassers may consist of: (a) a vacuum pumping system or (b) a distillation system or (c) devices for heating and stirring the solvents or (d) device for sparing in which the dissolved gases are swept out of solution by fine bubbles of an inert gas of low solubility.

Often there is a filter for removing dust and particulate matter from the solvents. An alternative way would be to filter them through a Millipore filter under vacuum before introduction into the solvent reservoir. The filter size used is normally 2 µm. This will eliminate the superfluous matter. In Analytical HPLC, the mobile phase is pumped through the column at flow rate of 1-5 ml/min. In HPLC, the mobile phase can be an aqueous organic mixture, a mixture of organic solvents or buffer solution, depending on the chromatographic method and on the detector used.

A separation that employs a single solvent of constant composition is termed *ISOCRATIC* elution. Frequently, separation efficiency is greatly enhanced by *GRADIENT* elution. Here two or more solvent systems that differ significantly in polarity are employed. The proportion of the two solvents is varied in a programmed way, sometimes continuously and sometimes step-wise. Modern HPLC equipment is often equipped with devices that introduce solvents from two or more reservoirs into a mixing chamber at continuously varying rates; the proportioning values that are provided alter the volume ratio of the solvents linearly or exponentially with time.

The advantage of gradient over isocratic elution is that the separation of the same five components of a mixture, the speed of separation increases (retention time decreases) with gradient elution without any deletion in resolution. Thus, this gradient elution produces effects similar to temperature programming in gas chromatography.

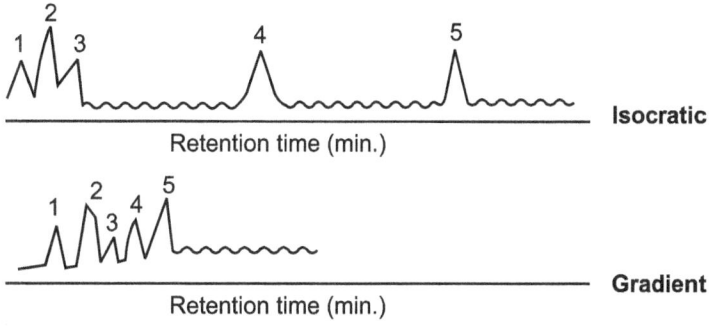

Fig. 7.2

2. Pumps:

The pumps are used to pass mobile phase through the column at high pressure and controlled flow rate. Furthermore, the pumps used in HPLC should have the following features: (a) Generation of pressures up to 6000 psi. (b) Flow rates ranging from 0.1-10 ml/min. (c) Flow control and flow reproducibility of ± 0.5%. (d) It should be composition resistant and give a pulse free output. (e) It should be easy to change from one mobile phase to another. (f) The pump should be easy to dismantle and repair.

These pumps are necessary to force the liquid (mobile phase) through the column with finely packed particles. It should be noted that the high pressures generated by the pumps should not lead to an explosion hazard as liquids are not very compressible. The pumps are categorized into:

1. Constant displacement pumps or syringe pumps.
2. Reciprocating pumps.
3. Constant pressure or pneumatic pumps.

(a) Displacement pump: It consists of a large, syringe like chamber equipped with a plunger that is activated by a screw driven mechanism powered by a stepping motor. The advantages of this pump are: first, the flow is independent of viscosity and column back pressure; second, the flow is pulse free. Disadvantage is the limited solvent capacity (200–500 ml) and it is not easy to change solvent for purposes of gradient elution.

(b) Reciprocating pumps: It consists of a small chamber in which the solvent is pushed back and forth with the help of a motor driven piston or pressure may be transmitted by a diaphragm which is hydraulically pumped by a reciprocating piston.

Advantages of this mechanism and pump are: (i) A small internal volume (35–400 µ*l*); (ii) High output pressure (up to 10,000 psi); (iii) Ready adaptability to gradient elution; and (iv) Constant flow rates independent of column back pressure and solvent viscosity.

Disadvantage is that reciprocating pump gives a pulsed flow which must be damped as it produces a baseline noise on the chromatogram.

(c) Pneumatic pumps: In this, the mobile phase is contained in a collapsible container housed in a vessel that can be pressurized by a compressed gas. Advantages of this pump are:

(i) Flow is pulse free; and

(ii) The equipment is inexpensive.

Disadvantages are:

(i) Limited capacity;

(ii) Pressure output and flow rate depend on solvent viscosity and column back pressure;

(iii) Gradient elution not possible with this pump; and

(iv) Pressure output is less than 2000 psi.

3. Precolumn:

Some HPLC instruments are equipped with a Precolumn, which contains a packing chemically identical to that in the analytical column. Particle size is large; hence the pressure drop across the Precolumn is negligible with respect to the analytical column. The Precolumn is mainly used to remove the impurities from the solvent and thus prevent contamination of the analytical column.

4. Sample Injectors:

Often the limiting factor in the precision of liquid chromatographic measurements lies in the reproducibility wherewith samples can be introduced into the column packing. It must be noted that overloading of the sample causes band broadening. Therefore, minimum amount of sample must be introduced. It is convenient to introduce the sample without depressurizing the system. The sample is usually injected at the head of the column with minimum disturbance of the column material.

The sample injectors are of the following types:

1. **Syringe injection:** This is the earliest and simplest technique. Hence, the sample is injected through a self-sealing elastomeric septum and the syringes are designed to withstand pressures up to 1500 psi. The disadvantage is that the reproducibility is poor.

2. **Stop flow injection:** This too is a syringe injection but here the solvent flow is stopped momentarily. After removing the fitting at the column head, sample is injected directly onto the head of the column packing at atmospheric pressure. Then the fitting is replaced and the system is again pressurized. This technique is extremely simple, and as diffusion in liquids is small resolution is not affected.

3. **Solvent flowing:** Here sampling valves or loops are used, which inject sample volumes more than 10 μ/. Currently, this type of injectors are usually used in all automatic systems. In the fill position the sample loop is filled at atmospheric pressure. Actuation of the valve and the sample in the loop occurs at once. Samples in the range of 1-9 ml can be handled without affecting column efficiency. [See Fig. 7.3].

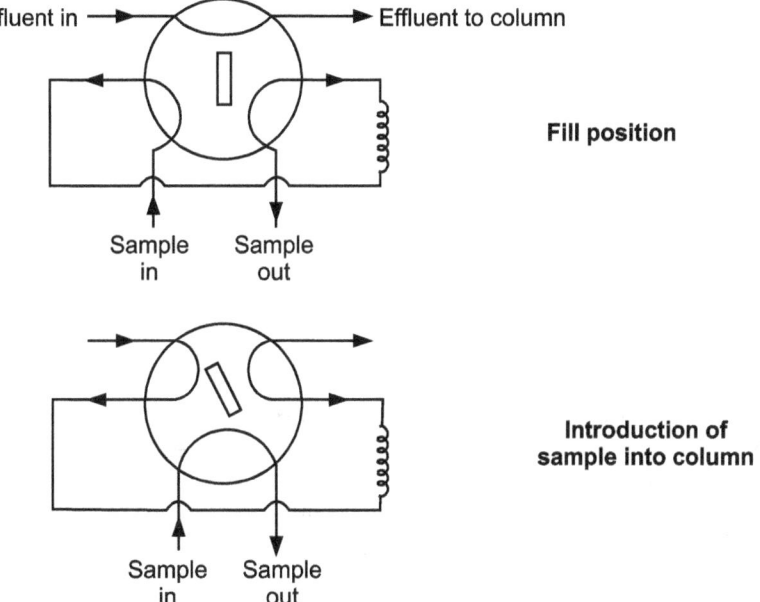

Fig. 7.3

5. **Liquid Chromatographic Columns:**

They are usually constructed from smooth bore stainless steel tubing or heavy-walled glass tubing. If prepared from heavy walled glass tubing, then pressure is restricted to lower than 600 psi. Occasionally, you may come across coiled columns, but their use is very limited.

The columns are of two types: *(a)* Analytical *(b)* Preparative.

For analytical columns:

Size: Length: 25–100 cm with internal diameter of 2-6 mm.

For preparative columns:

Size: Length: 25-100 cm and internal diameter of 06 mm or more.

The common particle size is 5-10 μm; recently manufacturers have been producing high speed, high performance micro-columns which have smaller dimensions.

Length: 3-7.5 cm and internal diameter of 1-4.6 mm; particle size: 3 or 5 μm.

The main advantage of these columns is speed and minimum solvent consumption. These columns should be provided with a system for temperature control to withstand high pressure.

6. Column Packing Materials:

Two basic types of packings have been used in HPLC

(a) Pellicular and *(b)* Porous Particle.

1. **Pellicular:** It consists of non-porous, spherical glass or polymer beads with a diameter of 30–40 μm. A thin porous layer of silica or alumina or ion exchange resin is deposited over it. Sometimes, a liquid stationary phase is held by adsorption over it; alternatively, the beads may be treated chemically to give an organic surface layer e.g. Silica beads which are esterified with alcohols (CORASIL).

2. **Porous Particle:** These particles have sizes ranging from 3-10 μm and are composed of silica, alumina or an ion exchange resin. These particles are often wetted with thin organic films which are physically or chemically bonded to the surface e.g. PORASIL, PORAGEL/STYRAGEL (Polystyrene and Polystyrene acetate beads which are used for non-aqueous solvents). ZIPAX particles are often coated with liquid stationary phase. ZIPAX may be coated with Carbowax, trimethylene glycol, etc. which serve as liquid stationary phase. Ion exchange resin beads are also used.

Presently, analytical HPLC is accomplished with micro-particulate column packings, which are small porous particles usually spherical or irregular silica with diameter 3, 5 or 10 μm. They have high efficiency and a large surface area. Micro-particulates are generally packed into columns using slurry of the material in a suitable solvent and under considerable pressure.

7. Detectors:

A detector is required to sense the presence, and the amount of sample component in the column effluent. A detector that measures property possessed by both mobile phase and solute is called **bulk property detector**, e.g. Refractive Index detector.

If the solute possesses the property e.g. absorption of UV/visible light of electrochemical property, the detectors are called a **solute property detector**.

A good detector should have the following features:

(a) It should respond to all components of the mixture in a wide range of mobile phases.

(b) It should not respond to mobile phase.

(c) It should be unaffected by changes in temperature and flow rate.

(d) It should have high sensitivity, i.e. larger detector signal for smaller amount of solute. Low noise and a wide linear response to solutes present.

(e) It should not constitute to zone spreading.

(f) Non-destructive, inexpensive, reliable and easy to use.

Generally two types of detectors are used:

1. Refractive index monitors detectors:

Since, every compound has its own refractive index, this property becomes a universal indicator. A differential refractometer continuously monitors the difference in RI between the pure mobile phase (reference stream) and the column effluent.

The advantages of these detectors are: (a) They respond to nearly all solutes. (b) They are reliable and unaffected by flow rate. (c) They do not require any double bond or aromaticity to be present in the structure for elucidating a response while disadvantage is that there must be a difference between the refractive index of the solutes and of the mobile phase. Besides, this is not a sensitive detector.

Construction of Refractive Index monitor detector:

1. Several different designs of a refractive index detector have been used in HPLC, one of which is deflection refractometer. [See Fig. 7.4].

Light from the source is focused on the cell, which consists of sample and reference chambers separated by a diagonal sheet of glass. After passing through the cell, the light is diverted to a beam splitter 'B' to two photocells P_1 and P_2. A change in the refractive index of the sample stream causes a change in the relative amounts of light falling on P_1 and P_2 and therefore a difference in their relative output. The difference is amplified, giving an error signal at the amplifier output that operates a servo-meter which rotates the beam splitter until the error is reduced to zero. The beam splitter movement is proportional to the difference in refractive index and is measured by the recorder.

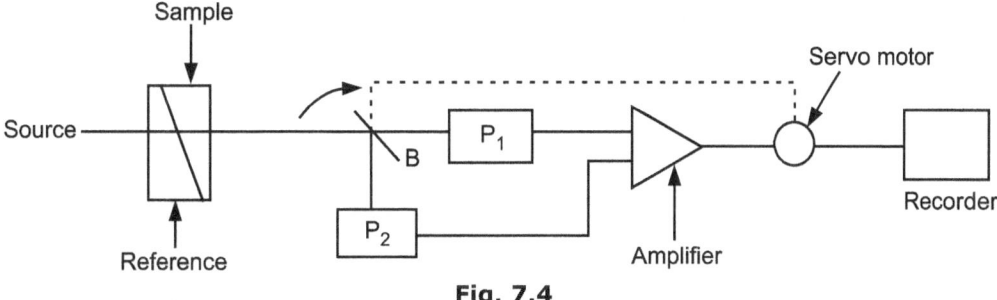

Fig. 7.4

2. UV-visible absorption detector:

The principle is that the mobile phase from the column is passed through a small flow cell held in the radiation beam of the UV/visible spectrophotometer. These detectors are selective, in that they detect only those solutes that absorb UV/visible radiation e.g. alkenes, aromatic compounds and compounds having multiple bonds between C and O, N or S.

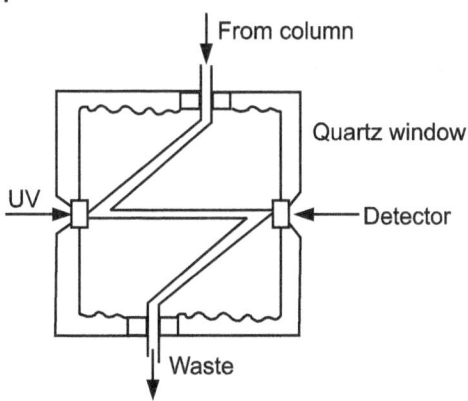

Fig. 7.5: Flow cell for UV/visible absorbance detector

This is 1000 times more sensitive than RI detectors. A low pressure mercury lamp acts as a source. Alternatively, a Deuterium lamp or a tungsten filament with intermediate filters can also act as a source.

Both fixed and variable wavelength UV/visible detectors are available, the latter can operate between 190–700 mm with number of absorbance ranges. Fixed wavelength detectors can operate at 254 nm, 280 nm or other wavelength where most organic compounds, double bonds/aromatic groups cause absorption. Since, most common solvents do not absorb in UV/visible region, the detector is sensitivity free from interferences. Other detectors used in HPLC are IR detectors, fluorescence detectors, electro-chemical detectors and mass spectrometric detectors.

8. Recorders:

The signals from a detector are recorded as deviations from a baseline. Two pen recorders are used with instruments having two detectors. The peak position along the curve relative to the starting point denotes the particular component. With proper calibration, the peak is a measure of amount of component in a sample.

APPLICATIONS OF HPLC

(a) Natural Products: HPLC is an ideal method for the separation of various components in plant extracts which resemble in structure and thus demand a specific and very sensitive method e.g. analysis of digitalis, cinchona, liquorice, ergot extracts.

(b) Stability studies: HPLC is now used for ascertaining the stability of various pharmaceuticals. With HPLC the analysis of the various degradation products can be done and thus stability indicating HPLC systems have been developed as in the case of stability studies of atropine.

(c) Bioassays and its complementation: Antibiotics and peptide hormones are mainly analysed by bioassay which is expensive besides it needs replicates. The biggest disadvantage is the poor precision and length of time required. Bioassays give an overall estimate of potency, but no clue about the composition. Thus, HPLC can be used to complement bioassays to give an activity profile. It has been used for analysis of chloramphenicol, penicillins, cotrimoxazole, sulfas and peptide hormones.

HPLC has been used for biopharmaceutics of the dosage form, and the pharmacokinetics of the drugs.

Assay of the following drugs can be performed by high performance liquid chromatography.

	Drug	Column	Mobile Phase
1.	Alprazolam and it's tablets	Stainless steel column packed with porous silica particles (5-10 μm)	Acetonitrile, chloroform, 1 butanol, water, glacial, acetic acid (850 : 80 : 50 : 20 : 05)
2.	Amitriptyline HCl tablets	Stainless steel column packed with octadecyl silica chemically bonded to porous silica or ceramic micro-particles (5-10 μm)	Acetonitrile: Water (Equal volume) + 0.03 M sodium hexane sulphonate pH adjusted to 4.5 by glacial acetic acid.

	Drug	Column	Mobile Phase
3.	Betamethasone sodium phosphate tablets	Stainless steel column packed with octadecyl silane chemically bonded to porous silica or ceramic micro-particles (5-10 μm)	Citrophosphate buffer pH 5.0 + methanol (55 : 45)
4.	Captopril tablets.	Stainless steel column packed with octadecyl silane chemically.	Methanol + water containing 0.05 volume of phosphoric acid (55 : 45)
5.	Cefadroxil and it's tablets, capsules and oral suspension.	Stainless steel column packed with octadecyl silane chemically.	Phosphate buffer pH 5 + Acetonitrile (96 : 4)
6.	Chlorambucil tablets	———— " ————	Acetonitrile + 0.02 M Potassium dihydrogen phosphate (60 : 40)
7.	Ciprofloxacin	———— " ————	0.025 M phosphoric acid previously adjusted with thioethanolamine to pH 3 and Acetonitrile (87 : 13)
8.	Diclofenac sodium injection.	Stainless steel column packed with octyl silane chemically bonded to totally porous silica particles (5 – 10 μm)	Methanol + 0.1 M sodium acetate solution (60 : 40)
9.	Diltiazem HCl and its tablets.	Stainless steel column packed with octadecyl silane chemically bonded to porous silica or ceramic micro-particles (5-10 μm)	Buffer (0.116% w/v d- 10-Camphorsulfonic acid in 0.1 M Sodium acetate pH adjusted to 6.2 by 0.1 M sodium hydroxide) + Acetonitrile + Methanol (50 : 25 : 25)
10.	Enalepril maleate and its tablets.	Stainless steel column packed with rigid spherical styrene Divinyl benzene copolymer (5-10 μm)	Phosphate buffer pH 6.8
11.	Folic acid tablets.	Stainless steel column packed with octadecyl silane chemically bonded to porous silica or ceramic micro-particles (5-10 μm)	0.05 M potassium dihydrogen phosphate + Acetonitrile adjusted to pH 6 with sodium hydroxide (93 : 7)
12.	Fusidic acid oral suspension	Stainless steel column packed with octadecyl silane chemically bonded to porous silica or ceramic micro-particles (5-10 μm)	Acetonitrile + 1% v/v solution of glacial acetic acid + methanol (60 : 30 : 10)
13.	Guggulipids and its tablets.	———— " ————	Acetonitrile + water (65 : 35)
14.	Haloperidol tablets	———— " ————	1% w/v solution of ammonium acetate + Acetonitrile (55 : 45)

	Drug	Column	Mobile Phase
15.	Insulin	———— " ————	0.1 M sodium dihydrogen phosphate adjusted to pH 2 with phosphoric acid + Acetonitrile (72.5 : 27.5)
16.	Methotrexate and its injection	———— " ————	Phosphate buffer of pH 8 + Acetonitrile (92 : 8)
17.	Norfloxacin tablets	———— " ————	0.1% v/v of phosphoric acid + Acetonitrile (85 : 15)
18.	Omeprazole and its capsules	———— " ————	Phosphate buffer pH 7.4 + Acetonitrile (65 : 35)
19.	Pyroxicam and its capsules	———— " ————	Methanol + Buffer solution prepared by diluting mixture of 7.72 g of anhydrous citric acid in 400 ml water + 5.35 g of sodium phosphate in 100 ml to 1000 ml with water (45 : 55)
20.	Ranitidine HCl and its injection, tablets.	———— " ————	Methanol + 0.1 M Ammonium acetate (85 : 15)
21.	Pyrimethamine and Sulphadoxine tablets	Stainless steel column packed with octadecyl silane chemically bonded to porous silica or ceramic micro-particles (5 to 10 µm)	0.1 % v/v glacial acetic acid + Acetonitrile (4 : 1)
22.	Salbutomol sulphate tablets	Stainless steel column packed with spherical particles of silica, surface of which has been modified by chemically bonded nitrile groups.	Water + 0.5 M Ammonium acetate + 2 Propranolol, pH of mixture adjusted to 4.5 (65 : 30 : 5)
23.	Thiamine HCl injection and tablets.	Stainless steel column packed with octadecyl silane chemically bonded to porous silica or ceramic micro particles (5 to 10 µm)	1 gm of sodium heptanes sulphonate dissolved in a mixture of 180 ml methanol and 10 ml of methyl amine diluting to 1000 ml with water and adjusting the pH to 3.2 with phosphoric acid
24.	Triamcionolone acetamide injection	———— " ————	Methanol + Water + (56 : 44)
25.	Vinblastine sulphate	Stainless steel column packed with octyl silane chemically bonded to porous silica particles (5 to 10 µm)	Methanol + 1.5% v/v diethyl amine + adjusted to pH 7.5 with phosphoric acid + Acetonitrile (50 : 38 : 12).

CHAPTER ... 8

GAS CHROMATOGRAPHY

INTRODUCTION

Gas chromatography is a widely used technique for separation of gaseous and volatile substances which are difficult to separate and analyse. It is a rather simple and inexpensive method, generally efficient in regard to separation. In gas chromatography, gas as a moving phase is passed through a column containing adsorbent or a liquid adsorbent supported on an inert solid. Thus, adsorption or partition is possible. In 'gas solid adsorption chromatography' (GSC), the components of the mixture distribute themselves between the gas phase and the adsorbent and the separation is due to the differences in adsorptive behaviour. While in 'gas liquid-chromatography' (GLC), the components of mixture distribute themselves between gas phase and the stationary liquid phase according to their partition coefficients, the solid functions only as a support for the liquid stationary phase, enabling it to present a large surface for the gas. Thus, GLC has a much greater application in analysis of most of the organic compounds, which have a measurable vapour pressure at the temperature employed.

Though fundamentally it is a separation technique, it provides identification of compounds and the quantitative estimation also. It finds application in analysis of varied type gases and pollutants, petroleum and petrochemicals, oils and fats, food and flavours, drugs and vitamins, steroids and alkaloids, blood and serum, pesticides and fungicides, radioactive isotopes and a number of miscellaneous purposes.

HISTORY

Gas chromatography is a very similar technique to column chromatography except the gas is used as mobile phase instead of liquid. Gas solid chromatography was initially developed by G. Damkohler and H. Thiele (1943), but gas-liquid chromatography was originated by Nobel Laureate: A. J. P. Martin with A. T. James who announced this technique in 1952. Martin has theoretically predicted feasibility of GLC in separation analysis. GLC was further developed with improved instrumentation and applications by various workers.

ADVANTAGES OF GAS CHROMATOGRAPHY

1. This technique has a very high resolution power. Complex mixtures can be resolved into it's components by this method. The separation, identification and determination of compounds with negligible differences in boiling points are possible by this technique e.g. separation of methyl esters of stearic, oleic and linoleic acids is possible.

2. Sensitivity in detection is very high with thermal conductivity detectors. One can detect down to 100 ppm, while flame detectors, electron capture and phosphorus detectors can detect ppm, parts per billion (ppb) or pictograms (10^{-12} g) respectively.

3. It is a micro-method hence small sample size is required. Micro-litre of sample is sufficient for complete analysis.

4. The speed of analysis is fast. The use of gas as the moving phase has the advantage of rapid equilibrium between the moving and stationary phases and allows use of high carrier gas velocities, leading to fast analysis in seconds, minutes or in hours.

5. It involves relatively simple instrumentation operation of gas chromatograph and related calculations do not require highly skilled personnel and thus this technique is suitable for routine analysis.

6. It gives relatively good precision and accuracy.

7. Qualitative and quantitative analysis at a time is possible. The area produced for each peak is proportional to that concentration.

8. The cost of gas chromatograph is very low compared to the data obtained.

TECHNIQUE OF GAS CHROMATOGRAPHY

Gas chromatography is a special form of chromatography wherein the moving phase is a gas and the stationary phase may be either liquid or solid. The technique is suitable for separation of materials which are volatile without decomposition.

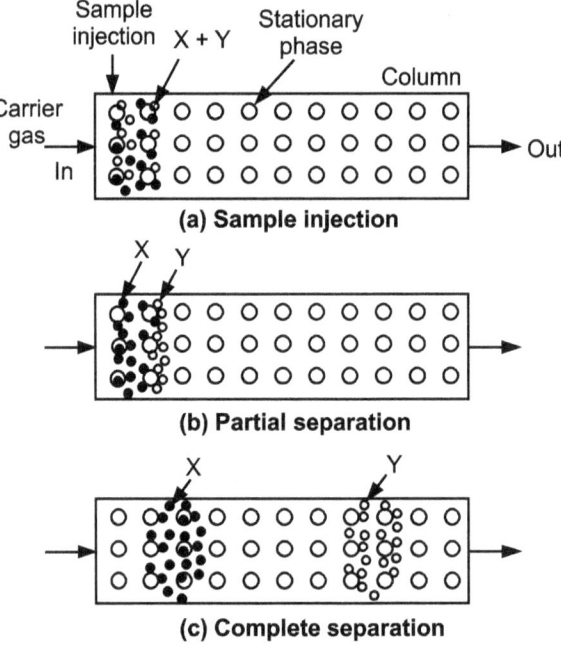

(a) Sample injection

(b) Partial separation

(c) Complete separation

Fig. 8.1

In this method, the sample is introduced into the moving carrier gas stream and is carried by it through the column. The column contains either the active solid (GSC) or a liquid of low vapour pressure held upon an inert solid (GLC). The active solid or non-volatile liquid acts as stationary phase whereas the carrier gas acts as mobile phase. The components of mixture sample distribute between two phases. The adsorption or solubility properties may differ from component to component and therefore the components are carried along the column at different rates, and finally they emerge at the outlet of the column in distinct zones (peaks) separated by the carrier gas. On emerging, the vapours of the components are detected by suitable detector accompanied by an automatic recording.

When the sample in the vapour phase is introduced into the column by carrier gas, some molecules of the sample get rapidly dissolved in liquid and a dynamic equilibrium is established. At equilibrium the concentration of molecules of each type is a constant ratio in two phases e.g. molecules of compound X distribute equally between the two phases and molecules of compound Y on other hand may be highly soluble in the liquid phase therefore a few molecules will be in the vapour phase when the equilibrium is attained. In this position, the carrier gas will drag molecules of X leaving those of Y behind in the column. Molecules of X will be carried to the region containing fresh liquid and some of them get dissolved until new equilibrium is reached. In the meanwhile, a fresh mobile gas comes over the liquid containing Y; some of molecules Y will again enter the gas to reach equilibrium. Thus, the volatile molecules are continuously dragged to the head while the less volatile molecules fall back, they too are picked up and forwarded by continuous gas stream and if conditions are right, a clean separation is achieved. [See Fig. 8.1].

The resolution of chromatography peaks depends on: column efficiency and solvent efficiency. The column efficiency is related to peak broadening of initially compact band as it passes down a column. The broadening results from the column design and operating conditions and can be quantitatively described by the height equivalent to a theoretical plate (HETP). Solvent efficiency results from the solute-solvent interaction and determines the relative position of solute bands on a chromatogram. However, improved separations can be obtained by controlling the variables that increase the band separation (increased solvent efficiency) and/or decrease the band broadening (increased column efficiency) as illustrated in Fig. 8.2.

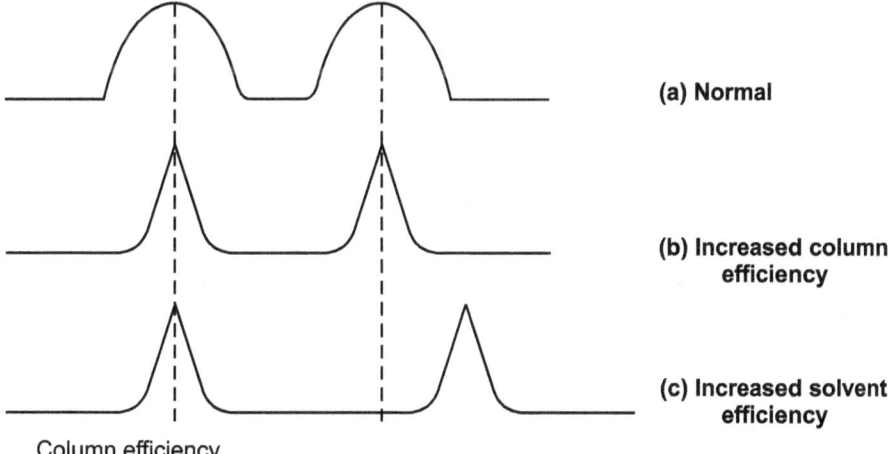

(a) Normal

(b) Increased column efficiency

(c) Increased solvent efficiency

Column efficiency

Fig. 8.2

Column efficiency:

Column efficiency is measured by the number of theoretical plates. The original theory of chromatography, i.e. plate theory was able to describe the effects of variables that influence the migration rates in quantitative terms. However, the plate theory is unable to describe the effects of factors which are responsible for band broadening. Hence, plate theory is now supplemented by rate theory which accounts for the latter variables also.

(a) Plate Theory:

The plate concept is adapted from the theory of distillation columns. According to the theory a chromatographic column is composed of discrete, but continuous, narrow, horizontal plates. It is assumed that, during chromatographic process the equilibration of the solute between mobile and the stationary phase takes place at each theoretical plate with the step-wise transfer of solute and solvent from one plate to the next.

As in distillation, in gas chromatography, the discrete plate is an artificial concept. The separation efficiency of chromatographic column increases with increasing number of theoretical plates. Thus, the number of theoretical plates N is used as measure of column efficiency. Theoretical plates can be easily measured from the chromatogram. The number of theoretical plates N, is given by

$$N = 16 \left(\frac{t}{w}\right)^2$$

Where 't' is the distance from injection to peak maximum (retention time) and 'w' is the peak width in units of time which can be determined by drawing the tangents about 2/3 of the height to the peak at the points of inflection. This is illustrated in Fig. 8.3.

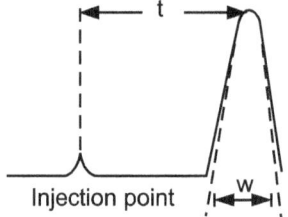

Fig. 8.3

The second term affecting column efficiency is Height Equivalent to Theoretical Plates (HETP); which is that length of column necessary for the attainment of solute equilibrium between mobile and stationary phase. HETP is related to the number of theoretical plates N by

$$HETP = \frac{L}{N} = \frac{L}{16} \left(\frac{w}{t}\right)^2$$

Where, 'L' is the length of chromatographic column, usually in centimeters. HETP calculations are useful in comparisons between columns of different lengths. Thus, HETP and N are the preferred measures of column efficiency.

(b) Rate Theory:

Several chromatographic theories have been developed to account for the shape of elution curves from chromatographic columns. The rate theory developed by Van Deemter et al. successfully describes the influence of variables that affect the band separation (retention time) and band broadening. Van Deemter equation is useful in optimizing the chromatographic performance and can be expressed as:

$$HETP = A + B/u + Cu$$

Where A, B and C are coefficients of Eddy diffusion, longitudinal diffusion and mass transfer respectively and 'u' the linear gas velocity (flow rate) through the chromatographic column. The linear gas velocity is measured by

$$\mu = \frac{\text{Length of column, (cm)}}{\text{Retention time of air, (second)}}$$

When HETP is plotted against u, we get a hyperbola with a minimum HETP. This minimum is the optimum flow rate (u) whereas the column efficiency is at the peak. (Fig. 8.4)

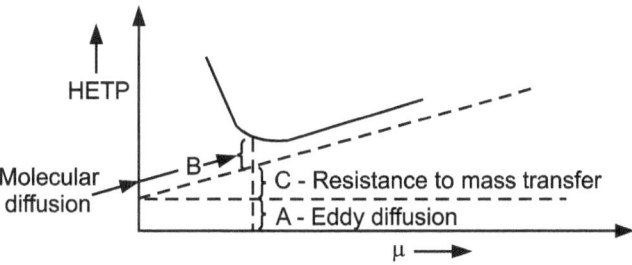

Fig. 8.4

The influence of the parameters of the equation on the separation efficiency has been discussed by Keulemans et al.

(a) Eddy diffusion (Multiple paths) 'A':

In packed columns the solute and carrier gas molecules travel along many paths of different length, thus solute molecules have different residence time. This results into peak broadening. which broadening depends upon the size of packing particles, the shape and the manner of packing and on the column diameter. (Fig. 8.5) The term *A*, i.e. 'Eddy diffusion' can be decreased by using smaller particle size but it is easier to obtain regular packing with larger particles; hence, the particle size should be optimum. Smaller particles also increase the pressure drop across the column leading to disturbance in linear gas velocity, which ultimately decreases column efficiency. Thus, the Eddy diffusion can be minimized by using small particles of uniform size and smaller diameter columns. Generally, the particle size up to 100-120 mesh range and the columns with 1/8 inch inner diameter are used for good resolution.

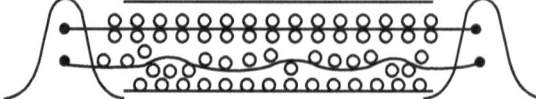

Fig. 8.5

(b) Molecular Diffusion:

Molecules from solution of high concentration tend to move to low concentration by diffusion. This phenomenon of broadening by diffusion occurs during the travel of band of solute on column. The diffusion by concentration gradient occurs on both upper and lower side of the band. This is known as longitudinal diffusion, This is proportional to the solute diffusivity in the carrier gas. High solute diffusivity leads to band broadening with consequent loss of efficiency. Solute diffusion in the liquid phase is negligibly smaller than the gas. Diffusivity is the property of both solute and carrier gas and may be reduced by increasing the density of the carrier gas. This can be done by increasing the pressure or molecular weight of the gas. Thus, the molecular diffusion can be decreased by using the optimum linear gas velocity (flow rate) and using high molecular weight of carrier gas, e.g. nitrogen, or argon than hydrogen or helium.

(c) Resistance to mass transfer 'C' term:

This term describes the effect of the amount and viscosity of liquid on the solid support. A low viscosity low vapour pressure solvent with good absolute and differential solubility for the sample should be used. Also, low liquid loadings (1-10 per cent) have the advantage of fast analysis and lower temperature operation. Low liquid loadings, however, reduce the sample capacity and may require highly inactive solid supports. Lowering the temperature improves the resolution and decreases decomposition of compounds but at the same time may increase the adsorption and time of analysis. Simultaneous reduction of liquid loading and temperature is generally beneficial.

Solvent efficiency: The major advantage of Gas chromatography over distillation is that one can use selective solvent or liquid phase and thus the substances having same vapour pressure can be easily separated. The selection of proper solvent can be facilitated by considering the following factors:

(I) Interaction forces and partition coefficient:

There are four interaction forces that can aid gas chromatographic separation viz. orientation, induced dipole, non-polar and specific interaction forces. Orientation forces result from the interaction between two permanent dipoles, i.e. hydrogen bond. Induced dipole or Debye forces result from the interaction between permanent dipole in one molecule and induced dipole in a neighbouring molecule. These forces are usually small. Non-polar forces result from synchronized variations in the instantaneous dipoles of the two interacting species. They are weaker than the first two types of forces. Specific interaction forces result from chemical bonding by complex formation between solute and solvents.

All these forces determine the solubility of solute and thus separation in chromatography. The combined effect of these forces is expressed by partition coefficient (K).

$$K = \frac{\text{Amount of solute/unit volume of liquid phase}}{\text{Amount of solute/unit volume of carrier gas}}$$

The higher value of 'K' indicates that most of the substance is retained in the liquid phase and only a small fraction of the substance will be eluted in the carrier gas, thus leading to slow movement of the substance down the column. The separation of two compounds is possible if their partition coefficients are dissimilar. The greater the difference in these partition coefficients, shorter is the length of column required for their separation.

(II) Solvent efficiency and temperature:

The solvent efficiency is measured by the relative retention (α) which is the ratio of adjusted retention times or partition coefficients. The relative retention differs from the separation factor (SF) which is the ratio of uncorrected retention times (Fig. 8.6).

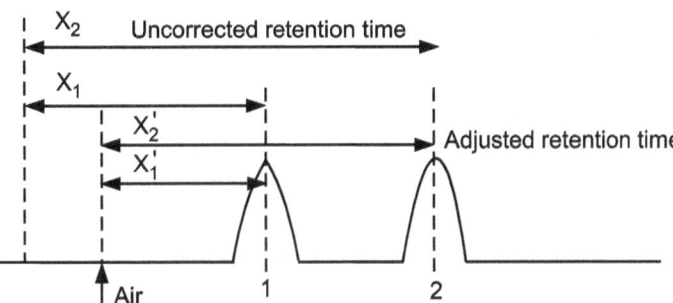

Fig. 8.6

$$\text{Solvent efficiency } \alpha \; = \frac{X_2'}{X_1'} = \frac{K_2}{K_1}$$

$$\text{Separation factor SF} \; = \frac{X_2}{X_1}$$

Both 'α' and 'K' are temperature dependent. The α is constant over a limited range of temperature while K decreases with increasing temperature. This will lead to decreased elution time and decreased separation since the substance will remain in gas phase for more time than in liquid phase which is responsible for separation. Thus to achieve better separations, lower temperature should be used. This will lead to more liquid phase interaction, more separation and longer analysis time. As a minimum, the solute should spend 50 per cent of the time in liquid phase.

(III) Resolution (R):

The true separation of two consecutive peaks on a chromatogram is measured by resolution. It is the measure of both the column and solvent efficiencies and accounts for both the narrowness of the peaks and the separation between maxima (Fig. 8.7).

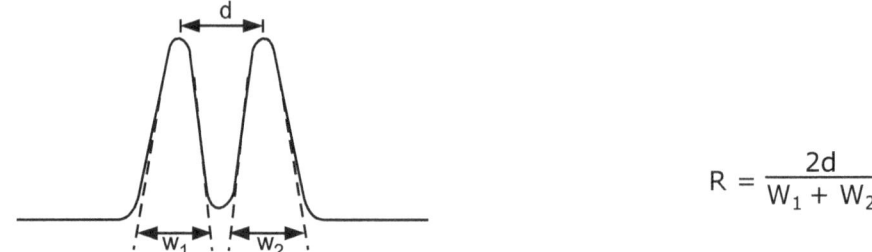

$$R = \frac{2d}{W_1 + W_2}$$

Fig. 8.7: Calculation of resolution

If   R = 1, the resolution of two equal-area peaks is approximately 98 per cent complete.

If   R = 1.5, baseline separation (99.7 per cent resolution) is achieved.

(IV) Number of plates for required separation:

The number of plates and thus the length of column required can be calculated by using the following equation.

$$N_{red} = 16\,R^2 \left(\frac{\alpha}{\alpha - 1}\right)^2 \left(\frac{K_2' + 1}{K_2'}\right)^2$$

Where, K_2' = Capacity factor for peak two

$$= \frac{\text{Adjusted retention time } X_2'}{\text{Retention time in air}}$$

R = Resolution

And α = Solvent efficiency

INSTRUMENTATION OF GAS CHROMATOGRAPH

The modern gas chromatograph consists of the following basic components illustrated in Fig. 8.8.

1. Carrier Gas:

The main purpose of the carrier gas is to transport sample components through the column. For selection of carrier gas, the factors should be ordered as follows:

(a) Chemically inert not to interact with sample or stationary phase.

(b) Suitable for the detector to be utilized and the type of sample analysed.

(c) Optimum column performance consistent with the desired speed of analysis.

(d) Readily available, cheap and of high purity.

(e) Risk-free of fire or explosion hazard.

The carrier gases commonly used are hydrogen, helium, argon and nitrogen. For most applications with thermal conductivity detector either hydrogen or helium is used. Between hydrogen and helium, the latter should be preferred for safety reasons. Hydrogen is used because it is cheap and when Helium is not available. With flame ionization, hydrogen is used in producing a flame in the detection system and hence nitrogen or helium is used as a carrier gas. For electron capture detector argon is used as carrier gas but argon is not readily available in India.

Purity of carrier gas is very important in gas chromatography. Usually, more than 99.9 moles per cent purity is desirable. Moisture and other gases contaminations are removed by using filter, drier and absorbing tubes. The commonly employed source of carrier gas is a compressed gas cylinder. Sometimes commercially available small units of continuous gas generators are also used. To the compressed gas cylinder, is fixed pressure regulator preferably double stage and a pressure gauge to read the pressure. It is recommended that a molecular sieve, filter drier, flow meter, needle valve should be incorporated in the carrier gas supply line.

A line diagram of GLC unit is shown in Fig. 8.8.

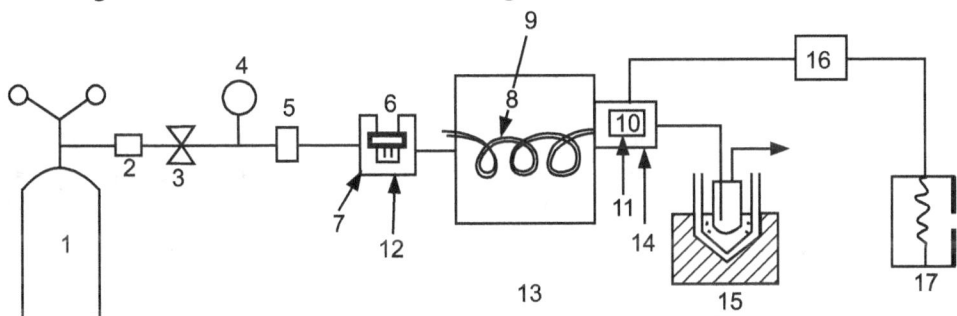

1.	Carrier gas	2.	Filter drier
3.	Pressure control valve	4.	Pressure gauge
5.	Flow meter	6.	Sample injector port
7.	Vaporizer heat	8.	Column
9.	Column oven	10.	Detector
11.	Detector oven	12. 13. 14.	Heater controls
15.	Fraction trap 1	16.	Detector electronic
17.	Recorder		

Fig. 8.8

2. Sample Injection System:

The sample is introduced in the column in the form of a sharp plug through an injection port, which contains a gas tight self-sealing type rubber septum through which the sample is injected by a syringe (Fig. 8.9). Immediately after injection, the sample has to be vaporized instantly and flown into the column with minimum pressure change, flow rate and back diffusion. For this purpose injection ports are heated and specially designed. The temperature of sample injection port is kept 20–50°C above the column temperature.

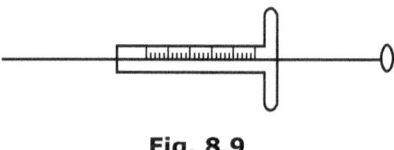

Fig. 8.9

To guard against sample deposition after long use narrow base glass or metal inserts are provided in the injection port.

The sample deposition on insert can be taken out and cleaned periodically. Sometimes, the sample is released just in the column using long needle syringe. Liquid samples are generally injected in μl quantities (0.1–10 μl) with a hypodermic syringe. Gases can also be injected by similar syringes which have gas tight (Teflon tipped) plunger, but are of larger capacity (01–10 ml). Material of construction of the injection port should not have any catalytic effect on the system.

   (a) Gas Samples: Gases are most conveniently introduced by a typical export gas sampling valve which is installed on the gas chromatograph. In these, only carrier gas flows through the column at a specific position while the sample gas flows through the standard volume loop and the gas trapped within the loop is carried into the column. Use of these sampling valves is particularly important to handle gases that contain lighter components where the syringe technique is not very satisfactory. The sample gas can also be injected at the top of the column by a hypodermic syringe. The Hamilton Teflon coated gas syringe is particularly suitable.

   (b) Liquid sample: Liquids are most conveniently introduced by a micro-syringe which is of different size. Sometimes, the syringe needle will take minute cores from the disc or cap and deposit them on the top of the column where they may give distorted peaks as they absorb the components. Small samples can also be introduced by micropipette. They may be made by fusing short lengths of very fine capillary into wider tubing. They can introduce small volumes up to 0.01 micro-litres.

   (c) Solid samples: Solid samples should be made to vaporize as quickly as possible by heating the injection port by means of a small coil. Generally, samples can be weighed into thin glass ampoules, sealed and placed in the gas stream and then crushed in the ancillary tube which is heated by heating coils to vaporize the sample. An alternative method is to dissolve the solid sample in a volatile solvent and inject like liquid sample. But in this case the sample size cannot be measured accurately.

3. Column Technology:

Column is the very important unit of GC, where the separation takes remarkably. The unit parts comprising the complete chromatographic column are the column, the support medium, and the liquid phase.

(a) The column: Depending upon the separation, the columns may vary in shape and dimensions. There are two types of column shapes as coiled helix and U-tube type. Coiled helical shape is most efficient shape but here the problem arises in uniform, even packing. U-tube columns are advantageous due to their short length and easy, even packing. The columns may be made up of glass, aluminium, copper, steel cupronickel or stainless steel. Nylon and other synthetic plastic tubings are also used but their use is prohibited at high temperature. Tubes may be 2-10 mm in diameter and from 2-4 metres in length. Glass is frequently used in U-tubes. W-tube columns are used for separation of compounds which are sensitive to catalytic action, e.g. biological products.

(b) Support medium: The purpose of solid support is to provide large and inert surface area for holding the liquid phase in thin and uniform film. It must be poor adsorbent and must be finely divided porous substance having a large surface area. It should also be chemically inert, heat stable and having sufficient mechanical strength to prevent fractionating with normal handling and be uniformly wetted by the liquid phase. No substance meets all these requirements perfectly. Most common supports are available from diatomaceous earth. Two types are available namely firebrick and Kieselguhr. The firebrick is commercially available as chromosorb P. Kieselguhr is more fragile than fire brick and sold under the name chromosorb W., Celite, Embacel and Celatom. Glass beads, porous polymers, unglazed tiles, sand, fluorinated resins etc. are also used as support medium.

(c) Liquid phase: There is no well accepted method for selecting the best liquid phase for a particular separation. The right selection is based on mainly experience and/or trial and error. The main requirements in choosing a liquid phase are:

    (i) Non-Volatility: It should be practically non-volatile and stable at the operating conditions.

    (ii) Selectivity: It should show selectivity for the components to be separated.

    (iii) Compatibility: It should have reasonable compatibility for the sample components.

(iv) **Low viscosity:** It should have low viscosity at the operating temperature.

(v) **Chemically inert:** It should be chemically inert towards the solutes at the column temperature.

(vi) It should dissolve in a volatile solvent and wettable on the support surface.

Generally, the upper temperature limit is set for a liquid phase, above which the liquid may start bleeding, causing the baseline disturbance. The liquid phase chosen mainly depends on the composition of the sample. For an efficient separation, the liquid phase should be similar in chemical structure to the components of mixture, e.g. hydrocarbons are best separated with hydrocarbon solvent, polar compounds with polar solvent.

Liquids may be classified as:

1. **Very polar:** Glycols, glycerols, amino alcohols, hydroxy acids, polyphenols, dibasic acids etc.

2. **Polar:** Alcohols, fatty acids, phenols, primary and secondary amines.

3. **Intermediate:** Ethers, ketones, aldehydes, esters, tertiary amines etc.

4. **Low polarity:** Chloroform, dichloromethane, 1, 2 dichloromethane, aromatic hydrocarbons etc.

5. **Islon-polar:** Saturated hydrocarbons, halo-hydrocarbons.

(d) **Preparation of Chromatographic Columns:** Three types of analytical columns are used in gas chromatography; packed, support coated open tubular, open tubular columns.

(i) **Packed columns:** These are prepared by packing metal or glass tubings with granular stationary phase. For gas solid chromatography the columns are packed with adsorbents or porous polymers, while in GLC columns are packed by coating the liquid phase over an inert solid support.

(ii) **Open tubular columns:** These columns are called capillary or Golay columns prepared from long (100–130 ft) capillary tubing having uniform and narrow internal diameter [0.01–0.03 inch]. The inside wall of capillary tubing is coated by liquid phase in the form of thin and uniform film. The carrier gas faces least resistance as there is no packing in the column. The sample capacity of this column is very low.

(iii) **Support coated open tubular columns:** SCOT columns are made by depositing a micron size porous layer of support material on the inside wall of a capillary column and then coating with a thin film or liquid phase. These columns have higher sample capacity and yield better resolution.

Generally, in the preparation of columns it is necessary to prepare the stationary phase by coating the liquid phase over the inert stationary support media. The coating is accomplished as follows:

1. Weigh out the required weight of solid support media of correct mesh size and place it in a rotary evaporation flask.

2. Calculate and weigh the appropriate amount of liquid phase to give the correct liquid loading.

3. Dissolve the liquid phase in sufficient volume of solvent to just wet the solid support media.

4. Add slowly the dissolved liquid phase to the support media in flask with stirring until an even slurry is formed and mixed properly.

5. Attach the flask to a rotary evaporator and allow the solvent to evaporate. Rotate the flask until uniform coating of liquid is confirmed.

6. Select a suitable column and plug one end with glass wool and to the open end, add the stationary phase. Uniformly packed columns are prepared with the help of an electric vibrator along the column or by constant tapping during the addition. U-tubes are packed by filling from one end towards the centre with vibrators.

7. The column is now fastened into the chromatograph and conditioned by passing carrier at about 25°C above the operating temperature for 24 hours or for fixed time. An ideally prepared column will maintain constant zero baseline on chromatogram.

(e) Equilibration of the column: Before introduction of the sample, complete equilibration or conditioning must be obtained. Column packed with stationary phase is attached to the instrument and desired flow rate of carrier gas is adjusted by flow regulators. The column temperature is set at desired temperature, but below the upper temperature limit of the liquid phase used. Conditioning is achieved by passing carrier gas for at least 6 hours or generally 24 hours. A properly conditioned column will show zero baseline on the recorder.

(f) Control of column temperature: Columns are usually operated above room temperature except for gaseous samples. A temperature programming is now used where the column is not kept at constant temperature but is subjected to controlled rise which reduces the retention time of the less volatile samples to be analysed more rapidly. For this, various methods have been used, i.e. vapour jackets, electrically heated air baths and liquid bath or metal block etc.

4. Detectors:

After the resolution of solutes, each vaporized component emerges in turn from the column and is carried into the detector mixed with carrier gas. The detector receives impulse from the elute of the column in the form of solute. Vapour is sensed by the detector. It converts this impulse into an electrical signal proportional to the concentration of the solute in carrier gas. This signal is amplified and recorded as a peak on the chromatograph. Thus, the detector is considered to be the brain centre of the instrument. A good detector should (a) be stable against the effects of the extraneous noise in detector system, (b) give a rapid and linear response to changes in solute vapour as the column effluent passes through the detector, and (c) have concentration reproducibility and sensitivity to a wide range of solute vapours. There are numerous types of detectors used in GC, but only three types are in common use.

(a) **Thermal Conductivity Detector:** This is also known as Katharometer or Hot wire detector. The TCD is based on the fact that the rate of loss of heat from body depends upon thermal conductivity of the surrounding gas and that the thermal conductivity of the surrounding gas is a function of its composition. Thus, the rate of loss of heat is related to the composition of the surrounding gas.

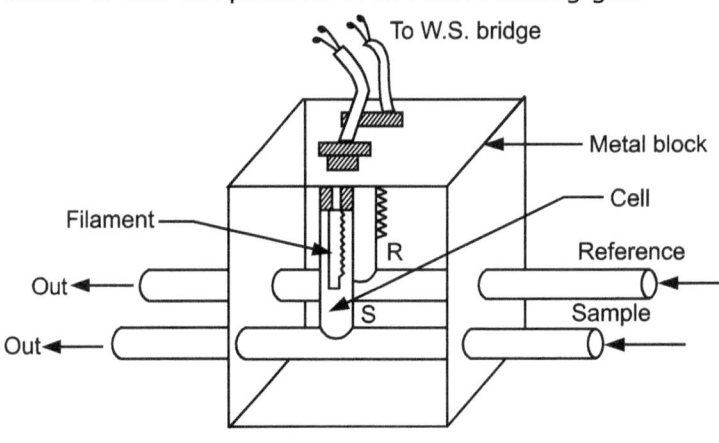

Fig. 8.10

TCD (Fig. 8.10) consists of two chambers of small volumes made within a metal block, each containing a resistance wire or a thermistor which have a high temperature coefficient of resistance. These resistances constitute the reference [R] and the sensing [S] elements respectively and are included in two arms of a Wheatstone bridge circuit. The carrier gas passes in both the cells and the arrangement is such that the column effluents are moved into the sensing side only, the filaments R and S which get heated due to passage of a small constant current, are quite matching when only a carrier gas is passing in both the cells. As the sample component enters the sensing cell, (Fig. 8.11) the temperature of filaments change due to widely different thermal conductivity of the sample component than that of the carrier gas. Consequently, the resistance of 'S' also varies and the bridge becomes unbalanced. This off-balance current is signalled to the recorder which is recorded on chromatogram. Now-a-days it is a common practice to provide four filament TCD, two for reference and two for sensing which improves sensitivity and stability of the instrument.

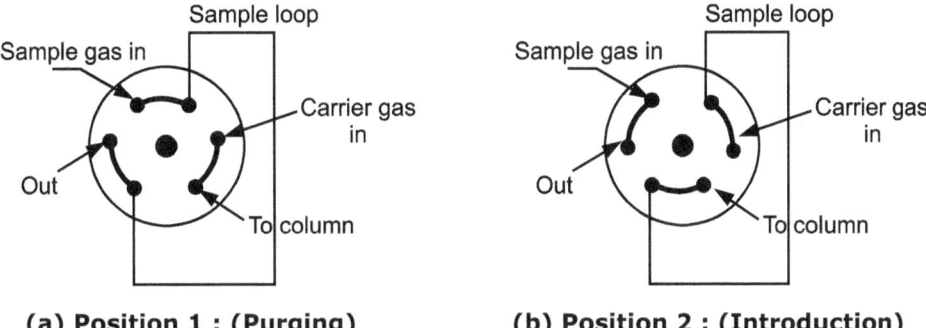

(a) Position 1 : (Purging)   **(b) Position 2 : (Introduction)**

Fig. 8.11

TCD filaments are made of platinum, tungsten or alloys having large temperature coefficient of resistance and corrosion resistant. Thermistors are made of oxides of manganese, cobalt or nickel to which some trace elements are added. It responds to all substances except carrier gas and its sensitivity depends upon the type of carrier gas, filament current, temperature and flow rate of carrier gas.

(b) Flame lionization Detector: A tiny flame of hydrogen is maintained at a capillary jet made of quartz or platinum, air or oxygen is introduced through a side by inlet for supporting the combustion. Column effluents are led into the flame wherein ionization of components may take place. An electrode system located close by picks up the ionization current which is then amplified and fed to the recorder (Fig. 8.12). When only carrier gas passes through the flame, there is no or very small and constant ionization current recorded as a steady baseline. When the sample component elutes and passes through the flame, its molecules are ionized and the resulting ionization current after amplification is fed to the suitable recorder. A FID is sensitive to almost all the organic compounds but insensitive to noble gases, oxygen, nitrogen, CO, CO_2, water, nitrogen oxides, H_2S, SO_2, CS_2 etc.

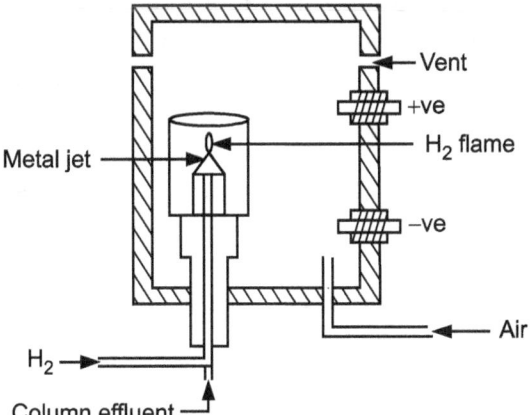

Fig. 8.12

The FID is not concentration sensitive but is rather mass sensitive, i.e. it gives the response proportional to total mass of component entering the detector and is therefore independent of carrier gas flow rate.

(c) Electron Capture Detector: It responds to only those compounds whose molecules have an affinity for electrons, e.g. chlorinated compounds, unsaturated compounds, etc. Nonetheless, it hardly responds to compounds such as hydrocarbons.

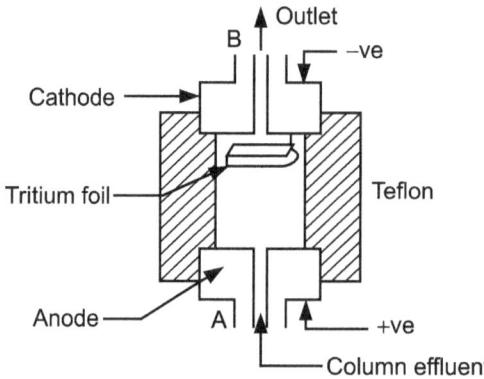

Fig. 8.13

A tritium (titanium tritide) or Ni^{63} foil placed inside the cell ionizes the carrier gas molecules to form electrons that move slowly towards the anode under a fixed voltage (Fig. 8.13) Thus, a standing current is produced which is amplified by an electrometer. When a component having affinity for electrons elutes out of the column and enters the detector, it absorbs some electrons causing drop in standing current. This loss of current is traced by the recorder as a peak.

The disadvantage of this detector is its temperature limitation (220°C) and requirement of very pure/ultra pure nitrogen and argon-methane mixture as a carrier gas.

(d) β-ray Ionization Detector: The principle of ionization in this detector is reverse of flame ionization detector. In this detector, argon which is used as carrier gas is ionized by subjecting it to ionizing radiations. The ionizing radiations, radium 226, strontium 90 or tritium not only ionize it, but also raise a considerable proportion of it to an excited state. The energy of those excited atoms is sufficient to ionize vapour molecules when collision occurs. Thus, the presence of molecules of eluted vapour will give rise to an increase in the current passing through the chamber. Generally, the body of the detector forms one electrode. The other collecting electrode is insulated by a plug of Teflon. The body of the detector is made of brass.

The Argon detector fails to give linear response in case of inorganic substances viz. H_2, N_2, O_2 noble gases, CO, H_2O, H_2, CS_2, nitrogen oxides etc.

5. Recorder:

The signal from a gas chromatograph is continuously recorded as a function of time, generally by a potentiometric recorder. In a potentiometric recorder, the input response is continuously balanced by a feedback response; a pen connected to this system moves proportionately along the width of the chart paper, thus recording the signal, even as the chart paper moves at a fixed speed along its length. Before operating a recorder, its zero should be adjusted with the input zero otherwise the baseline will shift.

6. Integrator:

An integrator is employed for simultaneous measurement of areas under chromatographic peaks by mechanical/electronic means. Manual techniques for measurement of peak area are time consuming, tedious and are less precise. Electronic integrators print out of the peak area digitally and give highest precision but they are quite expensive.

APPLICATIONS OF GAS CHROMATOGRAPHY
(I) Qualitative analysis:

Though gas chromatography is a potential method of separation, it does not yield characteristic symptoms as in case of the chemical or spectroscopic methods. Nevertheless having some data about the origin and the nature of the sample, gas chromatography can be used for the following types of qualitative analysis.

(a) The method can be used to confer identity of a suspected compound but it alone cannot establish the structure of unknown compound. It can provide evidence that two substances are not the same if they have different retention characteristics under identifiable conditions. But if two substances give coincident peaks, it indicates that two compounds may be same.

The retention characteristics of an unknown compound can be expressed mainly as relative retention.

$$r_{A/B} = \frac{V_{g.A}}{V_{g.B}}$$

Where, V_{gA} = Specific retention volume for 'A'

V_{gB} = Specific retention volume for 'B'

$r_{A/B}$ = Relative retention and

A = sample and

B = reference standard

Examples of reference standards include: ethanol, cholesterol, pentobarbital, Chlorpheniramine, Santonin, codeine etc.

Although relative retention is not highly reliable for identification of an unknown, it is useful for analysis of compounds in a mixture of known composition as in routine analysis of body fluids during therapeutic monitoring.

(b) To supplement identification of unknown by retention data, the suspected compound can be added to the unknown compound and to see if there is a concomitant increase in the peak height.

(c) Other approaches which aid in confirmation are: *(a)* derivative the unknown and see if the retention time of derivative compares with that of known derivative, *(b)* trap the material when it elutes and analyse it by standard procedure like UV, IR, NMR or chemical tests.

(II) Quantitative analysis:

The major application of gas chromatography is for quantitative analysis of individual components in a mixture. The method has advantages over titrimetric or spectrophotometry because the separation as well as qualitative-quantitative evaluation of a mixture can all be performed at once.

In most of gas chromatography detectors, the size of the peak is proportional to the amount of compound which has passed through the detector.

(a) External standardization: This involves calibration of the instrument by injection sample of known quantitative composition, i.e. by plotting a graph of peak area (or peak height) versus the concentration. That is how we get a standard curve. Then the peak area or height for the unknown is determined and the results are read from the graph.

(b) Internal standardization: This is the most used and preferred method in gas chromatography for its quantitative analysis. It involves addition of a compound called internal standard, which is not already present in the sample. The internal standard should have the following requirements:

(i)   Structurally similar to the compound to be analysed.

(ii) Separable from the test compound.

(iii) Internal standard peak should be similar to the sample peak.

Now we know that amount of a compound in a sample is proportional to the area of the chromatography peak.

$$A_1 = f_1 c_1 - \text{for sample}$$

$$A_2 = f_2 c_2 - \text{for internal standard}$$

$$\frac{A_1}{A_2} = K \frac{c_1}{c_2}$$

Where, $K = \dfrac{f_1}{f_2}$

$$f_1 = \text{Proportionality factor for } A_1$$

$$f_2 = \text{Proportionality factor for } A_2$$

Thus, a graph of peak area ratio $\left(\dfrac{A_1}{A_2}\right)$ versus weight ratio $\left(\dfrac{c_1}{c_2}\right)$ will be a straight line with a zero intercept and a slope of $\dfrac{f_1}{f_2}$.

If the amount of internal standard added in each sample is kept constant then c_2 becomes a constant and we will have

$$\frac{A_1}{A_2} = K_1 c_1$$

Where, $K_1 = \dfrac{f_1}{f_2 \, c_2}$

Thus, a plot of $\dfrac{A_1}{A_2}$ verses amount of sample will be a straight line which is used as a calibration curve for the analysis.

Further $\dfrac{A_1}{A_2}$ can be substituted by peak height ratio, i.e. $\dfrac{h_1}{h_2}$, thus a plot of $\dfrac{h_1}{h_2}$ Vs concentration can also be used as a standard curve for analysis.

(III) Application in Pharmaceutical Analysis:

Gas chromatography plays an important role in the analysis of pharmaceutical products and drugs. It is used in quality control, analysis of new products and in monitoring metabolites in biological fluids. Few of the applications include:

(a) **Antibiotics:** Penicillins and derivatives, gentamycin, kanamycin, neomycin, tetracycline, chloramphenicol,

(b) **Anti TB drugs:** Ionized, Ethambutol.

(c) **Antiviral:** Amantidine, Idoxuridine, cytarabin.

(d) **Antineoplastic:** Fluorouracil, 6-Mercaptopurine, Doxorubin etc.

(e) **General anaesthetics:** Ether, ethanol, chloroform.

(f) **Sedative hypnotics:** Barbiturates, Glutethimide

(g) **Tranquillizers:** Diazepam, flurazepam, chlordiazepam etc.

(h) **CNS stimulants:** Nikethamide, caffeine, theophylline.

Similarly vitamins, sulpha drugs, sympathomimetics, alkaloids, steroids, antipyretic etc. are analysed by gas chromatography method.

The assay of the following drugs can be possible by gas chromatography.

	Drug	Column	Carrier gas	Detector
1.	Atropine sulphate eye ointment, injection, tablets	Glass column packed with acid washed silanised diatomaceous support coated with 3 per cent w/w of phenyl methyl silicone fluid.	Nitrogen	FID
2.	Chloroxylenol solution	Glass column packed with acid washed silanised diatomaceous support coated with 3 per cent w/w of polyethylene glycol.	Nitrogen	FID
3.	Clove oil	———— " ————		

	Drug	Column	Carrier gas	Detector
4.	Econazole nitrate cream	Glass column acid washed silanised diatomaceous support coated with 3 per cent w/w of phenyl methyl silicone fluid glass column.	Nitrogen	FID
5.	Ethosuximide syrup	Glass column acid washed silanised diatomaceous support coated with 3 per cent w/w of cyano-propyl methyl phenyl methyl silicone fluid.	Nitrogen	FID
6.	Ethyloestrenol and its tablets and its tablets	Glass column acid washed silanised diatomaceous supported coated with 3 per cent w/w of phenyl methyl silicone fluid.	Nitrogen	FID
7.	Fenfluramine hydrochloride tablets	Glass column acid washed silanised diatomaceous support coated with 10 per cent w/w of polyethylene glycol and 2 per cent w/w of potassium hydroxide.	Nitrogen	FID
8.	Homatropine hydrobromide eye drops	Glass column packed with acid washed diatomaceous support coated with 3 per cent w/w of phenyl methyl silicone fluid.	Nitrogen	FID
9.	Hyoscine hydrobromide injection and tablets	Glass column packed with acid washed diatomaceous support coated with 3 per cent w/w phenyl methyl silicone fluid.	Nitrogen	FID
10.	Lincomycin Hydrochloride	Glass column packed with acid washed silicanised diatomaceous support coated with 3 per cent w/w of phenyl methyl silicone fluid.	Helium	FID
11.	Mianserin Hydrochloride tablets.	Glass column packed with acid washed silanised diatomaceous support coated with 3 per cent w/w of phenyl methyl silicone fluid.	Nitrogen	FID
12.	Stearic acid	Glass column packed with acid washed silanised diatomaceous support coated with 15 per cent w/w of diethylene glycol succinate polyester.	Nitrogen	FID
13.	Troxidone and its capsules	Stainless steel column packed with porous polymer beads.	Nitrogen	FID

CHAPTER ... 9

PROGRAMMED TEMPERATURE
GAS CHROMATOGRAPHY (PTGC)

INTRODUCTION

In ordinary gas chromatography separation of mixtures containing components of widely differing boiling points (polarity) under constant temperature (isothermal) column conditions is quite unsatisfactory. If the column temperature which adequately separates the low boiling constituents is selected, then the higher boiling component has high times and therefore will appear as broad, poorly defined peaks. If the column temperature is chosen to elute and separate high boiling components, then the more volatile (low boiling) components may not be resolved.

These problems can be solved by application of 'Programmed Temperature Gas Chromatography' (PTGC).

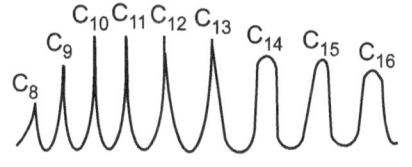 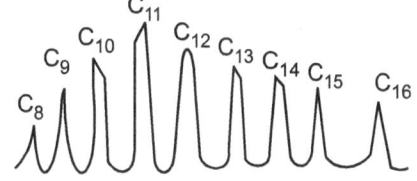

Fig. 9.1

In PTGC, a lower initial temperature is used and the early peaks are well resolved. As the temperature increases, each higher boiling component is "pushed" out by the rising temperature. High boiling components are eluted earlier as sharp peaks similar to earlier peaks. The temperature programming is simply a means for obtaining, automatically, the ideal temperature range for the separation of each narrow boiling point component thus resulting in well resolved, nicely shaped peaks, and a total analysis time is shorter than isothermal operation. Each component selects the temperature range in which to migrate and separate within the column. Prior to reaching this ideal temperature range, each substance is "frozen" or condensed at the head of the column, waiting for its turn to be separated at a higher temperature.

There are number of different methods to increase the temperature of column during chromatographic elution process:

(a) Temperature is increased immediately after sample injection and brought to program level and kept constant until high boiling component have eluted out and then temperature is returned to normal.

(b) The other temperature programming methods involve maintenance of initial column temperature for few minutes after sample injection and then increasing the temperature to a predetermined level and maintaining there, for required period.

(c) The third method involves, increasing the column temperature in several steps before reaching the final, i.e. gradient or step-wise increase.

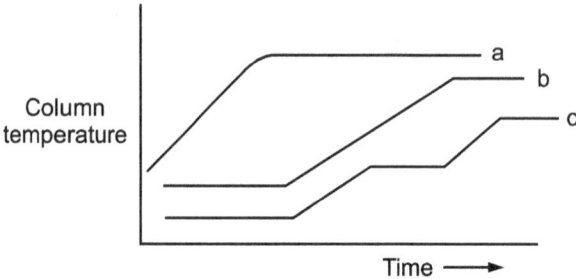

Fig. 9.2

This PTGC can be performed several times depending on the instrument and it permits the resolution of rather complex mixtures. The decision to use PTGC is based on the consideration of the boiling points of the sample components. Generally, if the range of boiling points is 100°C or more, programming is advisable. PTGC also helps in preparative scale, trace analysis and gas-solid chromatography.

One of the major disadvantages of PTGC is that as the temperature of column is increased, the bleed rate of liquid phase from column increases, causing an upward slope in baseline which may interfere with desired analysis.

This can be corrected by modern instruments which have two identical columns, with two identical detectors. The sample is introduced into only one column, i.e. analytical column whereas the other column is used as reference column. The reference column gives a steady baseline.

INSTRUMENTATION

The essential features for PTGC operation include:

(a) Separate heaters for injection port, column oven and detector.

(b) A temperature programmer (01/4°C–20°C per minute).

(c) A low mass oven.

(d) A suitable liquid phase.

(e) A differential flow controller and

(f) Pure, dry carrier gas.

The importance of each of these requirements for the PTGC technique is discussed as follows.

(a) Separate heaters:

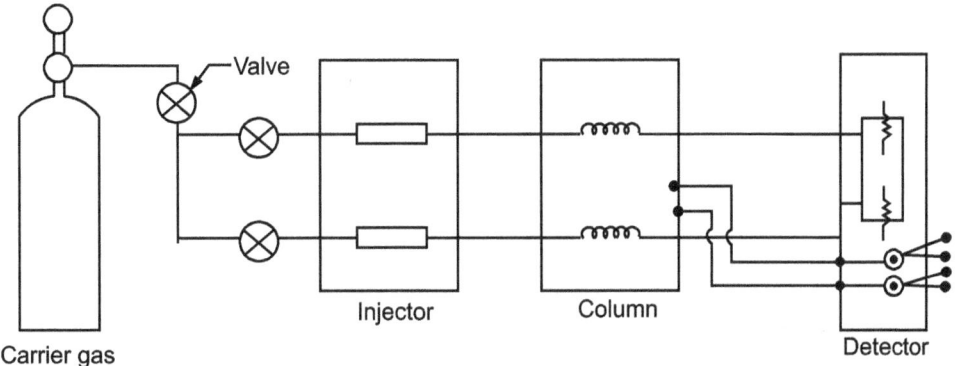

Carrier gas   Injector   Column   Detector

Fig. 9.3: Dual column gas chromatograph

The injection port, column oven and detector oven should be controlled by separate heaters and well insulated from the other. The change in the temperature of any one of these during the analysis is not desirable; particularly TCDs are affected by changes in temperature while FID is not sensitive to small temperature changes.

(b) Temperature programmer:

There should be a mechanism which can precisely reproduce a range of programming rates 1/4°C-20°C per minute which is essential for identification by retention time and for quantization by peak height.

The initial temperature is chosen much the same as for the isothermal analysis of low boiling component and this is normally less than the boiling point of the low boiling components.

The heating rate chosen is a compromise between resolution and speed of analysis. At lower rates, analysis time will be too long for high boiling and band deterioration will take place. At high rates, severe loss of resolution will cause typical rates for 6-10 feet columns of 1/8 and 1/4 inch diameter are 1°C–4°C per minute.

The final temperature chosen should be near the boiling point at the highest boiling component present in the mixture.

(c) Low mass column oven:

This is required to allow rapid heating and cooling of the column. Thin walled, short columns are recommended for programming. The temperature should be reproducible to within 1°C.

High mass ovens will not cool rapidly. Thin walled, stainless steel ovens with tight lid and high speed circulating air fans are an ideal choice.

A column length is chosen on the basis of resolution needed with packed columns; a typical length is 6-10 feet. Longer lengths are not beneficial in programming unless heating rates are used.

(d) Liquid phase:

The liquid phase must be stable at maximum operating temperature. Vaporization of the liquid phase is referred as 'bleeding'. Bleeding produces noise, shifting of baseline and changes in column characteristics. Following table shows the maximum allowable temperatures of some phases used in PTGC. See the table below:

Table 9.1

Liquid Phase	Maximum column temperature
(A) Non polar phases:	
1. Methyl silicone gum rubber (SE – 30)	350°C
2. Apiezon L	300°C
3. Fluor silicone (QF- 1)	250°C
4. Methyl silicone (OV-1)	350°C
(B) Polar phases:	
1. Versamid 900	250°C
2. Methyl phenyl silicone (OV-17)	300°C
3. Carbowax 20 M	250°C
4. Steroid analysis phase (STAP)	250°C

The use of low liquid loadings and narrow columns require low temperatures to elute high boiling peaks and thus helps to avoid bleeding. The total amount of liquid phase should be sufficient to provide column length allowing adequate resolution without requiring temperatures so high as to affect the sample, liquid phase or detector.

(e) Flow controller:

A differential flow controller is required to provide a constant carrier gas flow rate during programming. As temperature increases gas velocities increase, column resistance increases and flow rate decreases, under constant pressure conditions. Hence, differential flow controller, with increasing inlet pressure with respect to increased column temperature is employed.

(f) Pure dry carrier gas:

A 'molecular sieve filter' is recommended for temperature programming. This removes traces of water which produce ghost peaks under programmed conditions.

APPLICATIONS OF PTGC

PTGC is used where the volatilities of the solutes in the mixture may vary over a considerable range by starting at low temperature and increasing the temperature during the run. It is often possible to separate the most volatile component at low temperature range and low volatile component at high temperature.

Complex natural products can be resolved as sharper peaks. PTGC is also useful in preparative scale separations. The major disadvantage of gas chromatography is longer analysis time and peak tail. This can be minimized through temperature programming. PTGC can also be used for qualitative and quantitative analysis similar to gas chromatography.

✳✳✳

CHAPTER ... 10

GEL CHROMATOGRAPHY

INTRODUCTION

The different separation methods used in chromatography are based on different principles. However, in many chromatographic methods it is rather difficult to define the variables which govern the method of separation. In 1954, "Mould and Synge" showed that the separations based on molecular sieving could be performed on uncharged substances during the migration through gels. This formed the basis for separations based on the relative sizes of the molecules. The systematic use of this principle was introduced in 1954 by "Porth and Flodin" who termed it as gel filtration for their method of separating large molecules of biological origin by means of polysaccharide gel (*sephade x*). *Moore* used the term "gel permeation chromatography". In 1964, "Determann" suggested that the "gel chromatography" is the most appropriate term for this technique. This method is mainly based on the differences in molecular dimensions and has different names like gel filtration, molecular sieve filtration, restricted diffusion chromatography, exclusion chromatography, molecular sieve chromatography, etc.

Gel chromatography method separates different substances depending on their molecular size. This technique differs from other partition chromatographic techniques. In this technique, the particles which come from stationary phase in the column are an uncharged gel. The gel swells in the same solvent which percolates through the bed.

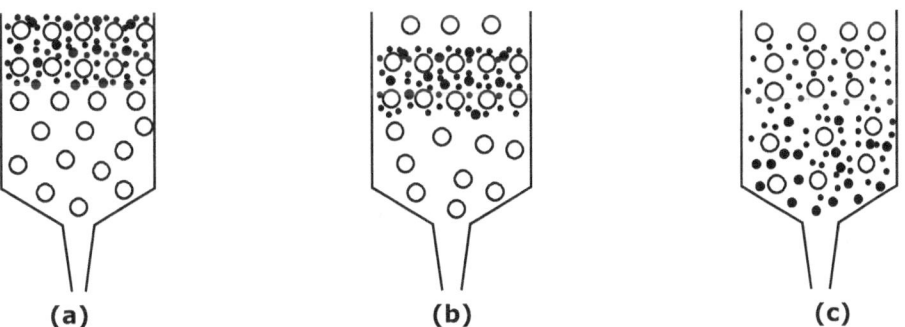

(a) (b) (c)

Fig. 10.1: Stages of separation

The stationary phase is a porous polymer matrix where the pores are completely filled with the solvent to be used as the mobile phase. The pore size is very important. The basis of the separation is the molecules above a certain size are totally excluded from entering and occupying the pores and the interior of the pores is accessible partly or wholly to smaller molecules. The flow of mobile phase will cause larger molecules to pass through the column unhindered without penetrating the gel matrix, whereas small molecules will be retarded because of their penetration in the gel (Fig. 10.1).

Thus, the components of the mixture emerge from the column in order of relative molecular mass, the largest first. The components which are completely excluded from the gel will not be separated from each other, and similarly small molecules which completely penetrate the gel will not be separated from the gel. The molecules of intermediate size will be retarded to a degree dependent on their penetration of the matrix. If the substances are of similar chemical type, they are eluted in order of relative molecular mass. Adsorption effects on the surface of gel particles are ignored and thus gel chromatography may be looked upon as a kind of partition chromatography.

MECHANISM

There are three mechanisms which have been proposed to describe the separation process. It is the process wherein solute molecules are distributed between two liquid phases (liquid in the gel pores and the liquid outside the gel).

(a) Stearic Exclusion Effect:

In this it is presumed that different fractions of the total pore volume are accessible to different size molecules because the gel particles contain a distribution of pore size. The large molecules get small number of pores into which they enter. Thus, small molecules can enter large number of pores.

The stearic exclusion effect is more prominent when major particles are larger than many pores of the gel.

(b) Restricted Diffusion Mechanism:

The process is diffusion controlled, i.e. there is no diffusion equilibrium. Retention volume will be affected by changes in flow rates. The absence of diffusion equilibrium is most pronounced at very high linear velocities.

(c) Secondary Exclusion effect:

If the mixture of large and small molecules is placed on the gel, small molecules diffuse rapidly into the pores of gel and the diffusion of larger molecules in unoccupied pores is reduced. Thus, the larger molecules move further down till they find unoccupied pores; this results in enhancement of separation.

Advantages of Gel Chromatography:

Gel chromatography as it is based on the separation on the differences in molecular dimensions, it has the following advantages:

1. It is very simple to perform.

2. It is not sensitive to eluent composition and the temperature.

3. The gel matrices do not cause degeneration of biological materials and hence can be performed under very mild conditions.

4. The range of separation can be varied by varying the contents of gel matrix.

5. The gels are very stable and can be used again and again without any change in their properties.

TECHNIQUE

Apparatus for gel chromatography is similar to that used for other forms of liquid chromatography. This is discussed below:

1. Column:

The column (Fig. 10.2) is similar to that used in column chromatography and consists of a straight glass tube with a bed support at the bottom. The bed support is of such type that it allows the liquid to flow through while the bed material is retained.

Some glass wool or filter paper is put at the bottom of the tube which is then covered with quartz, sand or glass beads. The diameter of the column is generally larger than those commonly used in partition and adsorption chromatography. The large column diameters and greater column lengths are preferred for high resolutions. The columns for gel chromatography are commercially available with diameters ranging from 1-20 cm.

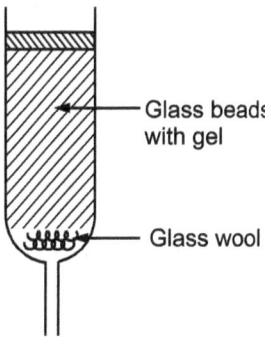

Fig. 10.2

2. Gel:

There are many gels but only a few of them can be used in gel chromatography. In general, the gel should satisfy some of the requirements so that it can be used in this technique. The requirements are:

(i)   The matrix of the gel should be inert chemically.

(ii)   The gel should be stable mechanically.

(iii)   The particle size should be uniform.

(iv)   The Content of the ionic groups should be low in the gel

(v)   The matrix of the gel should have the uniform porosity.

(vi)   The degree of swelling should also be small, since soft materials may bleed down while in use resulting in the alteration of the flow characteristics of the column. Also, it is easier to pack non-swelling materials on the column.

(a) Classification:

The gels are generally:

1. Rigid   2. Semi-rigid   3. Soft gel.

1. **Rigid gels:** Rigid gels have fixed, uniform pore volume, high column permeability. They also provide highly permeable columns with average capacity. Both hydrophilic and lyophilic ones have been prepared. Both silica gel and glasses, which are rigid substances, exhibit adsorption (Retarding especially polar species) which interferes with size separation.

2. **Semi-rigid gels:** These gels swell to about 1.1-1.8 times their dry volume, are open caged spheres, can withstand high pressures and provide a range of pore sizes. Semi-rigid gels are used primarily with aqueous solvents. These gels have been chemically and physically modified to render them wettable. These include cross-linked polystyrene, ion-exchange resins and polyvinyl acetate gels.

3. **Soft gels:** The soft gels imbibe large quantities of solvents into their pores and swell to many times their dry volume. They gain their porosity in proportion to the volume of solvent imbibed. They get easily deformed in the inertial field of moving solvent, resulting in enhancement of column pressure drop. At high solvent velocity, the gel bed gets compressed giving rise to voids in the column. Besides this, soft gels become more fragile with increase in porosity and thus they become useful for small molecules. While employing these gels, the solvent velocities must be kept low, giving high efficiency and capacity. Soft gels consist of cross-linked dextrans (sephadex), starch, rubber, lightly cross linked polystyrenes and polyacrylamide gels.

In general, the inorganic stationary phases such as porous glass or silica gel are available in a range of closely controlled pore sizes which do not swell and hence packing the columns becomes easier and the solvent can be changed without affecting the efficiency. They are stable at high temperatures. However they are less efficient than organic polymer gels. Xyrogels (obtained by the copolymerization of dextran with epichlor-hydrin and subsequent cross linking of the dextran chains by glyceryl bridges) such as sephadex are three dimensional hydrophilic product swelling strongly in aqueous medium. It is stable in pH range 2-10, but is hydrolyzed by concentrated acids and attacked by oxidants. Columns can be stored in 5 per cent formalin solution. Bacterial growth on it can be avoided by using buffers saturated with chloroform.

(b) Choice of Gel:

In gel chromatography, two types of separations are done:

1. The separation of high molecular weight substances from low molecular weight substances. This is called as group separations or desalting.

2. The second type of separation is called fractionation wherein the similar substances are eluted closer to another which may sometimes overlap.

The selection of column packing is generally based on the permeation range of the gel. In group separation, the groups are eluted with application of large volumes of samples whereas the sample size is limited in the fractionation method. For group separation sephadex G-25, Sephadex G-50, Bio-Gel P-6, Bio-Gel P-10 is used. In the fractionation method Sephadex G-25, Sephadex G-100, Sephadex G-500 are used.

(c) Particle size:

For routine work, the gel in the powder form with particle size of 70 µ in diameter is used, but the use of finer grade material gives further improvement in the resolution. The material with particle diameter less than 40 µ can be used in many cases. Sometimes, the commercially available gel may be improved by sieving.

(d) Gel preparation:

In gel preparation, the dry powder is allowed to swell in the liquid to be used as an eluent. The required weight of the dry powder is taken which is then mixed up with excess of liquid for swelling. This mixture is left as such till the equilibrium is achieved; this takes a very long time. The best way is to warm the gel slurry in a boiling water bath to about 100°C. By this method, the swelling will be complete in a couple of days and the bacteria and the fungus present in the suspension are killed and the dissolved air is also removed. The slurry is then cooled before packing.

(e) Drying of gels:

The gels can very well be stored in the wet state and thus there is no necessity of drying them. Agarose gels are not dried as it is difficult to bring them back to the original state. However, dextran gels (Sephadex), acryl amide gels (Biogel) can be dried without any damage and can be returned to the wet state without difficulty.

3. Packing of the column:

The general methods of packing the column as described in column chromatography are not used in gel chromatography. Dry packing of column followed by the liquid will result in the cracking of the column due to swelling of the gels. The most preferable method is to attach a large container to the top of the column. The column is filled with eluent and the thin slurry is poured from the top. The gel settles down in the column and packing is done; this however does not give an even packing.

The procedure for packing depends on the nature of the gel. Special efforts are needed to maintain uniform slurry. With soft gels more careful packing is needed while the hard gels do not require so many precautions. The gel is allowed to swell, and then deuterated under vacuum. The gel is then allowed to settle and the supernatural liquid is taken off. The gel is remixed and then poured in the column. Packing in many steps should be avoided as it gives uneven packing. Liquid should be carefully added; otherwise the gel surface will be disturbed.

With hard gels, the principle of the packing remains the same with slightly modified procedures. Agarose gels which are too thick to be packed directly into the column, are mixed with buffer solution, deuterated under vacuum and then packed.

Sometimes, the eluent is kept at 15–30°C above the column, which avoids the formation of bubbles. This is possible by placing an incandescent lamp just below the eluent reservoir.

4. Preparation of Sample:

The sample is dissolved in a proper solvent so that there will not be any solid particle or other substances which may be strongly adsorbed on the gel. The sample volume should be such which will give the required separations. In analytical applications, sample of 1-3 per cent of total bed volume is used. However, in group separation sample of 25-30 per cent of total column volume is used. The smaller the sample volume, the greater will be reduction of the component concentration in the eluate. The dilution effect must also be taken into account in deciding the column and sample sizes.

5. Application of the Sample:

In most cases, the sample is applied at the top of the gel bed and the flow is started. The sample solution is allowed to pass into the bed. A small amount of eluent is added to wash the traces of sample into the bed. The use of pipette with bent tip is preferable for the application. Viscous samples are introduced with the help of a valve loop. Commercial plunger type columns have special inlet arrangements for the sample.

6. Solvents:

The role of solvent in gel chromatography is less important than the other forms of the chromatography. The choice is often made based on the solubility characteristics of the sample and the type of detector used. In general the solvent should dissolve the sample and be sufficiently similar to the gel to wet it and prevent the adsorption. It must swell the soft gels. The important aspect is that the moving solvent, the trapped solvent and the gel must interact with the solute identically. The solvent viscosity restricts diffusion and affects the resolution. The solvent used must be compatible with the detector used and the system hardware. In many cases, the presence of salt as an electrolyte is important, as many a macromolecule change their size when the solvent composition or the electrolyte concentration is changed. In addition the pore size of soft gels changes with changes in electrolyte concentration. Thus, the solvent composition will affect elution behaviour.

7. Detector:

There are varieties of commercially available detectors. They are mainly based on a variety of physical properties of molecules in the solution. Many times multiple detectors are used. One type is used to indicate the elution of all components of the sample and the other to detect the specific component in the eluate. Thus, with the help of two detectors, information of both the molecular weight and the relation of sample can be obtained.

The differential refractometer is very sensitive in some units detecting difference of 107^7 or even 107^8 refractive index units. They are mostly used as they are not based on presence of specific functional groups. These detectors are temperature sensitive.

The visible and UV photometer is also used in cases where the solutes absorb radiation of wavelength, but the solvent does not; or those solutes which have high extinction coefficients. The detectors based on flame ionization, heat of absorption, electrical conductivity; IR absorption, Polarography, gravimetric etc. are also used.

CHAPTER ... 11

REFRACTOMETRY

INTRODUCTION

When the beam of light passes from one medium to a medium of different density, there is an abrupt change in the direction of beam, this is due to difference in velocity of the light beam in the two media. This bending of light beam from one medium to another is called refraction. See Fig 11.1.

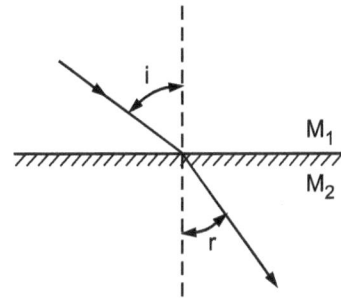

Fig. 11.1

The angle between the incident ray and the normal to the dividing surface is called the angle of incidence $\angle i$ whereas the angle between the refracted ray and the normal to the dividing surface is called the angle of refraction $\angle r$.

According to Snell's law

$$\frac{\sin i}{\sin r} = \text{constant} = n$$

The constant n is called the refractive index of the medium.

The refractive index of a substance is also defined as ratio of velocities of light in vacuum to that in a medium:

$$n_\lambda^t = \frac{V_{air}}{V_M}$$

Where,   n = absolute refractive index of the medium.

The refraction of light will occur, only when, the refractive indices of the two media are different and the angle of incidence is not zero. Refractive indices for various liquids as well as solids vary.

The refractive index for organic liquid ranges from 1.2-1.8, while those for organic solids from 1.3-2.5.

Factors affecting refractive measurements:

The refractive index of two given media changes with temperature, wavelength of light and also pressure, especially in cases of gases.

1. Temperature: The refractive index of the liquid varies with temperature; this is due to corresponding change in the density of the liquid. If the temperature increases by 1°C, refractive index decreases by 0.0004–0.0005. Hence, temperature control is essential for accurate measurements of refractive index. Generally, temperature should be controlled within ± 0.2°C.

2. Wavelength: The wavelength of light used in measuring the refractive index is another important variable. The refractive index of a transparent substance gradually decreases with increasing wavelength of radiation. This is called dispersion. Because of this, the wavelength must be specified in quoting the refractive index of a substance. The D line from the sodium vapour lamp (λ = 589.3 nm) is most commonly used as source of light in refractometry. The C and F lines from hydrogen source (λ = 653.6 nm and 486.1 nm) and G line of mercury (λ = 435.8 nm) are the other sources of light (wavelength) used in refractive index measurements.

3. Pressure: The refractive index of a substance is directly proportional to the pressure because of the corresponding increase in the density of a substance. This effect is most pronounced in case of gases, the change in refractive index with pressure amounts to about 3×10^{-4} per atmosphere. Thus variation in pressure is important in exact determination of refractive index.

If all these factors are kept constant, the refractive index is a characteristic constant and is used in identification and determination of the purity of substance and for determining the composition of homogeneous binary mixture of the known constituents.

MEASUREMENTS OF REFRACTIVE INDEX

Two types of instruments are used for measuring refractive index. They are:

1. **Refractometer:** This is based upon the measurement of positioning the critical ray (angle) or by the displacement of an image. The instruments from this category are very convenient to use for rapid measurement.

2. **Interferometers:** These instruments utilize the interference phenomenon to get differential refractive indices. The measurements by these are very precise.

When the beam of light passes from rarer medium to the denser medium, the angle 'r' will be smaller than the angle 'i'. If we successively increase the angle of incidence i, the angle 'r' also increases keeping the ratio sin i/sin r constant. Fig 11.2.

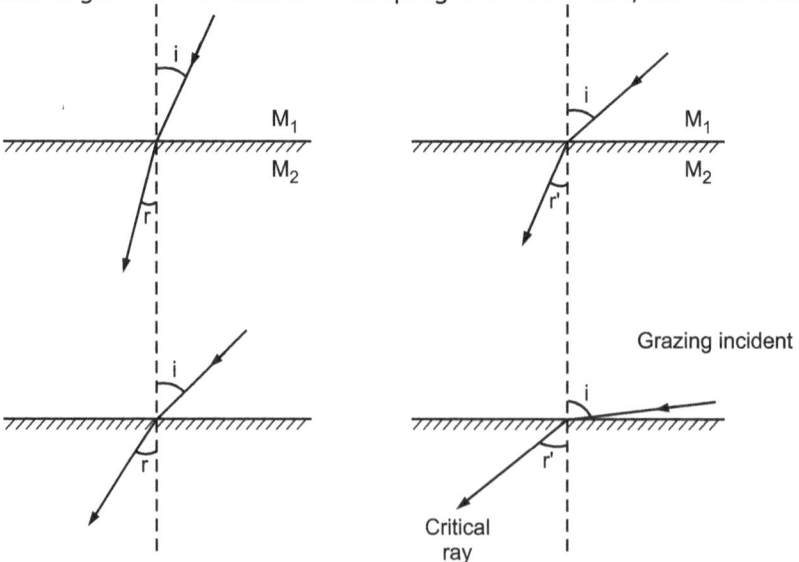

Fig 11.2: Refraction of a beam of light at increasing angle of incidence

When the $\angle i$ is made so large that it approximately equals to 90°, called grazing incidence, the angle of refraction achieves its maximum possible value. This angle is called 'critical angle' of refraction and the ray is called 'critical ray'. This forms the basis for the reference line used in many refractometers.

In actual practice, the light passing through a medium is not a single ray but a relatively broad beam. Part of this beam strikes the prism at grazing incidence while remaining at the smaller values of incident angle. All the area swept out by the critical ray, in the prism will be lighted while area beyond the critical ray will be dark. Thus, the critical ray forms the boundary between the light and dark portion of the prism. A telescope with circular field view and with its superimposed cross hairs is fixed on the prism. The field view is moved across the critical boundary, until the cross hairs center on the boundary (Fig 11.3).

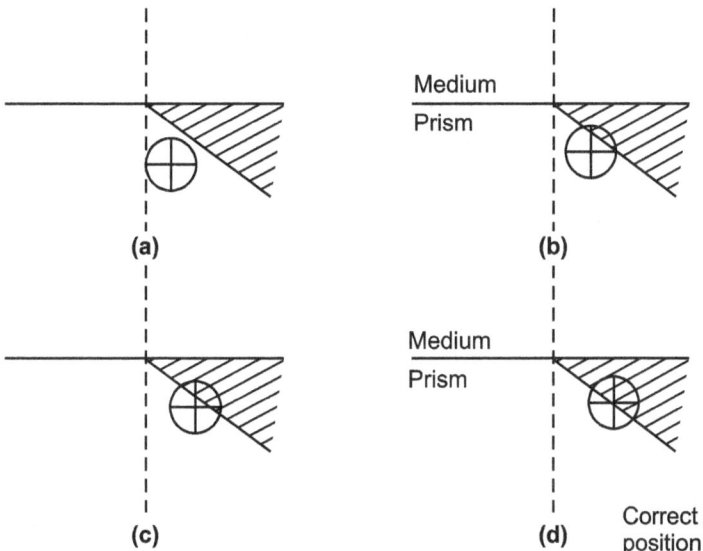

Fig. 11.3

The angle through which the field views are moved (r) will be used for calculating the refractive index.

SPECIFIC AND MOLAR REFRACTION

The specific refraction (r_D) is independent of temperature and pressure. The relationship between refractive index and density is given as $\dfrac{(n^2 - 1)}{d}$ which is approximately constant for number of substances but this depends on the arrangement of electrons in the medium. If the refractive index is corrected for density differences, then specific refraction should be a measure of electronic arrangements in the medium.

The specific refraction is given by the *Lorentz* and *Lorentz* equation as follows:

$$r_D = \frac{(n^2 - 1)}{(n^2 + 2)} \times \frac{1}{d} \text{ cm}^3/\text{g}$$

Where,   n = Refractive index

                                          d = Density of liquid

When specific refraction is multiplied by the molecular weight, we get molar refraction i.e.

$$r_M = \frac{(n^2 - 1)\ M}{(n^2 + 2)\ d}\ cm^3/mole$$

Where, r_M = Molar refraction/refractivity

                                          M   = Molecular weight of the substance

                                          d   = Density of the substance

The specific and molar refraction is characteristic of molecular structure and is constant at given temperature. This is useful in structural studies i.e. finding the nature of bonding in molecules and dipole movement.

Molar refraction is more or less additive property of the groups of elements comprising the compound and can be calculated by adding appropriate group refraction values which have been tabulated. The specific refraction, in homologous series of compounds increases systematically with increasing number of carbon atoms. The table 11.1 gives the appropriate atomic or group refractions.

Table 11.1: Retroactivities of Atom and Groups

Atom/Group	Molar/Group refraction
.C	2.418
.H	1.100
.C = C (double bond)	1.730
.C ≡ C (triple bond)	2.398
.O in C = O	2.211
.O in – OH	1.525
.O in ether, esters (R-O-R)	1.643
.F	1.000
.Cl	5.967
.Br	8.865
.I	13.900
.– NO_2 (aromatic)	7.30
.– OH	2.55
.– COOH	7.25
.–NO_2 (aliphatic)	4.71
.–CH_3	5.65
– C = O	4.60
. Five member ring	0.19
. Six member ring	0.15
N (amide)	2.65
N (Primary aliphatic amine)	2.322

Atom/Group	Molar/Group refraction
N (sec. aliphatic amine)	2.500
N (tertiary.) – do –	2.840
N (primary aromatic amine)	3.21
N (sec.) – do –	3.59
N (tertiary) – do –	4.36
– C ≡ N group	5.460
– S mercaptans (S – H)	7.69

Example 11.1:

Density of allyl chloride ($CH_2 = CH-CH_2 - Cl$) is 0.9 gm/c.c. at 20°C, calculate the refractive index.

Given: Molar refraction contributions for Na D line are C = 2.42, H = 1.1, Cl = 5.97.

$$-\overset{|}{C} = \overset{|}{C} - 1.73$$

Solution: First calculate the molar refraction

$$\text{Molar refraction due to 3 C atoms } 3 \times 2.42 = 7.26$$
$$5 \text{ H atoms } 5 \times 1.1 = 5.5$$
$$1 \text{ Cl atom } 1 \times 5.97 = 5.97$$
$$1 \text{ double bond } 1 \times 1.73 = \underline{1.73}$$
$$20.46$$

Therefore, Molar-refraction for allyl chloride = 20.46 cm^3/mole

$$\text{Molecular weight M} = 76.5$$
$$\text{Density d} = 0.9 \text{ g/c.c.}$$

Now,
$$r_m = \frac{n^2 - 1}{n^2 + 2} \cdot \frac{M}{d}$$

$$20.46 = \frac{n^2 - 1}{n^2 + 2} \times \frac{76.5}{0.9}$$

Therefore
$$\frac{n^2 - 1}{n^2 + 2} = \frac{20.46 \times 0.9}{76.5} = 0.2407$$

Therefore
$$(n^2 - 1) = (n^2 + 2) \times 0.2407$$
$$= 0.2407 \, n^2 + 0.4814$$
$$n^2 - 0.2407 \, n^2 = 1 + 0.4814$$
$$n^2 (1 - 0.2407) = 1.4814$$

$$0.7593\ n^2\ =\ 1.4814$$

$$n^2\ =\ \frac{1.4814}{0.75693}$$

$$n^2\ =\ 1.9510$$

$$n\ =\ 1.3967$$

Therefore, The RI of allyl chloride = **1.3967**

Example 11.2:

The refractive index of carbon tetrachloride at 20°C is 1.4573 and the density at 20°C is 1.595 g/c.c., calculate the molar refraction.

Ans. Given :

$$d\ =\ 1.595\ g/cc$$

$$n\ =\ 1.4573$$

$$m\ =\ 154$$

Now,

$$r_m\ =\ \frac{n^2 - 1}{n^2 + 2} \times \frac{M}{d}$$

$$=\ \frac{2.1237 - 1}{2.1237 + 2} \times \frac{154}{1.595}$$

$$=\ \frac{1.1237}{4.1237} \times 96.55$$

$$=\ 0.2724 \times 96.55$$

$$=\ 26.31\ cm^3/mole$$

Therefore, the molar refraction of CCl_4 = 26.31 cm³/mole.

Example 11.3:

A substance having the formula C_3H_6O might be either acetone or allyl alcohol. The molar refraction is 16.97. Find out whether it is acetone or allyl alcohol?

Given: Molar refraction contributions for C = 2.42, H = 1.1, carbonyl – O = 2.21,

$$\overset{|}{-}\ C\ \overset{|}{=}\ C\ =\ 1.73,\ OH\ =\ 2.55.$$

Solution: First calculate the molar refraction for acetone

$$\overset{\overset{\textstyle O}{\textstyle \|}}{CH_3 - C - CH_3}$$

Molar refraction due to 3C atoms = 3 × 2.42 = 7.26

Due to 6 H atoms = 6 × 1.1   = 6.60

Due to 1 carbonyl O = 1 × 2.21 = 2.21

16.07

Now, molar refraction for allyl alcohol $CH_2 = CH - CH_2 - OH$ comes to 17.04.

The given value of molar refraction, i.e. 16.97 is closer to 17.04; hence the compound is allyl alcohol.

INSTRUMENTATION

Refractometer determines the refractive index by measuring the position of critical ray. There are three types of refractometers: Abbe's refractometer, immersion or dipping refractometer and the Pulfrich refractometer. Out of these Abbe's instrument is most convenient and widely used refractometer.

(a) Abbe's refractometer:

It consists of a stationary telescope and two prisms held in contact with each other in a metal case. The prism system is attached with an arm which moves over the scale to read the refractive index. The Abbe's refractometer has a facility of controlling the temperature of prisms by circulating water of constant temperature. Fig 11.4 shows a schematic diagram of Abbe's refractometer.

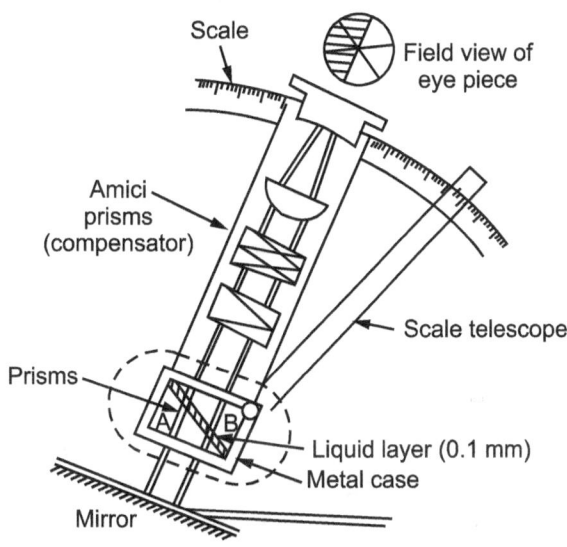

Fig. 11.4

A beam of white light reflected from mirror enters into prism 'A' called illuminating prism whose upper rough surface acts as a source of infinite number of rays which passes through 0.1 mm thin layer of liquid in all directions. These rays then pass through the polished surface of prism 'B' and produce a critical boundary like a rainbow. This is due to the dispersion effect. To eliminate the colour band, an auxiliary optical system called compensator is incorporated into the telescope which refracts the dispersed critical rays by exactly same value as for sodium D line critical ray. Thus, the optical compensator sharpens the boundary and produces a critical ray with white light which is equivalent to that with sodium D line critical ray. Thus, the refractive index measured with the Abbe's refractometer equals to n_D. The scale of the Abbe's refractometer is calibrated directly in refractive indices. The refractive index range is between 1.300 and 1.710.

(b) Dipping/Immersion refractometer:

It is quite similar to the regular Abbe's refractometer except that the telescope is fixed to the refracting prism and there is no diffusion prism. It is very simple to operate but requires about 10–15 ml of the sample. The single prism is mounted in the telescope containing compensator and eyepiece as shown in Fig 11.5. This is commonly used for analyzing solutions.

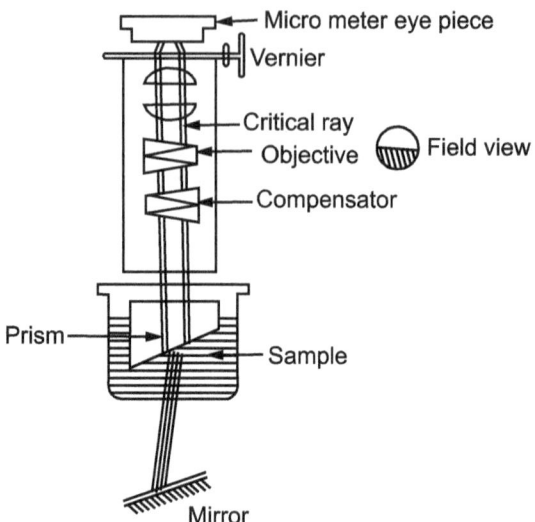

Fig. 11.5

The scale is mounted below the eyepiece inside the telescope tube. The lower surface of the prism is immersed in a sample contained in a small beaker. The mirror present below the beaker refracts the light through the liquid. The position of the critical ray emerging from the prism is read by a fixed telescope with a graduated scale mounted inside. The range of immersion refractometer is less but precision is more than Abbe's refractometer, i.e. + 0.000037 in n_D while for Abbe's it is ± 0.0002. The reading from the linear scale of dipping refractometer can be converted into refractive indices by using appropriate table.

(c) Pulfrich refractometer:

In Pulfrich refractometer, the refracting prism is located under the sample (Fig. 11.6). A beam of monochromatic radiation is allowed to pass along the surface of the prism at grazing incidence. Like Abbe's refractometer the refracted angle (r_c) is observed by a telescope connected to a graduated arc.

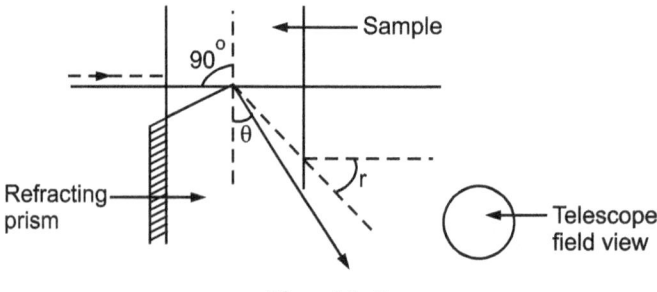

Fig. 11.6

The accuracy of this instrument is about 0.0001 units in n and the range of measurement is 1.33-1.60.

The other instruments used for measurement of refractive index include the image displacement refractometer and differential refractometer.

(a) Image Displacement refractometer: These are based on the principle that any prism spectrometer is a refractometer. If a prism shaped vessel containing sample is used instead of prism of a spectroscope, the image of the slit will be displaced proportional to the refractive index of the sample prism. The refractive index is read from the graduated arc attached to a movable telescope arm. The accuracy of the instrument is about $\pm\ 10^{-6}$ in units of n. A large range of wavelength from UV to IR can be used as source of radiation. These instruments can measure any refractive index value as compared to other refractometer.

(b) Differential refractometer: Differential refractometer detects any difference in the refractive index of the sample compared to reference when placed separately into two hollow prisms. Any difference in the refractive index values will cause angular deviation of slit image which can be measured by a stationary telescope. This method is used in gel-permeation chromatography.

The interferometer is a differential refractometer based on the interference phenomenon of light, i.e. velocities of light in reference and sample liquid are proportional to the refractive index of both liquids. The difference in the sample and reference cell will be measured by suitable means.

Calibration of Refractometer: The refractometer can be easily calibrated by using standard good grade liquids like water$\left(n_D^{20}\ =\ 1.3330\right)$, toluene and methyl-cyclohexane$\left(n_D^{20}\ =\ 1.4231\right)$.

APPLICATIONS

The refractive index measurements can be used for qualitative and quantitative analysis as well as in structural studies.

1. Refractive index is an intrinsic property of a substance. Hence, like b.p. and m.p. it is used in determining the identity and purity of a chemical.

2. The immersion refractometer is useful in determining the concentration of aqueous and alcoholic solutions. Refractometer can be used for analysis of binary mixtures, e.g. glycerine-water mixture. If the working curve of n against concentration is first prepared with solutions of known concentrations, then unknown solution can be analysed by measuring the refractive index and finding its concentration from the working curve.

3. Determination of sugar concentration, alcohol content in fermentation is routinely carried out by using refractometer.

4. It is also used in physiological chemistry. Only about 1-2 ml of serum is required to determine non-albuminous constituents, total globulins, albumins etc.

5. Refractometer can be used to follow the action of ferments in monitoring the effluent by HPLC. In this separation technique, the capability for resolving

mixtures into their components can be studied by detecting refractive index of solutes in a flowing stream.

6. The instauration in vegetable oils and the extent of fluorination in paraffin oil can be determined by recording specific refraction.

7. Besides the refractive index, the molar refraction r_m is also useful in studies of molecular structures.

A refractometer is also useful in controlling the analysis of commercial products and in identifying unknown substances.

CHAPTER ... 12

POLARIMETRY

INTRODUCTION

Polarimetry is the measurement of the beam of polarized light when passed through a certain substance. Polarimeter is an instrument wherein an interposed substance rotates the plane of a beam of polarized light. It is based upon the measurement of the physical property of rotation of plane polarized light. Optical rotatory dispersion and circular dichroism are the other techniques based upon the same principle.

The fundamental principle of polarimetry is based upon the existence of optical activity in a substance. In other words, polarimetry is based on the ability of a substance to rotate plane polarized light. To understand polarimetry, it is necessary to know more about optical activity and the meaning of plane polarized light.

OPTICAL ACTIVITY AND RELATED CONCEPTS

Structural requirements for the optical activity: Substances which refract and/or absorb right and left circularly polarized light to different extents are 'optically active' or show optical rotatory power. Such substances have molecules that lack a plane or centre of symmetry; hence they are said to be asymmetric. This absence of symmetry is the necessary criterion for optical activity as per Pasteur. A carbon atom with its four valencies satisfied by different groups which project to form the corners of a regular tetrahedron is said to be asymmetric. This is because it lacks both a centre and plane of symmetry. The two arrangements that fulfill the above requirements cannot be superimposed. These two are mirror images of one another, e.g. consider the simplest molecule with its atoms C, A, B, D, E. This may be represented as (a) and (b) which are non-superimposible mirror images of one another.

(a)   (b)

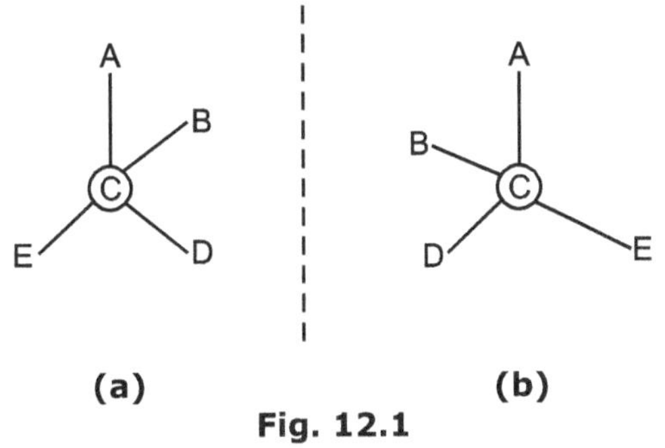

Fig. 12.1

(12.1)

The above figure shows two different molecules, each of which is optically active and rotates the light to the same extent but in opposite directions. Such isomers are called optical isomers or optical antipodes or enantiomers and the phenomenon is called as optical isomerism (i.e. enantiomeric). For every optically active asymmetric molecule, there exist one and only one enantiomers.

Enantiomers of the same substance (mirror images) have identical physical and chemical properties except that they differ in the sign of their optical rotations, e.g. α-aminopropionic acid (alanine).

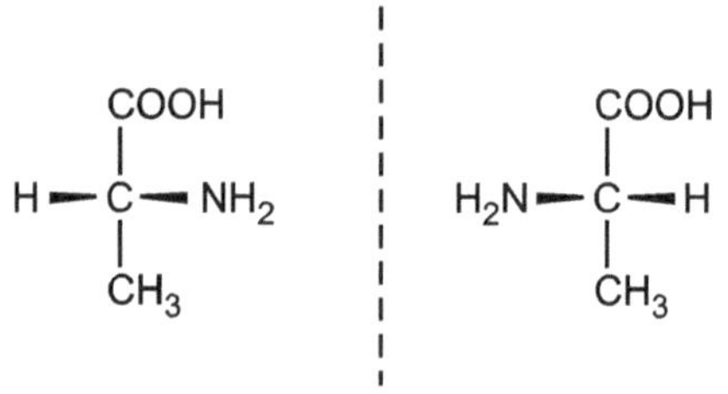

Configuration: The representation which shows the spatial arrangement of the groups of atoms constituting a stereoisomer is known as its configuration, e.g. Configurations of the optical isomers of lactic acid.

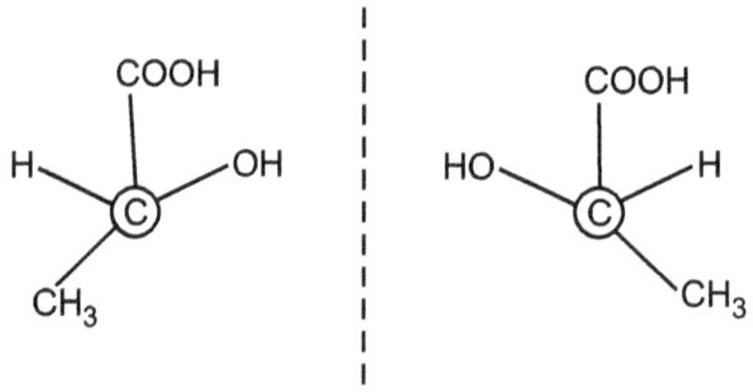

The three dimensional representation is inconvenient for regular use and therefore often replaced by a two dimensional projection formula (Fischer projection formula). In this method of representation, the molecule is so held that the central atom is placed in the plane of the paper, the groups at the bottom and top are equally inclined below the plane and the groups on the left and right are inclined equally above the plane, e.g. consider the projection formula of lactic acid.

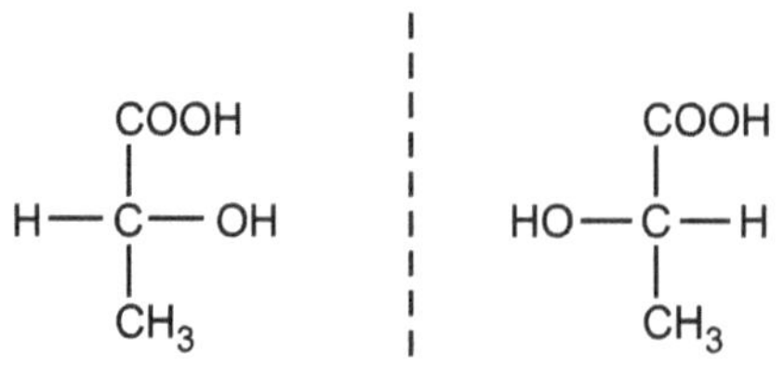

If the enantiomers contain an H atom attached to the central carbon atom and the projection formula shows the horizontal group other than H on the right hand of the C atom, it is said to have (+) D configuration. The other isomer in which the group other than H points to the left hand is said to have (−) L configuration.

Raceme modification: A mixture of equimolar solutions of equal quantities of the two optical isomers is called raceme modification. Such a modification is optically inactive since it is composed of equal number of molecules of both dextro and laevo rotatory molecules; hence the net effect or average rotation is zero.

Diastereomerism: This term is applied to all molecules which may be optically active and may exist in several asymmetric spatial arrangements that are not enantiomeric. In contrast to enantiomers, diastereomers have different physical and chemical properties.

Epimerization: This is another aspect involving the change in the configuration of one asymmetric carbon atom in a molecule which has more than one asymmetric atom. Epimerization usually involves the interconversion of diastereomers and the diastereomers that result differ in configuration at a single asymmetric atom and are called "epimers". e.g. Mutarotation of α (+) glucose, which involves change in configuration at C_1 carbon atom (anomeric C atom). A solution of α (+) glucose $\alpha_D^{20} = +113°$ with time undergoes spontaneous mutarotation to an equilibrium value of $\alpha_D^{20} = +52.5°$. This change involves hemiacetal formation at C_1, the hemiacetal (anomeric) carbon.

α (+) glucose
$(\alpha)_D^{20} = 113°$

Ketoform

β (−) glucose
$(\alpha)_D^{20} = 19.7°$

(epimers)

A molecule containing single asymmetric carbon atom exists as one of the only two possible enantiomers. But the situation is more complex when there are two or more asymmetric carbons in the molecule. For most of such compounds the number of stereoisomers is 2^n, where n = number of asymmetric C atoms. e.g. Tartaric acid. This has two asymmetric carbon atoms each linked to four different groups.

The spatial arrangement of various groups in tartaric acid is as shown as follows.

Mesotartaric acid
optically inactive

(−) Tartaric acid

(+) Tartaric acid

The first two forms of tartaric acid are optically inactive due to internal compensation in the molecule which produces a plane of symmetry.

Mutarotation: It is a process involving asymmetric atom that brings change with time in optical rotation of a solution of a pure optically active substance. Such a solution eventually reaches an equilibrium value of optical rotation which is not usually zero.

Theory behind plane polarized light:

Ordinary, natural, non-reflected light behaves as though it consists of a large number of electromagnetic waves, vibrating in all possible orientations around the

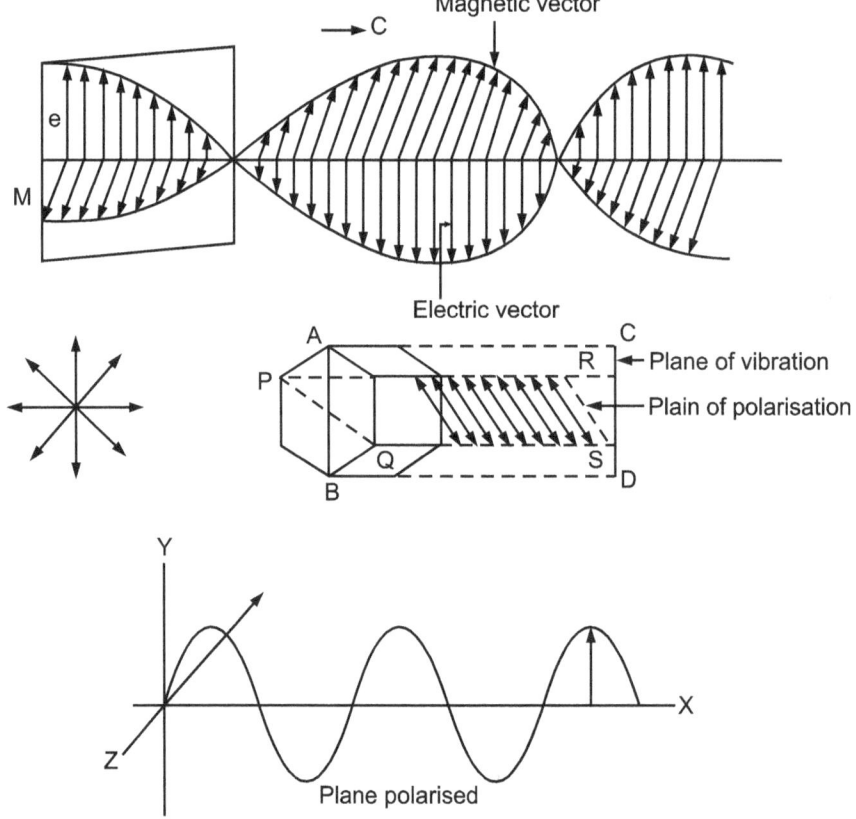

Fig. 12.1

direction of propagation. If, by some means we sort out from the natural conglomeration only those rays vibrating in one particular plane, we say that we have plane polarized light. Since, the light wave consists of an electric and magnetic component vibrating at right angles to each other, therefore the term "plane" may not be quite descriptive, but the ray can be considered planar if we restrict ourselves to noting the direction of the electrical component. Circularly polarized light represents a wave in which the electrical component (and therefore the magnetic component also) spirals around direction of propagation of the ray, either dextrorotatory or laevorotatory. Plane polarized light is obtained by passing a beam of light through an anisotropic crystal, i.e. if the ordinary ray of light is passed through a Nicol prism. The vector interacting with matter is the electric vector; hence the term plane is used.

The electric field of plane polarized light is composed of two components of fixed magnitude rotating in opposite sense with respect to one another (left circularly polarized and right circularly polarized light) and the plane beam is the vector sum of these two.

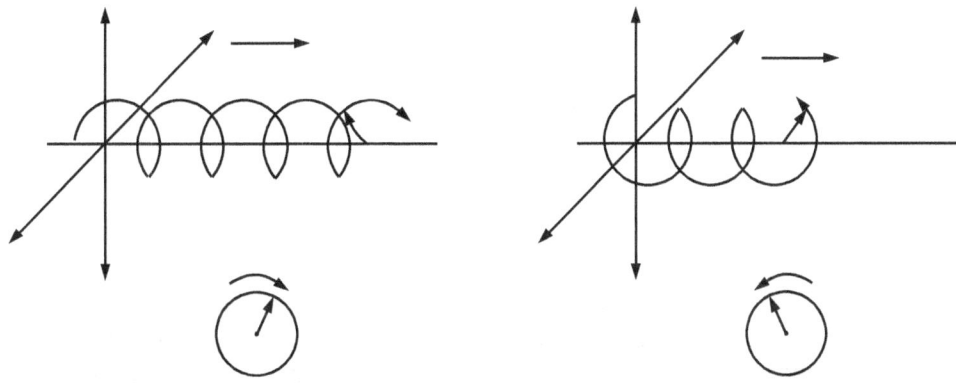

Right Circularly, Polarised (RCP)   **Left Circularly Polarised (LCP)**

Fig. 12.2

When plane polarized light passes through a medium, it is retarded to an extent which is indicated by the refractive index of the medium. When the medium is optically inactive, both the circularly polarized components are retarded to the same extent and the beam emerges from the medium-polarized in the same plane as the incident beam. If the medium is optically active, the components are retarded to different extents because the refractive indices of the medium for left circularly polarized light (n_L) and right circularly polarized light (n_R) differ. This phenomenon of the difference in the velocity of left and right circularly polarized light is called "circular birefringence". As a result of circular birefringence $\Delta_n = \Delta_L = \Delta_R$) the beam emerges from the medium still plane polarized but with the plane of polarization inclined at an angle $\theta°$ to the plane of polarization of the incident beam.

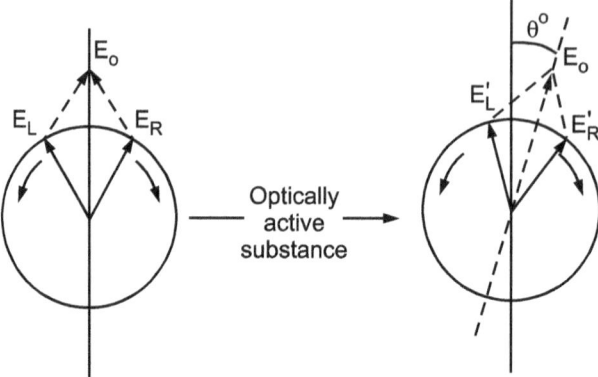

Fig. 12.3

It has been found that the magnitude of rotation depends upon the following factors:

- Nature of substance
- Length of liquid column (*l*) through which light passes
- Concentration of solution
- Temperature of the solution
- Nature of the solvent
- Wavelength of light used.

The rotary power of a given solution is generally expressed as specific rotation $(\alpha)_D^t$.

SPECIFIC ROTATION

Specific rotation is the number of degrees of rotation of the plane polarized light produced by a solution in one decimetre in length having one gram of the substance per 100 ml. The measurement is carried out at a temperature 't' using sodium light.

$$(\alpha)_D^t = \frac{100 \times \text{Observed angle of rotation}}{\text{Length in dm} \times \text{Grams of substance in 100 ml solution}}$$

$$= \frac{100 \times \theta}{Lc}$$

For very dilute solutions in any given non-active solvent, the specific rotation is constant. Comparison of rotatory power of compounds is facilitated by calculating molecular rotation (ϕ).

$$\phi = \frac{\alpha M}{Lc}$$

The specific rotation 'α' changes with wavelength and the rate of change of specific rotation with wavelength is known as optical rotatory dispersion 'ORD'.

Now, if we consider the absorption effect, if the absorptivities E_L and E_R are different, then the lengths of the clockwise and counter clockwise vectors will differ as one is absorbed more intensely than the other. Their resultant will not be therefore linearly polarized but will be elliptically polarized.

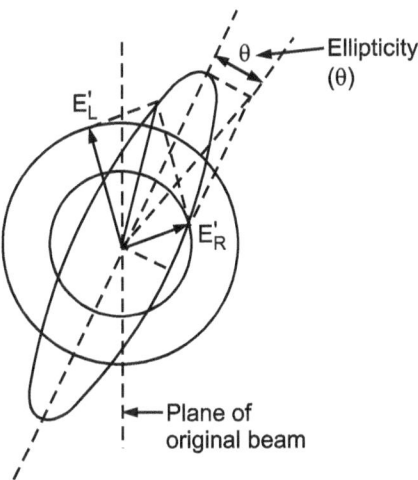

Fig. 12.4

The substance is then said to exhibit circular dichroism 'CD'. For a substance to exhibit circular dichroism, presence of optically active chromospheres is essential. "Chromospheres are a covalently bonded, unsaturated functional group in the molecule responsible for the electronic transitions".

The extent of circular dichroism can be expressed as the molecular ellipticity (θ).

$$(\theta = 3300 \ (E_L - E_R)$$

$$(E_L - E_R) = \text{differential dichromic absorption}$$

E_R is absorbed more than E_L. The resultant vector E_O represents an ellipse with major radius equal to $E_L' + E_R'$ and minor radius equal to $E_L' - E_R'$.

MEASUREMENT OF OPTICAL ROTATION

Natural light cannot be directly used for polarimetric measurements because it includes electric vectors vibrating in all the planes. The optical rotation of these planes results in another equivalent orientation that cannot be differentiated from the initial one. Hence, it is necessary to isolate light whose net electric vector is vibrating in only one plane, i.e. linearly polarized light. This is accomplished by using a polarizer.

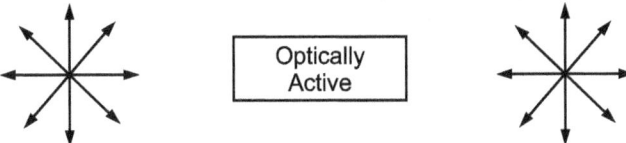

Fig. 12.5

Polarization involves the separation of natural light into its mutually perpendicular components. Either of these linearly polarized components may be used for polarimetric measurements. In certain crystals, e.g. calcite the velocity of light polarized in one plane is different from the velocity of light polarized in perpendicular plane. This indicates that the crystal has two refractive indices one for each linearly polarized ray (Double refracting crystal) e.g.

	η_o		η_e
Crystalline calcite	1.6583 and		1.4864
Quartz	1.544 and		1.553

The two polarized rays therefore do not separate (do not get refracted) although they differ in their velocities.

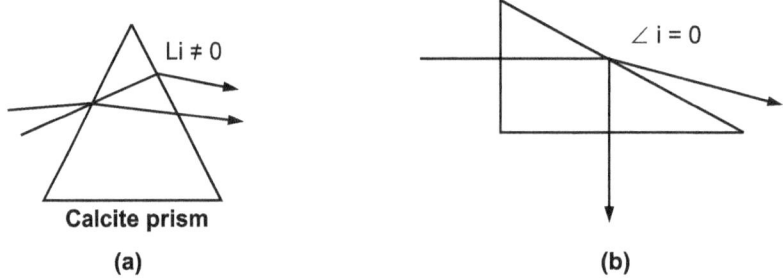

Fig. 12.6

However, in case of the prism as shown in Fig. 12.6 (a) it is difficult to select only one of the rays with the complete exclusion of the other. This may be accomplished, however, if a small but important modification is done in the prism as shown in Fig. 12.6 (b). As per this modification, the angle of incidence selected is such that the critical angle of reflection is exceeded for one ray but not for the other. Thus, the first ray will be totally reflected back into the crystal, whereas the second ray will pass through for use in the polarimetry.

In Fig 12.6 (b), the beam emerging out is not parallel to the incident beam and this is the major practical disadvantage of this polarizer. This problem may be overcome by cementing the second prism as shown in the Fig. 12.7 to re-reflect the polarized ray to be parallel with the incident ray. Other means like crystals of iodoquinone, i.e. Polaroid filters may also be used alternately.

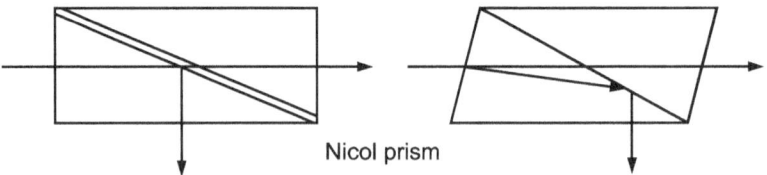

Fig. 12.7

The two prisms are cemented together with Canada balsam (RI 1.55) to reduce the loss of intensity of polarized ray by reflection at the prism interface. Other means of getting PPL are crystals of iodoquinone, i.e. Polaroid filters.

Determination of angle of rotation: If the linearly polarized light is passed through the optically active solution, the plane of polarized light will be rotated by an angle say α°. This may be measured using an analyzer. An analyzer is simply another nicol prism aligned to intercept the linearly polarized ray as it emerges from the sample solution. Maximum transmission of a linearly polarized ray by the analyzer is achieved with "parallel" Nicols. Fig 12.8 (a).

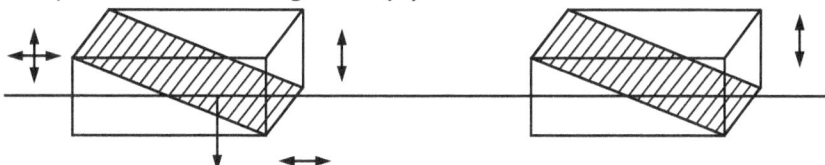

Fig. 12.8 (a)

If the analyzer nicol prism is rotated by 90° from the parallel position, the plane of linearly polarised ray will strike the analyser and get reflected by the analyzer. No light will be passed through this combination of analyzer and polarizer in this particular orientation. This situation is called as maximum extinction and is achieved by "crossed" Nicols Fig 12.8 (b).

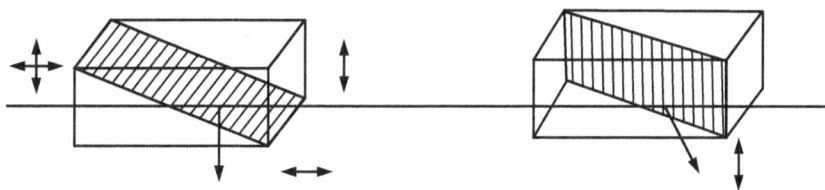

Fig. 12.8 (b)

The optical system for simple visual polarimetry is as shown in Fig 12.9.

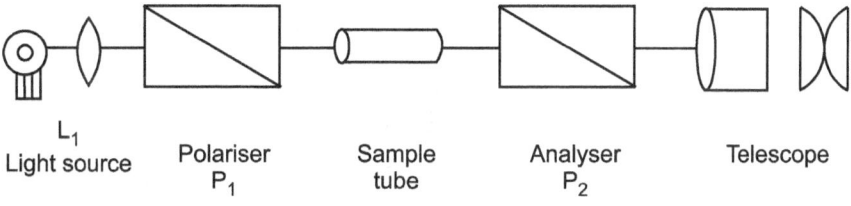

L₁ Light source	Polariser P₁	Sample tube	Analyser P₂	Telescope

Fig. 12.9

SOURCE

The light source is usually a sodium vapour lamp. The light obtained from this source is made parallel using lens L_1 and polarized by Nicol prism P_1.

Operating procedure: Initially, no sample is placed in the sample cell. The second Nicol prism P_2 may be rotated about the axis of the instrument so that the principle planes of P_1 and P_2 are mutually at right angles. Due to this the state of cross-Nicols is achieved and no light is transmitted by P_2 and the field view in the telescope is dark. Now fill the sample in the sample cell. As the sample is optically active, it will rotate the plane of polarized light by say $\alpha°$. Thus, some light will once more emerge through P_2. The previous extinction state can be restored by rotating P_2 through an angle $\alpha°$. This angle through which the analyzer must be turned to restore the condition of total extinction is therefore equal to the angle through which the sample has rotated the plane of the polarized light.

LIMITATION

It is difficult to determine precisely the angular position of P_2 where the illumination of the field is minimum. Because near the extinction point, change in the transmitted intensity per angular rotation is very less (may not be clearly distinguished or detected).

MODIFICATION

The above shortcoming can be overcome by making a small modification in the optical system.

A wedge shaped piece is cut out of the one half of the polarizer Nicol prism and the two parts are cemented together as shown in the Fig. 12.10 below.

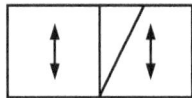 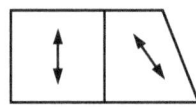 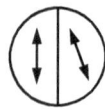

Fig. 12.10

An analyser Nicol prism crossed with the left half of the polarizer will show maximum extinction for half of the field of view, but since it cannot be simultaneously crossed with both halves of the polarizer, the other half of the field will be light in the Fig. 12.11 (a). Similarly is the case with the second half Fig. 12.11 (c).

Now when the analyzer is uncrossed to exactly the same degree with each half of the polarizer, both halves of the field will appear to be of equal intensity Fig. 12.11 (b). This state is called as "half-shade effect". It is a unique condition and highly reproducible. Therefore, better accuracy is obtained.

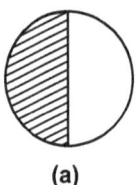  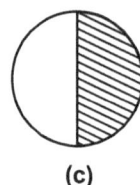

  (a)   (b)   (c)

Fig. 12.11

Applications of Polarimetry

The applications of polarimetry are:

1. Quantitative applications.

2. Qualitative applications.

Quantitative Applications:

Specific rotation is of importance in such applications:

1. If the specific rotation of a sample is known, its concentration in the solution can be estimated.

2. If the concentration of the material in the sample is known, then its specific rotation can be determined.

3. The technique may be extended to the determination of optical substances in the presence of optically inactive species.

4. As optical rotation is additive, readings can also be made in the presence of known amount of other active compound.

5. The observed specific rotation is a function of concentration. Therefore, quantitative analysis of optically active solutes may be carried out polarimetrically over a small range of concentration. The observed rotation is linear to a particular concentration. At higher concentration this linearity is lost. Quantitative analysis may be done by reading unknown concentration from the standard calibration curve of α vs Concentration obtained from solution of known concentration.

The formula used for all the calculations is

$$\alpha = \frac{100.\theta}{lc}$$

α = specific rotation $\qquad\qquad$ θ = observed rotation

l = layer thickness in decimetres $\quad$ c = concentration of solute in grams per 100 ml

Temperature of measurement is indicated by superscript and the wavelength by subscript.

6. Quantitative polarimetric analysis is of special importance in sugar industry and is called saccharimetry. In the absence of other optically active substances sucrose can be determined directly by measuring the angle of rotation, $(\alpha)_D^{20}$ being equal to + 66.5. If other active substances are present, it is required to measure optical rotation before and after hydrolysis in the acidic medium to give a resultant D and L mixture of isomers. This has an optical rotation of − 20.2°. The amount of sucrose present is calculated from the difference in rotation before and after inversion.

$$C_{12}H_{22}O_{11} \quad \xrightarrow{\text{Inversion}} \quad C_6H_{12}O_6 \quad + \quad C_6H_{12}O_6$$

$\qquad$ Sucrose $\qquad\qquad\qquad\qquad\qquad\qquad$ glucose $\qquad\qquad$ fructose

$\qquad$ (+ 66.5) $\qquad\qquad\qquad\qquad\qquad\qquad$ (+ 52.7) $\qquad\qquad$ (− 92.4)

$\qquad\qquad\qquad\qquad\qquad\qquad\qquad\qquad\qquad\qquad$ invert sugar

During 'inversion' the specific rotation changes from + 66.5 to −19.5 corresponding to equimolar mixture of product.

W_s = − 01.17 $\Delta\alpha$ − 0.00105 $(\alpha)_{D\ (x)}\ W_x$

W_s = Weight of source

$\Delta\alpha$ = Difference in rotation before and after the inversion

$[\alpha]_{D(x)}^{20}$ = Specific rotation of HCl

W_x = Weight of HCl

7. Simultaneous determination of penicillin and penicillinase enzyme can be carried out.

Qualitative applications:

These are few in number and not of much importance.

1. ORD and CD measurements can be used for studying configuration and conformation in UV region.

2. Optical activity is a physical constant specific to particular substance; hence an important criterion for the identification and determination of purity of substance.

3. Optical activity is the only parameter available for distinguishing between D and L isomeric forms.

Saccharimetry: The practical application of polarimetry for determination of concentration of sugar is known as saccharimetry. Sugar solutions of high concentrations can be estimated accurately. Impurities present in the solution do not affect optical rotation, thus it is possible to estimate sugar content.

It has been found that quartz shows same rotatory dispersion as the source in visible light. This fact is utilized in constructing a saccharimeter wherein quartz wedge is placed in light path of polarimetry. The wedge device is so adjusted that it compensates rotation of sugar solution. The usual polarizer and analyzer prisms are kept in same fixed orientation of path rays.

The saccharimeters are also called as "polariscopes". The quartz wedge compensating is calibrated in sugar degrees. The typical half shade device is used in the instruments. The graduated scale is °S from − 30 to + 110°S.

In the direct reading method the tube is filled with water and instrument balanced to read zero °S. Then the sugar solution is filled in the tube and rebalancing is done which shows reading in °S.

Cane sugar solutions or other sugar solutions; sometimes these are turbid and pose difficulty in readings. In such cases, the turbidity is removed by using clarifying agent like lead subacetate.

For cane sugar double polarization method is also adopted. In this, initial rotation is determined and then the sucrose is inverted by hydrolysis and second reading is taken. The total change of rotation is due to sucrose, as dextrose or fructose does not change rotation values. The inversion can be carried out by HCl or by enzyme invertase. Mixture of sugar solutions which are not very complex can be analysed by saccharimeter.

Polarimetric analysis is used in the assay of various drugs and pharmaceutical formulations. The drugs assayed by this technique are:

1. Adrenaline Bitartarate injection.

2. Anticoagulant Citrate Dextrose solution (For Dextrose)

3. Dextran 40 injection.

4. Dextran 110 injection.

5. Dextrose injection.

6. Iron Dextran injection (for Dextrans).

7. Sodium chloride and dextrose injection.

CHAPTER ... 13

MEASUREMENT OF POTENTIAL AND pH

INTRODUCTION

Different electrode systems are used in combination to measure potential or pH (hydrogen ion concentration) of a solution. A pair of electrode is commonly required for measurement. One electrode acts as an indicator electrode while the other serves as reference electrode. To understand this mechanism let us consider the concept of electrode potential and its measurements.

ELECTRODE POTENTIAL

When a metal rod (electrode) is immersed in a solution of its own ions a potential is established between the metal rod and its ions in solution, e.g. zinc rod dipped in zinc sulphate solution. The potential difference is given by the reaction

$$M^{n+} + ne \rightleftharpoons M \qquad \qquad ... (1)$$

This potential is expressed by Nernst equation as

$$E = E_O + \frac{RT}{nF} ln\ a^{Mn^+} \qquad \qquad ... (2)$$

Where in R = gas constant, T = absolute temperature, F = Faraday n = valency of ions, ln = natural log to base 10, a^{Mn^+} = activity of ions and E_O = constant dependant of metal ions.

By introducing standard values in the equation and also for ln, i.e. converting natural log to base 10 by multiplying by 2.302,

$$E = E_O + \frac{0.0591}{n} log\ a^{Mn^+} \qquad \qquad ... (3)$$

For most purposes a^{Mn^+} can be substituted by c^{Mn^+} (i.e. concentration in g ions/lit),

We get, $\qquad \qquad E = E_O + \frac{0.0591}{n} log\ c^{Mn^+} \qquad \qquad ... (4)$

In the above 'E_O' is standard potential of metal, n is the valency of ions involved and c is the ionic concentration.

In order to determine potential of a metal electrode (as described above), it is necessary to have another electrode whose potential is accurately known. Now, when these two electrodes are combined, it will form a voltaic cell, and the emf of first electrode can be measured.

In a Daniel cell, zinc rod dipped in zinc sulphate solution and copper rod dipped in copper sulphate solution forms a voltaic cell; as $Zn/ZnSO_4$ (solution) ‖ $CuSO_4/Cu$. In this cell at anode, $Zn \rightarrow Zn^{++} + 2e$ (oxidation) and at cathode, $Cu^{++} + 2e \rightarrow Cu$ (Reudction) occurs. The current flows from zinc to copper.

Electrochemical cells:

For a given electrochemical cell, the emf of it can be shown by

$$E_{cell} = E_{ind} + E_{ref} + E_{jf},$$

where E_{ind}, E_{ref} and E_j refer to potential of indicator electrode, reference electrode and the liquid junction respectively. The indicator electrode gives the measure of potential of a solution into which it is dipped; reference electrode furnishes standard or known potential while the liquid junction potential is an interface between dissimilar solutions. In most measurements, E_{ref} is constant and E_j is considered negligible thus E_{ind} gives measure of potential of a given solution.

In order to know the potential of metal electrode, it is necessary to have another electrode whose potential is standard or accurately known. The two electrodes then can be combined to form voltaic cell. The emf of metal electrode is then found out, since the emf is arithmetic sum or difference of electrical potential.

For the measurement of potential primary reference electrode is used. Most commonly normal or standard hydrogen electrode is used as reference electrode.

REFERENCE ELECTRODES

Normal Hydrogen Electrode (NHE):

This consists of a glass tube (A) having holes at its bottom. Inside this tube is another glass tube (D) having a platinum or copper wire with a platinum foil (B). The surface of platinum foil is coated electrically with Platinum black. Pure hydrogen gas at 1 atmosphere pressure is passed through the opening C of glass tube A and it escapes through small holes at the bottom of electrode. The electrode is dipped in a solution of standard acid like hydrochloric acid at unit activity (01.8 M of HCl at 25°C).

Some hydrogen gas is absorbed by Platinum black of electrode and it permits the exchange from gaseous to ionic of hydrogen and reverse process to occur without any obstacle. This way it acts as hydrogen electrode. Under fixed conditions of pressure of hydrogen gas passed and hydrogen ions in solution with contact of electrode, the hydrogen electrode possesses a definite potential. By convention this potential is taken as zero at all temperatures (Fig. 13.1).

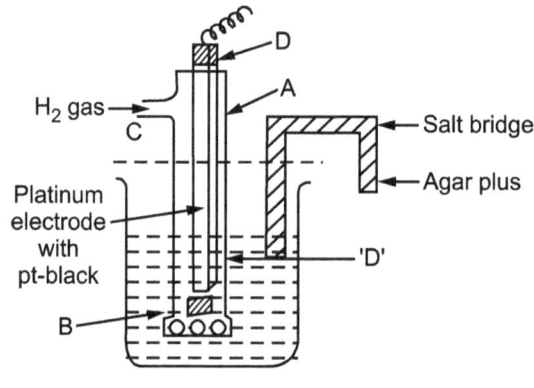

Fig. 13.1

When the normal (standard) hydrogen electrode is connected to any electrode by connecting through salt bridge, the potential of that electrode can be measured, e.g. when a zinc electrode (zinc metal rod in contact with a solution of zinc ion) is connected by potassium chloride salt bridge, we can write,

$$\text{Pt} \quad H_2 \,|\, H^+ \,(a = 1) \quad \| \; Zn^{++} \quad (a = \text{unknown}) \,\| \, Zn$$

NHE

And measure potential of zinc electrode. The cell reaction is

$$H_2 + Zn^{2+} \longrightarrow 2H^+ \,(a = 1) + Zn$$

And half cell reaction as

$$Zn^{2+} + 2e \rightleftharpoons Zn$$

In the similar way we can measure potential of any electrode.

By convention half cell reactions of electrode are written as reduction such as,

$$M^{n+} + ne \rightleftharpoons M$$

Or $$\qquad\qquad Zn^2 + 2e \rightleftharpoons Zn, \text{ For Zinc } E_O = 0.76 \text{ volts}$$

When activity of ion M^{n+} equals the unity (usually 1 M solution) the electrode potential E is equal to standard potential E_O.

When normal hydrogen electrode is connected by KCl salt bridge to another hydrogen electrode by dipping the latter into a solution of which pH is to be measured, the emf of resulting cell can be measured.

$$\text{Pt, } H_2 \,|\, H^+ \,(a = 1) \,\| \; H^+ = x, \, H_2 \,|\, \text{Pt}$$

The $$\qquad\qquad E = - \frac{0.0591}{n} \log \frac{x}{1}$$

The potential of hydrogen electrode 1 is given by

$$E = E_O, H_2 - \frac{0.0591}{n} \log (H)^+ \text{ as by convention}$$

$E_O (H^+, H_2)$ of NHE is zero.

Thus, $$\qquad\qquad E = - \frac{0.591}{n} \log (H)$$

Or $$\qquad\qquad E = 0.0591 \text{ pH} \qquad \text{as } - \log (H) = \text{pH}$$

It is clear that potential of a hydrogen electrode depends upon the pH value of a solution wherewith it is in contact. The pH value of a given solution thus can be calculated by combining it with NHE or with any standard reference electrode like saturated calomel electrode. The combined cell reaction of this type can be written as:

$$\text{Pt } H_2 \,(1 \text{ atm.}), \, H^+_{c \,(\text{unknown}) \,=\, \text{unkn}} \; \| \; KCl_{(sat)} \, Hg_2 \, Cl_{2(s)}, \, Hg$$

The emf of this cell can be measured by potentiometer; the E of the above reaction is given by

$$E_{cell} = E_{calomel} \,(sat) - E_{Hydrogen}$$

As E for calomel (saturated) = 0.242

$$E_{cell} = 0.242 - (0.0591) \, pH$$

Or

$$pH = E_{cell} \frac{-0.242}{0.0591}$$

Advantages of Hydrogen Electrode (NHE):

1. It is a fundamental electrode and is used as standard in pH measurements.
2. It can be used over wide pH range.
3. It exhibits no salt error.
4. It establishes equilibrium rapidly and gives accurate results.

Disadvantages of Hydrogen Electrode:

1. It cannot be used in solutions containing strong oxidizing or reducing agents.
2. It cannot be used in solutions containing metal ions that are below hydrogen in potential series (In such cases interaction with hydrogen will occur and the metal will be deposited on the electrode surface).
3. It gets readily poisoned by number of substances like proteins, tannins, mercury salts etc.
4. It is cumbersome to prepare and use in routine analysis.

Though hydrogen electrode (NHE) is a standard reference electrode ($E_O = 0$) because of its cumbersomeness it is replaced by other standard electrodes as reference electrode. Following electrodes are used as reference electrodes.

Calomel Electrode:

There are various forms of calomel electrodes. Some of these are shown in Fig. 13.2.

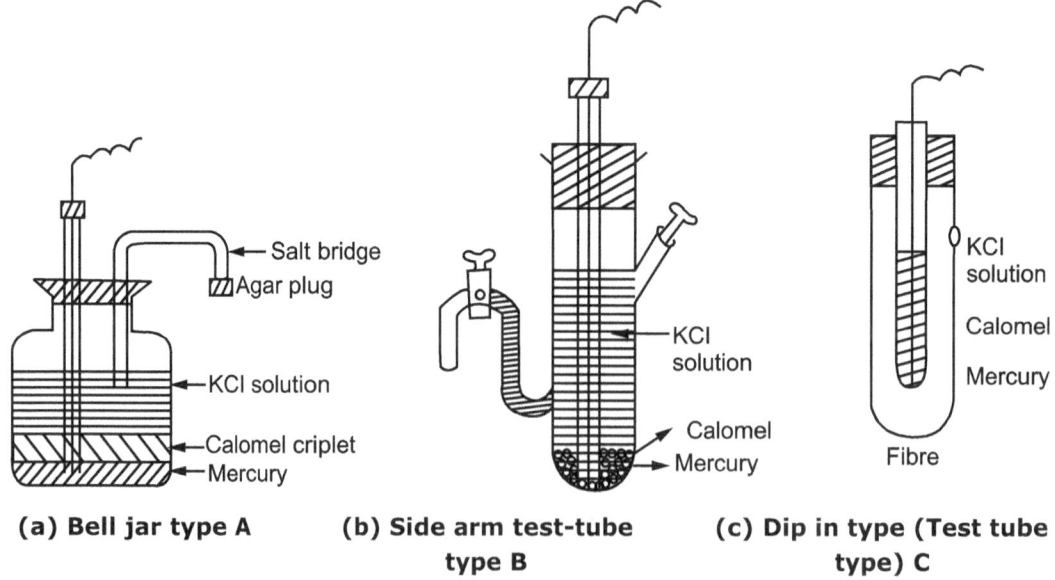

| (a) Bell jar type A | (b) Side arm test-tube type B | (c) Dip in type (Test tube type) C |

Fig. 13.2

Bell Jar type (A):

In a wide mouth bottle, mercury is placed at the bottom of jar. Above it is placed thick paste of calomel (mercurous chloride) with potassium chloride and sufficient saturated potassium chloride solution. Through the cork is placed a platinum wire sealed in glass tube which touches mercury. A siphon tube filled with saturated potassium chloride having an agar plug at one end is placed through the cork to make liquid junction connections.

Side Arm Test-tube type (B):

It consists of a glass tube having side arm with stopcock. A small amount of pure mercury is placed at the bottom of glass tube. It is covered with a thick paste of calomel and potassium chloride solution. The tube is then filled with potassium chloride solution through side arm. The same solution also serves to make connections through a salt bridge (in other side arm) for other electrode or half cell. The electrical connection with mercury is made by means of platinum wire sealed in a glass tube. The potential of calomel electrode depends upon the concentration of potassium chloride solution filled in electrode.

Test-tube type (C):

This electrode is easy to prepare and convenient to use. It consists of a tube of about 15 cm in length and 1-1.5 cm in diameter. It has a opening for filling potassium chloride solution. At the bottom of tube there is fine capillary plugged with asbestos fibre through this connection with solution is made. Inside the tube is an inner tube filled with mercury-mercurous chloride paste and having metal wire connections through mercury. This tube makes contact with saturated potassium chloride solution filled in the outside tube from the side opening. The electrode of this type has relatively high resistance of current carrying capacity. The half cell of calomel electrode can be represented by

$$Hg \mid Hg_2Cl_2 \text{ (saturated) } KCl \text{ (xM) } \parallel \ ;$$

In this, x represents the molar concentration of potassium chloride in solution. Most commonly (a) saturated potassium chloride (b) 1 M and (c) 0.1 M potassium chloride filled electrodes are used. The potentials of saturated KCl, 1 M KCl and 0.1 M KCl electrode relative to normal hydrogen electrode are 0.245, 0.284 and 0.338 volts respectively at 25°C.

Advantages of calomel electrode are: (a) It is sturdy and useful for measurement at wide pH range; (b) It can be employed in various solvents.

The disadvantages of this electrode are: (a) It is unstable at higher (above 80°C) temperature and (b) It is unsuitable where chloride ions show incompatibility.

When saturated calomel electrode (SCE) is connected to NHE for measuring H^+ ion concentration, we can write cell equation as

$$Hg \mid Hg_2 \ Cl_2 \cdot KCl \text{ (sat) } \parallel H^+ \ (a = 1) \ H_2 \mid Pt$$

And 25°C, then $\quad\quad\quad E_{obs} = E_{cal.\ sat.} - 0.0591 \log [H^+]$

Or $\quad\quad\quad\quad\quad\quad pH = \dfrac{E_{obs} - E_{cal\ .\ sat.}}{0.0591}$

Silver/Silver Chloride Electrode:

This is another reference electrode common in use. It is slightly difficult to prepare. It consists of metallic silver (wire or rod) or a silver coated/plated platinum or copper wire. The wire is coated externally by electrolytic method with a thin layer of silver chloride. This is dipped in a solution of KCl of known concentration. The potentials of 0.1 M and saturated with KCl-AgCl electrodes with respect to NHE are 0.290 and 0.224 volts. The half cell reaction is

$$Ag \mid AgCl_{sat}, KCl_{(xM)} \parallel$$

This electrode is sturdy and used similarly as calomel electrode. Where chloride ions interfere, this electrode cannot be used.

Mercury-mercurous sulphate electrode:

This is yet another reference electrode. This electrode is preferable where chloride ions have been found to interfere. It consists of mercury in a solution containing sulphate ion that has been saturated with mercurous sulphate. Standard potential when determined against NHE at 25°C has been reported as 0.680 volts.

INDICATOR ELECTRODES

In order to measure potential of a solution, an appropriate electrode is needed. This electrode measures potential when connected to a suitable reference electrode. An electrode which is used to measure potential or pH of a solution is called as indicator electrode. There are various types of indicator electrodes in use whereof some are described below:

1. Hydrogen electrode:

We have seen the construction of normal hydrogen electrode. This electrode is similar to the NHE; instead of using hydrogen gas at one atmospheric pressure and dipping the platinum wire of it in a solution of acid whose pH is to be determined, one can construct a hydrogen electrode. Since, this electrode is responsive to hydrogen ion concentration, it can be used for pH measurement. Platinum of the electrode does not take part in electrochemical reaction but only acts as the site for the transfer of electrons. The potential of the hydrogen electrode is given by,

$$E\ H^+, H_2 = E_{0_{(H^+,\ H_2\ =\ a)}} - \frac{0.0591}{n} \log [H^+]$$

$$= 0.0591\ pH, \quad as\ E_{0_{(H^+,\ H_2\ =\ a)}} = 0$$

2. Quinhydrone electrode:

This electrode is used in measuring pH of a given solution. It consists of a bright platinum wire dipped into a solution saturated with Quinhydrone. In solution Quinhydrone dissociates into equimolecular quantities of quinones and hydroquinone.

Hydroquinone   Quinone

The pH of a solution can be determined by the use of this red-ox system because reduction to hydroquinone or oxidation to benzoquinone involves H^+ ions. The potential of this electrode is given by,

$$E_{(H^+, Q, QH_2)} = E_{0(H^+, Q, QH_2)} - \frac{0.0591}{n} \log \frac{[QH_2]}{[Q][H^+]^2}$$

$$= E_{0(H^+, Q, QH_2)} + \frac{0.0591}{n} \log \frac{[Q][H^+]^2}{[Q H_2]}$$

$$= E_{0(H^+, Q, QH_2)} + \frac{0.0591}{n} \log H^+$$

The standard electrode potential of Quinhydrone electrode $[E^\circ]$ is + 0.699 volts. Thus the above equation becomes:

$E_{(H^+, Q, \text{and } QH_2)}$ = 0.699 – 0.0591 pH when we dip this electrode into a solution whose pH is to be determined and connect the electrode to any good reference electrode like SCE, the equation can be written as:

Hg, $Hg_2 Cl_2$ (s) KCl (sat) ∥ H^+ (a = unknown) Q, QH_2, Pt

The emf of this cell is given by

$$E_{cell} = E_{ele} \text{ (right)} - E_{ele} \text{ (left)}$$

$$= E_{(H^+, Q, QH_2)} - E_{(Hg_2 Cl_2, KCl_{sat})}$$

$$= (0.699 - 0.0591 \text{ pH}) - 0.242$$

Or 0.0591 pH = 0.699 – 0.242 – cell

$$pH = \frac{0.699 - 0.242 - cell}{0.0591}$$

Advantage of this electrode is that it attains equilibrium rapidly and can be used where hydrogen electrode is unsuitable. It gives accurate results also. Disadvantage of this electrode is that it cannot be used in more alkaline solution whose pH is above 8 as it readily gets oxidized by air in alkaline medium.

3. Antimony electrode:

This electrode is also used in pH measurements. It consists of an antimony rod coated or covered with antimony trioxide. The electrode is prepared by placing a stick or a rod of antimony metal covered with thin crust of its oxide. This rod is dipped into a solution whose pH is to be measured; and electrical connection made with reference electrode like SCE. The reaction involved is

$$Sb + H_2O \rightleftharpoons SbO^+ + 2H + 3e$$

$$Sb_2O_3{}_{(s)} + 6H + 6e \rightleftharpoons 2Sb_{(s)} + 3 H_2O$$

$$E_{cell} = E^o_{(Sb_2O_3, Sb)} - \frac{0.0591}{6} \log \frac{1}{H^+}$$

$$= E^o_{(Sb_2O_3, Sb)} - 0.0591 \ pH$$

The activities of solid antimony, antimony trioxide and of water are taken as unity. Advantages of antimony electrode include: (a) it can be used for measuring pH ranging from 2-8. (b) It can be used in viscous or turbid solvents. (c) It is sturdy and therefore it is very useful where continuous pH recording are made. (d) The electrode does not get readily poisoned. The disadvantages of this electrode are:

1. It cannot be used in measuring pH below 03 as the oxide gets dissolved.

2. It cannot be used in presence of strong oxidizing agents and complexing agents.

3. It cannot be used in the presence of metals such as Cu, Ag, and Au which are nobler than antimony (i. e. below in electromotive series).

4. It suffers from salt error. A modified micro antimony electrode is currently used in industry.

4. Glass electrode:

This is a very useful electrode for determination of hydrogen ion (or pH) of a solution. It involves no electron exchange but allows transfer of H ions through its membrane. It consists of very thin bulb made from glass membrane having high electrical conductivity. This bulb contains hydrochloric acid solution of definite concentration and/or Ag/AgCl wire to make electrical contract with it. Fig 13.3 (a) and (b).

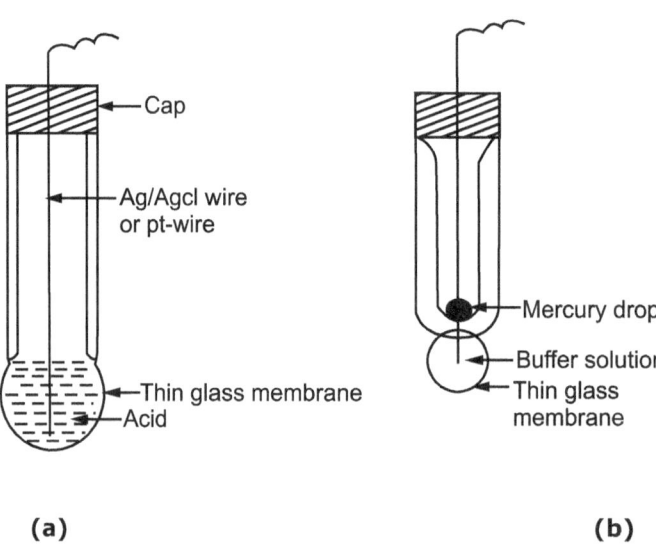

(a)   (b)

Fig. 13.3

The thin membrane of bulb is prepared from special type of glass sensitive and permeable to H ions. Generally, the glass membrane is made from soft soda lime glass containing lithium silicate with lanthanum and barium ions added to it.

The sensitivity of membrane of protons and other cations generally depends upon the composition of glass membrane. Corning glass contains 22 per cent Na_2O, 6 per cent CaO and 72 per cent SiO_2. The membrane of glass is specific to H^+ ions up to pH 9.0 above which it is somewhat responsive to Na^+ as well as other charged cations.

The surface of the glass membrane must be hydrated before it can function as pH electrode. The hydration of pH sensitive glass membrane involves an ion-exchange reaction between strongly charged cation in glass lattice and proton from the solution.

$$H^+ \quad + \quad Na^+ (Cl)^- \quad \rightleftharpoons \quad Na^+ \quad + \quad H^+ (Cl)^-$$

  Solution   Glass   Solution   Glass

Further, in order to serve as an indicator electrode for cations, the glass membrane must conduct electricity, for this hydrated gel layer or hydrated glass membrane is essential.

These ions act as lattice adjuster. Thus, glass bulbs function like a semi-permeable membrane permeable to H ions. The H ions enter glass lattice. It is known that on passing of electric current through glass is membrane, the amount of H^+ ions transferred through glass nearly in accordance with Faraday's law. For this, presence of water in the glass is essential. The pH function is impaired if the glass gets dried. To carry out pH measurement of a solution, glass electrode is dipped into it and connected to a suitable reference electrode like saturated calomel electrode and emf, recorded.

Each glass electrode has its own characteristic potential. This depends on several factors like composition of glass, thickness of glass bulb, size and area of glass membrane. The potential of glass electrode when immersed in a solution of which pH is to be measured is given by,

$E = K - 0.0591 (pH_1 - pH_2)$ where K = constant and characteristic (as stated above) pH_1 is pH of solution in bulb and pH_2 is the pH of test solution. Since, pH_1 is known, the equation is,

$$E = K - 0.0591 \ pH_2$$

Advantages of glass electrode:

1. It exhibits reasonably rapid response over wide pH range.
2. It is uninfluenced by presence of oxidizing or reducing agents
3. It can be used in viscous, coloured solutions, suspensions or colloidal solutions.

Disadvantages:

1. It is fragile and hence should be handled carefully, (minute scratches make electrode useless).

2. It is unsatisfactory in more alkaline (above pH 10) range as there is a partial exchange of other cations than hydrogen ion through membrane.

While handling glass electrode, care should be taken that it should never be allowed to remain dry. All glass electrodes must be conditioned for some time by soaking in water or in a dilute acid buffer solution. Before dipping into a test solution, it should be thoroughly washed with distilled water.

Besides the above referred indicator electrodes there are various electrodes which are used for analytical purposes. These are:

Electrodes of the FIRST kind:

This category electrodes are reversible with respect to the ions of its metal, e.g. a metal rod or wire in contact with a solution of its own ions. Silver rod dipped into silver nitrate solution. The half cell reaction is:

$$Ag^+ + e^- = Ag^0$$

According to Nernst equation

$$E = 0.799 - 0.0591 \log \frac{1}{(Ag^+)}$$

Electrodes of the SECOND kind:

These have two interfaces such as metal rod coated with a thin layer of its sparingly soluble salt. The reaction involved on its surface should be reversible. This category will include silver coated with thin deposit of silver chloride or mercury with mercurous chloride. Electrode of this type can be used for direct determination of the activity of metal ion or the anion used in coating, e.g. chloride ion in silver chloride.

Silver can serve as an electrode of the second kind for halide and halide like anions, i.e. Silver - Silver chloride electrode

$$Ag \mid AgCl\ (s) \mid Cl^-$$

The half cell reaction is $AgCl\ (s) + e^- \rightleftharpoons Ag\ (s) + Cl^-$, $E^0 = 0$

And potential is defined as

$$E_{ind} = 0.22 - 0.591 \log a\ Cl^-$$
$$= 0.222 + 0.591\ pCl^-$$

A chloride sensitive electrode can be prepared by using pure silver wire (anode) in an electrolytic cell containing KCl. The wire becomes coated with thin layer of silver chloride which will rapidly equilibrate with the surface layer of any solution in which it is immersed. Since, the solubility of AgCl is low, an electrode formed in this way can be used for number of measurements.

Electrodes of the THIRD kind:

This category includes a small mercury electrode with gold amalgamated wire in contact with solutions containing metal ions to be titrated by chelon such as EDTA. They are used to measure the activity (concentration) of desired metal ion in the test solution.

Metallic Redox indicator electrodes:

In Redox electrodes an inert metal is in contact with or solution containing the soluble oxidized and reduced forms of the Redox half reaction.

The inert metal used is generally platinum. The potential of such inert electrodes is determined by the ratio of the reduced and oxidized species in the half reaction.

$$M^{a+} + ne^- \rightleftharpoons M^{(a-n)+}$$

$$E_{ind} = E^0 M^{a+}, M^{(a-n)+} - \frac{0.0591}{n} \log \frac{aM^{(a-n)+}}{a M^{a+}}$$

For example, the potential of a platinum electrode in a solution containing Ce (III) and Ce (IV) ions is given by

$$E_{ind} = E^0 - 0.0591 \log \frac{(aCe^{3+})}{(aCe^{4+})}$$

Note: The electron transfer processes at inert electrodes are frequently not reversible hence, some inert electrodes do not respond rapidly and accurately.

Redox Electrode:

This electrode is used in a system to measure the concentration of oxidized or reduced form of the Redox.

Main advantages of this method of potentiometric measurement of emf are : (a) It employs null point method, therefore there is no deflection and no error. (b) It is a very simple method of measurement. (c) At null point no current passes through the cell that means the cell is not polarized and internal resistance does not affect reading.

Modified circuits are employed in commercial potentiometers. The details of which are available in standard text books of physics or physics/ chemistry.

Potentiometric pH meters:

A linear relationship exists between pH of a solution at a given temperature with potential E, employing a suitable indicator electrode and reference electrode. Thus,

$$E = K - 0.0591 \text{ pH or}$$

$$\Delta E / \Delta pH = -0.0591$$

In instruments, the calibration in millivolts is converted into pH units by dividing by 0.0591. Resistance values of wire are so chosen that divisor is 100. In commercial instruments (pH meters) there are auxiliary compensating devices in their electrical circuits. Most instruments e.g. incorporate a temperature compensating device in the form of a variable manually adjustance resistance or a thermistor for automatic model.

As per equation, K is a constant potential known as asymmetric potential and it is characteristic of cell used. In commercial pH meters it is allowed by adjusting a suitably placed auxiliary potentiometer by injecting a ~ k potential in the test cell circuit.

For standardization of pH meter, buffer solution of known pH is employed in which both the electrodes (glass/calomel) are dipped and dial of meter set to a known pH value. For most general type of instruments the sensitivity of the pH meters is adequate for the purpose.

POTENTIOMETRIC TITRATIONS

Potentiometric titrations are performed for solutions which show change in potential or pH by addition of a reagent or Titrant. In this technique, the absolute value of potential with respect to standard half cell is not required to be known. The changes occurring during the course of addition of Titrant are sufficient. The equivalence point of reaction is shown by sudden change in potential on a plot of emf readings against the volume of Titrant being added.

It is thus, clear that knowledge of actual potential of reference electrode need not be known accurately. Any electrode which furnishes a constant potential is useful as a reference electrode provided that its potential remains constant throughout the titrations. Depending upon the type of chemical reaction occurring, a suitable indicator electrode is used, e.g. glass electrode for acid-base titrations, platinum for Redox titrations etc. An apparatus involved in potentiometric titrations is shown in Fig. 13.4.

Apparatus consists of suitable sized glass vessel with lid having openings for passing nitrogen inlet tube, tip of burette and pair of electrode. The burette is mounted on a special stand and beaker placed on magnetic stirrer with speed control knob. Two suitable electrodes (one indicator and other reference electrode) are placed in beaker and their terminals connected to potentiometric unit. A solution to be titrated is placed in beaker and sufficient solvent added such that tip of electrodes dip in it. The potentiometric unit is a high resistance type with a compact galvanometer containing a lamp or magic eye. The potentiometer has two uncalibrated potential controls; a coarse with six steps of 250 mV and fine continuously variable potential.

Initial potential is applied and noted from galvanometer. A measured volume of Titrant is added, with stirring and corresponding values of emf or pH are recorded. In the instruments employing magic eye an approach of end point is indicated by closing or opening of magic eye and in case of galvanometer type a temporary deflection of needle. A small increment of volume should be added near the equivalence point which is found graphically by plotting burette reading corresponding to the maximum change of emf/unit change of volume.

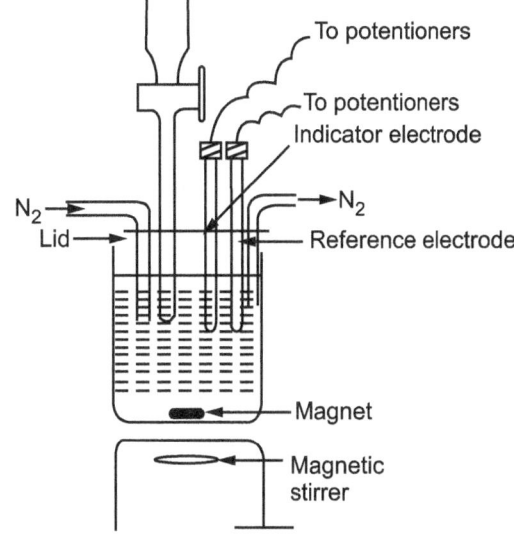

Fig. 13.4

Method of detecting end point:

There are different methods adopted to locate the end point. The critical problem in the location of end point is to know the point at which the quantities of reacting species are present in equivalent amounts at the equivalence point. It is generally found graphically. There are three methods used for this purpose: (a) In the first method values of emf (E) or pH are recorded on graph paper as ordinate and the volume of titrant (V) added as abscissa (Fig. 13.5 (a)). A smooth line is drawn for all the points and a point which gives the volume (V) corresponding to the maximum slope of curve is found out. It is also necessary to add small increments of titrant near the equivalence point for accurate results, since it involves drawing the best curve through the experiment observations. (b) In the second method, difference

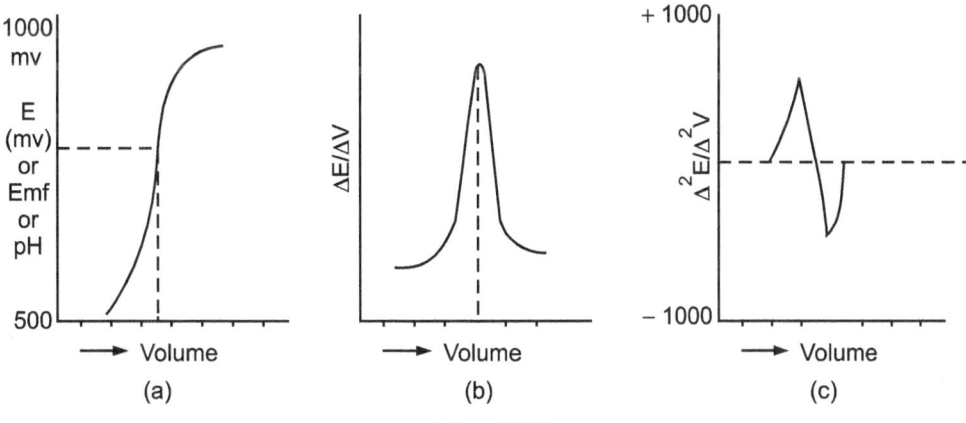

Fig. 13.5

of emf (E) or pH for the volume of titrant added (ΔE or ΔpH) is plotted as ordinate versus the volume of titrant (V) added as abscissa; in (Fig. 13.5 (b)). It becomes clear from the of emf curve of the graph that is maximum change in emf (E) or pH occurs at the equivalence point. The end point can be readily recorded by drawing perpendicular from the peak of the graph on volume axis (abscissa). (c) The third method uses second derivative, i.e. Δ^2E/Δ^2E where in the square of difference in potential or pH of the volume added vs the square of volume added is plotted (Fig. 13.5 (c)). The end point is shown as a zero point where the slope curve of Δ^2E/Δ^2E is the highest.

Gran's plots:

In this instead of plotting the electrode potential (which is log function of concentration) against volume, the concentration of sample remaining at each point in the titration is plotted. A straight line plot will be obtained wherein the concentration would decrease to zero at equivalence points.

This is because at 20 per cent titrated, 80 per cent of the sample will remain unused, and at 50 per cent titrated 50 per cent of sample will remain unused and so on. A plot like this can be obtained by a number of ways:

1. A calibration curve can be used to convert potential readings to concentrations or

2. The log scale on the potential measuring device (pH meter) can be used to read concentrated values directly (each $\frac{59}{n}$ mV being equal to 10 fold change in concentrated an initial calibration or at least one point would be required and preferably more points to establish the slope).

3. The antilog or the potential or pH reading can be calculated and plotted against the volume of Titrant. (E $\propto$ log C) (Antilog E $\propto$ C); such a plot is Gran's plot.

A typical Gran's plot is shown below:

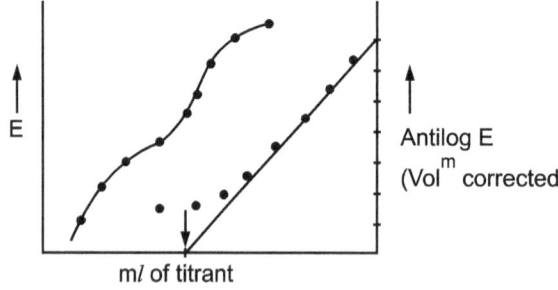

E

Antilog E
(Vol^m corrected

ml of titrant

Fig. 13.6: Gran's plot

Curvature of the straight line around the end point generally indicates appreciable solubility of the plot, dissociation or complex etc.

Advantages:

1. It is only necessary to obtain a few points to a definite straight line, and the end point is easily identified by extrapolating the line to the horizontal axis.

2. Points only need be accurately determined a bit away from the equivalence point, where the titrant is in sufficient excess to suppress dissociation of the titration product and where electrode response is rapid because one of the ions is at relatively high levels compared to the levels at equivalence point.

3. In case of small inflection points the end point is more readily defined by Gran's plot.

A Gran's plot is convenient in "standard additions" or "known additions" procedures.

Standard additions:

These are useful ways of calibration when the sample matrix alters the analyte signal. In this method, a signal recorded for sample and then a known amount of standard is added to the sample and the change in the signal is measured. This latter measurement provides calibration in the same matrix as the unknown analyte and the matrix should have the same effect on both unknown and standard i.e. electrode response calibrated.

By employing a Gran's plot a linear graph can be obtained. Here the potential of the sample is initially recorded and then known amounts of standard are added to the sample. The antilog values are plotted as a function of the amount of standard added and the best straight line is drawn through them. (Least-square analysis) Extrapolation to horizontal axis gives the equivalent amount of analyte is the sample.

(Determination of blank with extrapolation to get zero concentration may be done to get accuracy).

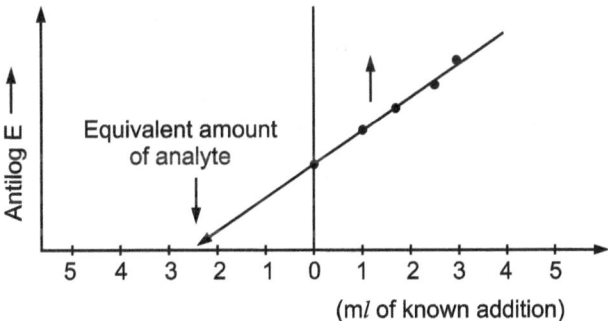

Fig. 13.7

Type of Reactions by potentiometer:

Various types of titrations involving different chemical reactions are possible to be covered and followed using potentiometer with appropriate electrode systems. Some such chemical reactions are recorded below:

1. Neutralization titrations:

In this type of reaction acid can be titrated against alkali and vice-versa. The indicator electrodes used may be hydrogen, glass or antimony or calomel as a reference electrode. The accuracy or end point depends upon the magnitude in the change of emf (E) in neighborhood of equivalence point. This depends upon the concentration (amount) and the strength of acid and alkali used. Less accurate results occur when acid or alkali are very weak ($K < 10^{-8}$) and dilute. Dibasic, tribasic and polybasic acids can be titrated with alkali to intermediate or full end point. This is possible provided that the dissociation constant for each stage in the titration is sufficiently apart. A difference of at least 2.7 pK units is required. In the titration of mixture of acids, the first inflection in the titration curve takes place when the strong acid is completely neutralized and the second when neutralization is complete.

2. Redox titrations:

Many redox titrations are possible using potentiometer provided no heating or cooling in the chemical reaction is involved. Indicator electrode most commonly employed is platinum. The potential of the indicator electrode is a function of the ratio of oxidized and reduced forms of an ion. The potential of indicator electrode is given by the expression,

$$E = E_O + \frac{0.0591}{n} \log \frac{Oxidation}{Reduction}$$

Where, E_O is the standard oxidation potential (or reduced potential) of the system. The equivalence point is indicated by sudden inflection in the titration curve. From the standard values of reduction potential and the observed values of potential the ratios of concentrations (Ox) / (Red) can be determined.

3. Precipitation titrations:

Potentiometric titrations are possible for certain types of reactions involving precipitations. The solubility product of the almost insoluble material formed during a precipitation reaction determines the ionic concentration at the equivalence point. The indicator electrode must rapidly come into equilibrium with one of the ions.

Silver electrode is used in the titration of halides against silver nitrate. The potential of the electrode is given by the expression,

$$E = E_O + \frac{0.0591}{n} \log (M^{n+})$$

Where (M^{n+}) is the ionic concentration present during the titration and in equilibrium with slightly soluble precipitate.

4. Complex formation and EDTA titrations:

When a particular metal ion forms a complex with ligand, its determination is possible using appropriate indicator electrode. In determination of mercury ions mercury-mercurous chloride electrode can be used. Similarly, EDTA titrations can be followed for determination of metal ions like Fe, Cu, and Cd etc.

Dead Stop-end Point Method:

Determination of moisture or water by Karl Fischer reagent method is most commonly carried out by dead stop end point type by technique. This method can be adopted for many chemical reactions. The principle of this method is that in a uniformly stirred solution of an analyte when two small but similar platinum electrodes are dipped and a small potential (1-100 mV) is applied, current flows as long as electrodes remain depolarized. When one component gets consumed or removed by the addition of titrant, the current ceases to flow. For the method to be applicable, only requirement is that a reversible oxi-red system be present either before or after the end point.

In the titration of iodine against thiosulphate when two platinum electrodes are immersed in the iodine solution and connected to the battery appreciable current flows through cell ($I_2 + 2e = 2I$). The amount of oxidized form reduced at cathode is equal to that formed by oxidation of the reduced form at anode. Both electrodes remain depolarized (seen by current flowing through galvanometer) until the oxidized component or the reduced component of the system is consumed by the titrant. Current thus, flows until end point. At or after the end point the current becomes zero. In the iodine against thiosulphate titration, a rapid decrease in current is observed near the vicinity of end point. Such titrations are given the name as "Dead stop end point". Other examples include titration of thiosulphate with iodine, nitrate ion by strong sulphuric acid medium, iron salt with ceric sulphate etc.

A circuit diagram of dead stop end point method is shown in Fig. 13.8.

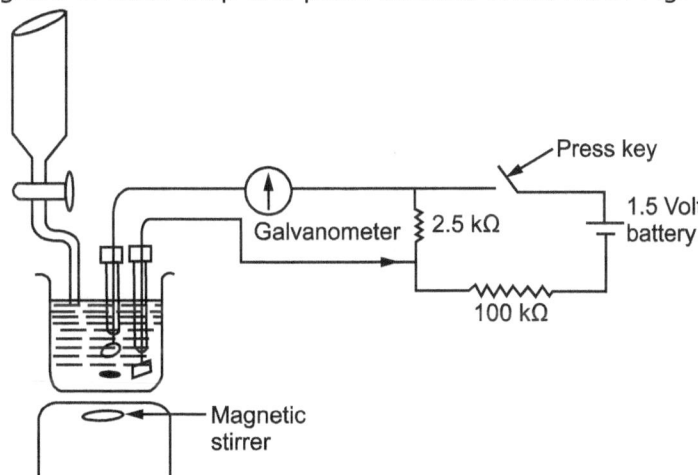

Fig. 13.8

The assembly consists of a beaker (vessel) of suitable size mounted on magnetic stirrer containing a solution to be titrated. Immersed in this solution are two bright platinum electrodes which are connected to a suitable potentiometer (shown in circuit) which in turn is connected to the 1.5 volt battery. A microammeter galvanometer is incorporated in the circuit. Small volume of titrant is added through microburette and current flowing through galvanometer is noted. When the current stops, the volume corresponding to it is recorded.

Ion Selective Electrodes:

In recent years, various types of ion selective electrodes have become available in the market. These are membrane electrodes. Just as in glass electrode, glass membrane is selectively permeable towards hydrogen ions; the ion selective electrodes are specific and permeable to certain selective ions. These are more useful for measurement of small concentration of ions in a solution.

Types of ion selective electrodes:

Various types of ion selective electrodes have been developed in recent years. As stated earlier, they are membrane electrodes. The construction and mechanism of some such electrodes is given below:

1. Glass membrane electrode:

These are similar in construction of the pH type glass electrode. The glass membrane of varying composition is used in these electrodes which permits low penetrability for various monovalent cations than H^+ ions. Selectivity for H^+ ions makes it pH sensitive. The construction of the electrode is shown in Fig. 13.9.

It consists of hard glass tube, to the end of which is a thin glass membrane permeable to selective ion. The internal filling solution is usually the chloride salt of the cation to which the electrode is most responsive. The composition of membrane will vary from type of glass used by manufacturer.

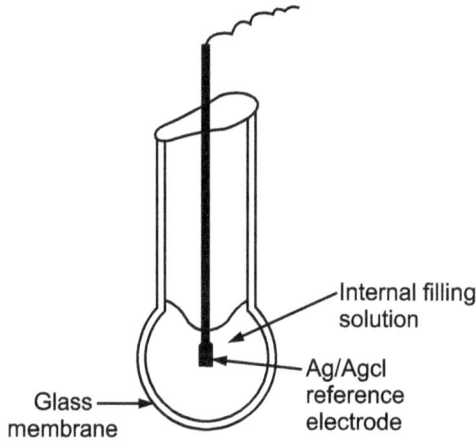

Fig. 13.9

In general the glass membrane will be any of the following three types:

(1) pH type:

This is similar to the conventional pH glass electrode. The membrane is permeable to H^+ ion selectively.

(2) Cation-sensitive type:

This responds favourably to monovalent cations. The order of selectivity is $H^+ > K^+ > Na^+ > NH_4^+$.

(3) Sodium sensitive type:

This is preferably selective to sodium ions. This is mainly used to measure the activity of sodium ions in presence of appreciable amount of other cations like potassium; the order being 3000 times or more in activity.

2. Liquid-Liquid electrodes:

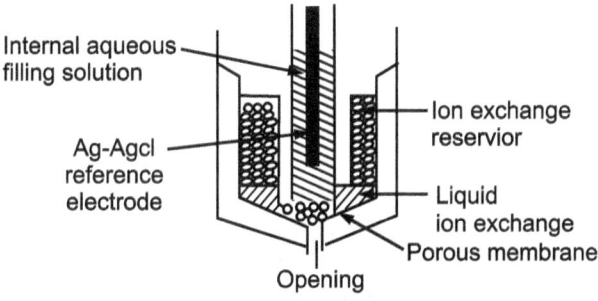

Fig. 13.10

The construction of this type is shown in Fig. 13.10. In this, the potential determining membrane is a layer of water immiscible liquid type ion exchanger held in place by an inert porous membrane. This porous membrane allows contact with test solution and ion exchange, but do not allow mixing. The internal filling solution contains the ion for which the ion-exchanger is specific. It also contains halide ion for the internal reference electrode. Calcium selective electrode is of this type. The selectivity for calcium ion is about 3000 over the sodium or potassium. It can be used in pH range of 5.5-11. Above pH 11, calcium hydroxide precipitates. Similar type of divalent cation electrodes are also prepared by using ion-exchange materials.

3. Crystal membrane electrode:

The construction of this electrode is shown in Fig. 13.11. It consists of hard glass tube which has opening at the bottom where a single crystal membrane is fitted. Inside the tube is filled internal filling solution and Ag-AgCl reference electrode. The crystal membrane is selective to a particular ion, e.g. Fluoride electrode. The membrane consists of a single large crystal of lanthanum fluoride containing little europium (II) ions to increase conductivity of the crystal. Lanthanum fluoride is very insoluble and has large selectivity for fluoride ions over chloride, bromide, iodide, nitrate etc. The crystals of this solid state type are prepared by making a pellet of required size and shape. Similar types of electrodes are prepared for sulphide, cyanide ions. Further other anion selective electrodes are also manufactured using either single crystal or liquid anion exchanger materials using liquid membrane technique.

Mechanism of ion-selective electrodes is not exactly known. It is based on membrane response phenomenon similar to that of glass electrode. The selectivity of cation electrode is due to the presence of anionic sites that show affinity towards certain cations. Similarly, anionic electrodes are due to cationic sites showing affinity for certain anions. The potential of electrode depends on the ratio of activity of ions at the membrane surface.

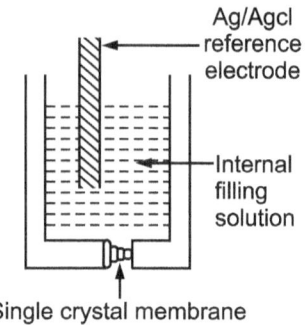

Fig. 13.11

Care and use of ion-selective electrode:

Similar to the pH glass electrodes, most ion-selective electrodes have high resistance and need electrometer to make measurements.

Further, response of ion-selective electrode is highly pH dependant. A suitable and selective buffer pH is necessary for accurate measurements. For most determinations a calibration curve of potential versus log activity is generally prepared. In certain concentration range determination of ions is very accurate.

It should be noted that response of many ion-selective electrodes is very slow and considerable time is required to establish equilibrium and readings. Further, it should be remembered that ion-selective electrodes are not specific, rather more selective towards particular ion.

Table 13.1: List of the drugs assayed by Potentiometric titrations

Drugs	Titrant	Electrode	
		Indicator	Reference
1. Amoxicillin sodium	Mercuric nitrate	Platinum/mercury	Mercury - mercurous sulphate
2. Acebutalol hydrochloride	Sodium hydroxide	Glass	Calomel/Silver-silver chloride
3. Dextromorphan hydrobromide	Sodium hydroxide	Glass	Calomel/Silver-silver chloride
4. Diphenoxylate hydrochloride	Ethanolic sodium hydroxide	Glass	Calomel/Silver-silver chloride
5. Disulfiram	Silver nitrate	Silver	Calomel
6. Hydralazine hydrochloride	Potassium iodate	Platinum	Calomel
7. Lomustine	Silver nitrate	Silver	Calomel
8. Metoclopramide hydrochloride	Sodium hydroxide	Glass	Calomel
9. Nalidxic acid	Ethanolic sodium of hydroxide	Glass	Silver-silver chloride
10. Phenobarbitone sodium	Sodium hydroxide	Glass	Calomel
11. Promethazine HCl	Sodium hydroxide	Glass	Calomel
12. Propranolol HCl	Sodium hydroxide	Glass	Calomel
13. Sodium Stibogluconate injection	Ferric ammonium sulphate	Platinum	Silver-Silver

CHAPTER ... 14

CONDUCTOMETRY

INTRODUCTION

Determination of conductance of an electrolyte solution by conductometer is called Conductometry. Solutions of electrolyte conduct electric current by migration of ions under the influence of electric field. Like a metallic conductor, the electrolyte solutions obey Ohm's law. The reciprocal of resistance $\frac{1}{R}$ is called as conductance and it is expressed in unit known as mhos or $ohms^{-1}$.

The standard unit of conductance is known as specific conductance (denoted by K). The specific conductance is defined as the reciprocal of resistance of 1 cm cube of liquid or solution at a specified temperature. The specific conductance of an electrolytic solution at a given temperature depends only on the ions present. When a solution is diluted, specific conductance decreases because less number of ions is present per cc in the solution.

The observed conductance of a solution depends directly upon the area (A) and inversely on the distance (d) between the electrode surfaces. Thus,

$$\text{Observed conductance} = K \frac{A}{d} \qquad \text{... (1)}$$

When a gram equivalent of a solute is present in a solution placed between two large parallel electrodes at 1 cm apart, the conductance is referred as equivalent conductance $\wedge$.

Equivalent conductance = Specific conductance $\times$ Volume in cubic cm

$$\wedge = KV$$

If C_s is the concentration of solute in gram equivalent / litre, it would be expressed as

$$\wedge = 1000 \times \frac{K}{C_s} \qquad \text{... (2)}$$

Similarly, the molar conductivity is defined as the conductivity of one mole per litre of solution.

The conductance at infinite dilution $\wedge_\infty$ is given by all the ions present in the solution. Thus, the total conductance given by an electrolyte solution is shown as

$$\wedge_\infty = \Sigma \left(\wedge^+ \right) + \Sigma \left(\wedge^- \right)$$

Where, $\wedge^+$ and $\wedge^-$ are the ionic molar conductances of cations and anions. At infinite dilution the ions are independent of each other and they individually contribute to the total conductance. The conductance value of ions changes with temperature. An increase of conductance is about 2 per cent per degree temperature. The conductance values of various ions (cations and anions) in water at 25°C at infinite dilutions have been reported in literature. Table 14.1 gives ionic molar conductance of some common ions at infinite dilutions at 25°C.

Table 14.1 Conductance of Ions at 25°C

Cations		Anions	
H^+	350	OH^-	198
Li^+	39	F^-	55
Na^+	50	Cl^-	76
K^+	74	Br^-	78
NH_4^+	73	I^-	77
Ag^+	62	HCO_3^-	45
Ca^{2+}	60	CH_3COO^-	41
Mg^{2+}	53	NO_3^-	71
Ba^{2+}	64	$C_6H_5COO^-$	32
Zn^{2+}	53	SO_4^{2-}	80
Hg^{2+}	53	CO_3^{2-}	69
Cu^{2+}	54	$C_2H_4^{-2}$	74
Fe^{2+}	54	CrO_4^{-2}	82
Fe^{3+}	54	PO_4^{-3}	80
$CH_3 NH_3^+$	59		

INSTRUMENTATION

For measurement of conductance of electrolytic solution, conductivity cell and conductometer are needed. After connecting conductivity cell to the instrument measurement can be made.

Conductivity cells:

Conductivity cells of various types are available. For precision measurements a number of factors are taken into consideration. Some common types of conductivity cells are shown in the Fig. 14.1.

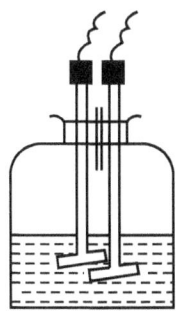   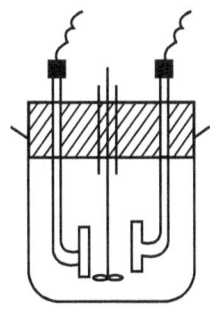   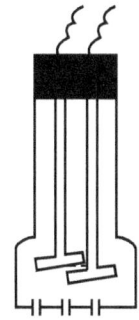

(A) For low conductance   **(B) For precipitating type**   **(C) Dip type**
measurement   **of reaction**   **(Electrode type)**

Fig. 14.1

In the A type, a wide mouth bottle with bark cork having holes for passing two platinum wires of 1 cm² size is used.

In B type, the electrodes are firmly fixed in the Perspex lid which is provided with opening for the stirrer and the tip of the burette. The stirrer may be replaced by magnetic stirrer. This type of cell is more suitable for precipitate giving reactions since the face of electrode plates are vertical and parallel.

The C or Dip type: In a wide bore glass tube of corning glass are fixed copper wires, the tip of which have two platinum plates of 1 cm² in size fixed at 1 cm apart. The terminals of copper wire are taken out for connections. The position of wire is fixed in glass tube by rosin. The two inside faces of platinum electrode of cell are plated with platinum black. This reduces polarization effect and allows absorption of ion on its surface.

For a given cell the ratio of d/A for fixed electrodes is a constant. It is called cell constant θ. The cell constant can be determined from the following:

$$k = \frac{\theta}{R} \qquad \qquad ... (3)$$

Where, k is specific conductance and R is the resistance of solution. For accurate determination of cell constant, cell is dipped in a standard solution of known specific conductance at 18°C or 25°C and resistance is measured. The cell constant is found from the equation (3). Potassium chloride solution of 1 M, 0.1 M or 0.01 M is employed as a standard solution for cell constant determination. Specific conductance values of the above solutions are recorded in literature and can be used for the calculations.

Conductivity meter:

The conductance measurements are made by using Conductivity bridge. The conductivity meters are made by using Wheatstone bridge circuit (Fig. 14.2). In this, cell is placed in one arm of the Wheatstone bridge circuit *ab* and resistance R_1 constitutes the arm *ac*. The arms *bd* and *dc* are in the form of calibrated slide wire resistor. The balance point of *d* is a sliding contact which shows no signal to detector *D*. This detector is a galvanometer, earphone, oscilloscope, magic eye or now-a-days calibrated digital display. A source of alternating current (V) with a frequency of 50-60 Hz or a mains operated oscillator giving a current with frequency up to 3000 Hz is used in the circuit by connecting *b* and *c*.

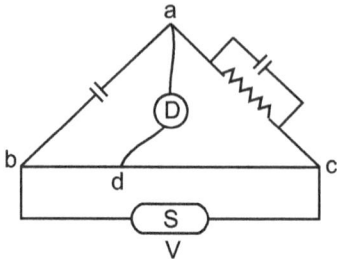

Fig. 14.2

Conductivity meters have a range switch (selector range) to select appropriate standard resistances (or standard conductances), a calibrate switch (calibrate) wherewith the instrument is calibrated to a desired value of conductance. A number of conductivity meters are commercially available.

To measure the conductance of electrolyte solution conductivity cell is dipped into it and terminals connected to test terminals of Conductivity Bridge. The selector switch is set to the appropriate conductance range and reading is recorded from the galvanometer or read out meter.

CONDUCTOMETRIC TITRATIONS

One of the most important applications of Conductometry is the conductometric titrations. Various types of acid-base titrations, replacement titrations, precipitations and complex formation reaction involving titrations are possible.

Principle of Conductometric Titrations

It is known that at infinite dilutions or in very dilute solutions, ions act independent of each other and they contribute to the conductance of the solution. Both cations and anions have varying degree of ionic mobilities (or conductance values). Thus, when a solution of one electrolyte is added (as a titrant) to the solution of another electrolyte the overall conductance (after addition) will depend whether a reaction occurs or not. If no chemical reaction occurs between the electrolyte solution and another added to it, the overall conductance of the solution will increase. All ions will contribute to the conductance of the solution for example addition of sodium nitrate solution to the sodium chloride solution.

However, when a chemical reaction occurs, replacement or substitution of ions takes place, and depending upon the ionic conductance of replacing and replaced ions conductance will either increase or decrease. For example, when a solution of sodium hydroxide is added to the hydrochloric acid solution, replacement of H^+ ion of high mobility with that of Na^+ with low mobility takes place and conductance is found to decrease.

The principle of conductometric titration is based upon the substitution of ions of mobility (conductance) by the ions of mobility. Thus,

$$A^+ B^- + C^+ D^- = A^+ D^- + C^+ B^-$$

the conductance will increase or decrease depending upon whether the mobility of C^+ ion is greater or lesser than that of ion A^+.

In conductometric titrations, titrant is added in small volume and conductivity is measured. The points thus obtained after the addition of each increment of titrant are plotted to give a graph which consists of two straight lines intersecting at the equivalence point. Naturally, accuracy of the methods is greater when the angle of intersecting line is more acute.

The volume changes by the addition of titrant should not be appreciable. For this, titrant of 10-20 times more concentrated in strength is employed. A correction for dilution effect is made by multiplying the readings of conductivity by factor $\dfrac{V + \bar{V}}{V}$,

where V is the original volume and $\bar{V}$ is the volume of titrant added. Conductance of weak electrolyte is largely dependant upon the degree of ionization, which in turn is dependant upon the dilution and temperature. Solutions of weak electrolyte are appreciably diluted before titration is carried out. For control of temperature thermostat arrangement may be employed.

TYPES OF CONDUCTOMETRIC TITRATIONS

Various types of acid-alkali titrations are carried out using conductometer. Some typical conductometric titration graphs which are observed are shown:

1. Strong acid with strong base:

In the titration of hydrochloric acid with sodium hydroxide, initial fall in conductance is due to replacement of hydrogen ions of high ionic mobility (350) with slow mobility sodium (50) ions. After the end point conductance rises due to excess of hydroxyl ions (199) being added.

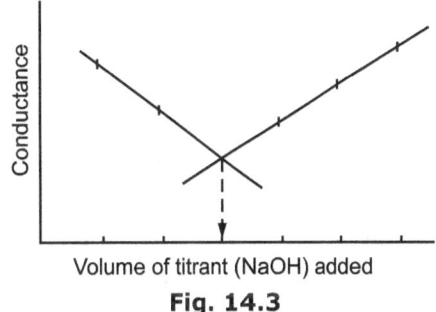

Volume of titrant (NaOH) added

Fig. 14.3

The shape of graph as shown in Fig. 14.3 is obtained.

2. Strong acid with weak base:

The titration of strong acid like hydrochloric or sulphuric with dilute ammonia solution gives the graph shown in Fig 14.4.

The progressive fall in conductance is due to the disappearance of hydrogen ions of high ionic mobility during neutralization. After the end point, the graph becomes almost horizontal because ionization of ammonia is prevented in the presence of ammonium chloride/ammonium sulphate formed during neutralization reaction.

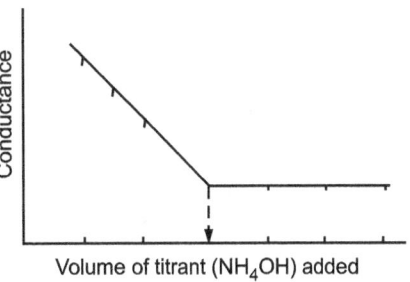

Volume of titrant (NH$_4$OH) added

Fig. 14.4

3. Weak acid with strong base:

In the titration of weak acid like acetic acid or boric acid with strong base like sodium hydroxide, the shape of graph will depend upon the concentration and dissociation constant of the acid. Thus in the neutralization of acetic acid, initial conductance is due to ionization of small amount of acetic acid. The progressive salt formation increases conductance which in turn repress ionization of acetic acid. These

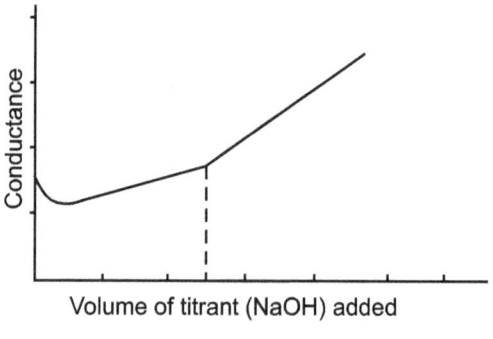

Volume of titrant (NaOH) added

Fig. 14.5

two opposing influences show fall followed by rise in conductance. After the neutralization, a break takes place showing rise in conductance due to hydroxyl ions. A shape of graph shown in Fig. 14.5 will be observed.

4. Weak acid with weak base:

Titration of weak acid like acetic acid or phenol with weak base like aqueous ammonia solution shows the graph as depicted in   Fig. 14.6.

The neutralization curve up to the end point of weak acid is similar to that obtained with sodium hydroxide. Conductance rises due to the salt formation of weak acid. After the equivalence point an excess of aqueous ammonia solution has no effect upon the conductivity because of suppression of ionization of ammonia by the salt formed.

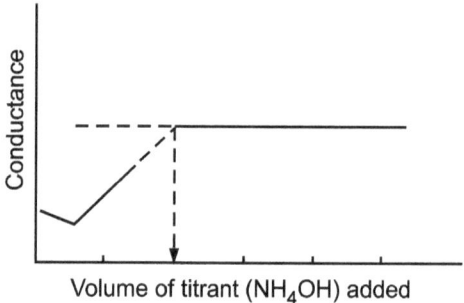

Volume of titrant (NH$_4$OH) added

Fig. 14.6

5. Very weak acid with strong base:

Fig. 14.7 shows the titration curve of very weak acid like boric acid with sodium hydroxide solution. Initial conductance is very small but increases progressively as neutralization proceeds. This is because of salt formation which accounts for rise in conductance due to hydrolysis. After the equivalence point the sharp rise in conductance is due to excess hydroxide ion added as titrant.

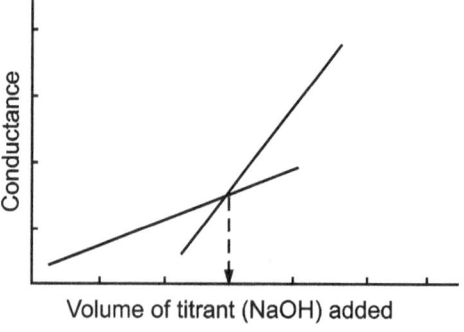

Volume of titrant (NaOH) added

Fig. 14.7

6. Mixture of hydrochloric acid (strong acid) and acetic acid (weak acid) with strong base:

This is shown in the Fig. 14.8. Initially, conductance falls due to neutralization of strong acid and then rises as the weak acid is converted into its salt. After the complete neutralization of both acids conductance finally rises more steeply as the excess of alkali (OH) ions are introduced. Two end points (a) and (b) for neutralization of strong acid and weak acid are observed respectively.

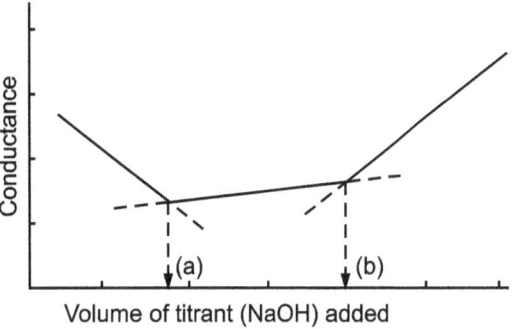

Volume of titrant (NaOH) added

Fig. 14.8

Titration of mixture of acids with weak base (like ammonia hydroxide) will show the graph similar up to neutralization of both acids. Afterwards conductance remains the same due to suppression of ionization of weak base.

7. Displacement titrations:

Titration of salt of weak acid (sodium acetate) with strong acid (Hydrochloric acid) *(a)* and that of salt of weak base (Ammonium chloride) with strong base (sodium hydroxide) *(b)* can be followed by conductometer. The shape of graph for these types is shown in Fig. 14.9. In the sodium acetate titration with hydrochloric acid, the initial increase in conductivity is due to slightly greater ionic mobility of chloride ions than that of the acetate ion. Until replacement is complete, solution contains sufficient sodium acetate to suppress the ionization of liberated acetic acid.

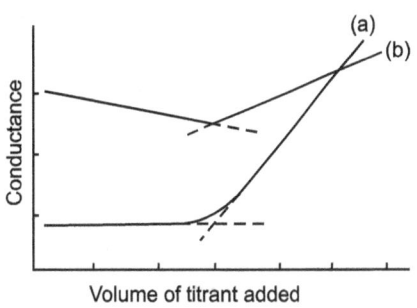

Volume of titrant added

Fig. 14.9

Near equivalence point the acetic acid is sufficiently ionized to give rise in conductance. Beyond equivalence point the excess of hydrochloric acid accounts for high conductance. Similarly, in titration of ammonium chloride with sodium hydroxide, the initial fall in conductance is due to replacement of ammonium ion (high mobility) by the sodium ion (low mobility). After equivalence point steep rise in conductance is due to hydroxyl ion of sodium hydroxide.

8. Precipitation and complex formation titrations:

Conductometric titrations of this type can be satisfactorily performed if:
1. The reaction product is sparingly soluble,
2. Forms stable complex, and
3. The precipitate does not have strong adsorbent properties.

In order to obtain satisfactory results, the solubility of precipitate (and its dissociation) is kept below 5 per cent by addition of ethanol. A slow rate of precipitation prolongs the time of titration. This is reduced by seeding technique. Titration of silver nitrate with potassium chloride or sodium sulphate with barium chloride gives the shape of graph as depicted in Fig. 14.10.

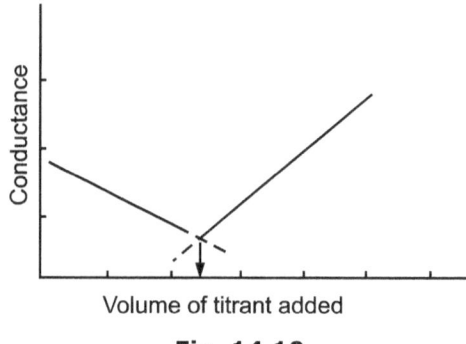

Fig. 14.10

9. Redox titrations:

The Redox type of titrations is not possible by conductometer. In most of Redox reactions a large excess of acid or base is used for completion of reaction. This interferes by masking the changes in conductance. Hence, redox titrations are not performed by using conductometer.

APPLICATIONS OF CONDUCTOMETER IN ANALYSIS

1. Determination of solubility of sparingly soluble material:

The specific conductance (K) of saturated solution of sparingly soluble salt is determined. The equivalent conductance Λ_e of sparingly soluble salt in saturated solution is considered practically equal to the limiting value Λ_∞ of conductance. This can be obtained by summation of limiting conductance of constituent ions. Thus, if S is the solubility in g/litre and K is specific conductance then,

$$\Lambda_e = \Lambda_\infty = \frac{1000 \, K}{S}$$

Thus from measuring specific conductance and limiting conductance of constituent ions of sparingly soluble material, solubility (S) can be determined.

2. Kinetic studies:

Kinetic studies of reaction are based upon the measurement of conductivity before, during, and at the end of chemical reaction. In any reaction wherein ions are produced, consumed or exchanged the course of reaction can be followed, e.g. in alkaline ester hydrolysis of ethylacetate, the initial conductance is due to excess of alkali and ester. During hydrolysis there is exchange of slow moving acetate ions by very mobile hydroxyl ions. Thus, during hydrolysis, conductance is due to excess base and acetate produced. At the end of reaction conductance is mainly due to acetate ions produced and residual base.

3. Degree of dissociation of weaker electrolytes (α):

The degree of dissociation of weaker electrolytes (α) can be found by use of following equation i.e.

$$\alpha = \Lambda_v / \Lambda_\infty$$

Where, Λ_v = Equivalent conductance at given dilution V

Λ_∞ = Equivalent conductance at infinite dilution

The value of Λ_∞ can be found from equivalent conductance table at infinite dilution and Λ_v can be found experimentally.

4. Basicity of organic acids (B):

This can be found by using empirical formula given by Ostwald as follows:

$$B = \frac{\Lambda_{1024} - \Lambda_{32}}{10.8}$$

Where, Λ_{1024} and Λ_{32} = equivalent conductance of the salt at 25°C and dilution of 1024 liters and 32 liters per gram equivalent respectively. This method is not correct in case of very weak acids whose salts are considerably hydrolyzed in solution.

5. Determination of concentration:

This determination is based on dependence of the conductivity of the solution on content of solute in it. A series of solutions with known content of electrolyte is prepared, determine their conductivities and plot the calibration curve of conductivity of solution against concentration of electrolyte. Then determine the conductivity of unknown solution and find the concentration by using calibration curve. Direct conductometric analysis is very convenient for routine analysis of solutions containing a single electrolyte, especially if the solutions are coloured or turbid. The industrial conductometers (concentration meters) are widely used for automatic control of solution concentration at chemical plant.

HIGH FREQUENCY METHOD

In the conductivity method, we have seen that migration of ions occurs under the influence of electric field. Thus, when low frequency current is applied to any molecule in solution containing two electrodes, the electrons of the molecule are attracted towards the positive end of electrode while the positive end of molecule is attracted towards opposite end. This orientation of molecule occurs upon ionization, dissociation in polar solvents. This effect is of short duration and disappears when the field is removed.

Some practical difficulties are encountered in the measurement of conductance for certain molecules by the conventional method. These are the effect of polarization (partial or incomplete) under the frequency of current used, poor ionizing solvent media like certain non-aqueous solvents and the effect of adsorption at the electrode surface.

Number of workers (Jensen, Parrack, Blake) suggested use of high frequency oscillator to induce ionic or polar motion in a molecule. In this method (a) direct introduction of electrode into a solution of substance is not involved, and (b) a high frequency alternating voltage is applied to the cell. Since, high frequency (radio frequency) electrical field is applied to the substance for measuring electrical conductance, the term 'High frequency methods' is given to this technique.

There are two types of high frequency methods. When the conductivity cell containing solution is placed between the plates of a capacitor carrying higher frequency current, method is called as capacitive cell method. In this type, two bands of copper are cohered around outside the vessel and these are connected to the high frequency voltage supply while in the other method known as inductive cell method, the vessel containing the solution is placed in the field of an induction coil. Since, the induction coil or capacitor is a unit of high frequency oscillator circuit, any change in composition of the solution is reflected as change in the plate and grid current and voltages.

Instruments:

Various types of instruments have been developed. Commercial type of titrimetric instruments is based on the design by Hall. A simple Blacke type titrimeter is shown in Fig. 14.11.

Blacke type instrument:

The basic units of instrument are oscillator (A), conductometric cell, (B) a rectifier tube (C) and microammeter (D).

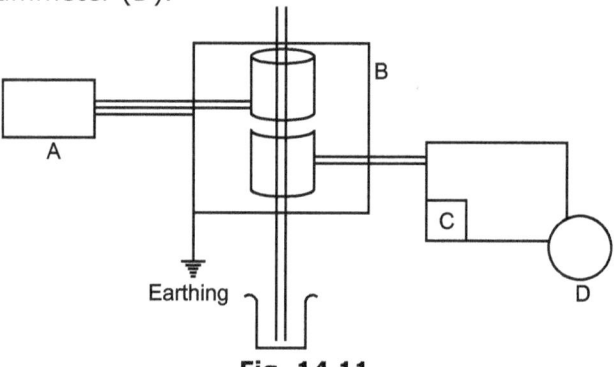

Fig. 14.11

The conductometric cell consists of narrow bore Pyrex thin walled glass tube through which solution under analysis can be drawn by syringe after addition of each volume of titrant. This tube is surrounded externally by two cylindrical metal electrodes which are separated from each other. The whole unit is enclosed in earthed metal box. Radio frequency current generated by suitable source is fed via screened cable from oscillator to one of the electrodes. The current passes across the electrode, through glass wall to solution and back across glass wall of other electrode. The current coming out of the second electrode is rectified and passed to microammeter for measurements.

Applications:

The various applications of high frequency methods are:

1. It is used to measure the dielectric constants of various solvents.
2. Direct high frequency analysis of binary mixtures, e.g. o- and p-xylene or acetone-water, benzene-hexane can be carried out by adopting calibration curves.
3. The technique can be used to study reaction rates, e.g. in the study of alkaline hydrolysis of esters or polymerization reactions etc.
4. The technique is useful to follow the course of titration. Neutralization reactions (Acid-base titrations), precipitation and complex formation reactions can be studied.
5. The other uses of high frequency titrations include determination of hardness of water by titration with standard soap solution.
6. In the oxidation-reduction reactions, oxidation of ferrous ion by permanganate and dichromate has been studied.
7. Titrations can be carried out for electrolyte or ion in presence of large excess of indifferent electrolytes, e.g. chloride and sulphate have been estimated in small samples of sea bed sediments.
8. Alkaloidal assays and non-aqueous titrations are also possible by high frequency method.

CHAPTER ... 15

POLAROGRAPHY

INTRODUCTION

The polarographic method of analysis has been developed by Jaroslov Heyrovsky, a Czech chemist in 1922, who received Nobel prize in chemistry in 1952. Since then this method has acquired immense importance in analytical chemistry for determination of metal ions and other electroactive organic compounds.

The term polarography is applied to the current voltage curves when dropping mercury electrode is used as an indicator electrode. This method comes under the category called as voltammetry, which is a general term used for all current voltage methods using micro-electrodes.

Polarography is essentially an electrolysis on a microscale for the solution of substances in a concentration range of 10^{-6} to 10^{-2} M. The method is based upon study of the current-voltage relationship by using polarographic apparatus. If a steadily increasing microvoltage is applied to a solution in a polarographic cell having a saturated calomel electrode or large mercury as an anode and dropping mercury electrode as a cathode, it is possible to obtain a current-voltage graph. The nature of graph (also known as polarographic wave) gives an idea about the nature and amount of material present in the solution. Thus, qualitative and quantitative analysis of substance is possible provided the substance under study is capable of undergoing cathodic reduction or anodic oxidation.

In polarography, dropping mercury is used as an indicator electrode. The reaction occurs at its surface. It is considered to be a polarised electrode. An electrode is called as polarised when it adopts a potential impressed upon it with no change of current. Once a chemical reaction has occured on the surface of electrode, it becomes depolarised. A large pool of mercury placed at the bottom of polarographic cell is a reference electrode. It is incapable of being polarised. This type is called as non-polarizable electrode in which the potential is independent of the current flowing.

THE POLAROGRAPHIC APPARATUS

A typical polarographic apparatus is shown in Fig. 15.1.

There are two main units of polarographic apparatus, a polarographic cell and an electrical instrument. Polarographic cells are of numerous types and different forms are available commercially. Simplest one consists of a beaker type of glass cell with a lid. A large pool of mercury at the bottom of cell has an electrical connection. This mercury electrode acts as an anode terminal. The lid has glass bend tubes for passing nitrogen gas and tip of dropping mercury electrode.

The dropping mercury electrode (DME) consists of a dropping funnel for mercury reservoir (about 100 ml capacity). It is connected to capillary tube of fine bore. The connection is made either by using heavy walled rubber tubing of about 80 cm long or by Neoprene tubing. The effective glass capillary tube has a length of about 5-10 cm and a bore diameter of about 0.05 mm. The outer diameter of capillary tube may be of 6-8 mm. The tip of capillary is cut fine and horizontal. The overall adjustment of DME is such that with a pressure of about 50 cm of mercury produces a drop weighing about 6-10 mg in a full time of 3-6 seconds.

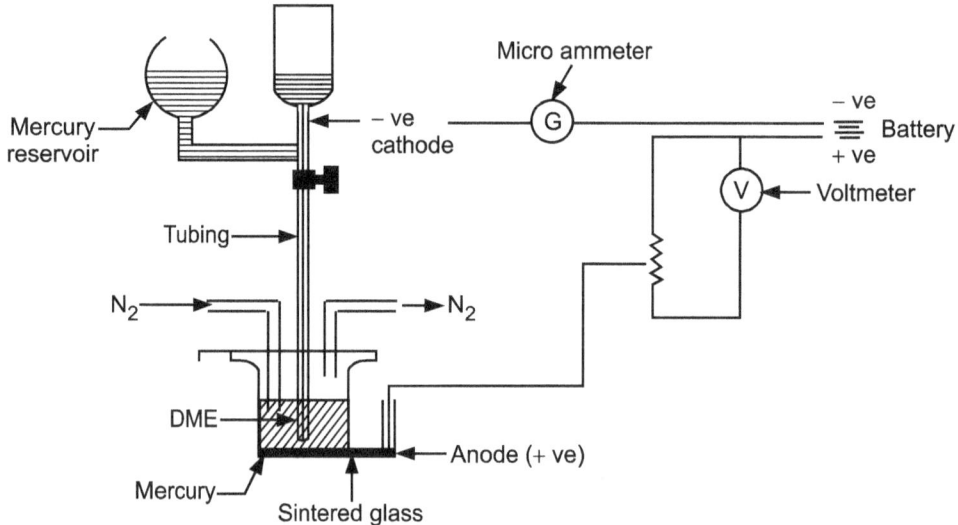

Fig. 15.1

The DME is fitted to the cell and the cell is mounted on a heavy stand on a platform free from vibrations. The instrument part consists of standard power supply from a battery, a variable potentiometer, emf indicating voltmeter and a galvanometer for measuring current.

A solution to be analysed along with solution of ground-inert electrolyte and maxima suppressor is placed in the cell. The anode and cathode are joined to the positive and negative terminals of a potentiometer slide wire. This enables a variable potential difference to be applied between the anode and cathode which is indicated by a voltmeter (V). The current flowing through the cell is indicated by the galvanometer (G). Air from the cell is driven off by passing a current of nitrogen before the measurement of current- voltage is made. The record of current-voltage (known as polarogram) is obtained by slowly increasing the applied voltage and measuring the current. In modern instruments, the applied voltage is supplied at a constant rate by a synchronous motor and record obtained on an automatic recorder.

The other form of polarographic cell of H-type deviced by Lingane and Laitinen is shown in Fig. 15.2.

It consists of H shaped tube, into one arm of which a capillary of dropping mercury electrode is inserted. A bent tube for passing nitrogen is also fixed in the stopper. A sample solution of about 10 – 50 ml is placed in the H tube into the other arm of cell, a saturated calomel electrode is fitted which makes a contact with the pool of mercury placed at its bottom. The two arms or compartments are separated by a sintered glass disc and a agar plug.

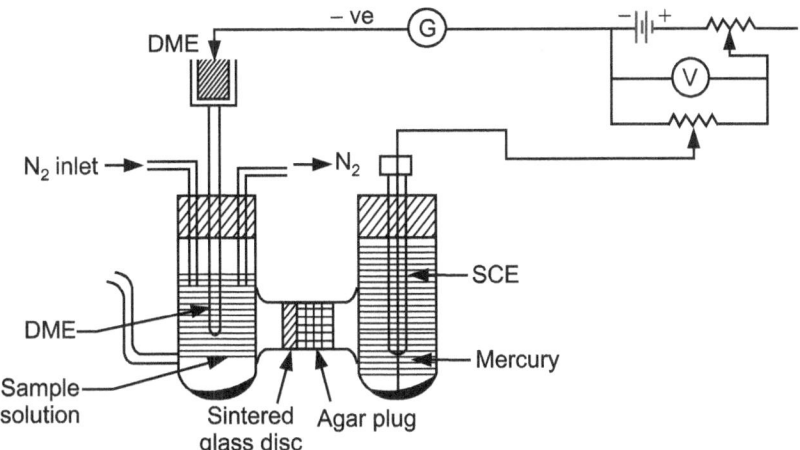

Fig. 15.2

THE BASIC PRINCIPLE

Polarography is the study of the current voltage relationship using polarographic apparatus. Let us consider a typical polarogram for a solution containing 10^{-3} M Pb^{+2} in 1 M KCl (as supporting electrolyte) and applying increasing negative potential. The 'polarographic wave' as shown in the Fig. 15.3 is obtained.

It will be seen that initially there is a very small gradual rise in the current between A and B. It is known as residual current (i_r). Though no electrolysis process takes place before the applied potential upto B, no current should flow through the galvanometer. The small background current which is usually observed is known as residual current. It is sum of faradic current (i_f) and condenser current (i_c).

$$i_r = i_f + i_c$$

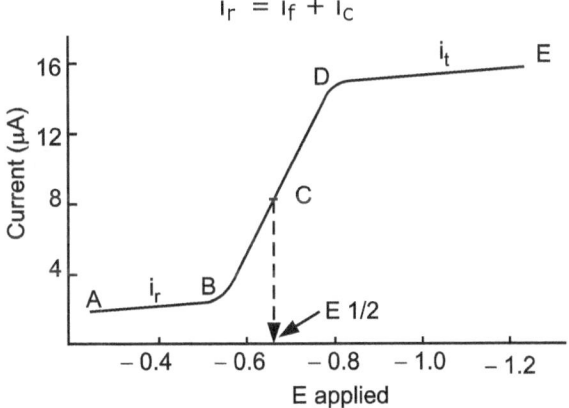

Fig. 15.3

The faradic current (i_f) is attributed to the reducible impurities present in the solution and condenser current because of the charge of each drop of mercury which it carries when it falls in the solution resulting in the formation of helmholtz double layer of positive and negative charged ions. This background or residual current should be deducted for diffusion current measurements. At point 'B' which corresponds to the decomposition potential of the electrolyte (Pb^{+2}) electrolysis commences and ions (Pb^{+2}) move to the electrode surface of DME and get reduced $Pb^{+2} + 2e = Pb^\circ$. At potential between $- 0.3$ and $- 0.5$ V the current increases rapidly because more number of lead ion from the solution carries current. The ions get reduced to metal lead that forms an amalgam with the mercury of DME. In the region of the polarographic wave, the electrode becomes depolarised. It obeys the Nernst equation. The current which flows is the result of reduction of lead ion to give appropriate ratio of [Pb amalgam] / [Pb^{+2}] at the electrode surface.

At a point 'C' the corresponding voltage is half-wave potential $(E_{1/2})$. At this point the concentration of oxidised and reduced forms at electrode surface is equal $(Pb^{+2}) = (Pb^{\circ})$. This potential is characteristic of the nature of reducing substance and is used for identification of unknown substance.

The straight line DE is known as limiting current i_l or diffusion current (i_d) in absence or presence of supporting electrolyte used. At the point 'D' electroreducible substance is reduced as rapidly as it reaches the electrode surface. Depending upon the concentration of reducing species (Pb^{2+} ions) the limiting stage of current is reached.

The reducible ions are supplied to the electrode surface by two independent forces :

1. a diffusion force which is proportional to the concentration gradient of ions at electrode surface and bulk of solution (i_d) and

2. electrical force which is due to the opposite electrical charge of ion. This is also called as electrical migration (i_m). Thus,

$$i_l = i_d + i_m$$

If a sufficient quantity of inert electrolyte (which is known as ground electrolyte or supporting electrolyte) is added to the solution under study the influence of electrical migration is reduced to zero ($i_m = 0$) then limiting current (i_l) becomes diffusion current (i_d). $i_l = i_d$. Thus, at potentials between − 0.5 to 0.9 V the current is limited by the rate of diffusion and is called as diffusion current (i_d). The substance reducing at the electrode moves only through a thin diffusion layer because of concentration gradient and not because of electrical migration (attraction). No further increase in current beyond point E is observed unless there is another electrolyte undergoing reduction at higher applied voltage. For example analysis of solution of lead 10^{-3} M and zinc 10^{-3} M concentration in 0.1 M KCl is shown in Fig. 15.4.

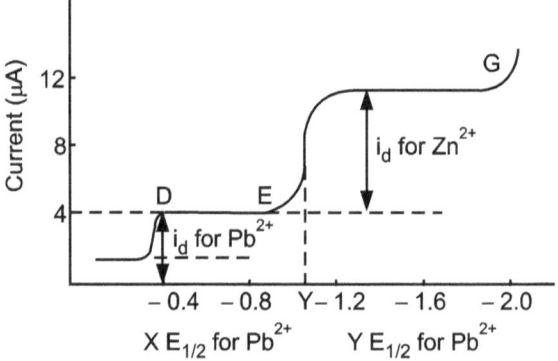

Fig. 15.4

The first wave on the polarogram is the reduction of lead ion to form lead-mercury amalgam $Pb^{2+} + 2e^- \rightarrow Pb - Hg$ (amalgam). The second wave is the reduction of zinc ion to metal zinc which also forms amalgam with mercury of DME.

$$Zn^{2+} + 2e^- \rightarrow Zn - Hg \text{ (amalgam)}$$

Between the points D and E no further increase in current occurs until the impressed voltage exceeds the decomposition potential of zinc ions (– 1.0 V). Finally current rises (after G) near – 2.0 V caused by the reduction of potassium ion used as supporting electrolyte.

For the reducible ions, often part of its charge gets reduced and the product is capable of further reduction at higher potential. This gives two steps polarogram. For example,

$$Cr^{3+} + e^- \rightarrow Cr^{2+} \qquad \qquad \text{... (i)}$$
$$Cr^{2+} + 2e^- \rightarrow Cr \qquad \qquad \text{... (ii)}$$

The Ilkovic Equation : The diffusion current at the DME is given by Ilkovic equation :

$$i_d = 607 \, n \, D^{1/2} \, c \, m^{2/3} \, t^{1/6}$$

where

i_d = the average diffusion current during the life of drop, in amperes.

607 = a constant of various numerical factors including π, the Faraday constant, density of mercury etc.

n = the number of electrons involved in the electrode reaction.

D = the diffusion coefficient of the substance in cm^2/sec.

c = the concentration of the substance in m.moles/litre.

m = the rate of mercury flowing through the capillary in mg/sec;

t = the drop time in seconds.

The Ilkovic equation holds for drop time of about 2 to 8 seconds. For this, adjustment of capillary length and mercury pressure is made to bring the drop time within the range. Accordingly with all other factors as constant (of drop assembly) i_d is proportional to the concentration or $i_d = kc$ wherein k = overall constant. The linear relationship fails when drop time is too short (fast falling) or too slow or when there is a stirring effect.

Factors effecting variables in Ilkovic equation :
1. The quantities m and t will vary with the capillary, its length and with the pressure of mercury.
2. It is important that the height of mercury column remains constant since the drop time depends upon the pressure exercised by the column of mercury at the tip of DME - solution interface.
3. Applied voltage causes changes in the surface tension, a drop at the tip of electrode.
4. Temperature and viscosity changes should be minimum since it disturbs diffusion coefficient most.

Some Practical Aspects of Polarography :

1. The Dropping Mercury Electrode : As stated earlier dropping mercury electrode (DME) is used as an indicator electrode for its unique nature. The advantages of DME are :

  (i)   It provides a smooth, fresh surface for the reaction.

  (ii) Each drop remains unaffected and does not become contaminated by the deposited metal.

  (iii) Mercury forms amalgam with most metals.

  (iv) Mercury has a high hydrogen overvoltage

  (v)   Diffusion equilibrium is readily established at mercury-solution interface.

Disadvantages of DME are :

  (i)   Surface area of a drop of mercury is never constant.

  (ii) Applied voltage produces changes in surface tension and hence change in drop size.

  (iii) Mercury has limited applications in analysis of more positive potential range; and

  (iv) Mercury is poisonous so care should be taken in its handling.

Precautions:

In using dropping mercury electrode following care should be taken.

  (i)   The DME assembly should be mounted vertical on a heavy stand to be free from vibrations.

  (ii) Tip of DME should be always immersed in water when not in use.

  (iii) Tip of DME should be cleaned by dipping in 50% nitric acid.

  (iv) It is essential to use clean and dust free tubing while setting the DME.

  (v)   Pure and triple distilled mercury should be used in DME.

  (vi) There should be sufficient mercury in reservoir so that the pressure changes are negligible.

The Supporting Electrolyte : The role of supporting electrolyte in polarographic analysis is to eliminate the influence of electrical migration on the reducing ions. The high concentration (10 to 20 times that of ions under study) of inert supporting ions eliminates the attraction or repulsion forces between the electrode and the analyte. The inert electrolyte ions are not electrolysed at the applied potential range. Potassium chloride, potassium nitrate or sodium chloride solutions are often used for this purpose.

Maxima suppressors : In the polarographic studies, it is observed that instead of S-shaped polarographic wave there is a distortion. The wave shows a sharp peak or a rounded hump as shown in Fig. 15.5.

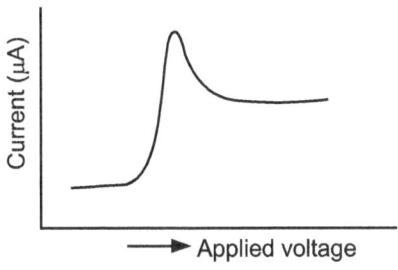

Fig. 15.5

(1) 0.001 M lead nitrate solution (without suppressor) with 0.01% gelatin as maxima suppressor.

This is known as polarographic maxima. The maxima phenomena is not completely understood. It is believed to be related to the phenomena of electrostatic stirring of the electrode surface and adsorption. The maxima can be suppressed by adding a small amount of surface active substance such as gelatin or agar in 0.005 % or using Trition x-100 in 0.002 percent. These substances are known as maximum suppressors. They are supposed to form a adsorbed layer on aqueous side of mercury solution interface which resists compression. This prevents maxima. Care must be taken not to add too much of maxima suppressors otherwise diffusion current may be suppressed.

Removal of oxygen : Dissolved oxygen in water is reduced in two steps, first to H_2O_2 and then to H_2O. In the first step in acidic conditions $O_2 + 2H^+ + 2e \rightarrow H_2O_2$ occurs at about -0.1 V. In the second step, reduction takes at 0.09 V,

$$H_2O_2 + 2H^+ + 2e \rightarrow 2H_2O$$

The interference of oxygen is eliminated by bubbling high-purity nitrogen through the solution for 5 to 10 minutes. A nitrogen atmosphere is maintained above the solution in cell while the polarogram is run.

In alkaline conditions reduction occurs as under :

$$O_2 + 2H_2O + 2e^- \rightarrow H_2 + 2 OH^-$$

$$H_2O_2 + 2e^- \rightarrow 2OH^-$$

Reference Electrode : A large pool of mercury at the bottom of cell is a anode and acts as reference electrode. Often saturated calomel electrode (SCE) is also used as reference electrode by connecting to the pool of mercury. This provides an accurately known potential of 0.245 mV. The potential (in mV) of polarised DME (E_m) at mercury solution is given by expression.

$$E_m = E_{ref} - (V - iR)$$

where E_{ref} is the potential of reference electrode (0.245 mV). V is the applied potential, i is current flowing through cell and R is the resistance.

Half-Wave Potential : Qualitative analysis by polarography is based on the 'Half wave potential' known as $E_{1/2}$ which is the potential at a point on polarographic wave where the current is one half of the diffusion current for a given substance.

Let us consider the reversible reduction of oxidant (metal ion) at the DME. This may be written as

$$E = E^\circ + \frac{RT}{nf} \log\frac{[OX]_o}{[Red]_o} \qquad \qquad ... (1)$$

It is further simplified as :

$$E = E^\circ + \frac{0.0591}{n} \log\frac{[OX]_o}{[Red]_o} \qquad \qquad ... (2)$$

The [ ]$_o$ denotes the concentration of oxidant or reductant at electrode surface. The current i at a point of polarographic wave is determined by the rate of diffusion of oxidant from bulk of solution to electrode surface under the concentration gradient $[OX] \rightarrow [OX]_o$ ... (3)

Thus $\qquad\qquad i = k\left([OX] - [OX]_o\right) \qquad\qquad$ ... (4)

where k includes capillary characteristic and the n, m and t terms of Ilkovic equation as constant. When

$$[OX]_o = zero$$

$$i = k[OX] = i_d \frac{1}{2} \qquad\qquad ... (5)$$

Now if reductant is water soluble or soluble in mercury (forming amalgam) its concentration at electrode surface is given by $[Red]_o \rightarrow [Red]$ under concentration gradient. Thus,

$$i = k[Red]_o \qquad\qquad ... (6)$$

Since [Red] is zero, now if

$$i = i_d \frac{1}{2} \text{ as per the Halfwave-potential}$$

the equation becomes

$$E = E^{\circ} + \frac{0.0591}{n} \log \frac{\left(i d_{(1/2)}\right)}{\left(i d_{(1/2)}\right)} \quad \dots (7)$$

or

$$E = E_{1/2} + \frac{0.0591}{n} \log \frac{\left(i d_{(1/2)}\right)}{\left(i d_{(1/2)}\right)} \quad \dots (8)$$

Thus the potential at point i when the diffusion current is half known as $E_{1/2}$, the concentration of oxidant and reductant at this point remains equal. This potential is a characteristic of electro reducible species and remains constant and is used for its identification.

MEASUREMENT OF WAVE HEIGHTS

For the quantitative evaluation of polarogram precise measurement of the height of each wave need be carried out. With the smooth polarographic wave the residual current plateau and limiting current plateau are almost parallel and measurement of diffusion current is simple. Subtracting the residual current from the limiting current by extrapolation of lines gives the measure of diffusion current. For measurement of wave height of diffusion current an extrapolation method as shown in Fig. 15.6 is carried out. As shown in the Fig. 15.6 the lines are constructed on the graph of current-voltage to find a point F for determining half wave potential. The height G for the diffusion current is also determined for quantitative work.

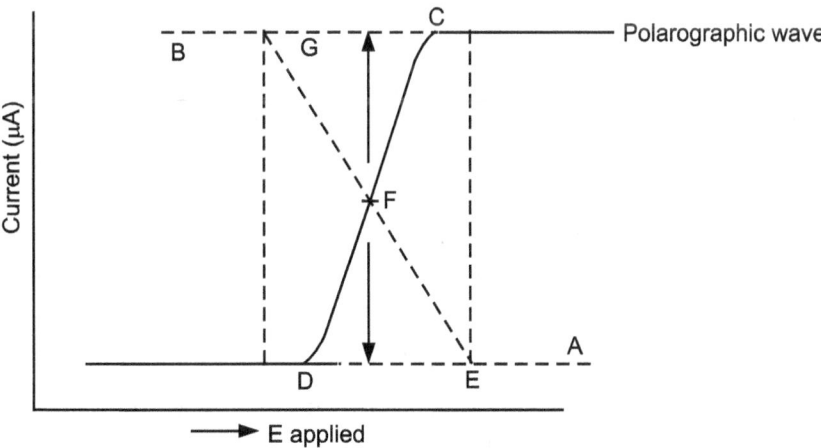

Fig. 15.6

QUANTITATIVE POLAROGRAPHIC METHODS

There are various methods by which quantitative estimation of drugs, metal ions etc. is made. Some such methods are described as under :

1. **Direct comparison method :** In the direct comparison method measurements of current of a standard solution of test ion with that of unknown or test ion is carried under the same condition of experiment. Then, using the Ilkovic equation, the diffusion current quotient i_d/C can be found out. The height of unknown wave when divided by quotient gives the concentration of unknown (test) ion. For accuracy of this method the conditions employed in experiment should be the same.

2. **Calibration curve method :** Various concentrations of standard solutions are analysed for determining their diffusion current. A plot of diffusion current vs. concentration is plotted. Diffusion current of unknown (test) sample is determined under the same conditions of experimentation of standard solution and the concentration of unknown is found out from the graph. This method gives accurate results provided same conditions are kept with respect to capillary characteristic, temperature, flow rate of mercury, concentration of maxima suppressors etc.

3. **Internal Standard (Pilot ion) Method :** This method is deviced by Forche. It is based on the fact that relative diffusion currents i are independent of capillary characteristic. For the pilot ion (standard ion) $i_{d_1} = I_1, C_1 m^{2/3} . t^{1/6}$

    where $I_1 = 607n.D^2$ and for test ion

    $i_{d_2} = I_2 C_2 m^{2/3} t^{1/6}$. Thus, ratio of $\dfrac{i_{d_1}}{i_{d_2}} = \dfrac{I_1 C_1}{I_2 C_2}$ the ratio of $\dfrac{I_1}{I_2}$ is known as pilot

    ion ratio, such a ratio of few concentrations of pilot (standard) ions with those of test ions are determined to find the concentration of unknown (test) solutions.

4. **Standard addition method :** This is considered to be a very simple and reliable method in polarographic analysis A polarogram of unknown (test) solution with a known volume is initially recorded. Then, an accurately measured quantity of standard solution of substance is added to another same quantity of test solution and second polarogram is run. The concentration of unknown solution is found out from increase in the diffusion current (by the addition of standard solution) using the following formula.

$$C_1 = \frac{C_2 \, i_2 \, V_2}{V_1 \, (i_2 - i_1) + i_2 V_2}$$

where C_1, V and i are concentration, volume and diffusion current and subscript 1 and 2 refers to test and standard solution.

For maximum precision the amount of standard solution added should be sufficient to give about double the original wave height.

Analytical Applications : Applications of polarography are limited to those species both organic and inorganic that can be oxidised or reduced at electrode. The potential range is limited to the positive direction by the oxidation of electrode material. Use of platinum micro electrode extends the anodic region considerably especially employing some non-aqueous solvents. Most of the metal ions and many inorganic anions are readily determined alone as well as in mixture.

Polarographic methods are applicable to several class of organic compounds possessing :

- (i)   conjugated double bonds,
- (ii) aromatic ring system,
- (iii) carbonyl,
- (iv) aldehyde,
- (v)   nitro and
- (vi) nitroso,
- (vii) quaternary ammonium groups,
- (viii) halogen groups.

Many compounds which contain carbon-nitrogen, nitrogen-oxygen, sulphur-sulphur, carbon-sulphur bonds can be analysed polarographically. From pharmaceutical point of view the drugs like acetazolamide, chlorthiazide, nitrofurantoin, chloramphenicol etc. are polarographically analysed.

RECENT ADVANCES IN POLAROGRAPHY

In recent years, some significant and useful advances in polarographic techniques have been reported. Some such advances are given below :

1. **Alternating current polarography :** This method has been developed in an attempt to have more rapid and accurate determination of half wave potential. The method enables estimation of small concentration of ion in presence of other reducible substances. In this technique alternating current is supplied to the electrode.

2. **Oscillographic polarography :** This method utilises alternating current coupled with oscillograph. The method is adapted for analysis of pharmaceutical products like antibiotics, vitamins, hormones from various materials.

3. **Chronopotentiometry :** This method involves measurement of potential time pattern. In this method, the working electrode is polarised with constant current and potential of indicator electrode with respect to reference electrode

is observed as a function of time. Thus chronopotentiometry is the study of time relation with the potential of working electrode during the electrolysis which occurs through the cell due to high current. Sand (1951) derived the following relationship

$$r_{1/2} = \frac{E^{1/2} \, nf \, D^{1/2} \, C}{2 \, I}$$

where,   r = Transition time (when conc. of species at electrode is zero.)

           E = Potential

           C = Bulk concentration in mole/lit.

           I = Current density in amp/sq. cm.

Thus $r_{1/2}$ is proportional to C (conc. of analyte sample). In instrumentation, a source of constant current, a device of recording potential as a function of time, a suitable cell/electrode system and galvanometer (ammeter) are required.

The analytical application of chronopotentiometry includes study of irreversible electrode process, study of mechanism of complex ions, in adsorption studies etc.

CHAPTER ... 16

AMPEROMETRY

INTRODUCTION

Like potentiometric, conductometric and photometric titrations, amperometric titration is a methodology for determination of ions and drugs up to 10^{-4} M concentrations. The principle of Polarography has been used as the basis for Amperometric titrations.

Principle:

In polarography, it is observed that diffusion current is proportional to the concentration of electroactive material present in the solution. If the concentration of such electroactive substance is decreased by interaction with another reagent, the diffusion current will decrease. Conversely, if the reagent gives diffusion current a rise will be observed. Thus, measurement of diffusion current as a function of volume of titrating solution at a fixed applied potential is the basis of Amperometric titrations. The titrations are termed amperometric as the current is measured in ampere *vs* the volume of titrating solution.

Apparatus:

The equipment needed for conducting amperometric titrations is simple. It may be the same as used in polarography or some suitable modifications are made. The basic unit is almost the same of polarographic cell. The titration assembly is shown in Fig. 16.1.

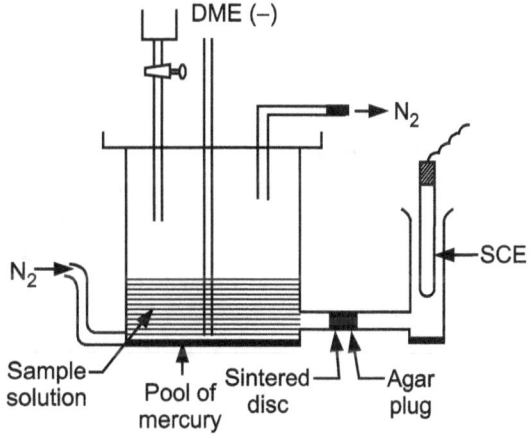

Fig. 16.1

It consists of a glass cell with a lid to allow the tip of a burette, dropping mercury electrode and gas vent to pass through. Dropping mercury electrode (DME) is the indicator electrode and is cathode. A saturated calomel electrode (SCE) is connected to the pool of mercury through sintered disc and agar plug. This acts as the reference electrode. The terminals of cathode and anode are connected to the negative and positive terminals of *g* volt battery. A slide wire potentiometer and galvanometer (to measure current in microamperes) is incorporated into the circuit.

METHODOLOGY

A small volume of test solution is placed in the polarographic cell and air is flushed out by passing pure nitrogen gas through it for 15 minutes. Electrical connections are made and applied voltage is adjusted to a fixed value. If the optimum value of voltage at which titration is performed is not known, the polarogram are determined for the test substance and the reagent solution separately. An appropriate voltage which gives diffusion current (beyond the decomposition potential of material) is selected. Diffusion current is noted. Reagent is added from the microburette in regular increments and diffusion current noted. A graph of current (in microamperes) *vs* volume of titrant solution is plotted. The lines of graph are extrapolated and the intersection point is taken as the end point. Corrections to the observed current due to volume changes involved during the titration is made by the following formula

$$I_{corrected} = i_{observed} \left(\frac{V + v}{V} \right)$$

Where, V is the original volume and v is the volume of titrant added.

TITRATION CURVES

The following types of amperometric titration curves are usually seen.

(A) Titration of reducible substance with non-reducible reagent:

A polarogram of solution of lead being titrated with sulphate ion is shown in Fig. 16.2. Voltage selected is −0.8 V. The lead ions present in the solution give diffusion current at the applied potential. The titrant sulphate ions exhibit no diffusion current at the applied potential. The increments of titrant remove lead ions and the current decreases. When all the lead ions have interacted and undergone a complete change, only the current flowing is a residual current characteristic of supporting electrolyte. The intersection of the extrapolated lines of titration curve gives the end point.

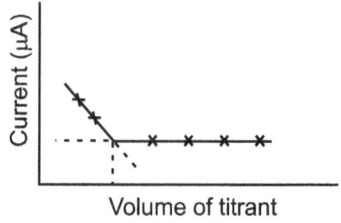

Volume of titrant

Fig. 16.2

(B) Titration of non-reducible substance with reducible reagent:

A polarographic curve as shown in Fig. 16.3 is obtained when a solution of lead nitrate is titrated with potassium dichromate in acetate buffer of pH 4.2. The applied potential is 0.0 V. In this case at the applied potential lead ions do not give diffusion current but the titrant dichromate ion (Cr_2O_7) does give. The titration curve thus shows little or no diffusion current up to the end point and thereafter the increase in the current is due to the excess dichromate ions added during the titration. Similarly, sulphate ion can be titrated against lead ions.

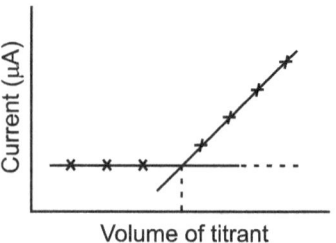

Volume of titrant

Fig. 16.3

(C) Titration of reducible substance with reducible reagent:

When both the substances and the titrant give diffusion currents at the applied potential, the current decreases up to the end point and then increase to give a V shaped titration curve. The titration of nickel ions with dimethylglyoxime solution gives the V shape of the titration curve as shown in the Fig. 16.4.

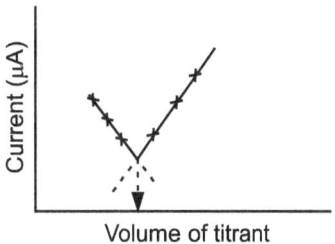

Fig. 16.4

(D) Titration of substance giving anodic diffusion current with the reagent giving cathodic diffusion current:

This type of titration shows zero current at the end point. Titration of potassium iodide with mercuric nitrate reagent shows this type of graph (Fig. 16.5). This anodic diffusion current is given by iodide ions. Its removal after the end point shows cathodic diffusion due to the mercuric ions added.

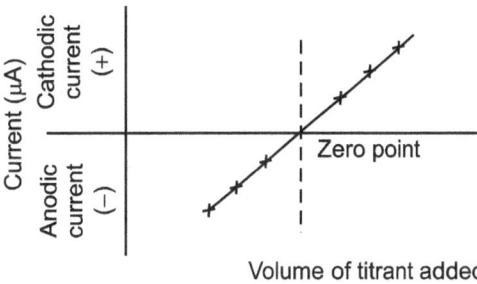

Fig. 16.5

(E) Titration of non-reducible substance with non-reducible reagent using reducible indicator:

When neither the substance nor the reagent gives diffusion current, indicators which show diffusion current at end point can be employed. Titration of aluminium salt with sodium fluoride can be followed by using ferric salt as indicator. A titration graph as shown in Fig. 16.6 is observed.

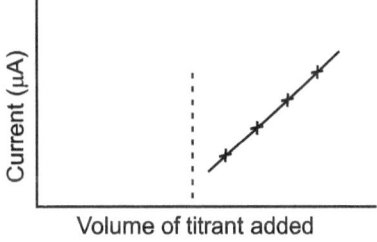

Fig. 16.6

Advantages of Amperometric Titrations:

Several advantages of Amperometric titrations are immediately apparent.

1. Titrations can be carried out for dilute solutions up to 10^{-4} M concentration of substance or titrant.

2. Presence of foreign salt or other electrolyte do not interfere in the analysis, contrariwise some electrolyte is added to eliminate the influence of migration current.

3. Titrations of solutions which cannot be analysed by other methods like potentiometric, colorimetry etc. can be carried out rapidly.

4. The end point is determined by extrapolation of lines which gives accurate results than a single point determination method.

5. The results are independent of the characteristic of DME and temperature effects are negligible.

APPLICATIONS OF AMPEROMETRIC TITRATIONS

Applications of amperometric titration are more general than the other classical methods. Many metal ions which are reducible at the selected applied voltage can be titrated using non-reducible reagent. Similarly, the anions can be titrated using metal ions solution as titrant-determination of lead against dichromate or oxalate, sulphate against barium acetate, oxalate against calcium, and zinc against EDTA etc.

Mixture of iodide, bromide and chloride can be successively titrated with silver nitrate solution at different pH.

Besides inorganic chemicals a large number of organic compounds of pharmaceutical interest can be analysed by amperometric titrant method. A list of some drugs analysed by this technique is given in the Table 16.1.

Table 16.1: Amperometric Titrations vis-à-vis Drugs

Drug	Titrant	Medium
1. p-aminophenol	$K_2Cr_2O_7$	1 M Sulphuric acid
2. Phenobarbitone	Mercuric acetate in acetic acid	Ethanol-water mixture
3. Thiourea	Silver nitrate	1 M sulphuric acid
4. Phenol	Pot. bromate	Methanol
5. Vitamin C	Ferric nitrate	Water
6. Strychnine Cocaine	Silicotungstic acid	0.3 N hydrochloric acid

CHAPTER ... 17

ELECTROMAGNETIC RADIATION
AND
ABSORPTION SPECTROSCOPY

ELECTROMAGNETIC RADIATION

Electromagnetic radiation is a form of radiant energy, which exhibits both wave and particle properties. The wave properties of radiation source include the phenomena of reflection, refraction, interferences etc. while the discrete particles called as photon have definite energies. Both these properties are inseparable and are a distinctive feature of electromagnetic radiation.

Nature of Electromagnetic Radiation

The electromagnetic radiation is considered as a form of radiant energy that is propagated as a transverse wave. It vibrates perpendicular to the direction of propagation and this imparts a wave motion to the light (Fig. 17.1).

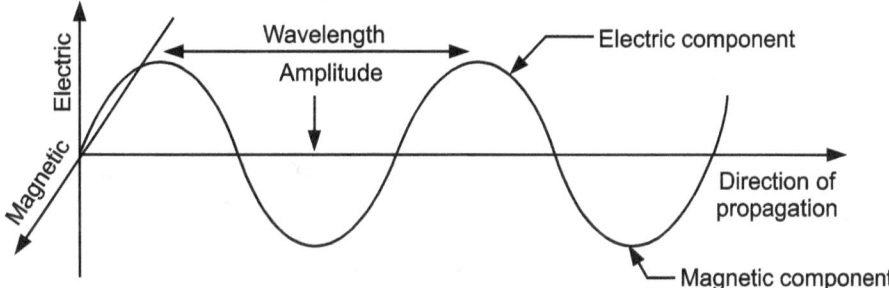

Fig. 17.1

The wave is described either in terms of wavelength (distance of one complete cycle or from on crest to the another) or in terms of the frequency, which is the number of cycles passing through a fixed point per unit time. The symbol of wavelength is λ and that of frequency is υ (hertz). The wavelength and the frequency are related to the velocity of light by the formula

$$\lambda\upsilon = \frac{C}{n} \qquad \text{... (1)}$$

Where c = Velocity of light in vacuum (2.99×10^{10} cm/sec) and n is the refractive index (the ratio of the velocity of light in vacuum to its velocity in the medium of study). For many purposes n is considered as uniform and hence,

$$\lambda\upsilon = c \qquad \text{... (2)}$$

Or
$$\lambda = \frac{c}{\upsilon} \qquad \text{... (3)}$$

The reciprocal of the wavelength is called the wave number. It is a number of waves in a unit length and is represented by $\bar{\upsilon}$ in cm^{-1}.

The wavelength of electromagnetic radiation varies from a few angstroms to several metres. The units and symbols used to describe the electromagnetic radiation are shown in Table 17.1.

Table 17.1: Relation of units and symbols in electromagnetic radiation

Nature	Unit	Symbol	Conversions
Wavelength λ	Angstrom	A°	1A = 10^{-8} cm
	Nanometer	nm	1 nm = 10^{-7} cm
	Millimicron	mμ	1 mμ = 1 nm
	Micron	μm	1 μm = 10^{-4} cm
Frequency υ	Cycles per sec	CPs	1 Hz = 1 cps
	Hertz	Hz	
	Megahertz	MHz	1 MHz = 10^6 cps
		cm^{-1} or $\bar{\upsilon}$	cm^{-1} = $\frac{1}{l}$
Intensity of radiation	Energy per sec.	I	

Electromagnetic radiation possesses a quantum of energy. The energy unit of light is called as photon, and is related to the frequency by,

$$E = h\upsilon = hc/\lambda$$

Where,   E is the energy of photon in erg

H is Planck's constant = 06.62 × 10^{-27} erg/sec.

It is apparent thus, that the shorter the wavelength greater the energy.

The various regions of the electromagnetic spectrum of use and importance are shown in the Fig. 17.2.

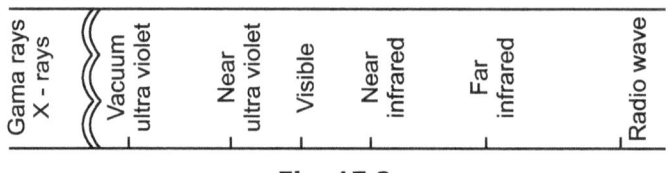

Fig. 17.2

The principal region of the electromagnetic radiation for the study of absorption spectrophotometry includes the ultraviolet region which extends from 10–380 nm, the most useful for analytical purpose is 200–380 nm, and is called as near ultraviolet region. Below 200 nm, the air absorbs appreciably and hence instruments are operated under vacuum. This region (120–180) is called vacuum region. The visible region comprises a very small part of electromagnetic radiation, and extends from near ultraviolet 380 to about 780 nm. This region of wavelength is visible to the naked eye, and is therefore called the visible region. This part of wavelength is extensively used in Colorimetry. The infrared region extends from 780 nm to 300 μ; of this the 2-5 to 25 μ is most frequently used for analysis. The lower energy regions of radio and microwaves do not concern us, especially in analytical work.

When a molecule is exposed to electromagnetic radiation, a certain amount of energy associated with the particular radiation is absorbed by the molecule. There is a transfer of energy from the beam of radiant energy to the molecule. This is called 'absorption' and the study of this is called as absorption spectrophotometry. When the process is reverse, in which the internal energy of molecule is converted into radiant energy, it is called 'emission'. There are other ways of energy instead being absorbed, scattered or re-emitted, which is of different consideration.

When a molecule is at rest, it is considered to be in ground state of energy level E_O. There are three basic internal energy levels in a molecule. First is the rotational energy that allows molecule to rotate about various axes. This energy is very small. The second is the vibrational energy level, which allows atoms or groups of atoms within a molecule vibrate relative to each other. Third, the electrons of molecule may be raised to higher electron energy, known as electronic transition. Thus, a total energy of molecule at ground state can be shown as

$$E_O = E_{electronic} + E_{vibration} + E_{rotational}$$

When a molecule at a ground state of energy level E_O is exposed to a radiation in ultraviolet to infrared region, a certain quantity of energy is absorbed by the molecule and it is raised to the excited state of energy E_1, E_2 etc. The quantity of energy associated with the wavelength of ultraviolet is more visible is small and with infrared it is very small. If radiation of wavelength corresponding to one of the natural frequencies of a molecule strikes it, the radiant energy may be absorbed to raise the molecule at excited state level. The amount absorbed would be

$$\Delta E = 286,000 \text{ kcal mole}^{-1}$$

A schematic energy level diagram for a simple diatomic molecule is shown in Fig. 17.3.

A given electronic transition may involve vibration as well as rotational changes, resulting in several photon energies being absorbed.

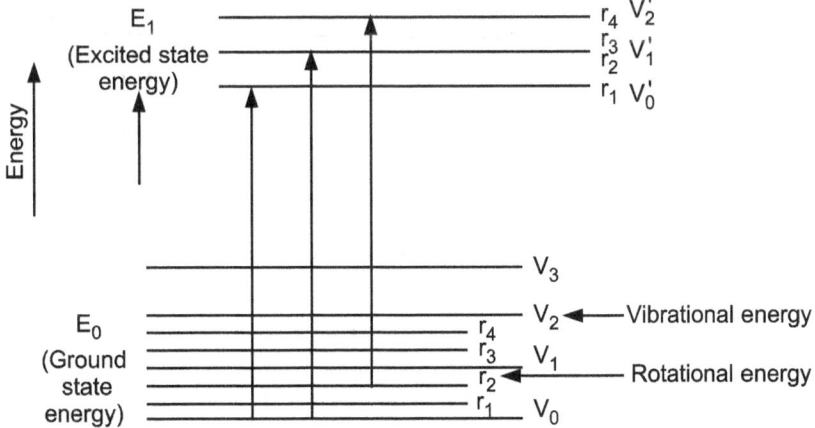

Fig. 17.3

Molecules from excited state of energy return to ground state in 10^{-9} to 10^{-8} seconds, and in the process the absorbed energy is released, if molecule returns to a ground state directly, heat is evolved, and if it returns by a way of second excited state then the energy is released in the form of heat and light.

ABSORPTION SPECTRA

Absorption of light in ultraviolet and visible regions gives rise to the absorption spectra. These spectra of molecules and ions are due to the transitions between electronic energy levels of certain types of groups present in the molecule. A group that gives rise to absorption in visible and near ultraviolet is known as a chromophore. The term chromophore was originally applied for unsaturated groups/atoms which were thought essential for colour (chrome = colour). Most unsaturated groups, heteroatoms carrying lone pair of electrons are potential chromophore. Now-a-days, the term chromophore is given to a group which when attached to a molecule shows absorbance in ultraviolet-visible region at a specified wavelength. Table 17.2 lists some common chromophores and their approximate wavelengths of maximum absorption. Although a chromophore shows absorption in a certain region of spectrum, the maximum absorption will depend on the particular molecule and the influence of other groups in the molecule.

Table 17.2: Absorption bands and electronic transitions for common chromosphores

Chromophore	System	Example	Maximum	Electronic Transition
Alkane	R – CH = CH – R	Ethylene	165 193	$\pi \rightarrow \pi^*$
Amine	R – NH$_2$	Aniline (cation)	203 254	$\pi - \pi^*$
Amide	R – CONH$_2$	Acetamide	220	–
Azo	R – N = N – R	Azomethane	338	–
Carbonyl (ketone)	$\underset{R}{\overset{R}{>}}C = O$	Acetone	188 279	$\pi - \pi^*$ $n - \pi^*$
Carbonyl (aldehyde)	$R - C \overset{O}{\underset{OH}{<}}$	Acetaldehyde	180 290 230	$\pi - \pi^*$ $n - \pi^*$ $\pi - \pi^*$
Carboxyl	R – C – OH	Benzoic acid	270	
Nitro	R – NO$_2$	Nitromethane	201	
Nitroso	R – N = O	Nitrosobutane	302	
Nitrate	R – ONO$_2$	n-Butylnitrate	270	

Changes in the absorption spectra can be brought out by certain groups attached to a fully saturated system. These groups do not absorb radiation at wavelengths > 200 nm. They do modify and shift the absorption bands. Such groups are called Auxochromes. The groups like – OH, – NH$_2$, – Cl etc. have non-bonding valency electrons. They show intense absorption in far ultraviolet region.

When an auxochrome is attached to a chromophore, the chromophore absorption band is shifted to longer wavelength. This is called bathochromic shift (Red shift), when there is increase in intensity of absorption it is termed as hyperchromic effect (The molar absorptivity increases). When a shift of absorption band is to a shorter wavelength the effect is termed as hypochromic shift (blue shift) and reduction in intensity is called hypochromic effect. (Fig. 17.4)

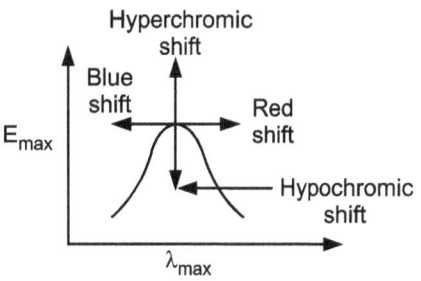

Fig. 17.4

The types of electrons involved in absorption of energy in the ultraviolet-visible regions are mainly of three types:

σ **(sigma) Electrons:** These are usually found in fully saturated system like alkane. These electrons require very large amount of energy for their excitation and hence do not show absorption in ultraviolet region. The absorption band given in some cases is due to their interaction with π* (pie excited) electrons to give hyper conjugation. The absorption band is encountered in vacuum ultra-violet region.

n-electrons: The valence electrons which do not participate in chemical bonding in molecule are called as n-electron or non-bonding electrons. These are located principally in the atomic orbital of nitrogen, oxygen, sulphur and halogens as lone pair electrons. Their transition from n to π* gives absorption in ultraviolet region.

π**-electrons:** These are found in unsaturated compounds in multiple bonds. The π electrons are generally 'mobile electrons'. The outer shell electrons, the atomic p-orbital electrons are responsible for pi bonds. The basic absorption occurs due to transition of π–π* which gives band in ultraviolet-visible region.

Transition of electrons to their excited higher energy levels gives rise to mainly four types of absorption bands.

K-band spectra arise from π–π structures due to π–π* transitions. These are characterized by high molar absorptivities (ε more than 100,00). In diene for example, K-band results due to resonance transition:

$$C = C - C = C \text{ to } C^+ - C = C - C^-$$

It also results in aromatic compounds possessing chromophore groups.

R—bands arise from n–π* transitions and show intermediate molar absorptivity. The weak intensity bands are found in non-aromatic compounds having chromophore auxochrome groups like OH, NH_2, – SH, – CHO, – C=) etc.

B—band spectra are characteristics of aromatic and hetro aromatic molecules. These give weak absorption bands and show very low molar absorptivity (250).

E—band spectra arises from oscillations of electrons in aromatic ring systems.

The energy level diagram (Fig. 17.5) shows the ΔE values for transitions from ground to excited state in the order.

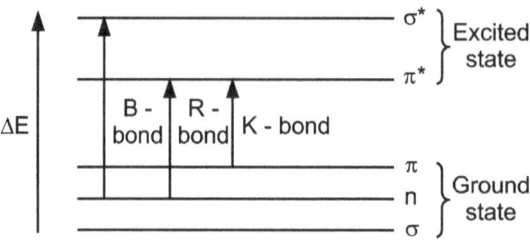

Fig. 17.5

Many molecules contain more than one chromophore and/or auxochromes. Interaction of radiant energy with such molecules and the resultant spectra depends upon the relative positions of two chromophores. In general it can be said that:

1. When two chromophores are separated by more than one carbon unit, then total absorption is sum of the absorption of each chromophore.
2. When two chromophores are adjacent to each other, absorption shifts to longer wavelength (bathochromic shift) and intensity of absorption (hyperchromic effect) increases.
3. When two chromophores are attached to same carbon atom, there results in summation of absorption and shift are towards longer wavelength. However, the degree of shift is less than shown by conjugated chromophore.
4. Auxochrome shifts and modifies absorption. The auxochromes encountered in covalently unsaturated moieties such as $-NH_2$ are more effective in modifying absorption.
5. The other auxochrome like $-OH$, $-\overset{+}{N}H_3$ or $-$ S also shifts absorption spectra to higher wavelength.

Some examples of chromophore showing basic absorption and shift of spectra are given below:

1. Dienes and Polyenes

These show shift of absorption to longer wavelength. Butadiene ( ) shows λ_{max} at 217 nm while hexatriene ( ) has λ_{max} at 256 nm. Woodward observed that the diene absorption is influenced by the groups and molecules and he worked out a rule (known as Woodward rule) for predicting the expected λ_{max} by calculations. Table 17.3 shows the rules for calculation of absorption.

Table 17.3: Absorption spectra calculations

Parent structure not having diene in ring	214
Parent structure having diene in ring	253
For each substituent double bond in conjugation	30
Alkyl substituent in ring	5
N-alkyl	60
S-alkyl	30
λ_{max} of Total	592 nm

2. Aldehydes and Ketones:

Simple aldehydes and ketones show absorption around 280 nm (weak) and 190 nm (medium) e.g. acetone, due to $\pi-\pi^*$, λ_{max} is at 188 nm and n – π^* transition shows λ_{max} at 276 nm. Similarly, acetaldehyde $\pi-\pi^*$ show λ_{max} at 194 and due to n – π^* 292 nm.

3. Aromatic and heterocyclic

Benzene exhibits three bands at 255 nm (low absorptivity), 200 nm and at 185 nm (high absorptivity). The substitution shows marked effect e.g. alkyl substituent—CH_3 in toluene by replacing –H of benzene shows bathochromic shift from 255–261 nm. The other groups like – OH, – NH_2 also cause bathochromic shift. The effect is more pronounced in polar solvents, e.g. in phenol, the – OH substitution

shows λ_{max} at 210 and 270 in water. The phenolate ion (in alkaline pH) shows λ_{max} at 235 and 287 nm.

Amino group is a powerful auxochrome and when attached directly to benzene ring shows shift in benzene λ_{max} from 200, 255–230, 280 nm, in Aniline. Aniline in acidic media forms aniline cation which is less effective as auxochrome (λ_{max} = 203 and 254 nm). In the case of heterocyclic compounds it is necessary to have spectrum of basic ring for comparison and interpretation.

4. Fusion of two rings

Fusion of two or more benzene rings causes bathochromic shift. This results because of conjugation of chromophore which modifies basic spectra e.g.

	Number of rings	λ_{max}
Benzene	1	255
Naphthalene	2	312
Anthracene	3	375
Naphthacene	4	471 (Yellow coloured)
Pentacene	5	575 (Blue coloured)
Pyridine	1	195, 250
Quinoline	2	275, 311
Isoquinoline	2	262, 317

5. pH effect:

The effect of pH is very striking, e.g. in Sulpha drugs . The intense λ_{max} is observed at 251 nm in 0.1 N sodium hydroxide solution. This is due to – NH_2 group which shows its powerful auxochrome. The peak is lost in 0.1 N hydrochloric solutions for the same sulpha.

Fig. 17.6 shows the effect of pH on the absorption spectra of sulpha drugs.

6. Solvent effects:

Solvents play a striking role on the absorption spectra of compounds. Many substances show fine structure bands when measured in solvents of low dipole moments. Thus, benzene shows number of bands in petroleum ether (low dipole) whereas in aqueous solutions the fine structures are lost. The electronic transitions of n – π^* are more pronounced in certain solvents. For example, the spectra of iodine in polar solvents like ethanol shows characteristic shift to shorter wavelength (showing brownish colour), whereas it appears as purple in chloroform. Solvents begin to absorb ultraviolet energy at some specified wavelength. Thus, those solvents which show λ_{max} at particular wavelength cannot be used as solvent for absorption studies of compound having λ_{max} near the solvent λ_{max}. Impurities in solvents show that it is essential to use good grade (spectroscopic grade) solvents for absorption studies. Some solvents are acidic or basic in nature and they do affect the λ_{max} due to their pH effect.

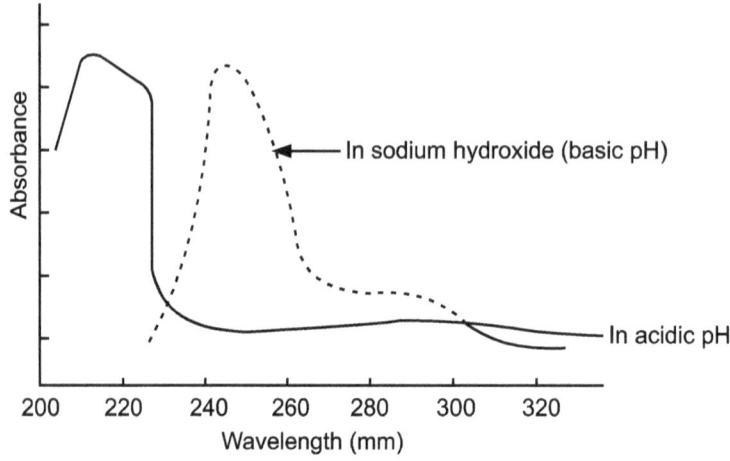

Fig. 17.6

Wavelength of absorption of common solvents is given in Table 17.4.

Table 17.4

Solvents	λ_{max} in nm
Acetone	188, 276
Benzene	200, 255
CCl_4	265
$CHCl_3$	245
Cyclohexane	210
DMF	270
Diethyl ether	220
Ethanol	210
N-Hexane	210
Toluene	261
Water	200
Xylene	266

7. Temperature effects:

At low temperatures the absorption bands of most substances are sharper than at room temperature. The solute-solvent interaction is decreased at low temperature and hence studies are carried out at 15–25°C.

CHAPTER ... 18

QUANTITATIVE ANALYSIS BY ABSORPTION SPECTROPHOTOMETRY

INTRODUCTION

Absorption spectrophotometry is the measurement of the absorption of electromagnetic radiation of definite and narrow wavelength range by molecules, ions and atoms of a chemical substance. The technique most commonly employed in analytical field includes ultraviolet, visible, infrared and atomic absorption spectrophotometry. For study of absorption spectrophotometry, it is essential to understand the fundamental laws of photometry. Two fundamental laws are associated with the practice of photometry.

FUNDAMENTAL LAWS OF PHOTOMETRY

When a beam of light falls on a solution or homogeneous media, a portion of light is reflected from the surface of the media, a portion is absorbed within the medium while the remaining is transmitted through the medium.

Thus if I_o is the intensity of radiation falling on the media, I_r is the amount of radiation reflected, I_a is the amount of radiation absorbed and I_t as the amount of radiation transmitted then,

$$I_o = I_r + I_a + I_t \qquad ... (1)$$

In most of the measurements the amount of radiation lost by reflection by the surface of media is small, and hence it is eliminated from consideration.

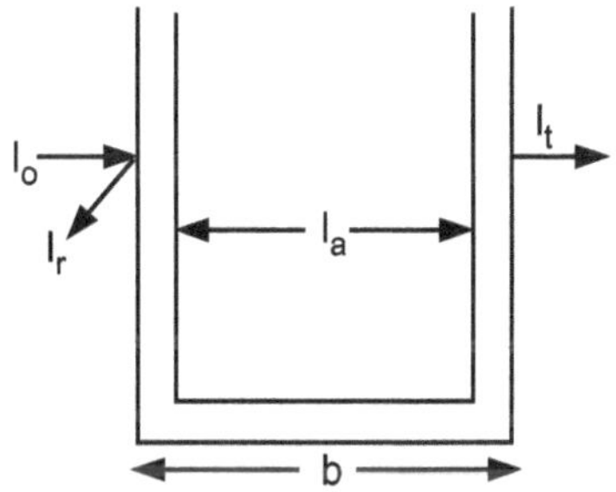

Fig. 18.1

Thus, $\qquad I_o = I_A + I_t \qquad ... (2)$

Now considering the relationship for the intensity of light falling upon a medium, its part being absorbed and transmitted, two laws play significant role.

THE BOUGUR (1729) OR LAMBERT (1760) LAW

When a monochromatic light passes through an absorbing medium at right angles to the plane of surface of medium or solution, the rate of decrease in intensity with thickness of medium (b) is proportional to the intensity of light. In other words the intensity of transmitted light decreases exponentially as the thickness of medium increases arithmetically. Thus by differential equation,

$$-\frac{dI}{db} = KI \qquad \qquad \text{... (3)}$$

Where,   I = Intensity of incident light of λ wavelength

b = Thickness of medium

K = Proportionality constant

Now integrating the equation, and putting $I = I_o$ when $b = 0$

$$I_n \frac{I_o}{I_t} = Kb \text{ or } I_t = I_o\, e^{-Kb} \qquad \qquad \text{... (4)}$$

Where, I_o = Intensity of incident light falling on thickness b

I_t = Intensity of transmitted light

K = Absorption coefficient for the given wavelength and medium

Converting from natural logarithms to base 10 logarithms

$$I_t = I_o \cdot 10^{-Kb} \qquad \qquad \text{... (5)}$$

Beer's Law: Bernard and Beer (in 1852) independently stated that 'The intensity of incident light decreases exponentially as the concentration of absorbing medium increases arithmetically. This is similar to Lambert's law and thus,

$$I_t = I_o \cdot e^{-K'c} \qquad \qquad \text{... (6)}$$

Where,   K' = Proportionality constant

c = Concentration

By converting from natural logarithms to base 10

$$I_t = I_o \cdot 10^{-Kc} \qquad \qquad \text{... (7)}$$

Now combining two laws, i.e. equations (5) and (7) we have

$$I_t = I_o. \, 10^{-\varepsilon\, cb} \qquad \qquad \text{... (8)}$$

Where,   K and K' = ε

c = Concentration

b = Thickness of medium

Thus, $$\log \frac{I_o}{I_t} = \varepsilon\, c\, b \qquad \qquad \text{... (9)}$$

Where ε is the absorptivity, a constant dependent upon the wavelength of incident radiation and the nature of absorbing material. The value of ε (which is also referred as a = absorptivity) will depend upon the method of expression of concentration. If c = gram mole/litre and b = thickness in cm then ε = molar extinction coefficient. This is also called as molar absorptivity or molar absorbancy index.

The ratio of $\frac{I_t}{I_o}$ is a fraction of light transmitted by a thickness 'b' of a medium and is called as transmittance or transmission. Its reciprocal, i.e. log of $\frac{I_o}{I_t}$ is called opacity or optical density denoted by letter A or E or D.

Absorbance (A) is thus product of absorptivity, the optical path length and the concentration of solution.

$$A = abc$$

Or $$A = \varepsilon cb \qquad\qquad ...(10)$$

The term specific extinction coefficient (E_s) is called by absorbancy index and is defined as extinction or optical density per unit thickness per unit concentration. The term $E_{1\ cm}^{1\ \%}$ refers to the absorbance of 1 cm layer of solution whose concentration is 1 per cent at a specified wavelength. Thus, we can define the terms as:

1. The optical density D or absorbancy A as log ratio of intensity of incident light to that of transmitted light and is

$$D = A = \log \frac{I_o}{I_t}$$

This is also written as $\log \frac{1}{T}$ or $- \log T$.

2. Transmission T (Transmittance) is a ratio of intensity of transmitted light to that of incident. $T = \frac{I_t}{I_o}$. The percent transmittance = 100 T.

3. Transmittancy T_s is a ratio of transmittance of a cell containing a solution to that of identical cell containing solvent blank or blank solution.

4. Specific extinction coefficient is optical density of unit concentration of unit length solution $E_s = A/cb$.

5. Molecular extinction coefficient (Molar absorptivity) is optical density of 1 gram mole per litre of solution of 1 cm path length i.e.

$$\varepsilon = \frac{A}{cb}$$

It is also a product of absorptivity 'a' × molecular weight i.e.

$$\varepsilon = a \times M$$

The relationship between transmittance, absorbance and concentration of solution is shown in Fig. 18.2.

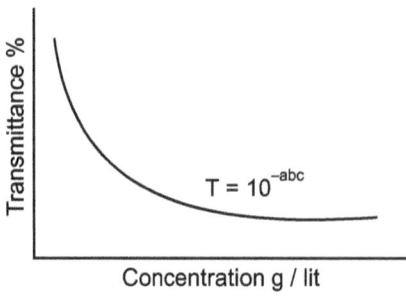 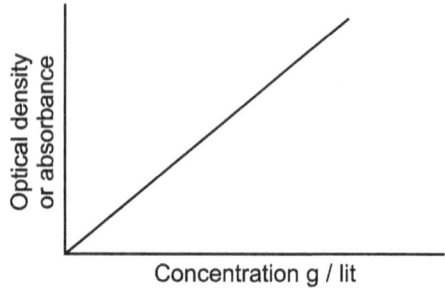

Fig. 18.2

We can summarize the terminology as

$$\text{Absorbance 'A'} = \text{Optical density} = -\log T \text{ or } \log \frac{I_0}{I_t}$$

$$\text{Absorptivity 'a'} = \text{Absorbancy index} = A/cb = a \times M$$

Where, c = g/lit, M = mol. wt., b = 1 cm

$$\text{Molar absorptivity '}\varepsilon\text{'} = \varepsilon \text{ molar absorbancy index} = A/cb$$

Where c = g.mol/lit., b = 01 cm

$$\text{Transmittance T} = \text{Transmission} = \frac{I_t}{I_0}$$

DEVIATIONS FROM BEER'S LAW

There are no deviations or exceptions to Lambert's law since it relates to the thickness of medium. Usually, thickness of medium is considered to be homogeneous in nature. This is because in experiments matching cells or cuvettes of uniform thickness are employed. However, deviations to Beer's law are frequently observed. To verify the validity of this law a plot of absorbance *vs.* concentration should be plotted. It should give a straight line passing through origin with a slope = ab.

The deviations to Beer's law may be due to the following reasons:

1. Dilute solutions only follow Beer's law more closely. When the concentration of absorbing species is high, the molecules will react or interact with each other by collision and each molecule will not then absorb the radiant energy in the same manner as in the dilute solution. The index of refraction for the absorbed radiation is changed at high concentration, and hence Beer's law is not obeyed. This type of deviation from Beer's law is called 'True deviation'.

2. Instrumental deviation: In determination instrumental variations may show deviation which may be due to:

   (a) Stray radiation reaching the detector;

   (b) Sensitivity changes in detector employed;

   (c) Fluctuation of radiation source, and

   (d) Defect in detector amplification system etc.

3. One of the causes of instrumental deviation is the working with a broad band of wavelength rather than using truly monochromatic radiation. Beer's law assumes the radiant power to be of monochromatic light. Though in case of spectrophotometer it is possible to isolate a wavelength specified for the filter type of instruments, the solutions are exposed to broad range of wavelength of varying radiant energy. Furthermore, the slit width (exit) of instrument allows varying wavelength to enter the solution. With wide slit width accuracy will be less as what the detector measures is the average intensity, whereas what is wanted is the average of the log of intensity. The average of the logarithms of a set of values is not equal to the logarithm of the average. Thus with narrow slit width and with monochromatic light of selected wavelength Beer's law is obeyed and deviations are less.

4. Chemical deviation: The absorbing species in the solution may undergo ionization, dissociation or even may react with the solvent. These processes may produce two or more species in the solution with varying absorptivity values. For example, acidic or basic medium may produce hydrolysis of the species into entities of varying absorptivity. In other cases, exposure to intense radiation may cause irradiation effect which in turn may bring out cleavage or breakdown of the absorbing species. This type of deviation encountered in certain cases can be corrected by the use of (i) buffers (ii) choosing suitable solvent, and (iii) by selecting appropriate narrow band of wavelength for measurements.

SPECTROPHOTOMETRIC METHODS FOR ESTIMATION OF DRUGS

(A) One Component analysis:

(i)   For one component analysis, the absorbance of standard (As) and unknown (Au) are compared at λ_{max} of compound in particular solvent, provided that Beer's law is obeyed. The contents of unknown are calculated by the following formula:

$$Cu = \frac{Au}{As} \times Cs$$

Where,   C = Concentration

                          A = Absorbance

                          u = For unknown and

                          s = For standard

(ii) A standard calibration curve is plotted using series of standard solutions as concentration against absorbance and concentration of sample is determined from the graph.

(iii) To establish absorptivities values E (1 per cent 1 cm) for standard at selected wavelength (usually λ_{max}) in particular solvent.

(B) Methods for multi-ingredient analysis:

1. Simultaneous equation method or "Vierodt's" method.

2. Multicomponent method of analysis.

3. Derivative spectrophotometry.

4. Geometric correction method.

5. Absorption factor method (Absorption correction method)

6. Difference spectrophotometry.

7. Orthogonal polynomial functional method.

8. Absorbance ratio method.

9. Two wavelength/three wavelength method.

1. Simultaneous equation method or "Vierodt's" method:

If a sample contains two absorbing drugs (x and y) each of which absorbs at the λ_{max} of the other (Fig. 18.3, λ_1, λ_2), it may be possible to determine both the drugs by the techniques of simultaneous equation provided that :

(a) Two absorbing drugs (x and y), each of which should absorb at the λ_{max} of the other.

(b) The λ_{max} of two drugs should be reasonably dissimilar.

(c) The two components should not interact chemically.

Application spectra of two hypothetical substances x and y are shown below:

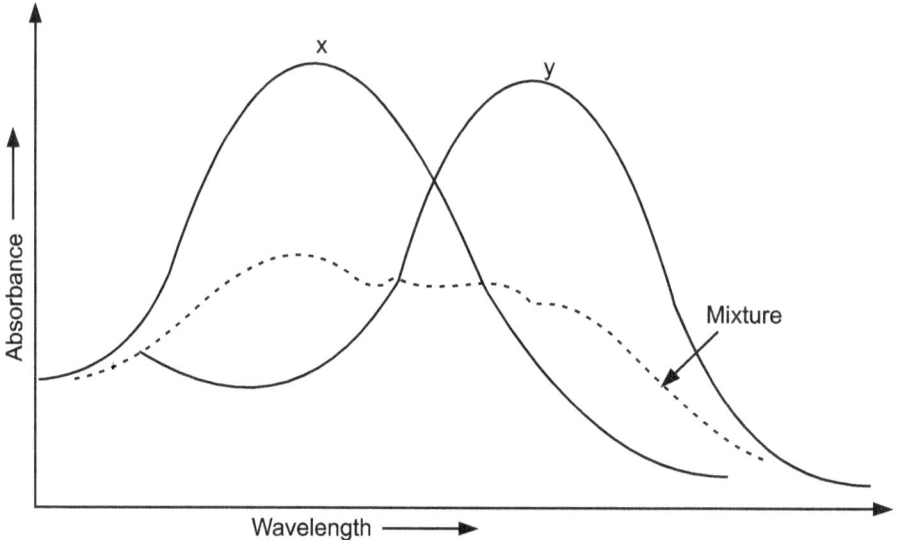

Fig. 18.3: The individual absorption spectra of substances x and y showing the wavelengths for the essay of x and y in admixture by the method of simultaneous equation

The two equations are constructed based on fact at λ_1 and λ_2 the absorbance of mixture is sum of individual absorbances x and y.

At λ_1 $A_1 = ax_1\ bc_x + ay_1\ bc_y$ ... (11)

At λ_2 $A_2 = ax_2\ bo_x + ay_2\ bc_y$ ... (12)

Rearranging equations (11) and (12) gives

$$c_x = \frac{A_2\ ay_1 - A_1\ ay_2}{ax_2\ ay_1 - ax_1\ ay_2}$$

And $$c_y = \frac{A_1\ ax_2 - A_2\ ax_1}{ax_2\ ay_1 - ax_1\ ay_2}$$

Where, c_x and c_y are concentrations of x and y respectively, ax_1 and ax_2 are absorptivities of x at λ_1 and λ_2 respectively, and ay_1 and ay_2 are absorptivities of y at λ_1 and λ_2 respectively.

A_1 and A_2 are absorbances of diluted mixture at λ_1 and λ_2 respectively.

2. Multicomponent method of analysis:

Multicomponent analysis is done earlier by using online computers with an UV detection system to collect and compare spectral data 10. The absorbance values at several wavelengths are processed by means of matrix equation to obtain concentration of two or more drugs known to be present in the sample solution. Another approach applying multicomponent least square calculation to the output from spectrophotometer is also reported.

The present day sophisticated spectrophotometers like the SHIMADZU Mode UV – 1601 have an in-dash built computer for spectral data processing. The instrument gives accurate results within a short time. The concentrations of each of the components in the mixture are printed out after all the required processing computation is done by the instrument. The successful utilisation of this mode of analysis involves the following steps:

(i)   Selection of scanning range.

(ii)   Selection of sampling wavelengths.

(iii) Study of Beer-Lambert's law.

(iv)   Analysis of laboratory mixture.

(v)   Analysis of marketed formulations.

(vi)   Recovery studies.

3. Derivative spectrophotometry:

This method is very useful when the sample of drug shows large irrelevant absorption. It is found that in many a drug like Benzenoid drugs which show very narrow bands of fine structure in pure form, or due to large excipients/drug ratio, low doses and also weakly absorbing molecules, show broad band absorption. In such cases, derivative spectroscopy enhances the resolution and bandwidth discrimination permits selective determination of certain absorbing substances in the sample were non-specific interference may prohibit application of simple spectroscopic method.

It involves conversion of normal spectrum to its first, second or higher derivative spectra where the amplitude in the derivative spectrum is proportional to the concentration of the analyte provided that Beer's law is obeyed by the fundamental spectrum. The measured value in quantitation is the largest amplitude that is unaffected by presence of other absorbing component of the sample. For quantitative purpose, second and fourth derivative spectra are most frequently employed.

4. Geometric correction method:

A number of mathematical correction procedures have been developed which reduce or eliminate the background irrelevant absorption that may be present in the samples of biological origin. The simplest of these procedures is the three-point geometric procedure which may be applied if the irrelevant absorption is linear at the three selected wavelengths.

5. Absorption factor method (Absorption correction method):

It is modification of simultaneous equation method where quantitative determination of one drug carried out by E (1 per cent 1 cm) value and quantitation of another drug carried out by subtracting absorption due to interfering drug using absorption factor. This method includes the following steps:

(a) Selection of wavelengths.

(b) Study of Beer-Lambert's law.

(c) Study of additivity of absorbances.

(d) Determination of absorptivity E (1 per cent 1 cm) value

(e) Estimation of drugs in laboratory mixture.

(f) Analysis of marketed formulation.

(g) Recovery studies.

6. Difference spectrophotometry:

The essential feature of difference spectrophotometry assay is that the measured value is a difference absorbance (dA) between two equimolar solutions of the analyte in different chemical forms which exhibit different spectral characteristics.

The criteria for applying difference spectrophotometry to the assay of substances in the presence of other absorbing species are:

(a) Reproducible change may be induced in the spectrum of the analyte by the addition of one or more reagents.

(b) The absorbance of the interfering substance is not altered by the reagent.

7. Orthogonal polynomial functional method:

The technique of orthogonal polynomial is another mathematical correction procedure which involves complex calculation. The basis of this method is that an absorption spectrum may be represented in terms of orthogonal function as follows:

$$A(\lambda) = P_0 P_0 + P_1 P_1(\lambda) + P_2 P_2(\lambda) + \ldots P_n P_n(\lambda)$$

Where 'A' denotes the absorbance at wavelength belonging to set of n + 1 equally spaced wavelength at which the orthogonal polynomials $P_0 (\lambda)$, $P_1 (\lambda)$, $P_2 (\lambda)$ . . . $P_n (\lambda)$ are each defined.

8. Absorbance ratio method:

This method is modification of the simultaneous equation procedure. It depends on the property that, for a substance that obeys Beer's law at all wavelengths, the ratio of absorbances at any two wavelengths is a constant value independent of concentration or path length.

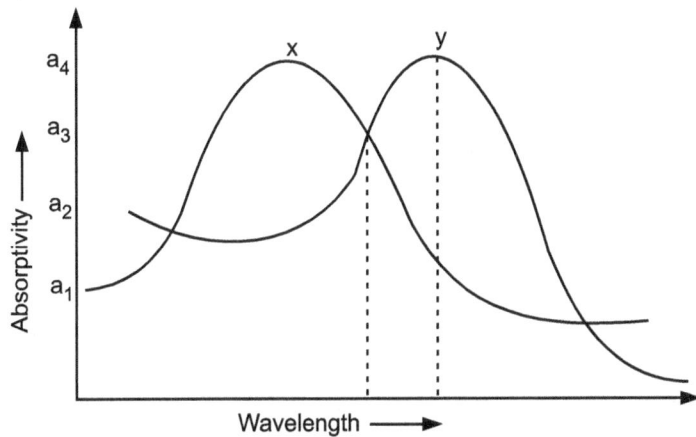

Fig. 18.4: Wavelengths for the assay of x and y in admixture by the method of absorbance ratios

At λ_2, $A_3 = a_3 bc_y$ ... (13)

At λ_2, $A_2 = a_2 bc_y$ ... (14)

Dividing equation (13) by (14),

$$\frac{A_3}{A_2} = \frac{a_3 bc_y}{a_2 bc_y} = \frac{a_3}{a_2} = Q$$

The ratio of two absorbance values is equal to ratio of two constants (that is absorptivities values) and therefore, is equal to a constant Q.

The ratio of absorbance at any two wavelengths (Q) is constant value independent of concentration or path length. This can be used to assess the purity of pharmaceuticals as well as identity of various official drugs, e.g. Cyanocobalamin, Promazine HCl, and Noscapine, etc.

Quantitative estimation of two components in admixture by absorbance ratio method was first reported by Pernarowski, et al. in 1961. In this method, absorbances are measured at two wavelengths, one being λ_{max} of one of the component (λ_2) and other being wavelength of equal absorptivities of the two components (λ_1) i.e. an Iso-absorptive point (Fig.18.4).

From Beer's law, the total absorbance at λ_2 is equal to the sum of absorbances due to x and y and therefore,

At λ_2, $A_3 = a_3 \, bc_y + a_1 \, bc_x$ ... (15)

Similarly at λ_1, $A_2 = a_2 \, bc_y + a_2 \, bc_x$ ... (16)

$$\frac{A_3}{A_2} = \frac{a_3 \, bc_y + a_1 \, bc_x}{a_2 \, bc_y + a_2 \, bc_x}$$

Dividing each term by $c_x + c_y$ and

$$F_x = \frac{c_x}{c_x + c_y}$$

And $$F_y = \frac{c_y}{c_x + c_y}$$

i.e. F_x and F_y are equal to fraction of the respective components present in the mixture.

$$\frac{A_3}{A_2} = \frac{a_3 \, F_y + a_1 \, F_x}{a_2 \, F_y + a_2 \, F_x}$$ ... (17)

However, $F_y = 1 - F_x$

$\therefore$ $$\frac{A_3}{A_2} = F_x \left(\frac{a_3}{a_2} - \frac{a_1}{a_2} \right) + \frac{a_1}{a_2}$$ ... (18)

Where, $\frac{A_3}{A_2}$ is equal to Q_m, the absorbance ratio of binary mixture. Similarly $\frac{a_3}{a_2}$ is

equal to Q_x, the absorbance ratio of pure x and $\frac{a_1}{a_2}$ is equal to Q_y, the absorbance

ratio of pure y.

$\therefore$ $Q_m = (Q_x - Q_y) \, F_x + Q_y$ ... (19)

Equation (19) is equation of straight line having a slope value of $Q_x - Q_y$ and intercept value of Q.

If the absolute concentrations of x and y are required, the equation is derived as

At λ_1, $A_2 = a_2 \, (c_x - c_y)$

$\therefore$ $$c_x + C_y = \frac{A_2}{a_2}$$

Rearranging equation (19),

$$F_x = \frac{Q_m - Q_y}{Q_x - Q_y}$$ ... (20)

Where, F_x represents the fraction of component x in the binary mixture and $\frac{A_2}{a_2}$

represents the total weight of x and y. Therefore, from equation (20),

$$c_x = \frac{Q_m - Q_y}{Q_y - Q_x} \cdot \frac{A_2}{a_2}$$ ... (21)

$$c_y = \frac{Q_m - Q_y}{Q_x - Q_y} \cdot \frac{A_2}{a_2}$$ ... (22)

Equations (21) and (22) give the exact concentration of x and y in terms of absorbance ratio (Q_m), the absorbance of mixture at its absorptive wavelength (A_2) and absorptivity of the compounds at isoabsorptive wavelength (a_2). Accurate dilutions of sample and standard solution of x and y are necessary for accurate measurement of A_2 and a_2 respectively.

The above method was used to assay of Trimethoprim and Sulphamethoxazole (Co-trimoxazole) tablets by Ghanem, et al.

9. Two wavelength/three wavelength method:

This method is based on the photometric modes of functioning. This method involves the estimation of two components, each time considering the second one to be the interfering one.

A prior criterion for this method is the existence of some absorption in the spectrum of the interfering component, where the component of interest has its λ_{max}. The spectra of components overlap partially.

SPECTROPHOTOMETRIC TITRATIONS

The absorbance of a solution is proportional to the concentration of absorbing species. For a monochromatic light passing through a solution, according to Beer's law, Absorbance $= \log \dfrac{I_o}{I_t} = \varepsilon$ cb, where, I_o is the intensity of incident light, I_t is the transmitted light, ε is absorptivity, c is the concentration of absorbing species and b is the path length of solution. The spectrophotometric titrations are carried out in a small vessel for which path length is constant, absorptivity remain same, and hence the absorbance is proportional to the concentration.

The titration in which the titrant, analyte or a reaction product absorbs, the plot of absorbance versus volume of titrant added will consist, if the reaction is complete, two straight lines intersecting at the end point. Thus, determination of changes in absorption to follow the changes in the concentration of light absorbing constituents in solution, during titration is the basis of spectrophotometric titrations.

For spectrophotometric titrations two points are of considerations:

1. The volume changes should be negligible. This is achieved by using Titrant 10-20 times concentrated and adding it by means of micro-pipette. The correction in volume is made by applying a factor $\dfrac{(V + v)}{V}$, where V is the initial volume of solution; v is the volume of titrant added.

2. Selection of wavelength for analytical studies is based on *(a)* Avoidance of interference by other light absorbing substance, and *(b)* Need for molar absorptivity which shows change during the titration to fall within convenient range.

For accuracy of the results by titration, appropriate concentration of solution of analyte ($10^{-4} - 10^{-5}$ molar) and titrant is employed. Stray light causes error and affects linearity of titration curve. Similarly, light leakage must be avoided.

Titration assembly:

A special type of titration cell which fits in cell compartment of spectrophotometer is employed. The titration cell is constructed of perspex material or of vycor with 20-100 ml capacity. See Fig. 18.4. The cell has a cover with two small openings for a tip of micro-burette/pipette and other for a micro-stirrer. For analysis in ultraviolet region the cell has two small quartz windows on opposite side for the light to pass through to photocell. For avoiding the stray light interference, the whole cell is covered with black paper (exception of the quartz window). Other components of the assembly, i.e. light source, a series of narrow-band filters, lenses, photocell remain the same as present in spectrophotometer.

The shape of titration curve will depend upon the optical properties of analyte, titrant and reaction product. Possible shapes of titration curves are shown in Fig. 18.5.

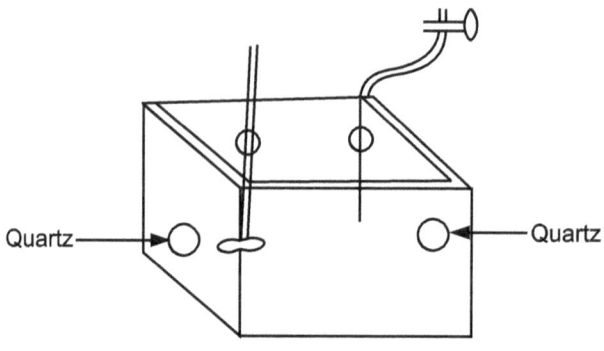

Fig. 18.5

Fig. 18.5 is characteristic of absorbable analyte converted into non-absorbable product by non-absorbing titrant. For example, titration of iron with salicylic acid at pH 2.4 with standard EDTA solution at 525 nm. The deep violet colour of iron salicylate complex gradually disappears as the end point is reached. The excess EDTA do not show colour.

The Fig 18.6 is typical of only titrant showing absorbance. In the titration of arsenic (III) with bromatebromide titrant the absorbance increases after the end point. The readings are taken at wavelength nm where bromate-bromide absorbs.

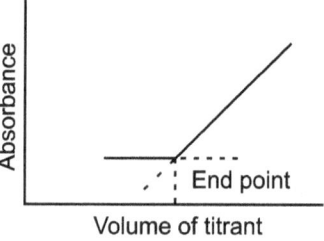

Fig. 18.6

The Fig. 18.7 is an example where analyte and Titrant are non-absorbing and the product alone absorbs. Titration of Cu (II) with standard EDTA at pH 2.4 at wavelength 745 nm shows this type of graph. The Cu-EDTA complex only shows absorbance up to the end point. Determination of nickel with EDTA at pH 4.0 and measurement at wavelength 1000 nm shows similar graph.

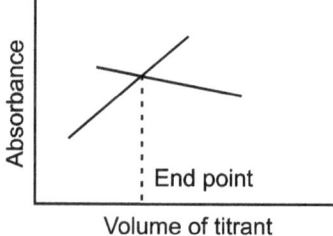

Fig. 18.7

The shape of graph obtained in Fig. 18.8 is of coloured analyte converted into colourless product by a coloured titrant, e.g. brominating of red dye.

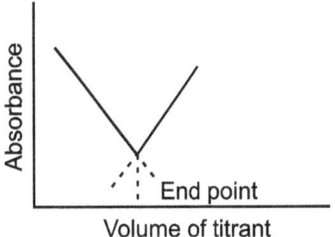

Fig. 18.8

Advantages of Spectrophotometry titration:

1. Presence of other absorbing species at the analytical wavelength does not cause interference, as only changes in absorbance are important.
2. It can be applied to those reactions which tend to be incomplete near end point.
3. Excellent results are obtained in dilute solutions (10^{-4} to 10^{-5} molar).
4. Precision of 0.5 per cent is attainable because more readings are pooled in construction of graph to obtain end point.

In spectrophotometric titrations care should be taken that

(a) Only single absorbable entity need to be present
(b) Absorbance of non-titratable components must not be intense
(c) There should be linearity of chemical reaction.

REFLECTION MEASUREMENTS

When a narrow band of incident light, after passing through filter, slit, enters the reflectance chamber and falls on opaque solid or particle or on coloured sample, a small part of light is absorbed while rest is reflected. The reflected light is directed by integrating sphere of chamber to the phototube, where it is measured and shown on the meter. The measurement of reflected light of a solid sample and its comparison to the standard reflectance material is the basis of reflection measurement.

Attachments for measuring reflection of various types are now-a-days available for many spectrophotometers. These are used in many industries like paints, textiles, plastic, glass, and tile, ceramic and in cosmetic, and pharmaceuticals. The variety of products with glossy or shining surface reflects light and the extent of reflection gives a measure of whiteness. The extent of brightness of sample is compared with the light reflected by a block of magnesium oxide or barium sulphate as a standard reflecting material.

Reflection occurs when a light ray encounters a reflecting surface. If the surface is mirror like then specular reflection or gloss results. Surfaces with intermediate property give diffuse reflection and even under unidirectional illumination shows constant luminance, regardless of the angle from which it is viewed. To have uniform reflection it is necessary.

(i) To have monochromatic light of incident radiation or of a narrow band wavelength.
(ii) Solid material should have uniform surface or particle size.
(iii) Sample material should be small and regular.

It is all essential to have integrating sphere in reflectance attachment to collect reflected radiations and direct them to photodetector.

There are various optical arrangements for reflectance measurements. A simple reflectance type is shown in Fig. 18.9.

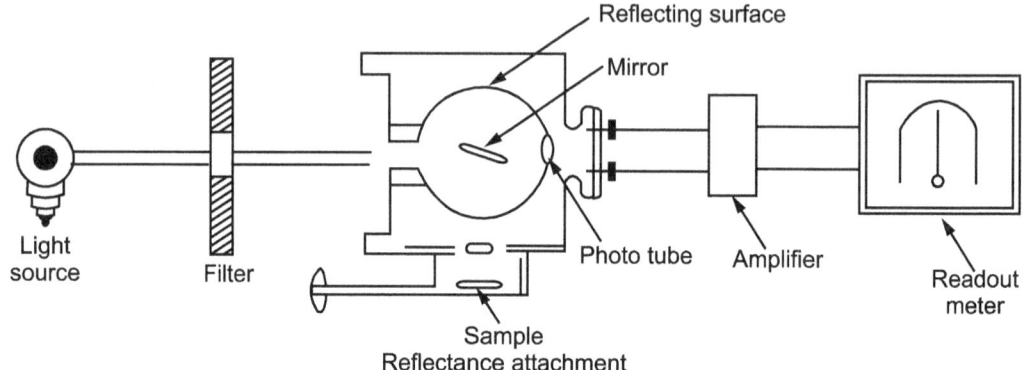

Fig. 18.9

In operation of the instrument a light from source is passed through filter and entrance slit into reflectance chamber. With the receiver dark (blank) a dark current or zero control is adjusted to balance the circuit with the reading scale of galvanometer to record zero. Now the reference solution or brightest sample is placed in the instrument. The light falling upon it is reflected by integrating sphere to the detector and reading adjusted at 100 per cent Transmittance (zero absorbance). A slit width control or amplifier control or both are adjusted to balance the circuit once again. Now, series of standards of different brightness are inserted in the instrument into light beam and scale readings are recorded. A calibration curve is plotted of reflectance transmittance versus different samples (Fig 18.10). Reflectance given by sample is measured to find its whiteness from the graph.

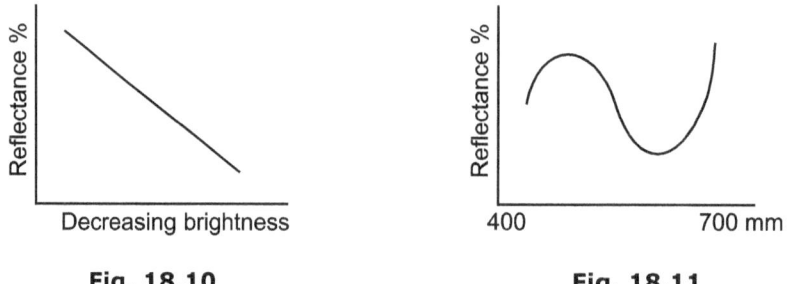

Fig. 18.10   **Fig. 18.11**

In reflectance measurement if colour filters are used to pass incident radiation, reflectance curve as shown in Fig. 18.11 is observed. This curve arises as a result of series of measurements made at different wavelength (using filters). The increase in brightness with blue filter indicates its importance in reflectance measurement.

CHAPTER ... 19

UV-VISIBLE SPECTROPHOTOMETRY

The essential components of a colorimeter or spectrophotometer include the following:

1. A suitable source of radiant energy.
2. A system consisting of lenses, mirror, slits etc. which collimate and focus the beam on sample.
3. A monochromator system.
4. A sample holder or container to hold sample.
5. A detector system of collecting transmitted radiation and
6. A suitable amplifier or readout galvanometer. A block diagram of any model of spectrophotometer will represent the features as shown in Fig. 19.1.

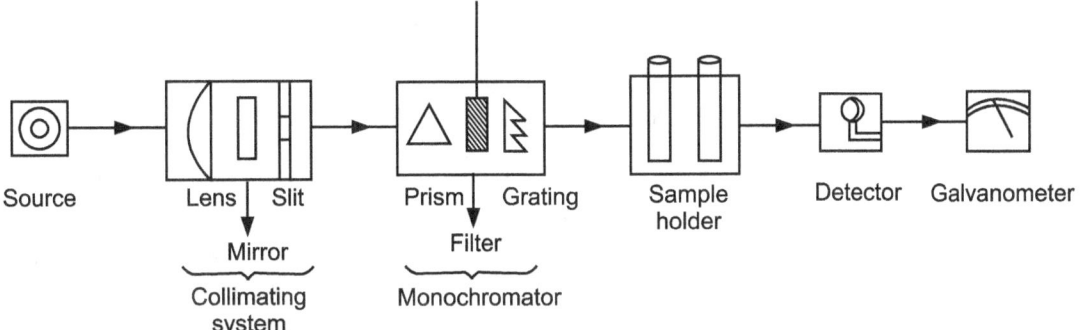

Fig. 19.1

The selection of components in fabrication of instrument involves many factors. A source of radiant energy is selected on the basis of nature of work, stability, wide range and operating temperature. The associated optical system including the selection of device for obtaining monochromatic radiation is based upon sensitivity sophistication and cost of instrument. The detector and galvanometer for readout are now-a-days developed with wide sensitivity and digital reading with recording device.

(A) SOURCES OF RADIANT ENERGY

Wide range of sources which provide radiant energy are available. A source of radiant energy should have the following features:

1. It should be stable and should show no fluctuations.
2. It should provide incident light of sufficient intensity.
3. It should emit a continuous spectrum of high and uniform intensity.
4. It should be appropriate for the purpose of work.
5. It should not show fatigue on continued use.

As almost all sources of radiant energy operate on electricity, a power supply of these sources should be of stable type resisting voltage fluctuations. A power supply stabilizer unit is helpful in this respect.

For ultraviolet radiation:

The hydrogen lamp and deuterium lamp are the most common sources of ultraviolet radiation. In hydrogen lamp, a pair of electrodes is enclosed in a glass tube provided with silica or quartz window (for ultraviolet radiation to transmit through) and is filled with hydrogen gas at low pressure. When current is passed through these electrodes maintained at high voltage, discharge of electron occurs which excites hydrogen gas to high energy states. The electrons return to their ground state and emit radiation in the region of 180–350 nm. When deuterium replaces hydrogen, similar excitation and relaxation of gas results in emission of radiation of ultraviolet region, but the intensity is of high order. Similar to hydrogen or deuterium lamp, a xenon discharge lamp is used as a source of continuous plus additional intense radiation. The lamp since operates at high voltage becomes very hot during operation and hence needs thermal insulation. Emission of visible region radiation also occurs along with ultraviolet radiation. A heat absorbing filter is often inserted between the lamp and sample holder to absorb the heat radiation.

For visible radiation:

A glass enclosed tungsten filament incandescent lamp is most widely used source for visible and near infrared region. The filament is heated by a stabilized power supply or by storage battery. It is available in various sizes and shapes suitable for fixing in the instrument and operates from 3-220 volts. The tungsten lamp emits continuous radiation in the region of 350-2500 nm. About 15 per cent of radiant energy falls within visible region. This source of radiation being inexpensive is very common in most spectrophotometers.

A mercury discharge lamp in glass tube for visible and in fused silica envelope for ultraviolet-visible region is also employed. The lamp on excitation emits continuous radiation in 350-800 nm. A very high intense radiation given out at 366, 405, 436, 546, 578 nm can be obtained using appropriate filter.

(B) COLLIMATING SYSTEM

The radiation emitted by the source is collimated (made parallel) by lenses, mirrors and slits. The lenses and mirrors are seldom used in combination to have radiation collimated. Materials used for lenses must be transparent to the radiation being used. The absorbance of such material should be less than 0.2 per cent at the wavelength of use. Ordinary silicate glass transmits between 350–3000 nm and is suitable material for visible and near infrared radiation. Quartz or fused silica is used as a material for lenses for work below 300 nm. The limit of quartz is about 210 nm, which is satisfactory for the purpose.

Similar to lenses, prisms are used for collimating purpose. Prisms made from glass are used in visible region while those made from quartz or fused silica is used in UV visible region.

Mirrors are used to reflect, focus or collimate light beams in spectrophotometer. Front surfaced mirrors are used to minimize light losses. For this, mirrors are aluminized on their front surfaces. Half-silvered mirrors are invariably employed in double beam instruments. To reduce the scattering by reflections, glass surfaces are coated with magnesium fluoride in a thin film. In infrared regions, mirrors are used because most materials are not sufficiently transparent and cause significant energy losses.

Slit width is an important device in resolving polychromatic radiation into its individual wavelength or into monochromatic radiation. To achieve this entrance slit and exit slit are used. The width of slit plays an important role in resolution of polychromatic radiation. Narrow slit widths isolate narrow bands; however, it limits the intensity which reaches the detector. Fig. 19.2 depicts the distribution of wavelengths leaving the slit. The nominal wavelength is that set on the instrument and is the wavelength of maximum intensity passed by the slit. The intensity of radiation at wavelengths on each side decreases. The effective band width is defined as the range of wavelength over which the transmission is at least one half of its maximum value. The spectral slit width is theoretically twice the nominal band width and is a measure of the total wavelength spread that is passed by the slit.

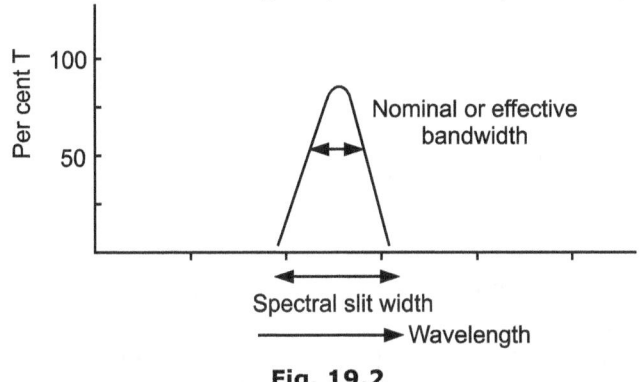

Fig. 19.2

If the intensity of the source of radiation and sensitivity of the detector are satisfactory, the spectral purity can be improved (i.e. the band pass decreased) by decreasing the slit width. However, at very narrow slit openings the reduction in the slit width does not cause a proportional reduction in the spectra isolated.

(C) MONOCHROMATOR

The purpose of employing devices is to resolve wide band of polychromatic radiation into a narrow band of monochromatic radiation. There are many types of dispersing devices employed for this purpose.

Filters:

Filters are used for isolation of narrow band of radiant energy of desired spectral region. Filters allow transmission of only limited wavelength regions while absorbing most of the radiation of other wavelengths. The filters are of many types like glass filters, gelatin filters and interference filters etc. Selection of filter is usually a compromise between peak transmittance and band pass width, in which the former should be as high as possible and latter as narrow as possible.

Glass filters:

These are the pieces of coloured glass which transmit limited wavelengths. Glass filters transmit radiation with an effective band width between 20–50 nm. The colours in the glass filters are produced by incorporating oxides of metals like V, Cr, Mn, Fe, Ni, Co, Cu etc. The colours produced are with Co-blue, Cu-blue-green, Mn-purple, Fe-green, and Cd-yellow. The glass filters are unaffected by heat and light. The only disadvantage of glass filters is that they allow broadband transmission through it. The filters are manufactured by many companies: Kodak, Alford, Corning and so forth and carry numbers on them. The transmission wavelength of the Corning brand filters is as given below in Table 19.1.

Table 19.1: Filters used indicating wavelength in nm

Number	Spectrum	Transmitted wavelength in nm
601	Violet	380 – 470
602	Blue	440 – 490
603	Blue-green	470 – 520
604	Green	500 – 540
605	Yellow-green	530 – 570
606	Yellow	560 – 610
607	Orange	570

Selection of filter is based upon constructing a calibration curve of optical density or transmission versus concentration using each filter. Best filter is the one that gives maximum absorption or minimum transmittance for the given concentration of absorbing solution. Alternatively, a concept of colour wheel is followed. In the colour wheel as shown in Fig. 19.3, main six colours found in rainbow are arranged. The main colour and its complementary colour are just opposite. Thus for example, solution to be analysed is blue in colour, a filter having a complementary colour orange is used in the analysis.

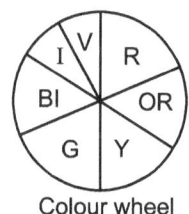

Colour wheel

Fig. 19.3

Gelatin filters:

Gelatin filters are manufactured from thin gelatin sheets, which are coloured with organic dyes during their manufacture. The thin sheets of gelatin filters transmit 10–30 nm band of wavelength which is slightly superior over glass filters. The gelatin sheet is sandwiched between a pair of clear glass to obtain the filter. Since, gelatin gets affected by heat radiation, heat absorbing filters are used along with gelatin filters.

The gelatin filters are now-a-days outdated because

(i)   They tend to deteriorate with time

(ii) They get affected by heat and moisture and

(iii) The colour of dye gets bleached.

Interference filters:

Narrow bandwidths are obtained with interference filters. Interference filters are constructed by using two parallel glass plates which are silvered internally and separated by thin film of transparent dielectric spacer of low refractive index. Magnesium fluoride (n_D = 1.38) is commonly used as dielectric material. Light incident upon the face of filter at 90° is reflected back and forth between the metal films. Constructive interference between different pairs of light rays occurs. The transmission of a spectral band by interference when light is incident sin 90° = 1 is given by equation:

$$m\lambda = 2d\,(n)\,(\sin\theta) \qquad\qquad \ldots (1)$$

Where, d is the thickness of dielectric spacer whose refractive index is n. Since sin θ = sin 90° = 1, the equation is

$$m\lambda = 2\,dn \qquad\qquad \ldots (2)$$

Where, m is integer. By adjusting the suitable thickness between the plates the suitable wavelength for transmission is obtained. These filters have a bandwidth of 10–15 nm with peak transmittance of 40–60 per cent.

Prisms:

Next to filters, prisms made from glass, quartz or fused silica is employed as dispersing devices in spectrophotometer. Since, glass has dispersing power about three times that of quartz, it is used in the visible portion of the spectrum. Quartz or fused silica prisms are the choice materials for ultraviolet spectrum. The mechanism in dispersing polychromatic beam of radiation into small bands of wavelengths by prism depends on the variation of the index of refraction with wavelength. Dispersion is defined as $\dfrac{d\theta}{dx}$ i.e. the change in angle of deviation with respect to the change in wavelength. When a beam of radiation passes from air into the dense material of prism, it will be refracted and bend towards perpendicular and further will show opposite effect when it emerges into air. Fig. 19.4 shows ∠ i as incident angle; ∠ r

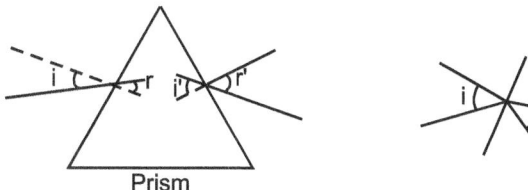

Prism

Fig. 19.4

as reflected from air to prism, ∠i' as incident in prism and ∠r' as refracted from prism to air. Since, the index of refraction depends on the wavelength, the shorter wavelengths are refracted more than longer wavelengths. It will thus be **seen** that when white light from electric bulb is passed through glass prism, dispersion of polychromatic light (white) in rainbow occurs as shown in Fig. 19.5 (a).

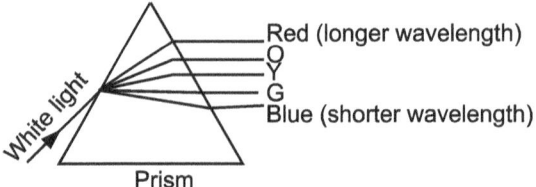

Fig. 19.5 (a)

Now, by rotation of the prism, different wavelengths of the spectrum can be made to pass through an exit slit on the sample. A prism monochromator mechanism is shown in Fig 19.5 (b).

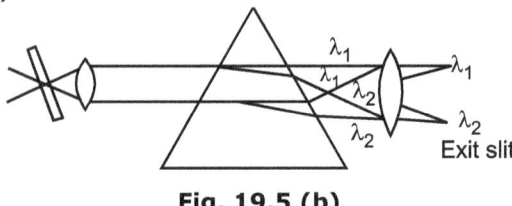

Fig. 19.5 (b)

The effective separation of wavelengths depends on the dispersive power of the prism material and the apical angle of the prism. For most satisfactory work it is 60°. There are two types of mounting of the prisms in an instrument. One type is called as Cornu-type [Fig. 19.6 (A)] which allows the light beam to pass through the prism in the cornu-type mounting prism has an apical angle of 60° and it is so adjusted that on rotation the emerging light is allowed to fall on exit slit. The other type is called as littrow type [Fig. 19.6 (B)]. In this the apical angle of prism is 30° and its one surface is aluminized which reflects light back to pass through prism and to emerge on the same side of light source, i.e. light does not pass through the prism on the other side.

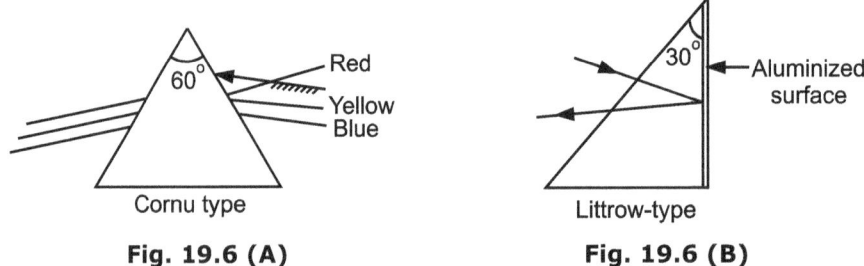

Fig. 19.6 (A)   **Fig. 19.6 (B)**

In both these types of mounting of prisms, the two surfaces of prisms must be carefully polished and cleaned.

Diffraction Gratings

More refined nature of dispersion of light is obtained by means of a diffraction grating. These consist of large number of parallel lines or grooves about 15000–30,000 per inch are ruled on highly polished surface of aluminium. The lines or grooves drawn on plate are the scattering centers for light beam impinging on it. Because of constructive interference the light rays are dispersed and employing exit slit the separation of desired wavelength is accomplished. The resolving power of grating depends on the number of lines ruled per inch on the surface and increases with increasing number of lines. Generally, resolving power of grating is better than that of prisms, and hence grating is used in all regions of the spectrum.

Generally, gratings are difficult to prepare and original gratings are expensive. The master grating is used as a mould to prepare replica gratings. On to the master grating of aluminium, an epoxy resin is applied. When the epoxy resin has hardened and set, the replica is taken out and its surface made reflective by aluminizing. The replica gratings are less expensive. Advantages of gratings are:

1. It provides a light of narrow wavelength.
2. With reflection gratings there is no loss of energy due to absorption by the material.
3. Gratings are sturdy and are less affected by water vapours.
4. Gratings are employed for calibration of wavelength dials of the instrument. A simple line diagram of grating monochromator is shown in Fig. 19.7.

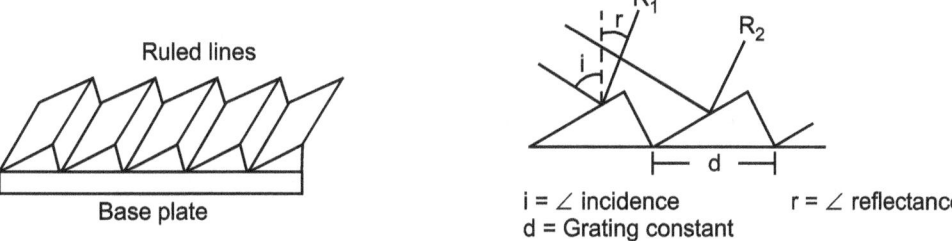

Fig. 19.7

(D) SAMPLE HOLDER

The cells or cuvettes or test tubes are used for handling the liquid samples. For the use in visible region, the cell may either be rectangular or cylindrical in nature. These are prepared from good quality glass like corning which shows uniform transmission. Test tube types are employed for routine use. The rectangular types are either 1 cm, 4 cm in internal diameter. For study in the ultraviolet region the cells or cuvettes are prepared from quartz or fused silica. Larger size cells are prepared from good quality glass with quartz window. The internal diameter of cells is either 0.5 cm, 1 cm or 2 cm. Microcells are employed for small samples. The cuvettes with lid are used for handling volatile type solvents and solutions.

The surfaces of absorption cells must be kept scrupulously clean. No fingerprints or blotches should be present on cells. Cleaning of the cells can be carried out by washing with distilled water or with dilute alcohol, acetone or detergent solutions.

(E) DETECTOR DEVICES

The light or the intensity of transmitted radiation by a sample is collected on a detector device. This is to measure the amount of transmitted radiation. Most modern detectors generate an electrical current after receiving the radiation. The generated current is often amplified and passed on to a meter, a galvanometer or a recorder. The detectors are of many types. They give different signals. Some important requirements of a good type of detector are:

1. It should give quantitative response.
2. It should have high sensitivity and low noise level.
3. It should have a short response time.
4. It should provide signal or response quantitative in wide spectrum of radiation received.
5. It should generate sufficient signal or electrical current which can be measured or easily amplified for detection by meter.

The following types of detectors are employed in instrumentation of absorption spectrophotometry.

(a) Barrier layer cell:

This detector is most simple and sturdy in nature. A barrier-layer cell is also photovoltaic cell. It is simple to construct and easy to operate. [Fig. 19.8] On a base plate (A) of iron or copper is deposited a thin layer of selenium (B).

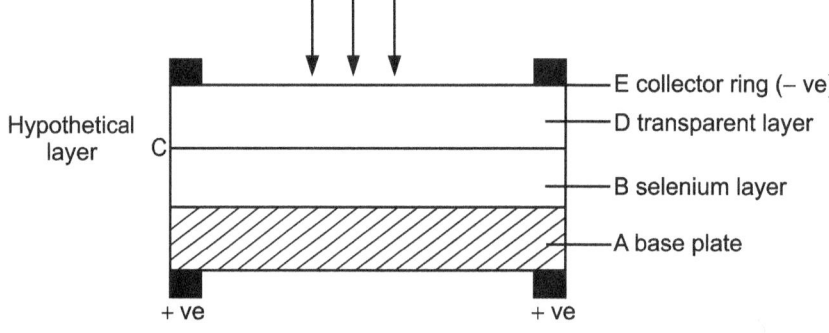

Fig. 19.8

Over this layer is a very thin transparent layer of silver (D) is spread. It has over it, a collecting ring (E) to collect electrons. Between the layer of selenium (B) and silver (D) is a hypothetical barrier layer (C). When light or a radiant energy falls on the surface of barrier layer cell, the light passes through transparent metal layer D and through hypothetical layer C to delay the progress of action on selenium layer B. On striking selenium layer it excites electrons from selenium which pass through hypothetical barrier layer and are collected on collector ring E. As a result of giving out of electrons from selenium layer spread on base plate, the latter possess a positive charge. Thus, the barrier layer cell generates its own electromotive force. If the cell is connected to a galvanometer, a flow of current is observed. This cell is simple, sturdy and does not require any external power supply. At low level of illumination it produces photo-current proportional to the radiant power received on it. The current produced by barrier-layer cell is small (in µA) and hence amplification is carried out to read on galvanometer. Barrier layer cell has disadvantages of (a) slow response (b) fatigue effect and (c) poor modulation and adaptability.

Photo-tubes:

Photo-tube detector is also known as photo-emissive tube. This consists of spherical shaped vacuum bulb containing photo-emissive cathode and an anode. The inner surface of semi-cylindrical cathode mounted inside the bulb is coated with photo-sensitive material like cesium oxide. A metal wire nearby is an anode. A high voltage is impressed (90–100 V) between them. When radiant energy falls on the surface of photo-sensitive cathode, electrons are emitted which are attracted to the anode causing current to flow. This current is amplified and measured. The response of phototube is dependant on the material used for coating and wavelength of light striking it. Different photo-tubes are used for different regions of spectrum of light. A construction of phototube is shown in Fig. 19.9. Current produced by photo-tube is generally small, and hence requires amplification. A small current known as dark current is usually observed when phototubes are used as detectors in the instrument. This is attributed to the scattered electron emission from photosensitive cathode due to stray radiation striking its surface. Naturally, the magnitude of it increases as the surface area of cathode is more. A compensating device to eliminate this 'Dark current' is usually employed in many instruments.

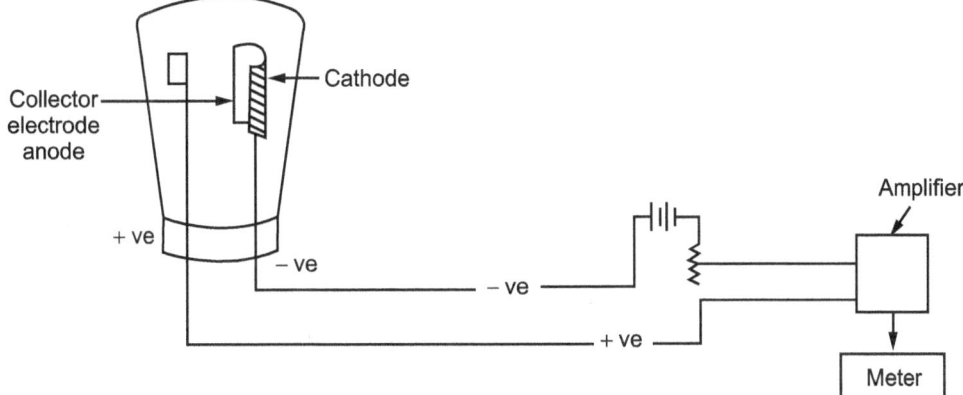

Fig. 19.9

Photo-multiplier Tubes:

This is more refined and sensitive device developed over the concept of photo-tube. In the mechanism of photo-tube it is seen that on striking the photo-sensitive material of cathode, electrons are released. If the released electrons are under the accelerated electric potential brought to another electron-active surface, it will release more electrons. These in turn, by acting on another electron-active surface will produce more and more electrons. Thus, a large current is generated by photo-multiplication. This mechanism is utilized in photomultiplier tubes. A schematic diagram is shown in Fig. 19.10. In a vacuum tube, a primary photo-cathode is fixed which receives radiation from the sample. Some eight to ten

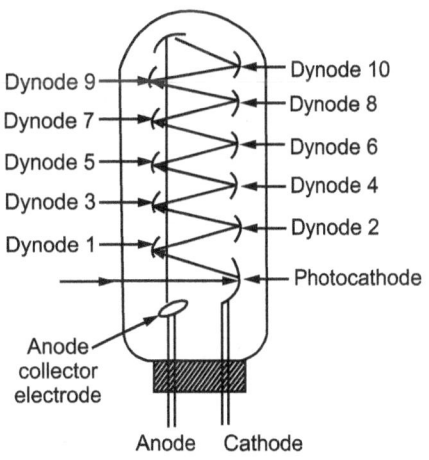

Fig. 19.10

dynodes are fixed each with increasing potential of about 90 V. Near the last dynode is fixed an anode or electron collector electrode. A high voltage is maintained between the cathode and anode.

The light received by cathode releases electrons which through series of dynode produce more electrons. These released electrons by last dynode are collected by anode and photo-current is produced. Photo-multiplier is extremely sensitive to light and is best suited where weaker or low radiation is received.

COMMERCIAL INSTRUMENTS

The instruments used in absorption photometry can be classified into three categories:

1. Visual comparators
2. Simple filter photometer and
3. Spectrophotometers.

Further, the instruments have been constructed as single beam and double beam type, direct reading or balanced circuit (null point) type with power stabilization circuit etc. In the selection of an instrument one should consider the cost, maintenance, ease of operation and adaptation to special situations under various conditions.

(a) Visual comparators:

These are colour comparators useful in the visible region only. In the methodology a series of standard coloured solutions are prepared and one placed into one comparator tube to a constant height. The sample or test solution of same colour is placed into another comparator tube and dilution made till both colours are matched. For this method, colour matching is done by eye, keeping the tubes side by side and viewing of light from a common source (or daylight).

The comparator tubes are made from good quality pyrex or corning glass of same thickness and are usually spherical in shape (like test tube). They are of same size and diameter. Nessler's tubes (Fig. 19.11 A) of 50 or 100 ml capacity with gravitation marking are commonly used as comparator tubes. The other types of tubes are Hehner cylinder [Fig. 19.11 (B)] which have stopcock on the side of the base.

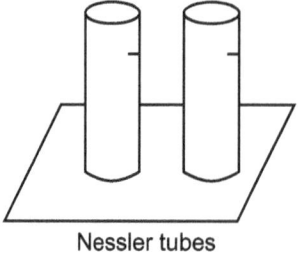

Nessler tubes

Fig. 19.11 (A)

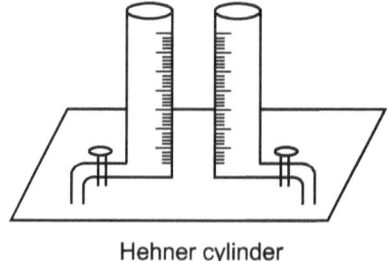

Hehner cylinder

Fig. 19.11 (B)

When the colour between the unknown (test) and the standard is matched, the concentration of unknown is found by noting the depth of two solutions (height) and from concentration of standard by a formula

$$C_u \, h_u \;=\; C_s \, h_s$$

$$C_u \;=\; C_s \times \frac{h_s}{h_u}$$

Where, C_u and C_s denotes the concentration of unknown and standard solutions and h_u and h_s refers to respective height of solutions. For more details of various methods in visual comparator refer colorimetric analysis.

(b) Filter photometer:

A line diagram of single beam, direct reading filter photometer is given in Fig. 19.12.

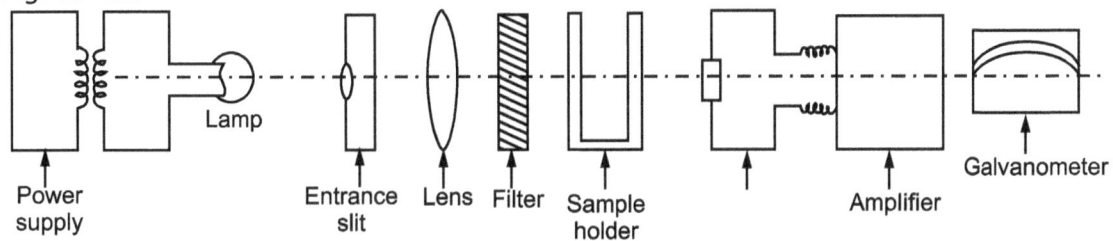

Fig. 19.12

The essential components of filter photometer are

(a) light source
(b) lens/entrance slit
(c) filter
(d) sample holder
(e) detector and
(f) galvanometer or readout meter.

Light source can be ordinary electric bulb or a lamp of 6 or 12 V storage battery by regulated voltage transformer to minimize voltage fluctuations.

Light from the source is carried through lens and/or through aperture to pass through a suitable filter. The type of filter to be used is governed by the colour of the solution. The sample solution to be analysed is placed in a test tube or cuvettes known as sample holder. After passing through the solution, the light strikes the surface of detector (barrier-layer cell or phototube) and produces electrical current. The output of current is measured by the deflection of needle of light-spot galvanometer or microammeter. This meter is calibrated in terms of transmittance as well as optical density. The readings of solution of both standard and unknown are recorded in optical density units after adjusting instrument to a reagent blank.

(c) Spectrophotometer:

Several models of various instrument manufacturers are available in market. A line diagram of single beam spectrophotometers is given in Fig 19.13 (a) and

19.13 (b) while a schematic diagram for double beam instrument is shown in Fig. 19.14.

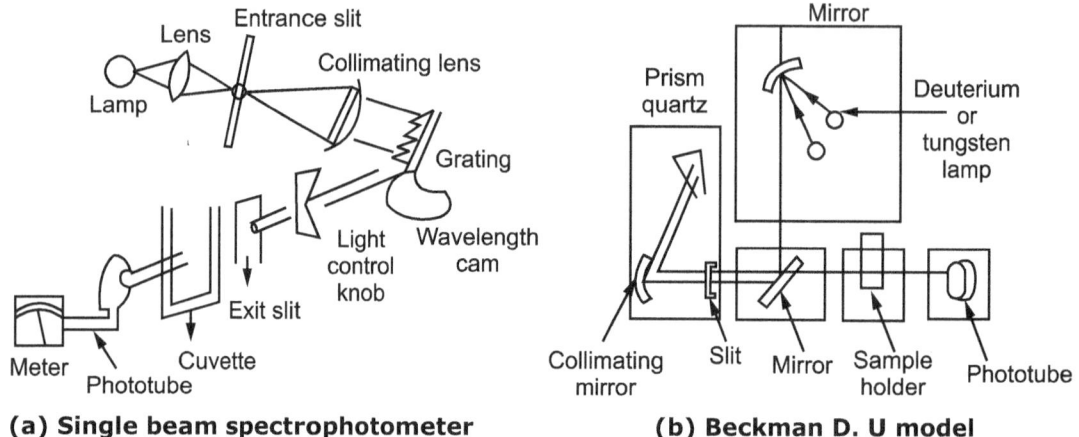

(a) Single beam spectrophotometer

(Bausch and Lamb)

(b) Beckman D. U model

Fig. 19.13

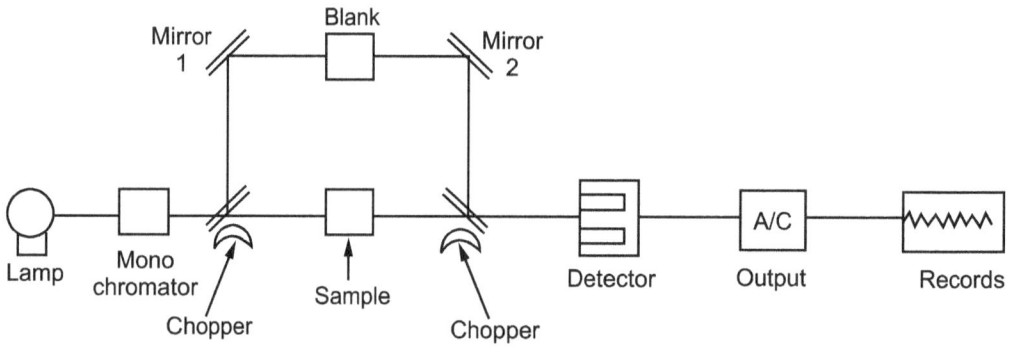

Fig. 19.14

The essential features of a spectrophotometer are:

- Source radiation
- Collimating system
- Monochromator (mainly prisms or gratings)
- Sample holder
- Detector
- Read out meter.

(a) Source of radiation:

For the visible region, tungsten lamp is commonly employed in an instrument. It emits continuous, incandescent radiations. For UV region, a hydrogen (or deuterium) discharge lamp is used. Some instruments also provide mercury vapour lamps to give intense radiation of specific wavelength both in UV-visible region. Commonly, a voltage establisher is incorporated in instrument to give radiations without fluctuations or fatigue.

(b) Collimating system:

It consists of lens, mirrors and/or aperture of entrance slit in spectrophotometer. This allows a narrow beam of collimating light and directed either on quartz or silica prisms or a grating to render monochromatic radiations.

(c) Monochromator:

Some instruments make use of prism in a form of 30°–60°–90° triangle with apical angle of 30°. This prism has its back aluminized which reflects the refracted ray through Littrow mounted prism back to the same collimating mirror at a different height (so to give different wavelength). Alternately, a grating device having aluminized back surface is employed to obtain monochromatic radiation.

(d) Sample holder:

It is a slot in instrument which holds test-tubes, cuvettes of different size and capacity. The sample tubes are made from good quality glass having uniform transmittance. The tubes or cells are of uniform size, shape and internal diameter. For study in UV region the cells or cuvettes are made from quartz or fused silica. For handling volatile solvents or solutions, the cells have cover or lid.

(e) Detector:

Detector unit is usually a barrier layer cell or a photo-tube. In some instruments two interchangeable photo-tubes are employed to be useful in red region (625–1000 mμ) and blue region (210–625 mμ) of wavelength. In double beam instruments two photo-tubes or photomultiplier tubes are employed.

(f) Galvanometer or meter:

It is to record the current generated and amplified by detector. These have coarse and fine adjustment knobs through which adjustment of dark photo-current between zero and 100 per cent transmittance with respect to blank or solvent is adjustable. The meter is generally calibrated in transmittance and absorbance (optical density) units. In some instruments (double beam type) a null point technique is used in readout meter.

The assay of following drugs can be performed by UV-visible spectrophotometry:

		Solvent used	Wavelength in nm
1.	Amodiaquine hydrochloride	HCl 0.1 N	343
2.	Amoxicillin trihydrate capsules	Water	325
3.	Ampicillin capsules	Water	325
4.	Carbimazole	Water	291
5.	Chloramphenicol	Water	278
6.	Digitoxin tablets	Water	550
7.	Dithranol	Glacial acetic acid	450

	Solvent used	Wavelength in nm
8. Folic acid	0.1 M NaOH	550
9. Furazolidine	DMF	367
10. Griseofulvin	Ethanol	291
11. Hydrochlorothiazide tablets	0.1 M NaOH	273
12. Isoxsuprine hydrochloride	0.1 M HCl	274
13. Labetalol hydrochloride tablets	0.05 M H_2SO_4	302
14. Methandienone	Ethanol	287
15. Nifedipine capsules	Methanol	350
16. Phenformin hydrochloride	Water	520
17. Psoralen	Methanol	247
18. Quinidochlor tablets	Methoxyethanol	650
19. Rifampicin	Methanol	475
20. Reserpine	Ethanol	388
21. Spironolactone	Methanol	238
22. Stilbesterol	Ethanol	418
23. Triamcinolone acetamide	Ethanol	240
24. Imidazole tablets	Methanol	310
25. Tubocuranine chloride	Water	280
26. Tomfool maleate tablets	0.05 M H_2SO_4 + Carbonate Buffer	295
27. Verapamil hydrochloride tablets	0.1 M hydrochloric acid	278

CHAPTER ... 20

COLORIMETRIC ANALYSIS

INTRODUCTION

Colorimetry is concerned about the measurement of light in the visible region. We see objects because they transmit or reflect a certain portion of the light in this region. When an ordinary light of visible spectrum (380–760 nm) is passed through an object or solution, it absorbs certain wavelength, leaving the unabsorbed wavelengths to be transmitted. This transmitted light (wavelength) will be seen as colour. This colour is complementary to the absorbed colour. We see a solution blue because from visible spectrum the wavelength of yellow colour (complementary) is absorbed by the solution. Similarly, opaque objects will absorb certain wavelengths, leaving a residual colour to be reflected and seen. Table 20.1 summarizes the wavelength, absorbed colour and transmitted colour.

Table 20.1: Colours of Different wavelength

Wavelength (nm)	Absorbed colour	Transmitted colour
380–450	Violet	Yellow-green
450–495	Blue	Yellow
495–570	Green	Violet
570–590	Yellow	Blue
590–620	Orange	Green-blue
620–760	Red	Blue-green

The basic principle of colorimetric analysis is the measurement of colour of a solution and its correlation to the determination of its concentration. The measurement is made by comparing or reading the colour produced for the substance with the same colour produced by a known amount of standard material under well-defined conditions. When the colours are compared by eye, it is called visual Colorimetry, The visual colorimetry is similar to the limit tests of impurities of pharmacopoeia substances.

When human eye is replaced by a photocell (or photoelectric cell) in an instrument then the instrument is called as colorimeter or photocolorimeter. The colorimeters are mainly of two types:

1. Filter colorimeter and
2. Spectrocolorimeter

In colorimeter, a suitable source of light of visible region, arrangement of obtaining narrow band of wavelength (monochromatic light) and suitable detector is employed. When a narrow band of monochromatic light is obtained by employing filter then the instrument is called filter colorimeter. Alternatively, when a monochromatic light is obtained by using grating/prism then the instrument is referred as spectro-colorimeter or spectrophotometer.

For quantitative analysis by visual colorimetry, one must be able to distinguish different intensities of light, its clarity and hues (shades). Human eye can detect best hue and brightness in 500–580 nm range. Because of fatigue effect and failure to compare intensely coloured solutions, visual Colorimetry is largely replaced by instrumental method, i.e. colorimeter.

SOME GENERAL REQUIREMENTS AND CONDITIONS

For satisfactory analytical work of quantitative nature, solution of substance must have certain general requirement and conditions. These are:

1. **Intensity and sensitivity of reaction:**

   Solutions should be intensely coloured and the intensity and sensitivity should be complementary to each other.

2. **Stability of the colour:**

3. The colour produced should be sufficiently stable to be readable. Suitable conditions for stabilization of colour like the use of buffer solutions, adjustment of pH, temperature, etc. must be adopted.

4. **Reaction time:**

   Reaction for the formation of colour should be quick and quantitative. Excessive use of heat, acid-alkali or corrosive treatment should be avoided.

5. **Specificity and selectivity of colour reaction:**

   The chemical reaction adopted should be specific for the particular substance. The other compounds or related materials should not give colour which will interfere in colour measurement. Use of buffer solutions, control of pH, altering oxidation state, removal of interfering material by suitable devices may be adopted.

6. **Reproducibility:**

   The colorimetric method should give reproducible results under the specified conditions.

7. **Beer's law obeyance:**

   The colour should obey Beer's law in the concentration range under study.

To obtain satisfactory results by colorimeters, it is essential to control and adopt the operational procedure so that the colour produced is specific for the substance under examination. Removal of interfering substances by extraction with suitable solvent, precipitation, suppression by formation of complex ions, volatilization, electrolysis etc. are followed in order to obtain best results.

Drugs, chemicals and substances can be analysed by colorimetric method for the following categories:

1. If it has its own colour, e.g. dyes like amaranth, crystal violet, methylene blue, or the coloured chemicals and drugs. For the analysis of such substances, solution is prepared in a suitable solvent and absorbance measured by using colorimeter at a wavelength of maximum absorption or by comparing in Nessler's cylinder with standard solution visually.

2. Substances which do not have inherent colour are allowed to react with suitable reagent to produce a colour, e.g.

   (a) Iron salt reacts with ferricyanide to produce Prussian blue coloured complex.

   (b) Salicylates react with ferric ion to give violet coloured complex.

   (c) Lead ions react with dithizone reagent to form pink-red complex.

3. When suitable reagent is not available for a substance to produce a coloured complex, the substance is converted into a derivative which in turn is caused to react with an appropriate reagent to form coloured complex, e.g.

   (a) Sulphonamides or primary aromatic amine class of compounds is diazotized in acidic medium and the diazotized moiety is caused to react with β-naphthol or N-Naphthylethylenediamine to give colour.

   (b) Saccharin is fused with alkali and converted into salicylic acid, which on reaction with ferric ion produces violet colour.

   (c) Acetophenatidin on hydrolysis gives phenatidine, which on chromic acid oxidation forms, coloured solution.

METHODS OF COLOUR MEASUREMENT

Measurement of colour of a solution can be done by many methods of visual colorimetry or by using instrument like colorimeter or spectrophotometer. In the visual colorimetry, the basic principle is to compare colour of unknown or test solution standard colour solution under identical and well-defined conditions. In the method, natural or artificial light (from electric bulb) is used. The coloured solutions of test and standard are placed in identical Nessler's cylinders of clear corning glass or in cups of identical size and shape and comparison made. The following comparometric methods can be adopted.

1. Standard series method:

The test solution is taken in Nessler's cylinder, colour developed and volume adjusted to a definite mark (25–50 ml). The colour is compared with a series of standard solutions of varying concentration similarly prepared. The concentration of test is found from the standard solution whose colour it matches exactly. For matching the colours, cylinders are viewed vertically. The accuracy of method is between ±3 and ±5 percent. The disadvantage of this method is that series of standard solutions of varying concentrations are to be prepared for comparison.

2. Duplication method:

The test solution after development of colour is taken in a Nessler's cylinder and volume adjusted to the mark (50 ml). Into another Nessler cylinder solvent, reagent, etc. is taken and to it standard solution of compound is added gradually until the colour matches that of unknown sample. The concentration of test is found from that of standard with which it matches colour. This method is also not very accurate.

3. Balancing method:

This method utilizes two cups and two plungers as in Dubuque colorimeter in which the height of solution can be adjusted by rotating plunger. The height of colour is compared, and when it balances, the concentration of test is found out from the height and concentration of standard solutions by the formula,

$$C_1\, l_1 = C_2\, l_2$$

Where C_1 is the concentration of test, l_1 is the height of unknown and C_2 and l_2 are the concentration and height of standard solution. The Dubuque colorimeter (Fig 20.1) is like a microscope. Light from source of illumination (bulb) is split into two beams of equal illumination. One passes through left side cup/plunger and other through right side cup/plunger. Solution of test is placed in either of cup and standard solution into another cup. By rotating the plunger, it is fixed to a known height (in mm) for standard. Now, by slowly rotating the other plunger (for test solution) by raising or lowering, the balancing of colour is obtained by viewing through eye piece. The height of solution is recorded and concentration found out from the formula

$$C = C_2 \frac{l_2}{l_1}$$

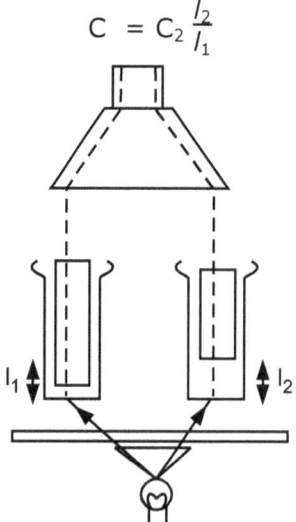

Fig. 20.1

By adjusting different heights for standard solutions corresponding heights for test solutions are determined for finding concentration of test solution. About 08–10 readings are recorded to determine the average. If solutions (both test and standard) are intensely coloured, suitable dilutions are made so that Beer's law holds true. After the work, the cups, plunger is cleaned with distilled water and the colorimeter kept scrupulously clean.

4. Photoelectric colorimeter method:

The method utilizing colorimeter is more reliable and accurate than the visual comparison methods. The visual comparison methods are subject to human errors because of obtaining exact comparison and of fatigue effect. In colorimeter human eye is replaced by photocell or photoelectric cell, which measures the amount of light falling on it. Photocells measure the light absorbed (in true sense transmitted by the solution) and not the colour. The instrument is therefore also called 'absorptiometer' or 'photoelectric comparator'.

The essential components of many models of colorimeter comprise:

(a) A light source,

(b) Suitable mechanisms for obtaining monochromatic light (filters, prisms, grating, lens, slits etc.),

(c) Glass cell for holding solution,

(d) Photocell,

(e) A galvanometer for measuring the radiation of optical density and/or transmission.

Two methods are frequently followed using colorimeter. In one method *standard curve* or *calibration curve* is plotted for the series of solutions of known concentration versus the reading of absorbance. The concentration of the test solution is then determined by recording the optical density and referring to the calibration curve. The various quantities of standard are treated in the same way as the sample (test) solution for the development of colour. The measurement of absorption is done at suitable wavelength or by using appropriate filter. The plot of absorbance $\left(\log \frac{I_0}{I_t}\right)$ against concentration should be straight line indicating obeyance of Beer's law. The graph can be used as standard for routine determination of samples. However, the standard graph should be checked at intervals. While plotting, solvent blank is used for 100 per cent transmission. Frequent checking of instrument is necessary to observe any 'fatigue effect' with respect to source of light, photocell, stray radiation effect etc.

The other method adopted is the 'reference standard method'. In this method, a definite quantity of test material is treated with appropriate reagent, and colour is produced. Simultaneously, a known concentration of 'reference standard' material is identically treated with reagent and readings of optical density or absorbance of both test sample and reference standard are taken at a specified wavelength or by employing filter.

According to Lambert-Beer's law

$$A = \log \frac{I_0}{I_t} = \varepsilon \, cb$$

Where, A = absorbance, since 'ε' remains constant for the same species of solution, b = path length of solution which usually is 01 cm, and hence also remains constant; then $A \propto C$. Thus by using the mathematical relationship $C_u = \frac{A_u}{A_s} \times C_s$, where C refers to concentration, A to absorbance, u for test or unknown solution and s for standard, the concentration of test solution is found out.

5. Spectrophotometer method:

Spectrophotometer is more sophisticated form of photoelectric colorimeter. It permits the use of continuously variable and monochromatic light of narrowband of wavelength. Thus accuracy of result is better than filter colorimeter. Furthermore, spectrophotometer can be used in ultraviolet visible region.

It is not necessary to prepare a calibration curve (standard curve) or adopt the reference standard method using spectrophotometer. According to Lambert-Beer's law,

$$A = \log I_0/I_t = \varepsilon \, cb$$

Where 'ε' is molar extinction coefficient if concentration is expressed in moles per liter or if molecular weight is not known then as specific extinction coefficient (absorbance for unit path length). The value of ε is characteristic of the substance. It can be found out by $\varepsilon = A/Cb$ (C is concentration of 1 mole/liter and b = 1 cm). The method of $E_{1\,cm}^{1\%}$ at specified wavelength is commonly adopted for determining the concentration of test sample. The values of $E_{1\,cm}^{1\%}$ for number of drugs have been recorded in literature.

For example:

1. Paracetamol 1 per cent solution in 1 cm cell at 257 nm has extinction value of 715.

2. Riboflavin 1 per cent solution in 1 cm cell at 444 nm has extinction value of 323.

3. Rifampicin 1 per cent solution in 1 cm at 476 nm has extinction value of 188.

4. Verapamil has extinction 118 for 1 per cent solution in 1 cm at 378 nm.

The spectrophotometry method is thus a most suitable method for determination of solutions in ultraviolet visible region.

CHAPTER ... 21

NEPHELOMETRY AND TURBIDIMETRY

The techniques of nephelometry and turbidimetry are concerned about the analysis of collidal or fine suspension system. When a light of incident radiation is allowed to fall on a fine dispersed suspension, a part of light is absorbed, a part is reflected and refracted and remainder is transmitted out. The optical property of a fine, stable suspension will depend upon the concentration of dispersed phase. The measurement of the intensity of transmitted light of a suspension in relation to the concentration of dispersed phase is the basis of Turbidimetric analysis.

If the suspension or colloidal sample is viewed at right angles to the direction of incident light, the system appears cloudy because of scattering of light from the particles of suspension. This scatter is due to Tyndall effect. Because of the scattering the colloidal system appears milky, hazy or cloudy. The measurement of the intensity of scattered light of suspension in relation to the concentration of dispersed phase forms the basis of Nephelometry analysis.

The Nephelometry and Turbidimetric are meant for determination of concentration of dispersed phase of a suspension. They differ in that in nephelometry, the amount of light scattered by the particles is measured by viewing at right angles to the incident light while in turbidimetric the amount of light transmitted by the suspension is measured.

Turbidimetry is similar to colorimetry since both methods measure the amount of transmitted light.

For the quantitative determination by Nephelometry or Turbidimetry the following conditions are necessary:

1. The suspension should be dilute.

2. The suspension should be stable and not allow the particles to settle down.

3. The particles of suspension should be small and fine.

4. The particles should have a uniform shape and size to allow uniform scattering of light.

5. For the stability of suspension addition of other salt and protective colloid should be used.

6. Viscosity and temperature should be such as to maintain stable suspension.

Both the Turbidimetry and Nephelometry are very sensitive in dilute solutions. For the determination of concentration of dispersed particles a calibration graph is plotted. After a particular concentration the optical property is not very linear.

THEORETICAL PRINCIPLE

Theoretical principle of Nephelometry and Turbidimetric analysis is similar to colorimetry. The intensity of light scattered or transmitted by a suspension is a function of the concentration of scattering particles of uniform shape and size. In dilute suspensions the amount of scatter depends upon the number of particles intersecting the beam of light. Provided no multiple scatter occur, the total scatter is simply the sum of the individual scatters by the particles. Thus, the Beer's law as applied in colorimetry can be applied.

$$\frac{I_t}{I_o} = 10^{-RBC}$$

Where 'r' is the turbidimetric coefficient, b is path length; c is the concentration in g/litre. The correlation of concentration of dispersed particle to that of transmission or scattered light will hold provided that

1.   there is no settling of particles
2.   no coagulation of dispersed particles
3.   no nucleation and crystal growth and
4.   absence of interfering ions, etc.

The Nephelometry or Turbidimetric analysis is carried out for a system which gives turbidity by itself. The sample material in a fine particle form is dispersed in a suitable solvent to get a stable suspension. Alternatively, turbidity is produced by addition of suitable reagent into a solution. The turbidity so produced is compared with standard turbidity produced in similar manner under similar conditions.

INSTRUMENTATION

Usual type of photoelectric colorimeter can be used for turbidimetric analysis. The sample holder allows large size cuvettes or cells to accommodate in instruments. Ordinary electric bulb or a light source of 6 volts or 6 watt bulb can be used in the instrument. A phototube or Barrier layer cell can be employed as a detector. A line diagram of simple type of turbidimeter is shown in the Fig. 21.1.

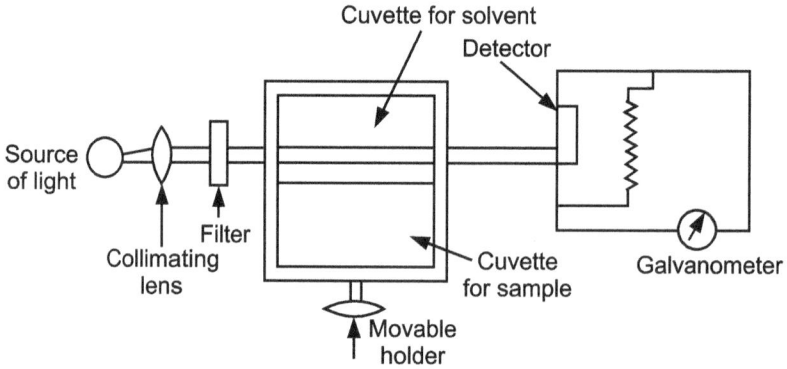

Fig. 21.1

Nephelometer (Fig. 21.2) is designed on the Tyndall effect. In an instrument, a suitable source of light 6-8 volts tungsten lamp is focused by lens and/or prism on the side of test tube or cuvettes containing a sample solution under test. The scattered light at 90° to the path of incident light is collected on a photocell. The current so produced is amplified and supplied to an indicator meter graduated from 0–100 divisions. The meter is also calibrated with corresponding standard solutions in Nephelometry-Turbidimetric Units (NTU) of sulphate or phosphate standards. The calibration is done from 0–40 or 50 divisions on meter with respect to NTU. The sensitivity of meter is adjusted to fine or coarse in various ranges from 04–100 NTU. The line diagram of simple Nephelometry is shown in Fig. 21.2.

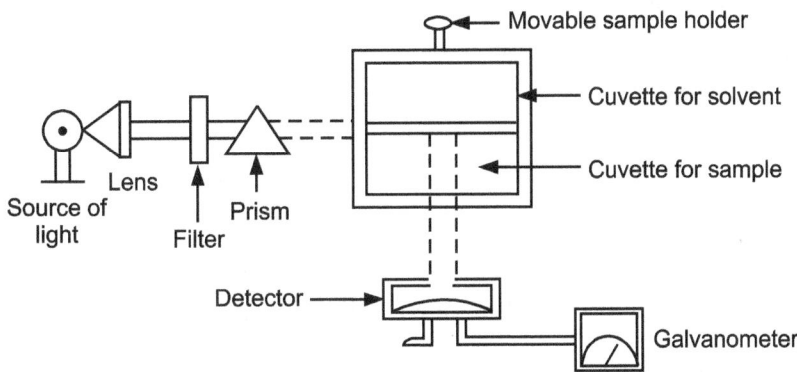

Fig. 21.2

Working of the Instrument:

Light source is started on and an appropriate filter (in case of filter type instrument) is inserted in the instrument. With pure solvent or distilled water zero setting is adjusted to '0' of galvanometer. With the standard turbidity or highest expected turbid solution, instrument is set to 100 divisions. Various solutions/ suspensions of intermediate turbidity are put in the sample tubes and readings recorded. A calibration graph is drawn for the various concentrations of turbid solutions. Now a sample of unknown or test is inserted in the instrument and turbidity reading is recorded. The concentration of unknown is found from the graph.

TURBIDIMETRIC TITRATIONS

Turbidimetric titrations can be carried out in a manner similar to photometric titrations. A sample solution which forms a finely colloidal type of precipitate on addition of titrant (reagent) can be analysed. In the titration, sample material is taken in cell (50–100 ml capacity having stirring mechanism) and regular volume of titrant is added by using microburette. A graph of absorbance is plotted against the volume of titrant added. [Fig. 21.3].

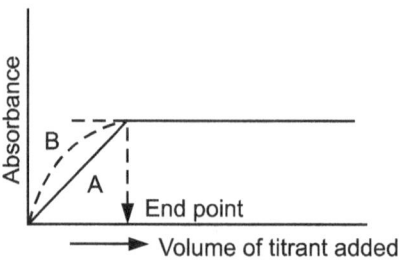

Fig. 21.3

In an ideal situation, absorbance increases linearly as the precipitate forms on addition of reagent to a point and then remains same. The intersection of the two straight lines gives an equivalence point.

This holds true only if the number of particles increase linearly to the end point and size and shape of particles remain same throughout. In practice, however, it is found that the added reagent may simultaneously form some new particles or get added to those previously formed giving distortion of lines (Fig. 21.3 curve B).

Some important determinations by this method include carbonates as $BaCO_3$, chloride as AgCl, calcium as calcium oxalate, zinc as ferricyanide, etc.

APPLICATIONS OF NEPHELOMETER AND TURBIDIMETER

There are numerous applications of the use of Nephelometer or turbidimeter in various industries including pharmaceutical industry. Some examples are:

1. For determination of ions like sulphate, chloride, carbonate, magnesium, calcium etc.

2. In determination of impurities in pharmacopoeial substances.

3. In determination of growth of bacteria in culture media and nutrient media.

4. In determination of growth of micro-organism in vitamin and antibiotic assays.

5. In determination of particles or solids in aerosols, injections and liquid preparations.

6. It is employed in soap and detergent industry in determination of cloud point.

7. It is used in determination of sediment and particles in water treatment tank and sewage tank.

8. The above instruments are used for various purposes in other industries like paper, pulp making, beverages, an oil refinery, petroleum, dye and paints etc.

CHAPTER ... 22

FLUORIMETRIC ANALYSIS

When certain molecules are exposed to the electromagnetic radiation they exhibit fluorescence. Fluorescence is a process of re-emission of radiant energy absorbed in the form of visible light. In this process, the light emitted is always of higher wavelength than that absorbed. In fluorescence, absorption and emission of light takes place in very short time (10^{-12} to 10^{-9} seconds). If there is delay in the emission of light then the phenomenon is called phosphorescence. The delay period may range from fraction of a second to few days. Both these processes of re-emission are generally designated as luminescence. The quantitative determination of fluorescence is the base of fluorimetry analysis.

THEORETICAL PRINCIPLE OF FLUORESCENCE

A molecule at rest or in ground state has three energy levels, i.e. rotational, vibrational and electronic. When an electromagnetic radiation falls on the molecule, it brings changes into its energy levels during the process of absorption. This is illustrated in Fig 22.1. Within each electronic level of the ground state, there is large number of vibrational energy levels (v_0, v_1, v_2 ...). Electrons of a molecule prefer to remain at the lowest vibration level of the ground electronic state. Absorption of ultraviolet or visible light by a molecule brings it into its excited electronic state. Each of the excited electronic states of molecule has many different vibrational energy levels $\left(v_0^{'} , v_1^{'} , v_2^{'} \ldots\ldots \right)$. During the absorption of radiation, electrons are promoted to an excited electronic energy in one of these vibration levels (hv_1). Most usually and common is a singlet state, i.e. one in which all electrons are paired and in each pair two electrons spin about their axis in opposite directions. Average lifetime of a molecule in excited state is short, usually 10^{-8} to 10^{-6} sec. During this period molecule at each vibrational level of excited state would lose energy by other two processes. Molecule may lose energy by emitting photon or radiation and fall to the original ground state. The energy of emitted light would be exactly the same as that absorbed. (This is shown by usual absorption). However, the other process may be that usually some molecules initially undergo radiation loss of energy because of collision and fall to lowest vibrational energy of the excited state. The vibrational energy is considered to be lost to the solvent molecule ($h\upsilon_3$). From lowest vibration level of excited state, molecules usually return to ground state by photoemission of energy $h\upsilon_2$. This energy is lower than the energy absorbed and so the emitted radiation is of longer wavelength. This emitted light is called fluorescence. Thus, fluorescence is defined as a radiation emitted in transition of a molecule from lowest level of singlet excited state to singlet ground state.

In certain cases, the electrons cross over from excited vibrational singlet state to excited vibrational triplet state. Triplet state is a metastable electronic level lower than singlet state. When this occurs, the lifetime is much longer, often from fraction of a second to seconds. The energy emitted from triplet state to vibrational ground level ($h\upsilon_4$) is called phosphorescence.

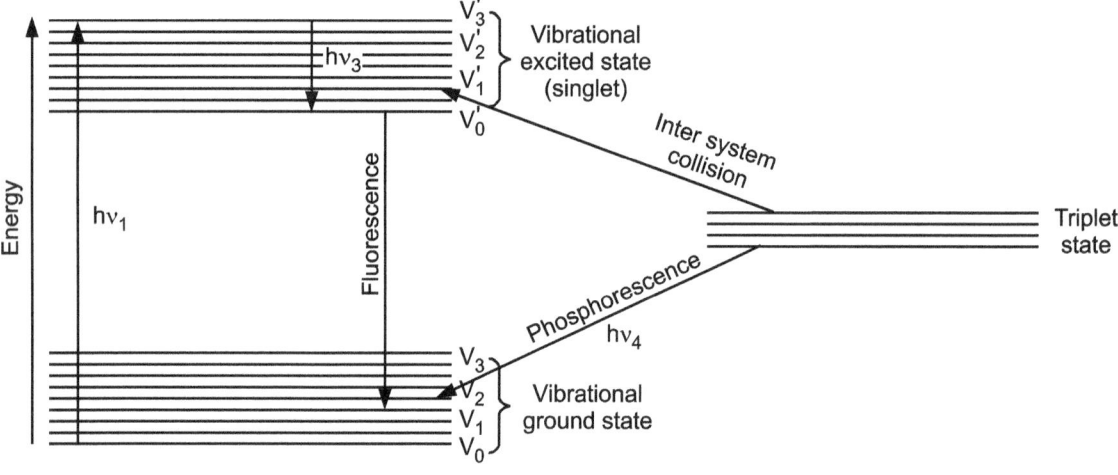

Fig. 22.1

Fig. 22.1 shows Energy level diagram illustrating energy changes on absorption of electromagnetic radiation showing fluorescence and phosphorescence phenomena.

MOLECULAR STRUCTURE AND FLUORESCENCE

It is observed that all substances do not show fluorescence. Some exhibit fluorescence under suitable conditions of excitation by themselves while others show it only when converted into suitable fluorogenic moiety. Thus, there appears a certain requirement in molecular structure for exhibiting fluorogenic activity. A generalization is as under:

1. Fluorescence is shown by those molecules which have absorbancy. Certain types of electrons present in the molecule show high absorbancy value and hence fluorescence.

2. Compounds with multiple double bond and conjugated bonds show fluorescence. A high degree of resonance stability is necessary. Any group or substituent that alters resonance stability affects fluorescence.

3. In many aromatic and heterocyclic compounds fluorescence is shown by the presence of certain substituted groups. There should be at least one or more electron donating groups such as – NH_2, – OH, – OCH_3 on the resonating nucleus.

4. Electron withdrawing groups like – COOH, – NO_2, – N = N–, –Cl, –Br, –I diminishes or destroys fluorescence.

5. Ring closure is conducive to the fluorescence in aromatic compounds, e.g. fluorescin, eosin etc.

6. Polycyclic compounds such as vitamin K, nucleosides, purine and the polyene such as vitamin A exhibit fluorescence.

7. Formation of metal chelates also promotes fluorescence. This is because of rigidity of molecule preventing excitation energy being dissipated in other ways than fluorescence.

8. Position of chromophore has important influence on fluorescence. Sharp changes of fluorescence occur both in intensity and degree with change in pH and solvent.

9. Ionization and dissociation of molecule which leads to increased resonance energy enhances fluorescence. The ionized or unionized form may be fluorescent and this is affected by pH changes, e.g. the violet fluorescence shown by aniline base in neutral or alkaline solution is lost in acidic solution.

FACTORS WHICH AFFECT FLUORESCENCE

Fluorescence is a very sensitive phenomenon exhibited by a substance in a given solution. There are number of factors which directly and indirectly affect fluorescence and decrease its intensity and sensitivity which is termed as 'quenching'. There are substances which by their presence compete for the electronic excitation energy and decrease the fluorescence. Some factors which affect fluorescence are:

(i) Concentration of substance:

Fluorescence is best given in dilute solution. In concentrated solution, the intensity of fluorescence is reduced and is not quantitative. This is called concentration quenching.

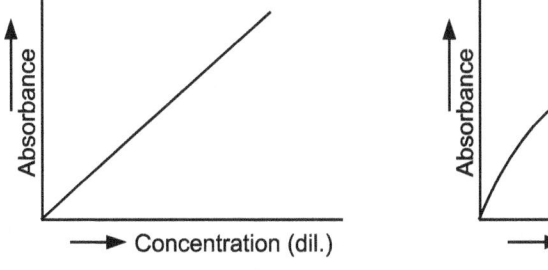

Fig. 22.2

The reason is that in dilute solutions, the absorbed light is distributed equally through the entire path length of the solution. But at higher concentrations the first part of the solution in the path absorbs more of radiation and less is available for the remaining path. Thus, in concentrated solution the fluorescence decreases because of

(a) vibration loss due to intramolecular collision, and

(b) By reabsorption of the emitted fluorescence.

(ii) Oxygen:

Presence of oxygen causes decrease in fluorescence. The interference is due to direct oxidation of fluorogenic material into non-fluorogenic and also indirectly due to quenching of fluorescence.

(iii) Photodecomposition:

In Fluorimetry, generally a high-intensity of radiation is required for excitation. This high intensity radiation may bring irradiation changes or photochemical changes in a substance destroying fluorescence. The light used must be of such suitable wavelength that it is not strong enough to cause photodecomposition. The measurement of fluorescence should be done rapidly.

(iv) pH:

Alteration of pH affects fluorescence significantly since it brings changes in the ionized and non-ionized form of fluorogenic material, e.g. phenol shows fluorescence in both ionized and unionized forms. In neutral and alkaline solution it ionizes and gives weak fluorescence. While in strongly acidic pH, phenol shows intense fluorescence.

(v) Temperature and viscosity:

Increase in temperature and decrease in viscosity is likely to cause collision between the molecules and thus decrease in fluorescence by deactivation of excited molecule. Low temperature and appropriate dilute solution are necessary for quantitative results.

(vi) Impurities and other substances:

Certain substances act as impurity and show fluorescence quenching, e.g. iodide ion is an extremely effective quencher. Organic substances, especially aromatic type in dilute solutions (1-2 ppm) have tendency of adsorption on the surface of cell. Addition of small amount of polar solvent usually eliminates this effect.

(vii) Chemical quenching

The quenching in fluorescence may also occur due to:

(a) Collision of excited molecule with other molecule/ion or impurity which results in the transfer of fluorescent intensity from excited molecule to other molecules or

(b) The quencher molecule forms a stable complex with the ground state molecule known as static quenching.

(viii) Inter filter effect:

There may be presence of non-fluorogenic material in the sample which absorbs light and thus shows filter effect. The presence of such materials should be kept minimal and constant both in standard and test sample.

RELATIONSHIP BETWEEN CONCENTRATION AND FLUORESCENCE

For the quantitative studies there should be a definite relationship (linear) between the concentration of species and the fluorescent intensity which is emitted. Such a relationship exists for very dilute solutions and fluorescent intensity. The Beer's law can be applied and thus,

$$F = K (I_0 - I_t) \qquad \text{... (1)}$$

Where,

$$I_0 = \text{Intensity of incident radiation}$$
$$I_t = \text{Intensity of transmitted radiation}$$
$$I_0 - I_t = \text{Intensity of radiation absorbed by the solution}$$
$$F = \text{Intensity of fluorescent radiation}$$
$$K = \text{Proportionality constant}$$

F is assumed proportional to the intensity of radiant energy absorbed $(I_0 - I_t)$

Now, according to Beer-Lambert's law

$$I_t = I_0 . 10^{-abc} \qquad \text{... (2)}$$
$$a = \text{Absorptivity}$$
$$b = \text{Path length in cm}$$
$$c = \text{Concentration in gm/lit.}$$

And

$$(I_0 - I_t) = I_0 (1 - 10^{-ABC}) \qquad \text{... (3)}$$

So

$$F = K I_0 (1 - 10^{-ABC}) \qquad \text{... (4)}$$

If

$$KI_0 = F_0 \qquad \text{... (5)}$$

Then

$$F = F_0 - F_0 10^{-abc} \qquad \text{... (6)}$$

$\therefore$

$$\text{Log} \frac{F_0}{F_0 - F} = abc \qquad \text{... (7)}$$

If abc is small > 0.01 then F = Kc. Thus, for low concentrations fluorescence intensity is directly proportional to the concentration and it is also proportional to the intensity of the incident radiation.

This equation holds for concentrations of the order of a few parts per million or less, depending on the substance. At higher concentrations, the fluorescent intensity generally decreases. It is noted that the fluorescence is concentrated near the entrance of cell and there is less and less in the remainder of the cell. Although the exciting light does penetrate through the solution it is not evenly distributed along its path and hence the fluorescence emission is not related to the absorption phenomenon.

According to equation it is assumed that the fluorescence is measured in the same path as the incident radiation. In practice, however, the fluorescence is measured at right angles to the incident light. The equation still holds true when b is replaced by b', the depth of cell in the direction of the detector.

INSTRUMENTATION

An instrument used for measuring fluorescence is called as fluorimeter. In fluorescence measurement, it is necessary to separate the emitted radiation from the incident and this is done by measuring the fluorescence at right angles to the incident radiation. There are different types of instruments depending upon the sophistication employed in them. However, fluorimeter in general are of two types;

1. filter fluorimeter and

2. spectrofluorimeter

In the filter type, two filters are used, one to isolate exciting wavelength from its source and another for emission wavelength. In the spectrofluorimeter, instead of using filters, the instrument incorporates two monochromators, one to select wavelength of excitation and other to select the wavelength of fluorescence.

A line diagram of a simple filter type fluorimeter is given in Fig. 22.3. The components of a typical fluorimeter are given in Fig. 22.3

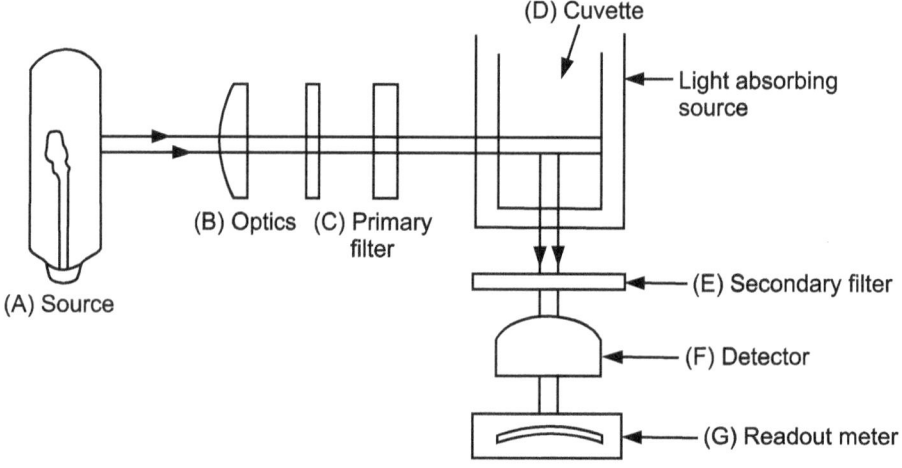

Fig. 22.3

In fluorimeter, an ultraviolet light is required as a source of illumination (A). A mercury vapour lamp with glass or fused silica envelope is commonly used as a source. When a spark is passed through mercury vapour at low pressure principle lines of wavelength are emitted. By isolating one of the principle lines at 366, 405, 436, 520 or 580 nm high intensity radiation can be isolated using suitable filter (primary filter). In more sophisticated instruments, a high pressure xenon lamp is used as a source of radiation.

The radiation from the source is collected on lenses, which are made of either quartz or glass and passed through a slit (B). The radiation is then passed through filter termed as primary filter (C). The primary filter allows the passage of wavelength required for excitation. In simple instruments, glass filters are used as they allow appreciable amount of wavelength to pass through. Interference filters are superior as they allow narrow band of wavelength to pass through.

The cuvette or cell (D) is usually 1 cm^2 type and is made of good quality glass for routine work. The cuvettes have a lid to prevent vapourization of volatile material. The cuvette unit is mounted in a chamber having light absorbing surface.

The fluorescent radiation is emitted in all directions. The radiation at right angles to the incident is allowed to pass through second filter known as secondary filter (E). The secondary filter allows the passage of wavelength of emission and absorbs the excitation wavelength. The fluorescent beam is collected on detector (F) which is usually a photomultiplier tube. This detects and measures even a weak fluorescence. To protect detectors from measuring reflected or scattered exciting radiation, secondary filters are placed just in front of photodetector. The signals from detector are fed to the readout meter (G) which is a galvanometer.

It is to be borne in mind that since it is difficult to measure an absolute fluorescence intensity, measurement of fluorescence of sample is made with reference to a fluorescence produced by a standard substance. Frequently, instrument is calibrated with various concentrations of standard solutions, including for solvent and cuvettes to find true value of fluorescence. The sample solution is treated under identical conditions for recording the fluorescence. From the plot of fluorescence concentration curve, concentration of sample solution is determined.

Commercial fluorimeter are more sophisticated and are filter or spectrometer type. Further, these may be a single beam or double beam in design. A number of popular name like Colem, Klett, Lumetron, Hilger-sppekker, Hitachi, Beckman are available in the market.

APPLICATIONS

One of the important features of fluorescence analysis is its sensitivity. And in this respect it is considered to be superior to absorption spectrophotometry. In absorption spectrophotometry, the difference between the two final signals I_o and I_t is measured. The sensitivity is thus governed by the ability to distinguish between these two, which is dependent on the strength and nature of the instrument, besides other factors. In Fluorimetry, however, we measure the difference between zero and finite number. Thus in principle the limit of detection is governed by the intensity of source and sensitivity of detector. It is thus possible to measure fluorescence in very dilute (10^{-8} M) solutions.

Fluorimetric analysis is possible for wide variety of drugs. Those substances which are intrinsically fluorescent are readily determined simply by dissolving in appropriate solvent or media, e.g. Aminocrine in 0.1 N hydrochloric acid, Ergometrine in 1 per cent tartaric acid, Riboflavine in aqueous buffer of pH 6, quinine in 0.1 N sulphuric acid etc.

Substances which by themselves are non-fluorescent can be converted into fluorogenic by chemical change. Such change can be carried out both in organic and inorganic compounds, e.g. Thiamine (vitamin B_1) is oxidized to thiochrome adrenaline to adrenochrome.

In other cases, fluorogenic reagent is allowed to react with organic or inorganic compounds to form fluorogenic complexes. Thus, substances like allyl morphine, para-amino salicylic acid, chloroquine; folic acid, menadione, phenobarbitone; procaine, thymol, aluminium, selenium, etc. can be analysed by coupling with suitable reagent.

It is possible to estimate one drug in presence of other fluorimetrically by adopting suitable technique; e.g. by changing pH, thus converting ionic to non-ionic and vice-versa. Morphine, codeine, atropine can be estimated by preparing derivative which are fluorogenic in nature.

CHAPTER ... 23

FLAME PHOTOMETRY
AND
ATOMIC ABSORPTION SPECTROPHOTOMETRY

(A) FLAME PHOTOMETRY

It is a well-known observation that several elements like sodium or potassium when burned in Bunsen flame emits a characteristic colour. The brightness of the colour varies with the amount of element introduced into the flame. A method of quantitative determination of a particular element using flame has been developed and is known as flame photometry. Thus, flame photometry or flame emission spectroscopy is a technique involved in detection of characteristic radiation emitted in flame by individual element and the correlation of emitted intensity with the concentration of that element.

The method of excitation of sample in flame is simple and is carried out as under. A small volume of sample, dissolved in water or in a suitable organic solvent is placed in a cup of automizer. Air, oxygen and combustible gas is fed to automizer under controlled conditions. This allows solution of sample to be sprayed into flame. Vapourization of solvent as well as excitation of element takes place in flame and radiations are emitted. The radiation from flame is allowed to pass through dispersing device to isolate the desired region of the spectrum. The intensity of isolated radiation is allowed to fall on photocell and after amplification; the intensity of isolated radiation is measured. After calibrating the instrument for different concentrations of known element, the intensity of unknown is measured and the amount of element is found out.

THEORETICAL BACKGROUND

Flame photometry involves use of flame for bringing excitation of element. There are three important characteristics of flame in photometry:

1. It brings transformation of sample to be analysed from solution or solid state to undergo into gaseous (vapour) state.

2. The temperature of flame brings about decomposition of molecular compound into simple molecules/atoms or ions.

3. It electronically excites atom or ions to emit light resulting in giving atomic or molecular spectra.

To obtain emission spectra, suitable flames are required. There are some important requirements of flames:

1. It should have proper temperature to carry out function.
2. The temperature should remain constant throughout operation.
3. There should not be any fluctuation during its burning.
4. The spectrum of flame should not interfere with the observations when emission is being measured.

When an aerosol or spray of solution is uniformly delivered into a flame, the following sequence of events occur in rapid succession:

(a) Water or other solvent is vapourized leaving minute particles of dry salt.
(b) At the high temperature of the flame, dry salt vapourizes and then a part of all of the gaseous molecules is dissociated to give neutral atoms.
(c) Some of the free metal atoms react with other radicals or atoms present in the flame gases.
(d) The vapours of neutral metal atoms or molecules containing the metal atoms are excited by the thermal energy of flame resulting into ionization and excitation of neutral atoms.
(e) From the excited levels of the atom or molecule or ion, its reversion to ground state occurs during which the energy is released in the form of light. This is called emission spectra.

Thus for example, when a solution of calcium chloride ($CaCl_2$) is sprayed into the flame, the following steps occur:

$$CaCl_2 \xrightarrow{\text{Aspiration}} CaCl_2 \xrightarrow{\text{Vapourization}} CaCl_2$$
$$\text{(Solution)} \qquad\qquad \text{(Solid)} \qquad\qquad \text{(Gas)}$$

$$CaCl_2 \xrightarrow[\Delta]{\text{Dissociation by}} Cl_2 + Ca$$
$$\text{(g)} \qquad\qquad\qquad \text{(g)} \quad \text{(g)}$$

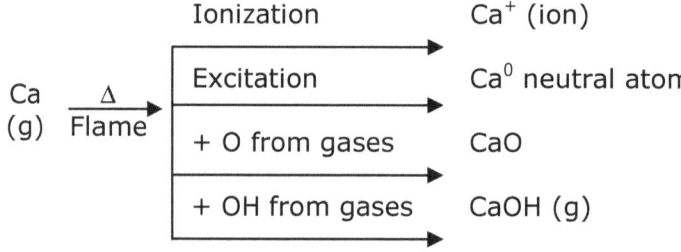

All the species, i.e. ionized atom and neutral atom of Ca as well as molecules of CaO and CaOH are excited by the thermal energy of flame. From this excited state when these ions, neutral atoms of Ca and their molecular species fall to the ground state emission spectra are produced.

The spectra fall into two main categories:

1.   Those consisting of lines originating from excited atoms or ions.

2.   The band spectra resulting from molecule.

When an electron falls to ground level from excited in neutral atom, emission occurs as discrete lines. The relation between the frequency 'υ' of radiation emitted to the energies E_1 and E_2 of two states of atoms is given as $E_1 - E_2 = h\upsilon$ (h = Planck's constant). The emission does not occur as single line spectra. If electrons fall to ground level through intermediate orbitals, then the emission of several spectral lines occurs. Spectra of ion of atom are different from the spectra of neutral atom. Due to high temperature of flame, atom from high excited energy gives emission because of transition of excited electrons of an atom to lower energy level. Due to high temperature of flame ion spectra is also given out as seen in alkaline earth metals.

The excited energy given out in case of neutral atoms is observed at (red) 671 nm for lithium, (yellow) 590 nm for sodium, (red) 767 and 769 nm for potassium and blue 422 nm for calcium etc.

Band spectra arise from electronic transitions involving molecules. Since molecules have internal vibrational, rotational and electronic excitation levels, the emitted energy is spread over wide band of spectrum known as band spectra.

INSTRUMENTATION

Flame photometer as measures the emitted radiation, the optical and electronic system used in spectrophotometer is similar. Any model of flame photometer consists of the following parts:

1.   Fuel gas, pressure regulator and flow meters

2.   The automizer

3.   The burner

4.   The optical system

5.   Photosensitive detectors

6.   Recording or reading meter.

Fuel gas, pressure regulators and flow meters:

In order to supply suitable thermal energy through flame, fuel gas is burnt in the burner. A structural diagram of a flame is shown in Fig. 23.1. The unburnt fuel gas emerging from region A, mixes with air/oxygen at outlet of burner comes into pre-heating region B.

Gases emerging from this mainly consist of CO, H_2, CO_2 and hydrocarbons. On burning, a steady temperature is provided throughout the outer mantle of flame.

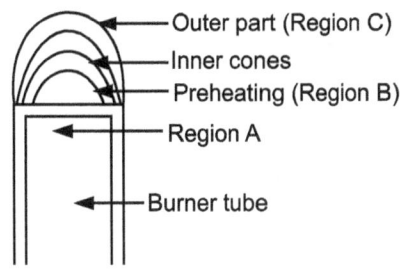

Fig. 23.1

To supply sufficient temperature between 1000–3000°C, various fuel gases like coal gas, illuminating gas, cooking gas and various hydrocarbon gases are employed. Using various mixtures of fuels with air or oxygen a sufficiently high temperature is obtained.

Table 23.1 records the temperature given for various fuels in air and in oxygen.

Table 23.1: Flame temperature with oxidants

Fuel	Temperature in °C	
	In air	In oxygen
Illuminating gas	1800	2800
Methane	2000	2700
Propane	1925	2800
Butane	1900	2900
Acetylene	2000	3050
Hydrogen	2100	2780

An ordinary air-gas flame gives about 1700°C which is sufficient to excite some alkali and alkaline earth metals. Higher temperature is obtained by using mixture of hydrocarbons and acetylene.

Fuel gas is generally obtained from cylinders where they are stored under pressure.

To obtain steady flame for giving emission, it is necessary that the gas pressure and gas flow is maintained constant. Usually 10 lb / in^2 of fuel gas and 30 lb / in^2 of air or oxygen are supplied. Flow rate ranges from 2-10 ft^3 / hr. This is adjusted by operating capillary flow rate meter or rotameter.

Automizer:

This is a very integral and important part of flame photometer. The purpose of automizer is to introduce liquid sample into flame at stable and reproducible rate. Automizer should be such that it should remain unaffected by solutions and solvents. Further, automizer should be such that it can be readily cleaned and should be sturdy in nature.

Automizers are classified into two types:

1. Those which introduce spray directly into flame and
2. Those which introduce spray into condensing chamber of automizer.

In the first type, two capillaries are sealed into wall of automizer burner and their bores are at right angles to each other. By the blast of air and combustible gas, solution is sprayed in the form of mist in flame. In the other type, air/oxygen and combustible gas is forced into chamber along with solution to be analysed. The sample is forced into the flame in the form of fine mist. Now-a-days combined automizer cum burner is employed in instruments.

Burners:

Main requirement of burner is that when fuel gas is supplied along with air/oxygen at a constant pressure, it should produce a steady flame. For low temperature flame Meeker burner is used. It carries a metal grid across the burner open tube which prevents flame from striking back down. There are two common types of automizer burner employed in flame photometer. These are:

1. Total consumption burner:

This is pneumatic nebulizer (Fig. 23.2). In this burner, the sample solution is passed through capillary tube under partial suction created in burner. The fuel gas and oxidizing gas i.e. air or oxygen is passed through separate tubes under pressure. When gas burns at the end of burner, solution gets drawn from fine orifice at the end in the form of mist.

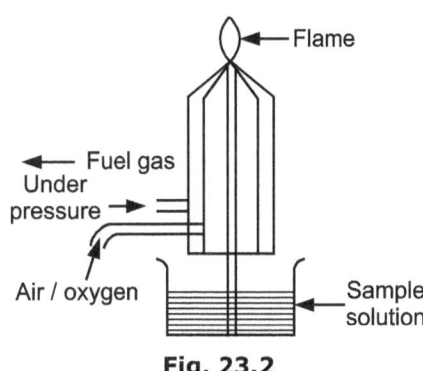

Fig. 23.2

2. Premix burner:

In this burner, the sample is aspirated into a large chamber by means of supply of fuel gas and oxidant under pressure. The fine droplets get carried out along with the fuel gas at outlet, the large drops of sample get collected in chamber and are drained out Fig. 23.3.

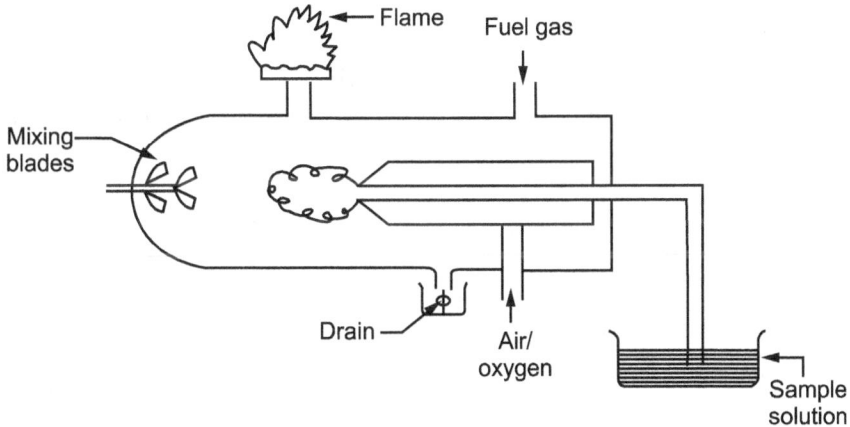

Fig. 23.3

The Optical System:

Function of optical system is to collect the light from steady fast flame, render it monochromatic by means of lens, prisms and focus on to the phototube. Concave mirror is frequently placed behind flame to collect scattered radiations and focus back into flame. By this mechanism intensity of emitted light is nearly doubled.

For isolation of spectral energy, filters and narrow slit width is commonly employed. In most simple flame photometers absorption or interference filters are used. Absorption filters of glass transmit rather wide spectral band. These are not suitable for analyzing samples giving lines to those which lie in close proximity to the analytical line. Interference filters are better in giving good resolution. These filters transmit the desired emitted wavelength energy and absorb the light of flame. Dispersion media can be quartz for operating in ultraviolet region. For finer separation of emitted light diffraction grating and/or prism is employed in an instrument which is commonly known as flame spectrophotometer.

Photo-detectors:

Most flame photometers or flame spectrophotometers mainly employ either Barrier layer cell or phototube or photo-multiplier as a detector. The latter provides a maximal signal for weak emission lines. RCA tubes operating in 200–700 nm are used while EM_1 tube in visible and above 800 nm are used.

Recorder or Readout meters:

The photo-current produced by the detectors is often amplified and fed to a light spot moving coil galvanometer. The sensitivity of this is adjusted through coarse and fine knobs, which adjust sensitivity ranging from 0.007–0.004 µ/mm scale divisions.

The double beam instruments usually are fitted with a strip chart recorder.

Commercially, flame photometers are available as

    (a) Single beam instruments

    (b) Double beam instruments.

Besides, these are either filter type (flame photometer) or spectrometer-grating type (flame spectrophotometer). A schematic line diagram for both types is shown in Figs. 23.4 and 23.5.

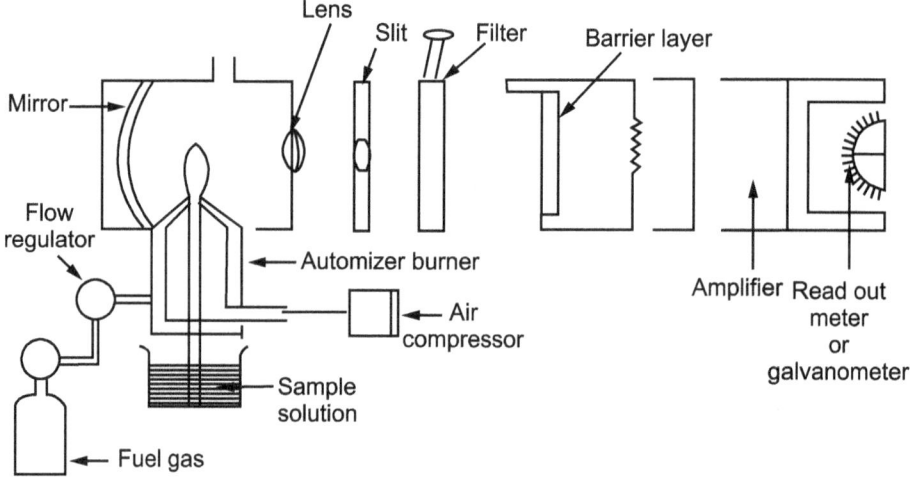

Fig. 23.4

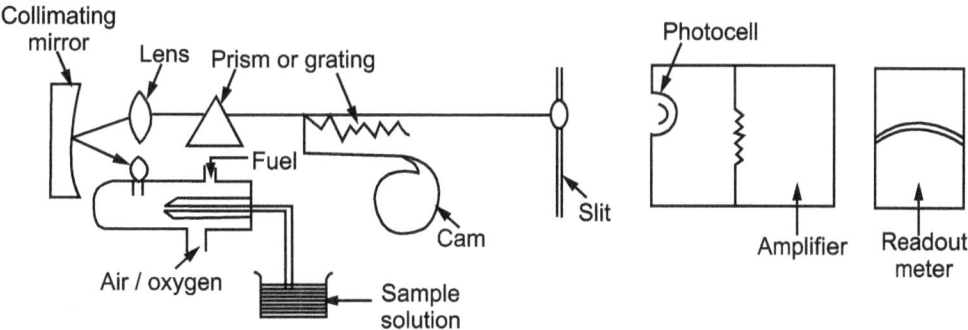

Fig. 23.5

Working:

Fuel gas is fed to burner at a steady rate of flow and air/oxygen is supplied to flame via air compressor. Distilled water or solvent is placed in cup of automizer-burner and it is allowed to be sprayed in flame. The radiation emitted in flame is collected via lens, slit and appropriate filter on photodetector. Adjusting coarse knob and fine knob, the galvanometer spot is adjusted to zero reading. Highest concentration of solution to be examined is now placed in cup and reading of galvanometer adjusted to 100. Intermediate concentrations are then atomized and readings are recorded (between 0–100). From the readings of galvanometer a calibration graph is plotted. Solution under test is run through automizer and reading of galvanometer is recorded. The concentration of unknown is found from the graph.

Double beam instruments:

A single beam instrument contains only one set of optics and detector. In double beam instruments a second light path is obtained from flame giving radiations by the added internal standard. The signal provided by one detector is opposed by the other detector. By adjusting indicator devices, ratio of concentrations of internal standard and analyte is found out.

Errors in Flame Photometry:

Flame emission photometry being an instrumental method, some errors does exist in this method. The cause and possible remedies for their removal is discussed as under.

Flame photometry is concerned about a molecule containing metal to undergo vapourization, dissociation into neutral atoms and ions, followed by excitation and releasing energy in the form of radiation. For good results, all the steps involved as above should occur in proper sequence. Some possible sources of error are:

1. Flame temperature:

It is very essential to have proper temperature of flame to bring about excitation and release of energy. If flame temperature is too low, it would be insufficient to cause vapourization, dissociation and excitation of atom. No lines or few weak lines would be obtained. The temperature should not be too high to have deteriorating effect.

2. Chemical interference:

When another component is present in the sample as impurity, error occurs. The magnitude of error depends upon the ratio of concentration of contaminant with the element under examination. In determination of certain metal ions (cations), anions present in the solution have depressant effect on the intensities of number of cation lines, e.g. more than 5 per cent oxalate, sulphate, phosphate ions bring decrease in emission intensities of alkaline earth cations. Thus, when contaminants are present, they need to be eliminated by precipitations/complexation or by other methods.

3. Radiation interference:

Sometimes, presence of certain element causes radiation interference by emitting light of wavelength identical to that of element under examination. The detector is thus unable to distinguish the lines and their intensities. This difficulty is generally eliminated by removing the interfering element or by adding an identical amount to the solution for constructing calibration curve.

APPLICATIONS

Flame photometry has been widely used in various industries like chemicals and pharmaceuticals, soils and agriculture, ceramics and glass, plant materials and water, oceanography, and in biological and microbiological laboratories.

1. Determination of sodium, potassium, calcium and magnesium in biological fluids like serum, plasma, urine etc. is routinely carried out by flame photometer.

2. Analysis of industrial water, natural water for determining elements responsible for hard water (like calcium, magnesium, barium etc.) is standard procedure in many laboratories.

3. Soil samples are routinely analysed mainly for sodium and potassium and also for calcium and magnesium (after removing other interfering elements) by flame photometer.

4. Some important elements which are commonly determined by this method are aluminium, barium, calcium, cesnium, chromium, copper, iron, lead, magnesium, manganese, potassium, sodium, strontium and zinc.

5. In glass industry, flame photometry is used in determination of sodium, potassium, boron, lithium etc.

6. In cement industry, this method is used in estimation of sodium (Na_2O), potassium (K_2O), calcium (CaO), magnesium (MgO), manganese (MnO_2) and lithium (Li_2O).

7. Flame photometry is extensively used in estimation of alkali-alkaline earth metals besides other metals present in metallurgical products, catalysts, alloys etc.

8. Flame photometry has also been used in determination of certain metals like lead, manganese, in petroleum products like gasoline, lubricating oils and organic solvents.

9. Analysis of ash by flame photometer is routinely carried out in various industries for estimating alkali and alkaline earth metals as their oxides.

(B) ATOMIC ABSORPTION PHOTOMETRY

Atomic absorption spectroscopy involves the study of the absorption of radiation by neutral atoms in gaseous state. For this the sample is first converted into atomic vapour and then absorption of atomic vapour is measured at the selected wavelength which is characteristic of each element under study. For quantitative studies the measured absorbance is proportional to the concentration of element in vapour state. Since, the technique involves spraying of a solution into a flame, it is also called absorption flame photometry.

This technique appears similar to flame photometry, the difference being, this method is based on absorption from the flame rather than emission into the flame. The principle of atomic absorption is similar to the absorption spectrophotometry of UV visible type; however, the instrumentation is of different types.

In the technique of atomic absorption analysis, the solution of sample in a suitable solvent is sprayed in a form of fine mist into a flame. Due to high temperature of flame, the element to be determined is reduced to element state in a vapour form. A suitable source of radiation is allowed to fall and pass through flame to the detector. Absorption of energy occurs by the vapour phase of element in flame and remainder is transmitted to the detector. The flame not only serves to convert element into its gaseous atomic form but also acts as a cell in the usual type of spectrophotometer.

In the absorption process by the gaseous atomic form, a series of well-defined lines occur due to electronic transition of outermost shell electrons of the element. In the absorption process the number of atoms capable of absorbing any transmitted light of characteristic wavelength is proportional to the product of concentration of atoms in flame and the path length in flame. In most determinations, concentration of sample solution, wavelength of radiation used for absorption studies, the temperature and height of flame is so adjusted to give accurate and quantitative results.

INSTRUMENTATION

A schematic line diagram of single beam atomic absorption spectrophotometer is shown in Fig. 23.6.

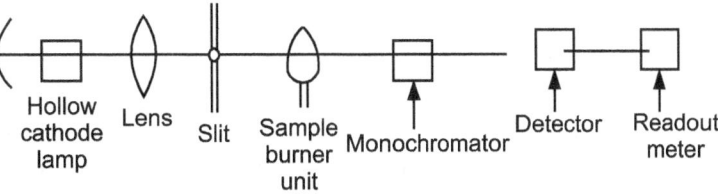

Fig. 23.6

The source of radiation is exceedingly important because the width of absorption line used in analysis is very small. The conventional sources such as tungsten lamp, xenon discharge lamp or mercury vapour lamp are not satisfactory because of broad-bandwidth emerging from those sources. The radiation source should give monochromatic light and it should not exhibit fluctuations. Most commonly, the hollow cathode discharge tube is used. The cathode discharge tube is now available for estimation of many elements. It consists of thick walled glass tube with a transparent window at one end. Inside the tubes are two tungsten wires one with hollow metal cylinder acting as cathode and the other as anode. The tube is filled with pure helium or argon gas at 1-2 mm pressure and potential of 600–1000 volts is applied to it. When the tube is on, the gas inside ionizes and current starts flowing. With an applied potential, gaseous cations acquire sufficient energy to dislodge some metal from the surface of cathode to give atomic cloud. This when excited emits characteristic radiation. During operation, some metal atoms diffuse back and redeposit on the surface of cathode. With proper applied potential desirable radiations of intensity can be obtained.

The optic system for separating the emitted radiation from hollow cathode discharge lamp consists of lens and/or entrance slit. The beam is focused on the centre of the flame.

The flame and sample burning unit are characteristics in atomic absorption spectroscopy. The burner has two main functions to perform:

1. It must introduce the sample in a fine mist at a constant and reproducible rate.

2. It must reduce the metal (element) to its atomic state in vapour form.

The flame shape is also important as it should give long path length so that more number of atoms is possible to come into path for absorption. Various types of automizers or nebulizers are commercially available. Furthermore, non-flame automizer involving introduction of heating devices to replace flame have also been marketed. Monochromator is another important device in atomic absorption spectrophotometry. Since, the radiation from the source consists of a line spectrum and the radiation emerging from gas is also given out, isolation of required line radiation is obtained by using grating monochromator. Separation of line from undesirable lines (from flame) is necessary to obtain accuracy and sensitivity. A glass filter can also be used for the same purpose.

The detector device, like UV-visible spectrophotometer is mostly a phototube or photomultiplier tube. The radiant energy received by detector is converted into electric signal. Photomultiplier tube is particularly useful when lines used for study lie in ultraviolet or blue region of visible light.

Amplification of current so produced is carried by amplifier and brought to the read out meter. Now-a-days in most of the models chart recorders are used as readout devices. A chart recorder is a potentiometer using a servometer to move the recording pen. The displacement of pen showing lines is proportional to the input voltage.

Operational procedure:

The operation of instrument will vary from one instrument to another. However, there are some common operational steps as:

(a) Preparation of samples:

A sample to be analysed needs to be in the form of solution. In most cases material is dissolved in suitable solvent (using acid/alkali) and resulting solution is diluted with water. This diluted solution is then sprayed directly into the flame. For substances which are not water soluble solutions are made in oil or other non-aqueous solvents and then diluted with semi-polar solvents. Usually, contamination and corrosion of the nebulizer burner results if the solution used earlier is not removed. Washing/spraying of water between the readings of each solution should be routinely carried out.

(b) Selection of radiant wavelength:

Light source generally gives out several emission lines. However, the line which shows greater sensitivity to the element under study should be selected. The lines or wavelength which are undesirable and which interfere are easily removed by chopping the exciting beam before entering into the flame.

(c) Fuel and Oxidants:

Natural gas, cooking gas, propane, butane, acetylene are very common fuel used in burner cum automizer. With the supply of air higher temperature can be obtained. Low temperature flames are satisfactory for certain elements like copper, lead, cadmium for which natural gas and air is satisfactory. The non-luminous acetylene-air flame which gives higher temperature (about 2200–2400°C) is best for elements like magnesium, calcium, iron and certain transition metals. Luminous acetylene-air flame which provides reducing conditions is used for barium, chromium etc. The total consumption burner and premix burner as used in flame photometry are also used in atomic absorption spectroscopy.

(d) Spraying technique:

The same technique as used in flame photometry is adopted in this method. The concentration of sample is so adjusted as to give absorption between 20-80 per cent (i.e. absorbance between 0.1–0.2).

(e) Standard solutions and calibration graph:

The concentrations for standard solutions vary according to the ppm and type of instrument employed. Standard solutions are prepared as per the instructions given. The calibration curve is obtained by the same way as per spectrophotometry method. Instrument is adjusted to zero (with water) and 100 or infinite with highest concentration of standard. The remaining intermediate concentration solutions are then sprayed and the readings are noted. The test solution is then analysed and its concentration found from the calibration graph.

The other method described by various pharmacopoeias is known as standard addition method. In this technique, known volumes (amounts) of standard solution are added to a fixed volume of sample solution and diluted to volume. The readings of these solutions are plotted in the normal way. Extrapolation of curve gives concentration of sample solution.

APPLICATIONS

1. Atomic absorption spectroscopy is very widely used in metallurgy, alloys and in inorganic analysis. Almost all important metals have been analysed by this method. It is an ideal method for analysis of many ores, minerals and alloys.

2. Biochemical analysis: A number of elements present in biological sample can be analysed by atomic absorption method. These include estimation of sodium, potassium, lead, zinc, mercury, cadmium, calcium, magnesium and iron.

3. Pharmaceutical analysis: Estimation of zinc in insulin preparations, oils, creams and in calamine, calcium in number of calcium salts; lead in calcium carbonate and also as impurity in number of chemical salts have been reported.

4. Sodium, potassium and calcium in Saline and Ringer solutions are estimated by this method.

5. In petroleum industry, metallic impurities in petrol, lubricating oils have been determined.

6. Analysis of ash for determining the contents of sodium, potassium, magnesium, calcium and iron is carried out in boiler deposits.

7. In cement industry, estimation of sodium, potassium, calcium, magnesium is carried out to determine the quality of cement.

8. Besides, atomic absorption, spectroscopy finds wide applications in various industries like agriculture, soil, forestry oceanography, fertilizer etc.

9. Atomic absorption spectrometry is used in the assay of *(a)* Intraperitoneal dialysis fluid (for calcium, magnesium), *(b)* Activated charcoal (for zinc), *(c)* Cisplatin (for silver).

CHAPTER ... 24

INFRARED SPECTROPHOTOMETRY

INTRODUCTION

The infrared absorption spectroscopy is concerned with the absorption of infrared radiation by a molecule and exhibits characteristic absorption spectra. The infrared region of the electromagnetic spectrum extends from the red end of visible spectrum to the microwave region of electromagnetic spectrum (0.8–200 µ). The most useful range is between 4000 and 400 cm^{-1}. This region is often called the fundamental region from the stand point of both application and instrumentation. The IR spectrum is usually subdivided into the spectrum of near infrared, middle and far infrared region, the limits of which are given below.

Region	Wavelength (λ) range µ	Wave number $(\bar{u})$ range cm^{-1}
Near IR	0.78–2.5	12800–4000
Middle IR	2.5–50	4000–200
Far IR	16–200	625–10
Infrared	2.5–16	4000–625
		(Most useful region)

We know that wave number is related to wavelength by the expression

$\therefore$ $$\bar{\upsilon} = \frac{1}{\lambda} \text{ and } \lambda = \frac{c}{v} = \frac{\text{Velocity of light}}{\text{Frequency}} \text{ cm/sec.}$$

$$= \bar{\upsilon} = \frac{v}{c}$$

Further, energy of quantum E corresponding to radiation of frequency υ is given by

$$E = h\upsilon, \therefore E = h\bar{\upsilon}c; \bar{\upsilon} = \frac{E}{hc}$$

In the above equation both h and c are constant. Thus, the energy of radiation is directly proportional to the wave number and inversely proportional to the wavelength.

As the IR radiation is of longer wavelength, it is associated with much lower energy than visible and UV radiation.

A chemical substance, when exposed to radiation in IR region, shows marked selective absorption bands. This is because after absorption of IR radiations, molecules of substance vibrate at many rates of vibrations giving rise to closely packed absorption bands, commonly known as IR absorption spectrum. The various bands seen in IR spectrum are due to characteristic functional groups and bonds present in a substance. Thus, an IR spectrum of a chemical substance is considered as a fingerprint and used for its identification. Band positions in an IR spectrum may be expressed conveniently by the number $\bar{\upsilon}$ where unit is cm^{-1}. The band intensities may be expressed either as Transmittance (T) or absorbance (A) on ordinate and wave number on abscissa.

THE ORIGIN OF IR SPECTRA

We have already discussed that UV-visible electromagnetic radiation results in changes of electronic as well as vibrational and rotational levels in a molecule. Since, infrared radiation is a weaker energy, it cannot bring out electronic changes but affects vibrational and rotational energy levels associated with a molecule. From wide region of IR radiation the 02.5–15 µ range has sufficient energy to cause changes in vibrational and rotational energies of a molecule. The higher region of IR (above 25 µ) can cause rotational transitions only. It is to be noted that since a change in vibrational level involves also changes in rotational levels, the resulting spectrum is known as vibrational-rotational spectrum.

Vibrational Changes

Exposure of a molecule to IR radiation (2.5–15 µ) results in stretching and bending vibrations into it. To understand these vibrations let us consider a diatomic molecule AB held by a covalent bond with mass m_1 and m_2 of the two atoms A and B. Each atom consists of nucleus corresponding to the atoms A and B, accompanying their electrons. The two atoms are connected by a covalent bond as a spring with two atoms at either end. The stiffness of spring is taken as a force constant k (Fig. 24.1).

In this spring-ball system if the spring connecting two balls is struck with a force, the vibrations are produced which can be described by Hook's law of simple harmonic motion.

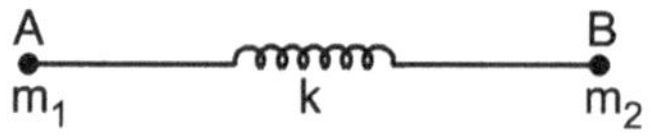

Fig. 24.1

The frequency of motion is

$$\bar{\upsilon} = \frac{1}{2\pi c}\sqrt{\frac{k}{c}}$$

Where υ = frequency, µ is the reduced mass of individual atoms.

As $\qquad \mu = \frac{m_1\, m_2}{m_1 + m_2} \qquad \therefore \quad \frac{1}{\mu} = \frac{1}{m_1} + \frac{1}{m_2}$ ... (2)

The force constant for a bond varies slightly from one compound to another. However, it can be calculated, e.g. C–O bond in methanol. It has f = 5×10^5 dynes per cm and µ = 6.85. It shows V = 1110 cm^{-1}. In spectrum, a strong band for methanol is observed around wave number 1034 cm^{-1}. It is thus seen that if force constant is known, approximate frequency of band can be calculated.

For vibrational mode to occur on striking IR radiation, it is essential that there is a change in dipole moment during vibration. In diatomic molecules if there is no change in dipole, no vibration is seen in IR region. Polyatomic molecules having no dipole moment of their own may be made to undergo vibrational rotational transition.

The vibrational energy of a chemical bond is quantized and is given by

$$E_{Vib} = \left(v + \frac{1}{2}\right) h\upsilon \qquad \qquad ...(3)$$

Where, v = Number of vibrational levels as 0, 1, 2

          h = Planck's constant

          υ = Vibrational frequency of the bond

The energy difference between two vibrational levels is given by

$$\Delta E_{Vib} = h\upsilon \qquad \qquad ...(4)$$

In summary, the absorption of IR radiation causes the excitation of molecule to higher vibrational levels and is quantized when transitions occur from lowest level ($v = 0$) to first level ($v = 1$). The frequency of that radiation is given by $h\upsilon = E_1 - E_0$ and is called fundamental vibration frequency; and when transition from ($v = 0$) to ($v = 2$) occurs it is called overtone frequency.

Polyatomic vibrational spectra:

In polyatomic molecules, the atoms and bonds are not rigidly linked and hence vibrate from their rest position to higher vibrational level giving fundamental and overtone bands.

The number of fundamental bands is related to the degree of freedom in a molecule. The number of degrees of freedom is equal to the sum of the coordinates necessary to locate all atoms of a molecule in space. Each atom has 3 degrees of freedom corresponding to the 3 coordinates (X, Y and Z) perpendicular to each other to show the position of atom. A polyatomic molecule containing N atoms thus has 3 N degrees of freedom. Three coordinates indicate the transitional motion and while three are required for describing the rotational motion. A non-linear molecule containing N atoms has 3 degrees of freedom is said to possess 3N–6 vibrational degrees of freedom while for linear 3N–5 vibrational modes, these are called normal or fundamental vibrational modes. Besides the fundamental modes, non-fundamental vibrations also occur which are termed overtone or combination tones.

The fundamental modes of vibrations are represented by stretching vibrations.

(a) Stretching vibrations:

The stretching vibrations are those in which two bonded atoms oscillate continuously, without altering bond axis or bond angles. They are of two types: (a) asymmetric and (b) symmetric.

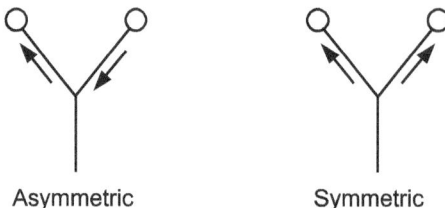

Asymmetric   Symmetric

Fig. 24.2

In symmetric, both atoms move away from central atom while in asymmetric one atom moves away from central atom while other moves towards it. Stretching vibrations generally require higher energies than bending.

(b) Bending (or deformed) vibrations:

These are characterised by continuously changing bond angle and axis with common atom. These are of various types as (positive indicates movement out of plane above and negative indicates movement back of plane).

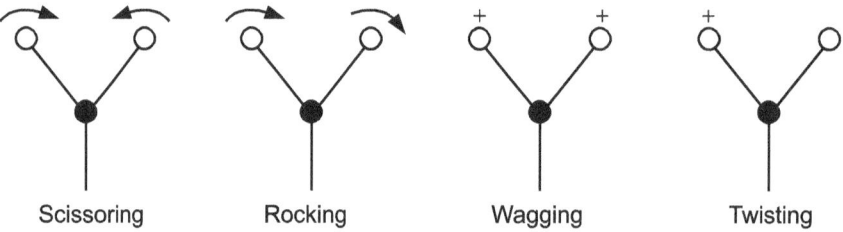

Scissoring   Rocking   Wagging   Twisting

Fig. 24.3

1. Scissoring vibrations occur when two atoms move back and forth towards each other.
2. Rocking vibrations occur due to oscillations of atoms back and forth out of equilibrium plane.
3. Wagging vibrations result when the unit oscillates in equilibrium plane-formed by the atoms.
4. Twisting vibrations occur when structural unit rotates around the bond which joins to the molecule.

Factors Influencing Vibrational Frequency:

From the discussion above we know that the probable frequency of absorption can be calculated by the Hook's law. However, it has been observed that the calculated value of frequency of absorption is not exactly equal to the experimental value. There are many factors which are responsible for shifts in vibrational frequencies.

1. The frequency shift may occur due to the effect of molecule in the immediate neighborhoods of bond,

2. Change in force constant of bond due to electronic structure and

3. Due to different states of the same substance, e.g. solid, liquid or gas (vapour).

The energy of vibration and thus the wavelength of its absorption peak are influenced by other vibrations in a molecule. The influence and extent of coupling of vibrations plays significant role.

EXAMINATION OF INFRARED SPECTRUM

Recorded infrared spectrum shows number of absorption peaks, some fine, some broad with varying intensities in its complete region (4000–650 cm^{-1}). The identification of unknown organic compound is usually done by examining certain region of the spectrum to get clues about the presence or absence of certain group frequencies. From the number of absorption peaks, some show distinctly the presence of particular group which helps in identification of a compound. While reading and interpreting spectra, it is to be remembered that no attempt to be made to assign for all peaks. Some important regions which are examined are described below:

(a) The region between 4000-1400 cm^{-1}:

This broad region shows presence or absence of many groups in the molecule. The important groups accounted for include NH, OH, C = O, C = C, C = N etc. The presence of aromatic nucleus (2000–1670) and hydrogen bonding O–H, N–H etc. are also encountered in this region.

(b) The region between 1400-900 cm^{-1}:

This is commonly known as finger print region. This region accounts for many absorption bands characteristic of functional groups. Since, location of different functional groups can be attributed in this region it is termed as fingerprint region. Absorption bands due to bending vibrations of different groups as well stretching vibrations of C – C, C – O, C – N are observed. Since, number of sharp bands of varying intensities is encountered in this regional close examination of bands for establishing identity is needed.

(c) The region below 900 cm^{-1}:

This region from 900–650 or 450 cm^{-1} gives few but sharp bands which can be accounted for the presence of specific groups. The presence of an aromatic nucleus is indicated in 1000–625 cm^{-1} region. The N–H, C–H rocking is also seen in this region.

Group frequencies:

Various authors have studied and tabulated frequencies of absorption of characteristic group, which information is available in number of standard text books. A very brief abstract of some principle absorption bands of selected functional groups is given in Table 24.1.

Table 24.1: Absorption peaks with intensity of some selected functional groups

Type of compound C–H stretching	Frequency range (cm^{-1})	Intensity
C – H stretching		
Alkane	2850–2970	s
Alkenes	3010–3095	m
Alkynes	3320–3310	s
Aromatic rings	3310–3100	m
Aldehyde	2900–2500	s
C = C and C ≡ C bond stretching		
Alkene	1680–1620	s – m
Alkynes	2300–2100	s – m
Carbonyl C = O stretching		
Saturated aliphatic ketone	1750–1700	s
α, β unsaturated aliphatic ketone	1685–1660	s
Saturated aliphatic aldehydes	1740–1720	s
α, β unsaturated aldehyde	1705–1680	s
Aryl aldehyde	1700–1680	s
Saturated esters	1750–1735	s
Unsaturated esters	1730–1715	s
Aryl aldehyde	1730–1715	s
Saturated carboxylic acids	1725–1700	s
Unsaturated carboxylic acids	1715–1690	s
Aryl carboxylic acid	1700–1680	s
Amide	1680–1630	s
Imide	1700–1670	s
Lacto	1720–1660	s
Thiocarbonyl C = S	1200–1050	s
Sulphone S = O	1180–1140	s
Sulphonamide	1350–1300	s
O–H (stretching)		
Alcohol (O–H) stretching free	3650–3450	s
Hydrogen bonded	3570–3450	s
Sec. and ter. (O–H) bending alcohol	1100–1050	s

N–H (stretching)		
Prim., Sec., Ter. amines	3500–3400	m
N–H bending		
Prim., Sec. amine	1650–1550	m
C–N Stretching		
Aliphatic	1200–1000	w
Aromatic	1350–1250	m
	and 860	m
$C \equiv N$ in nitrile	2280–2200	s
Halogen compounds		
C – F	1400–1000	s
C – Cl	800–600	s
C – Br	650–500	s
C – I	600–500	s

Aromatic compound:

The presence of aromatic nucleus in a compound is indicated in three regions: (a) 2000–1670 cm^{-1} (b) 1670–1430 cm^{-1} and (c) 1000–625 cm^{-1}. Very sharp and fine bands due to C–H bending occur in 1000–625 cm^{-1} region. Compared to parent benzene ring, monosubstituted compounds show absorption at 700 cm^{-1}, while disubstituted around 750 cm^{-1}, and para substituted around 860–800 cm^{-1}. Though presence of aromatic nucleus could be indicated by absorption bands in this region, the absence of it is more indicative of substance being non-aromatic.

Hydrogen bonding:

Hydrogen bonding between O–H, N–H groups is usually shown by strong absorption bands in 3700–2700 cm^{-1} region in stretching vibrations between hydrogen and other atom occurs. In OH, the O–H stretching vibrations appear at higher wave numbers and are broad than N–H band. Usually, hydrogen bonding tends to broaden the peaks and shows absorption at lower wave number.

Unstauration:

The unstauration in a compound could be due to triple bond which is indicated by peak for $C \equiv C$ at 2250–2275 cm^{-1} for $C \equiv N$ at 2180–2120 cm^{-1}. The double bond due to (C=O) carbonyl group show stretching around 1700 cm^{-1}. If absorption peak occurs in 1770–1725 cm^{-1}, it could be due to carboxyl stretching in esters, acid chloride, anhydrides etc.

Absorption peak around 1690–1600 cm^{-1} arises due to C=C and C=N stretching vibrations. Conjugation usually results in a lower absorption peak by 20 cm^{-1}. In case of carbonyl function (C=O) peak occurs at 1720 cm^{-1}. This may be attributed to the following chemical class of compounds (a) Ketone (b) aldehyde (c) ester

(d) lactone (e) anhydride (f) carboxylic acid. To differentiate these, examination for presence or absence of peaks at other region is carried out.

INSTRUMENTATION

Infrared spectrometers are composed of the same basic components as in the ultraviolet and visible regions, although the source of radiation, detectors and the materials used in the fabrication of the optical components are different. The standard infrared spectrophotometer is a filter-grating or prism-grating instrument covering the range from 4000–650 cm^{-1} (02.5–15.4 μ). The grating instruments offer high resolution that permits separation of closely spaced absorption bands, accurate measurements of band positions and intensities and high scanning speeds for a given resolution and noise level.

The radiation from a source emitting in the infrared region is interrupted (i.e. chopped, pulsed or modulated) at a low frequency level (10–26 Hz) and is passed alternately through the sample and the reference. This minimizes the effect of stray radiations emerging from the sample and cell before it reaches the detector. The temperature and humidity affects the performance of infrared spectrophotometer.

The following are the essential components of an infrared spectrophotometer:

1. Light source.
2. Monochromator and optical materials
3. Sample holder
4. Detector and
5. Instrument for recording the response (Recorder)

1. Infrared Radiation Sources:

The infrared radiation sources are the hot bodies, continuously emitting the radiations, which approximate a black body radiator in their emission properties.

(a) Incandescent lamp:

A closed wound nichrome coil can be raised to incandescence by resistive heating. A black oxide film formed on the coil give acceptable emissivity. In this, the temperature can be reached up 1100°C. The nichrome coil does not require water cooling. It requires little or no maintenance and gives long service. This source is recommended where reliability is essential. Though this source is simple and rugged, it is less intense than some other infrared radiation sources.

A rhodium wire heater sealed in a ceramic cylinder has also been used as a source of infrared radiations.

(b) Nernst glower:

In IR spectroscopy, Nernst glower is the most commonly used source of radiation. It is constructed by fusing a mixture of oxides of metals like zirconium, yttrium and thorium. They are moulded in the form of hollow tubes or rods about 1–3 mm in diameter and 2–5 cm in length. The ends of the rods are cemented to short ceramic tubes for mounting and short platinum leads are provided for power connections.

Nernst glowers are fragile. They have negative coefficient of resistance and they are preheated to be conductive. Thus, they are provided with auxiliary heaters. To prevent overheating they are provided with ballast, but they should also be protected from draught even as ventilation is needed to remove surplus heat.

The energy output of Nernst glower is predominantly concentrated between 1–10 µ with relatively low energy beyond 10 µ. Radiation intensity is approximately thrice that of nichrome and globar sources, except in the near infrared region.

The main advantages of Nernst glower are that it emits infrared radiations over wide wavelength range and the intensity of radiation remains steady and constant over a long period of time; second, it can be used in air as it is not oxidized.

(c) Globar Source:

It is a rod of sintered silicon carbide 6–8 mm in diameter and 50 mm in length. It is self starting and is electrically heated. The operating temperature is about 1300°C. It has a positive coefficient of resistance and can conveniently be controlled with a variable transformer. It is often enclosed in a water cooled brass tube, with a slot provided for the emission of radiations. It emits maximum radiation at 5200 cm^{-1}. In comparison with Nernst glower the Globar is a less intense source below 10 µ. The two sources are comparable to about 15 µ, and the Globar is superior beyond about 15 µ.

(d) Mercury Arc:

In the very far infrared region; i.e. beyond 50 µ (200 cm^{-1}), black body type sources lose effectiveness as their radiations decrease with the fourth power of wavelength. Mercury arc gives intense radiation in this region. It is enclosed in a quartz jacket to reduce loss. The output from mercury arc is similar to that of black body sources, but additional radiation is emitted from plasma which enhances the long wavelength output.

(e) Tungsten Filament Lamp:

This source is useful for near infrared region only.

2. Monochromator:

The radiation source emits radiations of various frequencies. As the sample in IR spectroscopy absorbs only at certain frequencies, it is therefore necessary to select desired frequencies from the radiation source and reject the radiations of other frequencies. This selection is achieved by means of monochromator. The monochromators are of two types: (a) Prism monochromator and (b) Grating monochromator.

(a) Prism Monochromator:

These are favoured because of greater range and simplicity. Neither glass nor quartz is sufficiently transparent to infrared radiations and therefore other materials like halogen salts are used in prism monochromators as they are transparent to infrared radiations.

Quartz prisms are used only in the near infrared region (0.8–3 µ). It is absorbed strongly beyond 4 µ.

The bulk of analytical work in the infrared region is done using crystalline sodium chloride as the prism material. It has high dispersion in the region between 5–15 µ and adequate up to 2.5 µ crystalline potassium bromide and cesium bromide are satisfactory for far infrared region (15 µ–40 µ). In the near infrared region (1–5 µ), lithium fluoride is used as prism material.

All the commonly used prism materials except quartz are water soluble and are easily scratched. These materials must be protected from moisture either by using desiccants or by placing in a sealed housing which is evacuated.

In the infrared spectrometers the focusing of the radiations is achieved by using concave mirrors rather than prisms. These mirrors can be prepared from various materials like metals or glass coated aluminium. The main advantage of these materials is that materials have no chromatic aberration and are sturdy. Besides concave mirrors plane reflecting mirrors are also used.

The prism monochromator may be a single pass monochromator or a double pass monochromator as shown in Figs. 24.4 and 24.5 respectively.

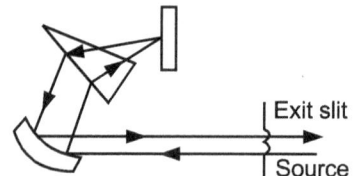

Fig. 24.4: Single pass monochromator

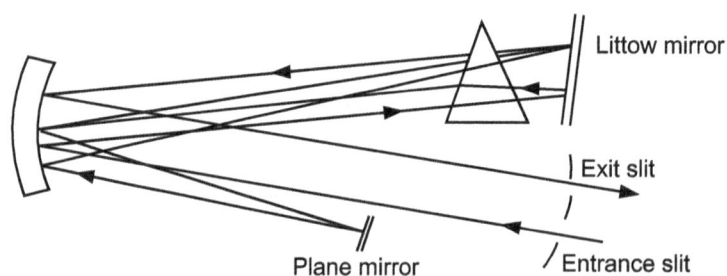

Fig. 24.5: Double pass monochromator

(i) Single pass monochromator:

The sample is kept at or near the focus of the beam, just before the entrance slit A to the monochromator. The radiation from the source after passing through the sample and the slit strikes the off-axis parabolic Littrow mirror 3. This renders the radiation parallel and is transmitted to the prism 'C'. The dispersed radiation after reflecting from a plane mirror 'D' returns through the prism second time and focuses into the exit slit of the monochromator and then to the detector part of the instrument.

(ii) Double pass monochromator:

In the double pass monochromator, there occurs a total of four passes of radiation through prism as shown (1) (2) (3) and (4) in the Fig. 24.5. The double pass monochromator produces more resolution of radiation than single pass monochromator.

In both single and double pass monochromators, sodium chloride (rock salt) prisms are employed for the entire region from 4000–650 cm^{-1} (2.5 to 15.4 μ).

Prisms of lithium fluoride and calcium fluoride give more resolution in the region where the significant stretching vibrations are located.

(b) Grating monochromator:

The grating is essentially a series of parallel straight lines cut out into a plane surface. It is usually constructed from glass or plastic which is coated with aluminium. To minimize greater amounts of scattered radiations and the unwanted radiations of other spectral orders, the gratings are blaze to concentrate the radiation into a single order. A grating is generally used in combination with a small prism which acts as order sorter. Sometimes filters transparent over a limited wavelength range are incorporated with gratings. Grating monochromator has certain advantages over prism monochromator as (a) the grating construction material is not attacked by moisture and is not subjected to etching where on the salt prisms are affected by moisture and can be subjected to etching; (b) grating mono-chromator can be used over considerable wavelength range and (c) grating monochromators are sturdy and long lasting.

Sample holders (sample cell) and Sampling of Substances:

As solvents used to prepare sample solutions have the tendency to absorb the infrared radiation, sample cells or sample holders are usually of much narrower (0.1–01 mm) than the one used in visible or ultraviolet region. The sample cells are usually constructed using pickle salt (sodium chloride). The sample cells are demountable and teflon spacers are used along with sample cell to adjust the path lengths. Fixed path length cells are also available and they can be filled or emptied with hypodermic syringe. As the sample cells are made of alkali metal salts, they become foggy due to moisture and thus they need polishing with buffing powder to render them useful again.

The sampling of the substance in infrared spectrophotometry depends upon the state of the sample, i.e. whether it is gas, liquid or solid. Depending upon the nature, various sampling techniques have been developed and used. The inter-molecular forces of attraction are more operative in solid phase than in gases. The sample of the same substance shows shift in the frequencies of absorption as it passes from the solid to the gaseous state. In some cases, additional bands are also observed with the change in the state of the sample. Therefore, it is always important to mention the state of the sample and the solvent to be employed for scanning in the infra region for correct interpretation of spectra. The samples whose spectra are to be recorded must be pure and free of water.

Sampling of solids:

Solid whose infrared spectra are to the recorded can be sampled in various ways:

1. Solid dissolved in solvent:

The solid samples are usually dissolved in a suitable solvent and this solution is used in one of the cells. This method cannot be used for all solids because suitable solvents are limited in number and generally no single solvent is transparent throughout the infrared region. The commonly used solvents are carbon tetrachloride, chloroform, alcohols, acetone, cyclohexane and carbon disulphide. Sometimes two solvents have complementary absorption region are used to cover the complete wavelength region. When the solutions of solids are used for scanning in the infrared region, the absorption due to solvent has to be compensated by keeping the solvent in a cell of same thickness as that of sample in that path of reference beam of a double beam spectrophotometer.

2. As solid film:

In this technique, sample solution is placed on the surface of a potassium bromide or sodium chloride and the solvent is allowed to evaporate. Thus, the solid sample forms a thin film on the surface of cell. This technique is useful for rapid qualitative analysis but not for quantitative analysis.

3. Mull technique:

In this technique, the solid sample is mixed with heavy mineral oil (Nujol) to form a paste. This paste is then sandwiched between two salt plates and then used for spectral measurement. Although Nujol is transparent in most parts of the infrared region but it has absorption maxima at 2915, 1462, 1376 and 719 cm^{-1}. This is the drawback in using Nujol for certain compounds which may have absorption in the region similar to Nujol. This technique is mostly used for qualitative work and not for quantitative estimations.

4. Pressed pellet technique (Disk method):

This technique is frequently used for the qualitative work. In this, a small amount of finely ground solid sample (dried) is intimately mixed with about 100 times its weight of powdered potassium bromide (IR grade and thoroughly dried) in a small agate pestle mortar. This mixture is pressed under a high pressure (25000 psi/g) in an IR tablet press to form a small pellet or tablet. The resulting pellet is transparent to infrared radiation and can be used as such.

This technique has some advantages over the Nujol Mull method. (i) It eliminates the problem of bands which appear in IR spectrum due to use of Nujol; (ii) The potassium bromide pellet if preserved properly can be reused for recording the spectra if required again; (iii) The resolution of spectrum in potassium bromide pellet is superior to the one obtained in Nujol mull technique. One disadvantage associated with this technique is that as high pressure is involved in the preparation of pellet, there could be polymorphic changes in the crystalline of samples like inorganic complexes, that can cause complications in the IR spectrum.

Sampling of Liquids:

A diagrammatic representation of sample cell is given in Fig. 24.6.

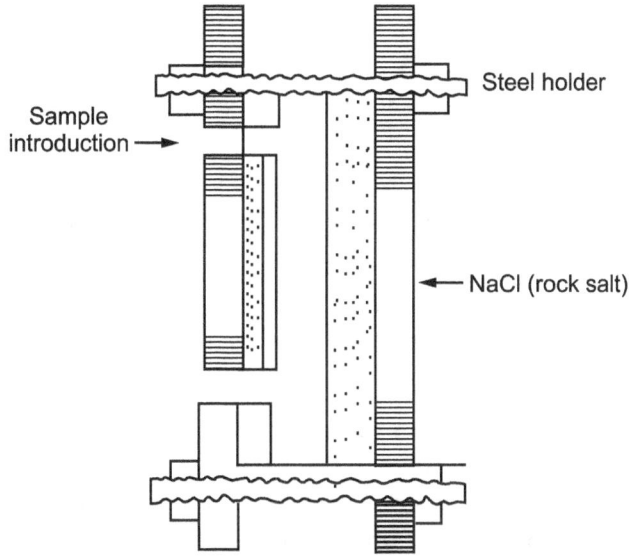

Fig. 24.6

The samples that are liquids at room temperature are usually handled in the pure form and free from moisture in the form of thin layers in variety of absorption cells. Various types of cells like sandwich cell, demountable cell and cavity cells are available for handling liquid samples. These cells are made up of sodium bromide, potassium bromide or thallium bromide. In demountable cell the salt plates are usually separated by a gasket and held together by a clamp. The thickness of liquid layer can be adjusted by spacers. The sample thickness should be such that the transmittance lies between 15–70 per cent. Usually for most of the liquids layer thickness of 0.01–0.05 mm is quite satisfactory.

Sometimes the liquid samples can be dissolved in a suitable solvent and scanned in the infrared region using any suitable cell. In double beam spectrophotometer, 'matched cells' are generally employed. In one cell, sample solution is placed while in other the solvent employed is placed. The cells used in this must have the same thickness. These sample cells must be protected from moisture.

Sampling of gases:

Gas samples are examined in infrared region after removing the moisture or water vapours. The dried gases are introduced via a stopcock and a system whereby a partial pressure of about 5–50 mm of mercury can be applied. The gas sample is introduced into the gas cell which is made up of glass or a metal cylinder of about 10 cm long. The end walls of the gas cell are made of sodium chloride. For measuring very low concentration of gases long path cells are required. However, the sampling area of most spectrophotometers is restricted in length. The gas cell is equipped with mirrors and used to bring about multiple reflections to increase the effective path length.

- Sometimes the GLC is coupled with IR spectrophotometers to analyse the elutes from GLC, for this purpose special cells are designed.

4. Detectors:

There are two types of detectors used in infrared spectrophotometry: (a) thermal detectors and (b) photo-detectors.

(a) Thermal detectors:

When the infra radiations falls on these detectors, they cause heating which gives rise to a potential difference which is measured. This potential difference depends upon the amount of radiation. The thermal detectors commonly used are thermocouples, bolometer and thermistors and Golay cell or Golay detector.

(i) Thermocouple:

It is the most commonly used detector in infrared spectrophotometry. Thermocouples are basically the dissimilar strips of metals joined together at one end. Thermocouples are constructed in various ways. In one of the thermocouple detectors two fine wires of metals which have different thermoelectrical properties are welded with blackened gold foil, and which absorbs the radiations. One welded joint (cold junction) is kept at constant temperature and the other welded joint (hot junction) is exposed to radiations. This exposure of hot junction causes a rise in its temperature. Thus, as the two junctions are at different temperatures, it causes a potential difference which is proportional to degree of heating of hot junction (or amount of radiations falling on the hot junction).

(ii) Bolometer:

They are constructed from metals or semiconductors. In this, large change of electrical resistance depends on temperature. When the radiations fall on bolometer, there is temperature change which causes change in the resistance of the conductor. This change in resistance depends upon the amount of radiations falling on the bolometer.

Bolometer is made in one arm of the Wheatstone bridge and a similar strip of metal is used as balancing arm of the bridge, which is not exposed to infrared radiations. When no infrared radiations fall on the bolometer, the bridge remains balanced. As the radiations fall on the bolometer, the bridge becomes unbalanced due to change in electrical resistance and thus the electrical current flows through galvanometer G. The amount of current flowing through galvanometer is a measure of the intensity of the radiations falling on the detector. The response time for bolometer is 4 m sec. The schematic representation is given below.

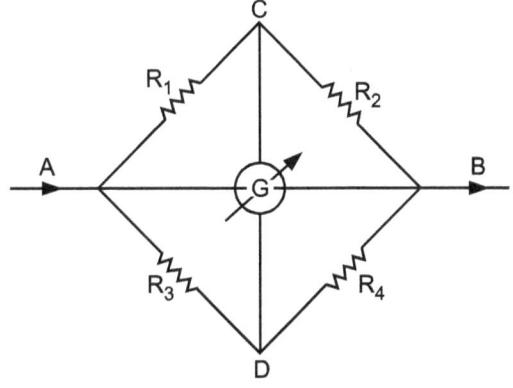

Fig. 24.7

Either thermocouples or bolometer is fitted in steel housing having potassium bromide or cesium iodide window and it is evacuated, which decreases the noise and increases sensitivity.

(iii) Thermistors:

These function similar to bolometer. They are the resisters made by fusing several metallic oxides. These show a negative thermal coefficient of electrical resistance.

(iv) Golay cell or Golay detectot:

Golay cell is now-a-days used in several commercial spectrophotometers. It consists of a small metal cylinder, one end of which closed by blackened metal plate and the other with a metalized diaphragm. A light beam falls on the diaphragm which reflects to phototube. The cylinder is filled with non-absorbing gas like xenon. When the radiations fall on blackened metal plate, it is heated, which causes the expansion of gas; this in turn affects the diaphragm (motion of the diaphragm). This causes the change in the output of cell received by the phototube, which can be modulated according to the power of the falling radiations on Golay cell. Thermocouples and Golay detectors possesses similar sensitivity in the mid infrared region.

(b) Photon detectors:

Photon detectors are widely used in near infrared region. They consist of suitable semiconductors like lead sulphide, lead telluride or germanium which are non-conducting at lower energy state. When the radiations fall on these they are raised to higher level which can conduct and produce a signal which is proportional to the amount of radiation. In these there is a drop of electrical resistance and if small voltage is applied there is a large increase in current which can be amplified and indicated on a meter or recorder.

5. Recorder:

In infrared recording spectrophotometers as the sample absorbs some energy, the sample beam and reference beam differ in their radiant energies. Then detector system generates the signal which is normally amplified and goes to servometer. The servometer which is connected to attenuator comb blocks the part of reference beam till energies of reference and sample beams are equal and thus beam balance is achieved (i.e. optical null). The attenuator comb is tied mechanically to the pen of the recorder and paper driver. They are synchronized with the automatic rotation of wavelength mirror. The transmittance of the sample is recorded as a function of wavelength.

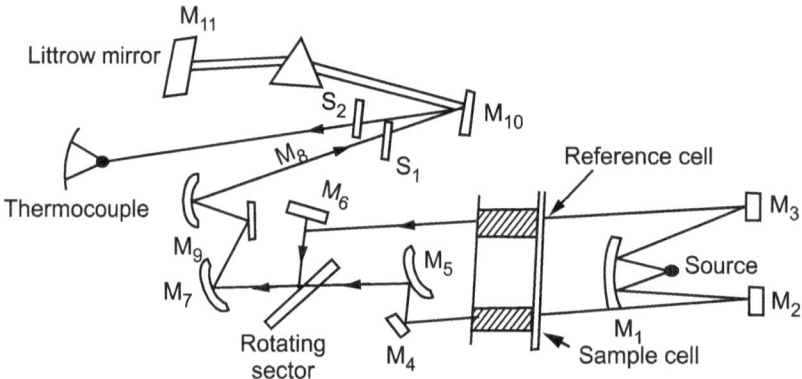

Fig. 24.8: Block diagram of infrared IR spectrophotometer

A schematic diagram of a double beam IR spectrophotometer is shown in Fig. 24.8. In the instrument 'S' is source (Nernst glower) of infrared radiation. Two beams of light of identical intensity are reflected by M_1 plane mirror and are picked up and reflected by mirrors M_2 and M_3. One beam passes through sample reflected by M_4 and M_5 to rotating sector mirror which reflects sample beam during one half of its rotation. The reference beam reflected by M_6 is reflected by rotating sector during other half of its rotation. Any difference between the two beams causes an out of balance signal. The rotating sector passes the reference beam and reflects the sample beam by mirror M_7, M_8 and M_9 and passes through slit-1 into the monochromator where it is dispersed by double passing through prism after reflector Littrow mirror M_{11}. The selected beam by M_{10} is allowed to fall on exit slit S_2 and then to the detector. An alternating potential signal from the detector is converted into frequency. The frequency of the alternating potential can be determined by rotation of rotating sector mirror. The magnitude of signal becomes zero when beams are equal. The output of the amplifier is used to rotate a small motor which drives a comb shaped attenuator. The comb is connected mechanically to the recording pen which records on paper. The rate of movement of paper is synchronized with the automatic rotation of the wavelength mirror.

PHARMACEUTICAL APPLICATIONS OF INFRARED SPECTROSCOPY

Infrared spectrophotometer is a very important tool used in qualitative identification and quantitative estimation of many drugs and chemicals. The instrument is particularly useful in pharmaceutical industry in identification of drugs and detection of impurities.

Qualitative analysis:

It is clear from earlier discussion that each compound or substance gives a characteristic IR spectrum. Thus, for identification, IR spectrum of a substance is compared with the IR spectrum of the authentic sample of the same substance. The sample spectrum is superimposed on the spectrum of authentic sample and if the spectra of both are identical then substance under examination and the authentic sample are the same.

Various pharmacopoeias like IP, BP and USP have included "IR spectra" as one of the test for identification of many drugs and substances.

Detection and identification of impurity in pharmaceutical substances can be ascertained by IR spectrophotometry. When a compound contains impurity, it reduces sharpness of individual bands, causes appearance of extra band or peak. Conditions for detection of impurity are most favourable when impurity possesses a strong band in IR region where main substance does not possess absorption band in that region, e.g. small quantity of ketone in hydrocarbon can be detected as a band near 1720 cm^{-1}, characteristic of ketone.

IR spectrophotometer is also useful in determining shape or symmetry of molecule, e.g. NO_2 (nitrogen dioxide) if linear, should show two bands and if nonlinear three bands. IR spectra of NO_2 gives 3 bands in 750, 1323, 1616 cm^{-1} region showing it is a bend structure and not a linear.

Presence of water in a sample can be readily detected by IR spectrophotometer. Small quantity water held will show three characteristic bands in 3600–3200 cm^{-1}, 1650–1620 cm^{-1} and 600–450 cm^{-1} regions. If water is held coordinated to metal ion additional band in 880–650 cm^{-1} region is observed. IR spectrophotometer is also widely used to analyse air contaminants in various fields.

Quantitative analysis:

In quantitative analysis studies by IR spectrophotometer records are obtained as percentage transmittance 'T', as a function of wavelength or frequency exposed. Concentration of substance, in solution or in solid (for disk method), cell path length, and slit width are selected such that 20–60 per cent transmittance is recorded.

Generally, all quantitative spectrophotometry measurements are governed by Beer-Lambert law. In IR spectrophotometry deviations to Beer's law are more due to (a) weak intensity of light source (b) weak detection by detectors and (c) by employing wider slit width as against UV-visible spectrophotometer. It is therefore necessary to check the plot of per cent transmittance *vs* concentration which should be a straight line before proceeding for IR spectrophotometric recording at a selected wavelength.

Another error usually encountered in quantitative methodology is fixing the base line. In most cases organic substances giving complex spectra the determination is a serious concern and a baseline technique (drawing a tangent to provide base line) is used.

For quantitative determination selection of suitable solvent for liquid cell method is most essential. Usually chloroform is considered as the best solvent. Carbon tetrachloride, carbon-disulphide, pyridine can also be used. The mull technique can also be used provided the sample and standard substance disks are prepared carefully.

In quantitative analysis, the substance used for obtaining spectra and the authentic sample are analysed simultaneously at a selected wavelength.

Detection and determination of complexes, polymorph, isomers and impurities are also carried out by IR spectroscopy.

In the research field, identification of unknown compound is mainly done by examining absorption peaks in various regions of IR spectrum and comparing those with the correlation charts of absorbance given in the books. In synthetic studies, completion of chemical reaction can be studied by recording IR of reactants and reaction products at a suitable interval, e.g. in reduction reactions of carbonyl group nitro group or instauration, the absence of characteristic peak will be evidenced.

CHAPTER ... 25

NUCLEAR MAGNETIC RESONANCE SPECTROSCOPY

INTRODUCTION

Nuclear Magnetic Resonance (NMR) is a form of absorption spectrometry. It is concerned with the absorption of certain energy by a spinning nucleus in a magnetic field when irradiated by certain energy radiation perpendicular to it. It thus permits identification of atomic configurations in a molecule. Absorption occurs when nuclei undergoes transitions from one alignment in the applied field to the opposite one. The proton of hydrogen gives Proton Magnetic Resonance (PMR) while that of Carbon-13 isotope as C^{13} NMR.

The wavelengths and energy required in NMR spectroscopy are far different from that of UV-visible and IR spectrophotometry. In NMR spectroscopy, radio frequency waves are used which are of long wavelength and therefore have less energy associated with them. These do not affect the electronic, vibrational or rotational levels of a molecule. However, they are able to interact with the nuclei of certain atoms when exposed to strong magnetic field.

The NMR spectroscopy enables us to record differences in the magnetic properties of various magnetic nuclei present in molecule thereby enabling to know the positions of these nuclei within a molecule. It enables to deduce different kinds of environment present in a molecule and also about the atoms present in neighbouring groups.

Thus, e.g. NMR spectrum of Toluene (Fig. 25.1) shows two signals corresponding to two different chemical and magnetic environments. Areas under each signal show the ratio of the number of protons in each part of the molecule.

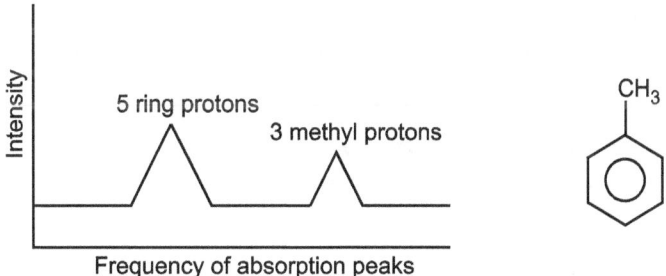

Fig. 25.1: Frequency of absorption peaks

The Spinning Nucleus

The nucleus of the hydrogen atom (proton) behaves as a tiny spinning bar magnet and it does so because it possesses both electric charge and mechanical spin. Any charged body will generate a magnetic field, and the nucleus of hydrogen is no exception.

Magnetic and Non-magnetic nuclei

All atomic nuclei contain nucleonic particles namely protons, the positively charged particles and neutrons which are neutral. As such the nucleus is positively charged. Like electrons, nucleonic particles spin on their own axis. This circulation generates a magnetic dipole along the spin axis. The angular momentum of the Spinning Charge can be described in terms of spin quantum number. Individual protons have spin quantum number $+\frac{1}{2}$ and $-\frac{1}{2}$ only.

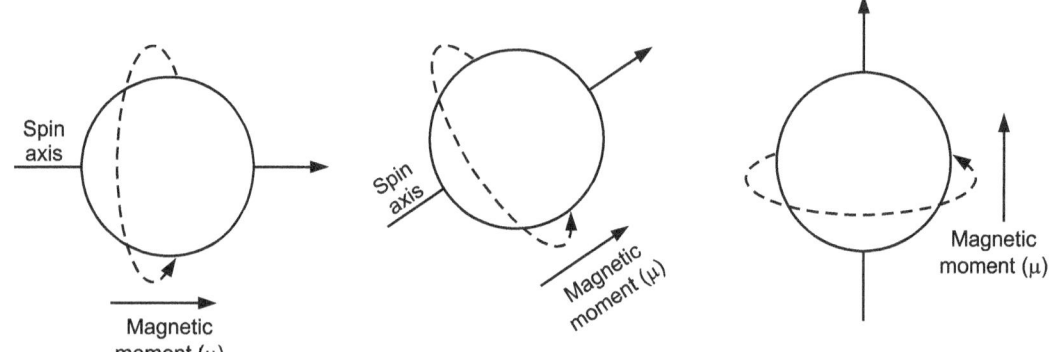

Fig. 25.2

The total of spin quantum number (I) is a characteristic of the nucleus and depends on the number of nucleons and on the symmetry of charge distribution.

Rules to find out Nuclear Spin:

1. Nuclei which have an odd mass number will have odd number of nucleons and thus they have half integral spin such as $\frac{1}{2}, \frac{3}{2}, \frac{5}{2}$ e.g. H^1, C^{13}, N^{13}, F^{19}.

2. Nuclei which have odd number of protons and neutrons (thus even mass number) have integral spins such as 1, 2, 3, e.g. H_1^2, N_7^{14}.

3. Nuclei which have even number of protons and neutrons (thus even mass number) always have zero spin, e.g. C_6^{12}, O_8^{16}.

Following Table 25.1 gives I values for some nuclei of elements commonly found in organic compounds.

Table 25.1

Nucleus	Number of protons Z	Number of neutrons N	Mass Number A = Z + N	Spin I
Hydrogen	1 (odd)	0	1 (odd)	1/2
Deuterium	1 (odd)	1 (odd)	2 (even)	01
Boron	5 (odd)	5 (odd)	10 (even)	03
Boron	5 (odd)	6 (even)	11 (odd)	3/2
Carbon	6 (even)	6 (even)	12 (even)	0
Carbon	6 (even)	7 (odd)	13 (odd)	1/2
Fluorine	9 (odd)	10 (even)	19 (odd)	1/2
Phosphorus	15 (odd)	16 (even)	31 (odd)	1/2

Thus, nuclei such as H^1, F^{19}, C^{13}, P^{31} have spin quantum number I > 0 behave like bar magnet while those with zero spin (I = 0) ^{12}C, O^{16O} are non-magnetic.

Effect of External Magnetic Field:

Like all bar magnets, the proton responds to the influence of an external magnetic field and will tend to align itself with that field (as a compass needle with earth's magnetic field). The proton can adopt only two orientations with respect to external magnetic fields: Aligned (lower energy state), i.e. parallel or opposed (higher energy state), i.e. Anti-parallel.

Precessional Motion:

Because the proton is behaving as a spinning magnet, not only can it align itself with or oppose an external magnetic field, but it will move in a characteristic way under the influence of the external magnet.

Consider the behaviour of a spinning top as well as its spinning motion. The top will (unless absolutely vertical) also perform a slower waltz like motion, wherein the spinning axis of the top moves slowly around the vertical. This is the precessional motion, and the top is said to be processing around the vertical axis of the earth's gravitational field. The precession arises from the interaction of spin that is gyroscopic motion with the earth's gravity acting vertically downwards. Only a spinning top will process while a static top will merely fall.

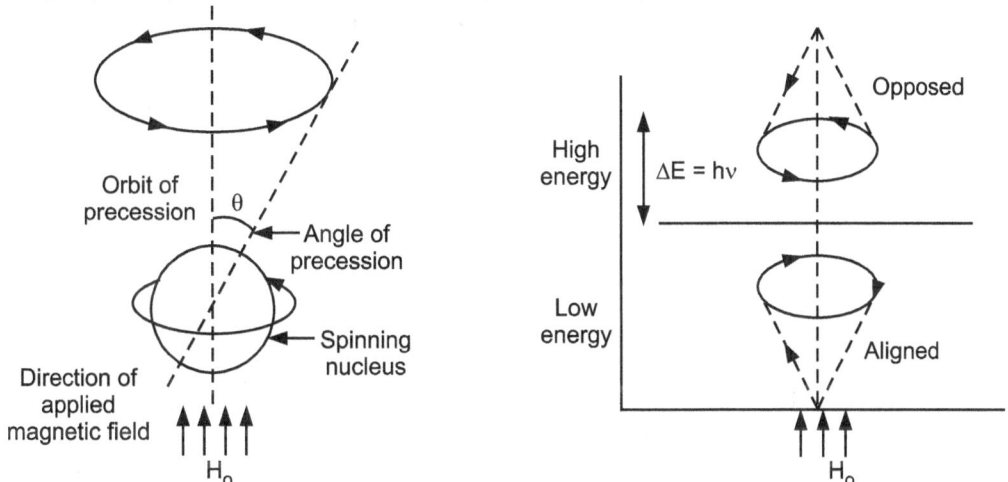

Fig. 25.3

As the proton is a spinning magnet, it will like the top process around the axis of an applied field in Z principal orientation either aligned with the field (low energy) or opposed to the field (high energy).

Precessional Frequency:

The precessional frequency of the nucleus is directly proportional to the strength of external field and also depends on the nature of the nuclear magnet. Magnetic nuclei of different atoms have different characteristic precessional frequency.

According to Larmor precession theory

$$\omega = \gamma H_o;$$

$\omega \rightarrow$ Larmor precession frequency

But $\qquad \omega = 2\pi V$

$\therefore \qquad 2\pi V = \gamma H_0$

$\therefore \qquad V = \gamma/2\pi H_0$ or $\gamma = \dfrac{2\pi V}{H_0}$

$\therefore \qquad V \propto H_0$

γ is gyromagnetic ratio:

Energy Transitions

As we know a proton when kept in an external magnetic field will process and can take one of the two orientations with respect to the axis of the external field, i.e., aligned (parallel) or opposed (Anti-parallel).

If a proton is precessing in the aligned orientation, it can absorb energy and pass into the opposed orientation and vice-versa by losing energy.

If we irradiate the precessing nuclei with a beam of radio frequency (energy of the correct frequency) the low energy nuclei may absorb this energy and move to a higher energy state. The precessing proton will absorb energy from the radio frequency source, if the precessing frequency is the same as the frequency of the radio frequency beam. When this occurs, the nucleus and the radio frequency beam are said to be in resonance, hence the term "Nuclear magnetic resonance".

THEORY OF NMR

The atomic nuclei which have the spin quantum number I > 0 will only exhibit the NMR phenomenon. The spin quantum number I is associated with the mass number and the atomic number of the nuclei.

Mass number	Atomic number	Spin quantum number	Atomic nuclei
Odd	Odd or Even	1/2, 3/2, 5/2	^1H, ^{11}B, ^{13}C, ^{19}F
Even	Even	0	^{12}C, ^{16}O, ^{32}S
Even	Odd	1, 2, 3	^2H, ^{10}B, ^{14}N

Under the influence of an external magnetic field, a magnetic nucleus can take up different orientations with respect to that field. The number of possible orientation is given by (2I + 1), so that for nucleus with spin ½ i.e. ^1H, ^{13}C, ^{19}F only two orientations are possible.

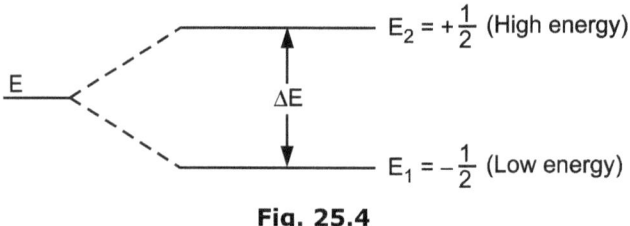

$E_2 = +\dfrac{1}{2}$ (High energy)

ΔE

$E_1 = -\dfrac{1}{2}$ (Low energy)

Fig. 25.4

Deuterium ^2H and ^{14}N have I = 1 and so can take up three orientations; these nuclei do not simply possess magnetic dipoles, but possess electric quatrapoles (non-spherical charge distribution).

In an applied magnetic field, magnetic nuclei like proton process at a frequency υ and when this frequency matches with the radio frequency, the exchange of energy takes place between radio waves and spinning nuclei. This leads to a transition of nuclei from $E_1 \rightarrow E_2$ and also from $F_2 \rightarrow F_1$.

In general, for a nucleus with spin quantum number I, the difference in energy is given by

$$\Delta E = \frac{\mu H_o}{I} \qquad \text{(i.e. energy of transition)}$$

And the energy of radiowave is given by the Einstein Planck equation as

$$E = h\upsilon$$

When resonance takes place, this energy is absorbed to bring about the nuclear transition. Therefore at resonance, Energy of radiation = Transition energy

$$\therefore \qquad h\upsilon = \frac{\mu H_o}{I}$$

$$\upsilon = \frac{\mu}{h.I.} \cdot H_o$$

At equilibrium the population of the nuclear energy upward and lower is given by Boltzmann distribution as

$$\frac{n \text{ upper}}{n \text{ lower}} = e^{-\mu H_o / IKT}$$

Where K is Boltzmann constant, T is absolute temperature.

However, normally the population of nuclei in the lower energy state is slightly greater than that in the higher energy state. This slight excess population, oriented along the direction of magnetic field H_o is directly proportional in magnitude to the precessional field strength. This is responsible for the net absorption of the radiowaves.

The absorption of energy from radiowaves boosts the nuclei from $E_1 \rightarrow E_2$ level and thus reduces the equilibrium ratio of low energy state to high energy state nuclei. The populations of the two states may approach equality and there is no further net absorption of energy and consequently the intensity of the NMR signal will diminish. This situation is called saturation of signal. However, in recording of NMR spectrum, the population of two spin states does not become equal because higher energy nuclei are constantly returning to low energy state (relaxation).

The high energy nucleus can undergo energy loss (relaxation) by two mechanisms:

1. **Spin-lattice relaxation (or longitudinal relaxation):** This occurs by transferring ΔE to some electromagnetic vector present in the surrounding environment, e.g. nearby solvent molecule.

2. **Spin-Spin relaxation (or transverse):** This takes place by transferring energy to neighbouring nucleus. A nucleus in the upper energy state can transfer its energy to a neighbouring nucleus by mutual exchange of spin.

INSTRUMENTATION

A line diagram of the instrument of NMR spectrophotometer along with its components is shown in Fig. 25.5.

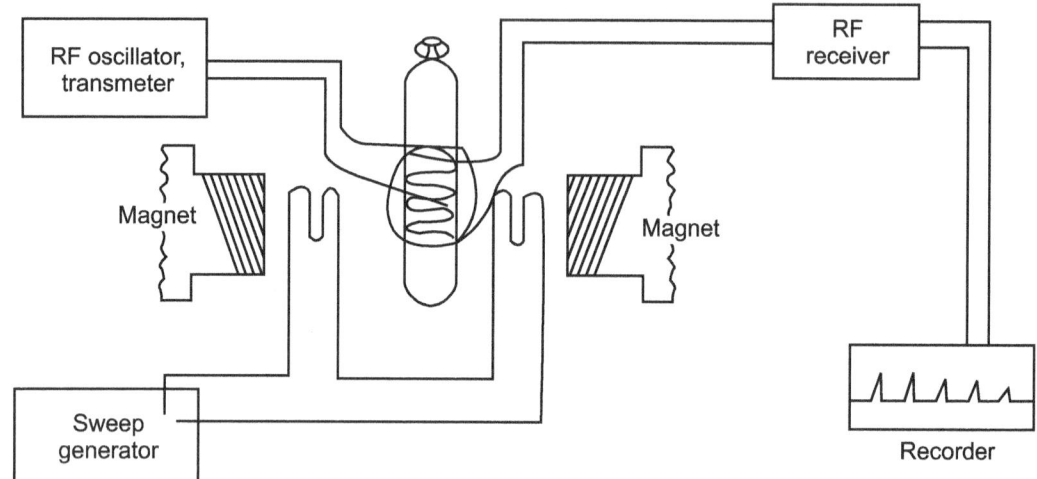

Fig. 25.5

Magnet:

The strong magnet provides stable and homogeneous field. The magnet size is 15 inches in diameter and is capable of producing strong fields (up to 23,500 gauss for 100 MHz work). If the magnetic field is not homogeneous, the nuclei in the different parts of the sample process with different frequencies, thereby producing broad signals.

Radio Frequency Oscillator (Transmitter) and Sweep Generator:

The RF oscillator coil is installed perpendicular to the magnetic field and transmits radiowaves of some mixed frequency such as 60, 100, 220 or 300 MHz.

Since, the large magnet as well as the Radio Frequency oscillator both produce fixed fields, a sweep generator is installed to supply a variable DC current to a secondary smaller magnet. This allows us to vary (or sweep) the total applied magnetic field over a small range.

RF receiver (detector) and Recorder:

The coil of the RF receiver or detector is installed perpendicular to both the magnetic field and the oscillator coil and is tuned to the same frequency as the transmitter. When the precession frequency is matched with the radio frequency the nuclei induce electromagnetic field (emf) in the detector coil by virtue of the change in magnetic flux following nuclear flip over. This signal is amplified and sent to a recorder.

The recorder gives a spectrum as a plot of the strength of the resonance signal on the Y axis *vs* strength of the magnetic field on X axis. The strength of the resonance signal is directly proportional to the number of nuclei resonating at that particular field strength. The area of the peak is therefore a direct measure of number of resonating nuclei and hence most of the instruments are equipped with automatic integrator which can record peak areas in the form of a superimposed integration trace on the chart.

The measurement of exact strength of continuously sweeping magnetic field is difficult task; hence it is difficult to assign a peak position on absolute scale. Thus, the method used is to record the peak position in relation to the position of an arbitrary standard lines (internal standard).

The tetra methyl silane (TMS – $(CH_3)_4$ Si) is used as internal standard for most of protons and is added to the sample before recording the spectrum.

Sample and Sample Holder:

A 1–30 mg sample is generally used in the form of dilute solution (2–10 per cent). The solvent should not contain hydrogen of its own.

Sample holder is a glass tube about 5 mm in diameter and is 15–20 cm in length.

Solvent:

Solvent should have the following characteristics:

1.   It should not contain proton.

2.   It should be inexpensive.

3.   It should have low boiling point, should be non-polar and chemically inert.

Generally, deuterated chloroform CCl_3 is used as a solvent.

If the sample is soluble only in polar solvent then Deuterium Oxide (D_2O), Dimethyl Sulfoxides (DMSO) CCl_4, CS_2, CF_3, COOH are used as solvents. TMS is commonly used as internal standard because:

1.   It has twelve equivalent protons which give an intense signal.

2.   Even a small quantity gives a strong peak.

3.   It is less electronegative than carbon.

4.   Protons of TMS are highly shielded and are chemically inert.

5.   TMS is volatile and can be removed by evaporation thus sample recovery is possible.

6.   TMS is soluble in most organic solvents.

7.   Signals of TMS are taken as zero and the signals of sample are recorded with reference to TMS in downfield.

CHEMICAL SHIFT

It was first observed in ethyl alcohol by Packard in 1951. It was found that the precessional frequency of all the protons in the same external field is not the same and depends on number of factors.

Ethyl alcohol shows 3 signals corresponding to 6 protons. It was thus concluded that the 3 different signals were due to 3 different chemical environments in ethanol, i.e. CH_3, CH_2 and OH.

Similarly, toluene shows 2 signals due to two different chemical environments of protons as C_6H_5 and CH_3.

Measurement of Chemical Shift:

The measurement of precessional frequency of a group of nuclei in absolute frequency units is extremely difficult. Hence, the differences in frequency are measured with respect to some reference group of Nuclei, e.g. for protons and ^{13}C, tetramethylsilane (TMS)

The signal of TMS is sharp at low concentration and is taken as zero. The other signals are compared with it. All other signals of the sample nuclei fall to the left of TMS signal. One to the left is called as downfield, while to the right is called up field.

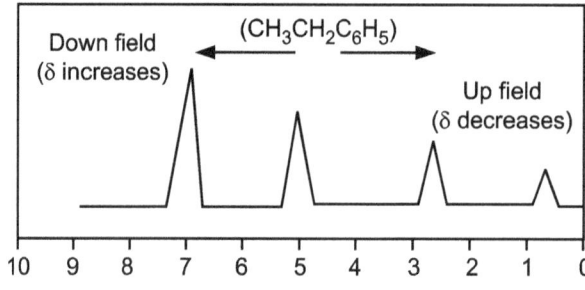

Fig. 25.6

The units are generally measured in δ (delta). High δ values represent downfield and vice-versa.

τ (Tau) value is also used sometimes and is opposite to that of δ. High τ value indicates upfield.

$$\tau = 10 - \delta$$

SHIELDING AND DESHIELDING EFFECTS

In hydrogen, nucleus is surrounded by electronic charge which shields the nucleus from the influence of the applied field. In an applied magnetic field the circulating electrons generate a small local magnetic field proportional to but opposing the applied field.

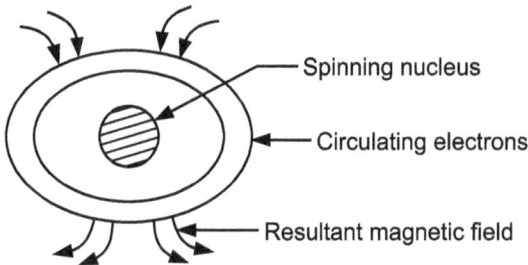

Spinning nucleus

Circulating electrons

Resultant magnetic field

Fig. 25.7

This is called diamagnetic shield because it shields the nucleus to some degree from the effect of applied field. The nucleus thus finds itself in an effective field which is somewhat smaller than applied field H_0. In order to attain the resonance condition the applied field must be made greater than H_0 depending upon the magnitude of diamagnetic shielding effect. The extent of shielding is represented in terms of shielding parameter (α). When absorption occurs, the field H left by the proton is represented as

$$H = H_0 (1 - \alpha)$$

Where H_0 is applied field strength. Thus, the field left by the proton does not correspond to the applied field. Greater the value of α greater will be the value of applied field strength which has to be applied to get the effective field required for absorption and vice-versa.

If the near neighbour is electron repelling, +ve, inductive effect will be observed, i.e. greater the electron density around the proton and greater will be the diamagnetic shielding effect, e.g. TMS silicone is electropositive and it pushes electrons into the $-CH_3$ groups of TMS and this powerful shielding effect means that TMS protons come to resonance at high field (upfield).

Presence of electronegative atoms or groups causes reduction in electron density around the proton (Deshielding), e.g. in CH_3F, F is electronegative, and it draws the electronic cloud towards itself. Thus, the electron density around CH_3 is less and it is deshielded, i.e. lower value of applied field is needed hence signal appears at downfield.

$$\begin{array}{c} H \\ | \\ H - C - F \\ | \\ H \end{array} \qquad \text{electron cloud}$$

Thus in case of olefins, acetylenes, aldehydes, ketones, acids, esters, nitrile if the proton is present in +ve region, it will be shielded and absorption occurs upfield. On the other hand, if the proton lies in negative region, its absorption is observed downfield.

FACTORS AFFECTING CHEMICAL SHIFT

1. Inductive Effect:

A proton is said to be deshielded if it is attached with an electro negative group. Greater the electronegativity of the atom, greater the deshielding effect and more will be the δ value.

$$CH_3 - CH_3 \qquad 0.9 \; \delta$$
$$CH_3 - Cl \qquad 3.05 \; \delta$$
$$CH_3 - F \qquad 4.2 \; \delta$$

Thus, electronegative groups deshielded the proton. As the distance from the electronegative atom increases, the deshielding effect diminishes.

2. Van der Waal's Deshielding:

In overcrowded molecules it is possible that some proton may be occupying sterically hindered positions. Clearly, the electronegative cloud of bulky group will tend to repel the electron cloud surrounding the proton. Thus, such a proton will be deshielded and will resonate at slightly higher values of δ than expected. This is considered as Van der Waal's deshielding.

3. Anisotropic effect (Space Effect):

Magnetic field developed by π bond is stronger in one direction than other, e.g. in alkene it is oriented in such a way that the plane of the double bond remains at right angle to the applied field. The induced magnetic field around carbon is diamagnetic and paramagnetic in the direction of alkene proton. Thus proton will feel greater field strength causing effect at the lower field.

4. Hydrogen Bonding:

Hydrogen atom exhibiting the property of hydrogen bonding in a compound absorbs at a low field in comparison to the one which does not show hydrogen bonding. The hydrogen bonded proton being attached to highly electronegative atom will have smaller electron density around it (deshielded) hence resonate at downfield.

5. Concentration, Solvent and Temperature Effect:

In CCl_4 and $CdCl_3$ chemical shift of proton attached to carbon is independent of concentration and temperature while protons of $- OH$, $- NH_2$, $- SH$ groups exhibit a substantial concentration and temperature effect due to hydrogen bonding. Intermolecular hydrogen bonding is less affected than intermolecular bonding by concentration change. Both types of hydrogen bonding are affected by temperature variations.

Nuclear Overhauled Effect (NOE)

Magnetic nuclei also interact through space but it does not lead to coupling. The interaction is seen when one of the nuclei is irradiated at its resonance frequency. Then the other is detected as an intenser or weaker signal than usual or normal signal; this is known as NOE. This effect is seen over short distance (2–4 A°) between two nuclei.

The interaction is dependant upon the relaxation of the observed nucleus by the irradiated nucleus. The NOE effect shows molecular geometry. It tells us whether the two protons are in close proximity within the molecule or not. Line intensities observed in the normal spectrum may not be the same as in the decoupled spectrum.

Shift Reagents

Lanthanide series of elements are used as shift reagents. A lanthanide ion can increase its coordination number by interacting with unshared electrons. As a result the NMR spectrum of the compound that contains a group possessing unshared pair of electron undergoes change and large chemical shift as a difference in peaks is observed.

All the shift reagents are mild Lewis acids. Shift reagent separates NMR signals those normally overlap. Thus, it gives more simplified spectrum.

The commonly used reagent is dipivalamethanato complex of Europium Eu $(DPM)_3$, Prasmodium Pr $(DPO)_3$. These reagents are β dicarbonyl complexes of rare earth metals, e.g. n-Hexane shows peak in a slightly upfield region for methyl and one downfield peak triplet for –OH and it shows number of peaks for all methylene in the region 1.2–1.7. But when shift reagent is added, the spectrum resolves over 1.0–11.0 δ and is more simple.

Shift reagents are paramagnetic, so large chemical shifts take place. The shift is downfield with Eu and upfield with Pr-complexes.

Broadening of the peaks occurs due to rapid spin lattice relaxation and depends on temperature. At lower temperature as there is more relaxation, more is the broadening.

Shift reagent is normally used in non-polar solvents like CCl_3, CCl_4, CS_2, and DMSO.

Induced shift is directly proportional to the amount of added reagent. The optimum quantity of reagent is generally 1 : 9 moles.

SPIN-SPIN COUPLING

(Spin-Spin Splitting)

On observing the NMR spectra of compounds it is seen that the signals are split into number of lines; e.g. in CH_3CH_2 OH the signals given are:

Singlet for OH

Quartet for CH_2

Triplet for CH_3

We say that each signal will split into doublet, triplet, and quartet depending on the number of protons present on adjacent carbons. The multiplicity of lines is related to the number of protons on neighbouring groups. A simple rule (n + 1 rule) is used to find the multiplicity. Count the number of neighbouring protons and add 1.

Splitting of the spectral lines arises because of coupling interaction between neighbour protons and is related to the number of possible spin orientations that these neighbours can adopt. The phenomenon is called either spin-spin splitting/coupling.

Theory of spin-spin splitting:

Consider cinnamic acid representing two vicinal protons, H_A and H_B. These protons with different magnetic environments resonate at different positions in unit spectrum. They do not give rise to single peaks (singlets) but doublets. The separation between the lines of each doublet is equal; this spacing is called coupling constant 'J'.

The resonance position for A depends on its total magnetic environment, part of its magnetic environment is the nearby proton B, which is magnetic, and the proton B can either have its nuclear magnet aligned or opposed with proton A. The two spin orientations of B create two different magnetic fields around A. Therefore, the proton A comes to resonance, not once, but twice and proton A gives rise to a doublet.

Similarly, with proton B the mutual magnetic influence between protons A and B is not transmitted through space, but via the electrons in the intervening bonds. The nuclear spin of A couples with electron spin of $C-H_A$ bonding electrons these in turn couple with C–C bonding electrons and then with $C-H_B$ bonding electrons. The coupling is eventually transmitted to the spin of H_B nucleus.

SPIN-SPIN DECOUPLING/INDOR/DOUBLE RESONANCE SPECTRA

It is a powerful tool for simplifying a spectrum. In a complex molecule if several of the coupling constants have nearly the same values; or if the long range coupling is present or if complex absorption gives multiples then it becomes very difficult to determine structure.

A proton spin couples with neighbouring proton because it has sufficient lifetime in a given spin state. If lifetime of a spin is reduced, i.e. if the exchange between spin states of nuclei is speeded up then little information about the neighbouring nuclei will be obtained.

In case of such compounds, where H_a and H_b are in different environments

$$\begin{array}{c c}
H & H \\
| & | \\
-C - C - \\
| & | \\
H_a & H_b
\end{array}$$

therefore two doublets at different field strengths are observed. If H_a is irradiated with strong correct radio frequency so that the rate of its transition between the two energy states becomes larger then the lifetime of this nucleus in any one spin state will be too short to resolve coupling with H_b. In such a case, H_b proton will have one time average view of H_a and hence H_a will resonate only once and H_b will appear as a singlet and not doublet.

Time d_t is needed to resolve the two lines of a doublet which is related to J. Thus, formation of a doublet is possible if each spin state of H_a has a lifetime greater than d_t. Due to double irradiation lifetime becomes still less and thus coupling is not possible. So it results in a singlet by spin-spin decoupling.

APPLICATIONS OF NMR

1. It is used in identification of structural isomers such as

    $CH_3 - CH_2 - CH_2\ OH$ $CH_3 - CH - CH_3$

    4 signals |

    n-propanyl   OH

    3 signals isopropanol

2. It is employed in determination of hydrogen bonding. Intermolecular hydrogen bonding shifts the absorption to downfield. The extent of H-bonding varies with solvent, concentration and temperature. Intramolecular H-bonding also shifts the absorption downfield. It is not concentration dependant.

3. This method is used to detect aromaticity of a compound. Proton attached to the benzyl, polynuclear and heterocyclic compounds whose π-electrons follow Huckel rule (4n + 2π electron) are extremely deshielded due to the circulation of sextet of π electron. So signals appear at very downfield. From this aromatic character of a compound can be predicted.

4. The NMR technique is used to distinguish between cis and trans isomers. Protons in cis and trans isomers have different chemical shift values and different coupling constants.

J = 7 - 12   J = 13 - 18

Similarly axial and equatorial protons or groups carrying a proton can be distinguished because protons/groups are deshielded in axial.

5. Detection of electronegative atoms or group is easily done by NMR method. Presence of electronegative atom in the neighbourhood of proton causes deshielding, so, signal gets shifted to downfield. Greater the electronegative group greater is δ value.

6. Determination of some double bond character due to resonance: In some compounds molecules acquire a little double bond character due to resonance. Due to this, different signals are expected. These signals are due to the restricted rotation of the formed double bond which changes the geometry of molecule, e.g. N, N dimethyl formamide.

CHAPTER ... 26

MASS SPECTROMETRY

INTRODUCTION

Mass spectrometry, like other spectroscopic techniques has been used as a routine method for dealing with many analytical problems in organic and inorganic chemistry like determining stable isotopes, examining ionization phenomena, studying free radicals, etc. It is also used by physicists, in space research and biomedical research.

The development of mass spectrometry began when Wiens (1898) demonstrated that a beam of positive ions could be deflected by both electric and magnetic fields. The instrumentation and techniques of mass spectrometry have steadily progressed since the work by Thomson (1905), Aston and Dumpster (1979), who built the first mass spectrometer. In the early stages the mass spectrometer was mainly used for the accurate measurement of the masses and relative abundances of isotopes. Now-a-days due to the instrumental development, this technique is widely used practically in all branches of science and technology.

The mass spectrometer is an instrument in which the substance in gaseous or vapour state is bombarded with a beam of electrons, to form positively charged ions (cations) which are further sorted according to their mass to charge ratio to record their masses and relative abundances.

Both positive and negative ions can be studied using mass spectrometer but usually positive ions are analysed since they are produced in larger amount than negative ions. Negative ion spectra although less commonly used than positive ion spectra, can also be obtained.

Many commercial mass spectrometers are now available to measure the relative abundances and the exact masses of the ionic species with great accuracy and sensitivity.

The mass spectrum is a sorted collection of the masses of all the charged molecular fragments produced, the relative abundance of each is the characteristic of every compound. The mass spectrum can give detailed information about the composition of an organic compound and the position of functional groups. Mass spectrometer is also used for determination of molecular weight.

Mass spectrometer can be coupled with gas chromatograph. This has widened its applications for qualitative and quantitative analysis of organic compounds. It also finds its applicability as detector in both gas and liquid chromatography.

PRINCIPLE OF MASS SPECTROMETRY

In mass spectrometry organic molecules in gaseous state under the pressure between 10^{-7}–10^{-5} mm of Hg are bombarded with a beam of energetic electrons (70 eV) using tungsten or rhenium filament. Molecules are broken up into cations and many other fragments.

$$M + e^- \rightarrow \overset{+}{\overset{\bullet}{M}} + 2e^-$$
$$\text{Fast} \qquad \text{slow}$$

$$\overset{+}{\overset{\bullet}{M}} \rightarrow \overset{+}{M_1} + \overset{\bullet}{M_2}$$

$$\overset{+}{\overset{\bullet}{M}} \rightarrow \overset{\bullet}{M_1} + \overset{+}{M_2}$$

$$R - H + e^- \rightarrow \overset{+}{\overset{\bullet}{RH}} + 2\ e^-$$

These cations (molecular or parent ions) are formed due the loss of an electron usually from n or π orbital from a molecule, which can further break up into fragment ions or daughter ions. All these ions are accelerated by an electric field, sorted out according to their mass to charge ratio by deflection in variable magnetic field, and recorded. The output is known as mass spectrum. The mass spectrum is a plot of relative abundance versus mass to charge ratio. Each line upon the mass spectrum indicates the presence of atoms or molecules of a particular mass. The most intense peak in the spectrum is taken as the base peak. Its intensity is taken as 100 and other peaks are compared with it.

The mass spectrum of the compound can be obtained by using very small sample (0.1–1 mg). The main disadvantage of this technique is that the sample gets destroyed. Another disadvantage is the difficulty in introducing very small samples without disturbing the vacuum system. The instrumentation is complicated, expensive and requires skilled technicians for operation and maintenance.

INSTRUMENTATION

A mass spectrometer consists of the following basic components. The schematic diagram is given below.

1. Sample handling system
2. Ionization chamber
3. Ion separator or mass analyzer
4. Ion collector, detector and read out system
5. Vacuum system.

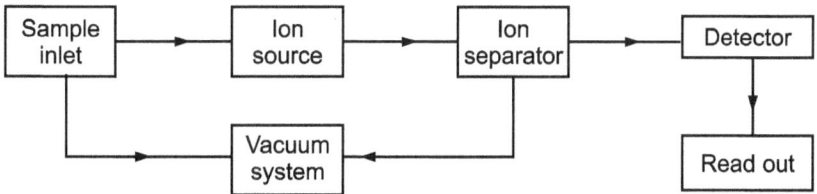

Fig. 26.1: Components of mass spectrometer

1. Sample Handling System:

The purpose of the sample handling system is to introduce the sufficient quantity of the sample into an ion source at constant rate without disturbing the vacuum. A micromole sample in gaseous state is slowly allowed to leak into ionization chamber. The pressure of the sample in the reservoir is greater than the ionization chamber to maintain the steady flow of gaseous sample. For different types of samples different sample inlet systems are used.

(a) Heated inlet system:

This type of inlet system is generally used for gaseous and less volatile liquid samples having boiling point less than 500°C. In heated inlet system the sample is vapourized externally and then slowly introduced into ionization source. Many types of vacuum locks are available for introducing sample into ion source without breaking the vacuum.

The volatile liquids are handled by 'freeze out' technique wherein the sample in the sample holder tube is frozen with liquid nitrogen or dry ice and after evacuation the tube is heated to room temperature or higher to evaporate the sample into sample reservoir. Low volatile samples like sugars, acids, amino acids, etc. are converted into volatile derivatives. For example, hydroxyl compounds into ethers, acids to esters etc.

(b) Direct inlet system:

Solids, non-volatile liquids and thermally unstable compounds are directly introduced into the ion source by means of sample probe which is inserted through a vacuum lock. Usually, the provision is made for both cooling and heating of the sample on the probe whereby sample can be slowly vaporized in the electron bombardment region. In this case, only a fraction of milligram or less of the sample is required to record the spectrum. Thermal decomposition of the sample is also eliminated in this technique. The non-volatile samples like steroids, polymeric substances, carbohydrates, etc. can be handled by this method.

(c) Gas chromatographic technique:

In gas chromatography and mass spectrometry, the sample requirements are similar, hence effluents from a gas chromatograph can be collected separately and analysed in the fast scanning mass spectrometer. Thus gas-chromatographic equipment can be directly coupled with rapid-scan mass spectrometer. The flow rate from capillary columns is generally low enough to be fed directly into the ionization chamber of the mass spectrometer.

2. Ion Source:

Ionization of the organic compound is the primary step in obtaining the mass spectrum. The minimum energy required to ionize the sample or organic molecule is called as its ionization potential. Several methods are available to induce ionization of organic compounds.

Ionization of the vaporized sample may be produced by the electron bombardment, field ionization, thermal ionization, chemical ionization, photoionisation or vacuum discharge ionization. Some of the common ion sources are discussed below.

Electron Impact Source (EI):

Electron bombardment is the standard and most widely used method of ion production. In this method, the bombarding energetic electrons are produced from electrically heated tungsten or rhenium filament (Fig. 26.2). These electrons are accelerated by an electric field to average electron beam energy of about 70 eV. The sample pressure is about $10^{-5}-10^{-6}$ torr. The vapour of the sample to be analysed is introduced at right angle to the electron beam through a molecular leak. Energy transfer takes place between the neutral sample molecules and bombarding electrons. If the transferred energy is equal to the ionization potential of the sample, ionization takes place. Ionization potential for most of the organic compounds varies between 8–12 eV.

The electron impact process suffers from the drawbacks that the sample first needs to be vaporized. This may result in the thermal decomposition of a part of a compound. Besides ionization and fragmentation, it may lead to complete destruction of the compound.

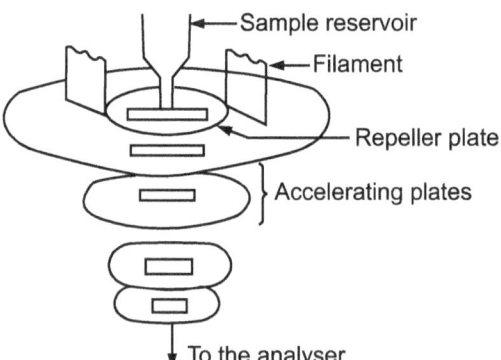

Fig. 26.2: Electron impact source of ions

Field ionization source (FI):

In field ionization, the molecules and atoms are ionized by evaporation over a potential barrier on the surface due to strong electric fields (10^8 V/cm). These strong electric fields are produced by using specially formed anodes of fine tungsten or other materials. The field ionization anode and cathode are arranged with a very fine gap (0.5–2 mm) which may serve as a slit. The gaseous sample introduced at the anode points where the electric field is concentrated. The ionization of the sample takes place by extraction of electrons from the sample by the micro-tips of the anode. In this process, fragmentation is less, leading to molecular ion as a major product which may be considered as advantage over EI process.

Chemical Ionization (CI):

The principle of chemical ionization is the use of ion molecule reactions. In this technique the gaseous sample is introduced into the ionization chamber at a pressure of 1 torr. The primary ionization of the sample is effected by impact with positive ions produced by electron impact method. Due to high pressure, the primary ions undergo ion-molecule reactions with the neutral molecules of the sample.

3. Mass Analyzer (Ion Separator):

Positive ions get accelerated at the end of the bombarding chamber by applying the acceleration potential (2–8 kV) between the accelerating plates. Some of the ions passé through slit and enter the magnetic field. As they enter the magnetic field, they get deflected in relation to their velocity, mass and charge. The lighter ions deflect more than the heavier. The mass analyzer should have the following characteristics:

(1) It should reduce the high ion current and

(2) It should have higher resolving power to distinguish very small masses. The mass analyzer is of two types:

(a) Single focusing analyzer with magnetic deflection and

(b) Double focusing analyzer with both electrostatic field and magnetic field.

(i) Single focusing magnetic deflection:

This is most widely used in mass spectrometer. It uses a permanent or electromagnet to sort the ions (Fig. 26.3). The separation of ions is based on the principle of velocity focusing means focusing of all ions of same mass and initial deflection but different velocities by employing successively electric and magnetic field. When the ions are accelerated by the electric field in the ion source they acquire the energy E given by the equation

$$E = eV$$

Where, e is the charge on the ion and V is the applied potential. When the ions are emerging out of ion source at that time the potential energy is converted into the kinetic energy represented by the equation

$$KE = \frac{1}{2} mv^2$$

Where m is the mass of the ion and v is the velocity.

$$\therefore \qquad eV = \frac{1}{2} mv^2$$

$$\therefore \qquad v^2 = \frac{2eV}{m} \qquad \qquad \dots (1)$$

When the ions enter the magnetic field (H) of the analyzer they assume circular path and are subjected to centripetal (magnetic) force of magnitude H.eV. At the equilibrium centripetal force will be equaled by the centrifugal force mV^2/r, where r is the radius of the circular path and H is the applied magnetic field strength.

$$\therefore \qquad \frac{mv^2}{r} = HeV$$

$$\therefore \qquad v^2 = \frac{Her}{m} \qquad\qquad ...(2)$$

Now by combining equations (1) and (2), we get

$$\frac{2eV}{m} = \left(\frac{Her}{m}\right)^2$$

$$\therefore \qquad \frac{m}{e} = \frac{H^2r^2}{2V} \qquad\qquad ...(3)$$

This is the fundamental equation for the single focusing mass spectrometer. From this equation we can see that the mass spectrum can be obtained by varying one of the three parameters H, r, and V while keeping the other two parameters constant. Since, in most of the mass spectrometers H and r are constant, m/e ratio is inversely proportional to accelerating voltage, so by suitable adjustment of voltage V any desired mass can be focused on exit slit.

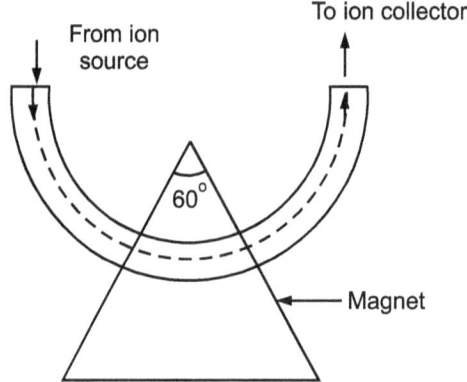

Fig. 26.3: Single focusing magnetic deflection mass spectrometer

(ii) Double focusing analyzer:

In single focusing mass analyzer, the separation of the ions is based on the assumption that all the ions enter the magnetic field with same kinetic energy. This means that all the ions with same mass to charge ratio possess same velocity. But in practice this is not true since the ions differ in their initial energy. Thus, single focusing analyzer fails to discriminate between small mass differences because of small variation in kinetic energy. To achieve better focusing, energy has to be reduced before ions are allowed to enter the magnetic field and increased resolving power can be obtained by using two mass analyzers in series.

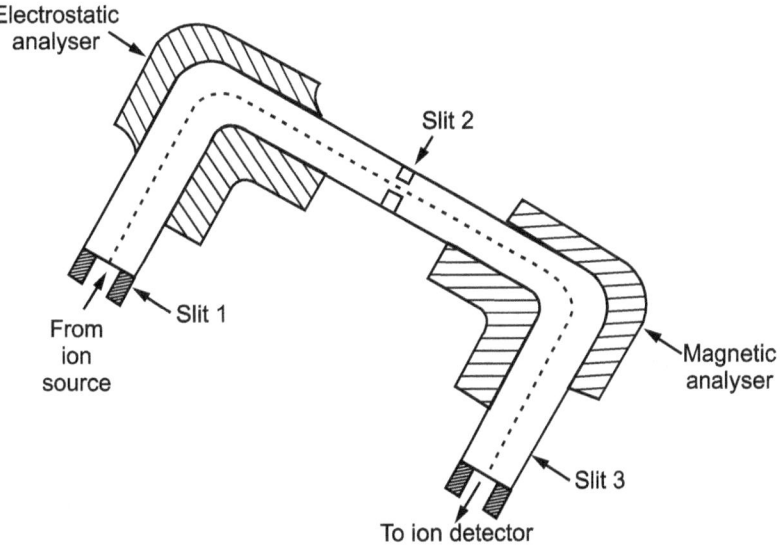

Fig. 26.4

In this mass analyzer, the beam of ions passes through electrostatic field which focuses the particles of same kinetic energy on slit 2 which then serves as a source for the magnetic analyzer. Then it goes to detector through slit 3.

The other devices used to sort the ions include cyclical focusing, time of flight analyzers and quadrupole analyzers.

Time of Flight Analyzers:

In this type of analyzer, the sorting of the ions is done in absence of magnetic field. It operates on the principle that, if the ions produced are supplied with equal energy and allowed to travel predetermined distance then they will acquire different velocities depending on their masses. In Bendix time of flight mass spectrometer (Fig. 26.5), a pulse of ions is produced in the ion source. An accelerating potential of the order of 2000 V is applied to a grid, in the form of a voltage pulse lasting μ sec or less and is repeated intermittently. This positive pulse accelerates the ions into a long field-free drift tube of about 1 meter, through which the ions move at their own velocities. Depending on the momentum, the ions reach the detector in the order of increasing mass.

In this instrument specially designed electron multiplier detector is used which consists of two glass plates coated with high resistance metallic film which acts as dynodes. The sorted ions get collected at the anode in order of their increasing mass. Time of flight spectrometers have resolution power of 500–600.

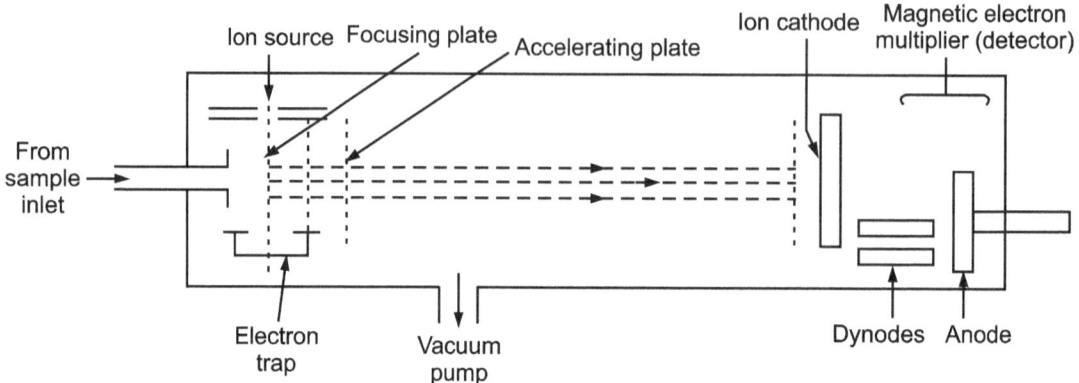

Fig. 26.5: Bendix time of flight mass spectrometer

Quadrupole Analyzers

In Quadrupole analyzers, the sorting of ions according to their m/e ratio is done without the need of magnetic field. The r_f field is used to modify the motion of the ions so that only those ions having a narrow range of velocities or masses can be detected.

4. Mass Detectors:

Three types of ion detectors are generally used in mass spectrometers, i.e. Faraday cup, an electron multiplier and the photographic plate detectors.

(a) Faraday cup collector:

It is a simple and least sensitive detector used in mass spectrometers where extreme sensitivity is not needed. It consists of an insulated conductor directly connected to an electrometer amplifier. Its cup shape reduces the chances of escape of secondary electrons liberated by the ion impact.

(b) Electron multiplier:

The operation of electron multiplier is similar to that of convention photomultiplier detector used in UV-visible spectrophotometer. It consists of the primary cathode optimized for the detection of ions rather than photons. The sensitivity of this detector is 1000 times greater than that of Faraday cup.

(c) Photographic detection:

This detector system is more sensitive than any other detector because the photoplate integrates the ion signal over a period of time. The photoplates are processed by the usual photographic techniques and read with the aid of densitometer. Photographic detection is used effectively for high resolution in double focusing spectrometers.

5. Vacuum system:

Since, the ions must travel a considerable distance through the magnetic field to the collector and also to avoid ion scattering and background, a very low pressure of the order 10^{-6}–10^{-7} mm of Hg must be maintained in the mass spectrometer. Loss of ions from the sample may take place due to collision with molecules of atmospheric gases resulting into superior result. Most of the vacuum systems use combination of mechanical and oil diffusion pumps to produce required vacuum.

RESOLUTION

The ability of mass spectrometer to separate the ions of different mass to charge ratio (m/e) reaching to the detector is described as its resolving power (resolution).

The resolution of mass spectrometer depends on two factors: mass dispersion and beam width at the focal plane. The two beams are said to be resolved when the beam dispersion is greater than the beam width. The dispersion of the mass analyzer is determined by its optics which cannot be changed. The beam width can be improved by reducing the width of the source and collector slits. Narrow slits give high resolution but an increase in the resolution is accomplished by a decrease in sensitivity of the mass spectrometer since the number of ions arriving at the collector is reduced by the use of narrow slit width.

The resolving power of a mass spectrometer necessary to separate two ions of mass M and M + Δ M giving adjacent peaks of approximately equal intensity is defined as

$$R = \frac{M}{DM}$$

Where,   ΔM = difference between the two mass numbers

The peaks are said to be resolved when the valley between them is less than a certain percentage of the peaks themselves. Generally, the resolution is expressed for a 2 per cent or 10 per cent valley. (Fig. 26.6)

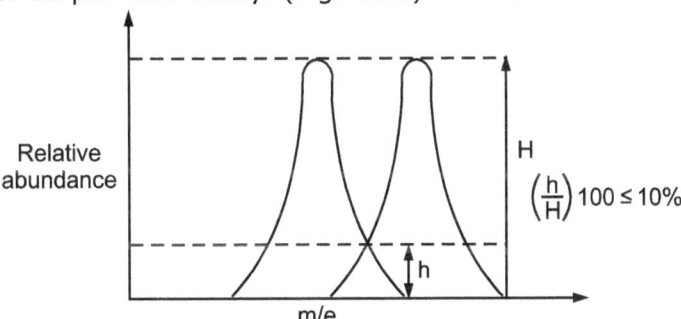

Fig. 26.6: Resolution of two ions with a 10% valley

Scanning of Mass Spectrum:

The sample is introduced into the ionization chamber very slowly to produce the positive ions. Then the accelerating voltage (V) is adjusted to the highest value (4000 V). At this time the ions with low m/e ratio will acquire the highest velocity and will be deflected by the magnet and finally recorded as a peak. The voltage V is then decreased progressively so that the ions with increasing m/e value will be brought into focus simultaneously. The scanning of mass spectrum is completed by decreasing the accelerating voltage slowly to zero.

MASS SPECTRUM

The mass spectrum of an organic compound is the plot of relative abundance or intensity on ordinate versus m/e ratio on abscissa. The most intense peak in the mass spectrum is the base peak and is given the value of 100 and the intensities of other peaks are expressed relative to this. The base peak in most of the cases is due to the molecular ion and is helpful in determining the molecular weight of the compound. Following are some examples of mass spectrum.

1. **Mass spectrum of methanol:**

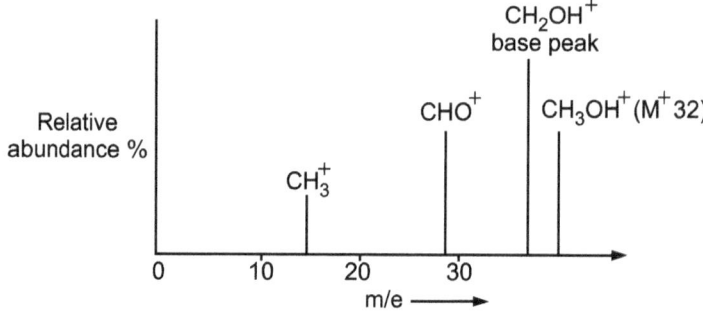

Fig. 26.7: Mass spectrum of methanol

$$CH_3\ OH + e^- \rightarrow \overset{+}{\underset{\cdot}{CH_3\ OH}} + 2\ e^-$$
$$m/e = 32$$

$$\overset{+}{\underset{\cdot}{CH_3\ OH}} \rightarrow CH_3^+ + \overset{\cdot}{OH}$$
$$m/e = 15$$

$$\overset{+}{\underset{\cdot}{CH_3\ OH}} \rightarrow CH_2\ OH^+ + \overset{\cdot}{H}$$
$$m/e = 31$$

$$\overset{+}{\underset{\cdot}{CH_2\ OH}} \rightarrow CHO^+ + H_2$$
$$m/e = 29$$

2. **Mass spectrum of n-butyl chloride:**

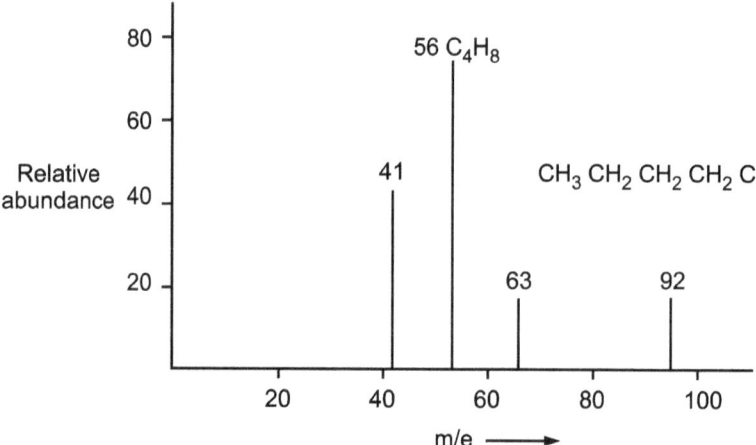

Fig. 26.8

3. Mass spectrum of ethyl benzene:

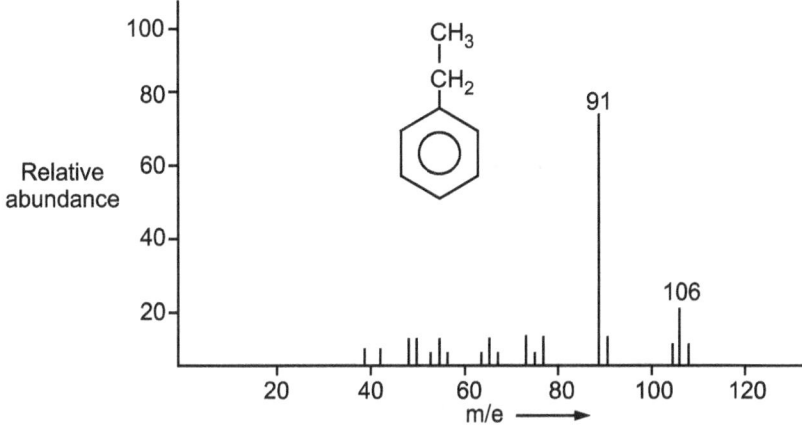

Fig. 26.9

TYPES OF IONS PRODUCED

The different types of ions are produced in the mass spectrometry, i.e. molecular ions, fragment ions, rearrangement ions, metastable ions, multiply charged ions, isotope ions and negative ions.

1. Molecular ion (Parent ions): If the electron beam energy is more than ionization potential electrons may be ejected from a lower lying molecular orbital leading to the formation of ions called molecular or parent ions.

$$M + e \rightarrow M^+ + 2e^-$$

Thus, molecular ions are formed in the ground state and in electronically excited states. The yield of molecular ions can be increased by increasing the electron beam energy.

The mass of such ions gives the molecular weight of the sample and also it is possible to determine molecular formula. The molecular ion patterns also give information regarding the number and nature of the types of atoms with characteristic isotope abundance present in the molecule. Hence, molecular ions are most important of all types of ions in mass spectrum. The molecular ion is located at high mass region of the mass spectrum.

The stability of the parent ion will determine its relative abundance with respect to the fragment ions. Its abundance can be increased by running the spectrum at low ionization energy. Aromatic compounds give rise to very intense molecular ion peak because of the presence of π-electron system. A molecular ion containing unsaturated functional groups will be more stable than that with saturated functional groups. In aliphatic compounds, branching results in the decrease in the abundance in the parent peak.

1. Fragment ion:

If the electron beam energy is further increased to the apparent potential of a molecule, then the excited molecular ions undergo decomposition to give rise to variety of fragment ions, which have smaller masses than the parent/molecular ion. The fragment ions are formed by both heterolysis and homolytic cleavage of bonds. They are formed by simple cleavage and rearrangement process. Bond dissociation energy stability of neutral fragments and steric factors are some of the major factors which determine formation of fragment ions, e.g. ethyl chloride.

$$CH_3\!-\!CH_2\!-\!Cl + e^- \longrightarrow CH_3\!-\!CH_2\!-\!Cl^+ + 2e^-$$

Parent ion

$$CH_3\!-\!CH_2\!-\!Cl^{+\bullet} \Big\langle \begin{array}{l} CH_3\!-\!CH_2^+\!-\!Cl^\bullet \\[4pt] CH_2\!-\!CH_2^+ + HCl \end{array}$$

Fragment ion

2. Rearrangement ions:

Fragment ions formed by the intramolecular rearrangements involving migration of hydrogen atoms from one part of the ion to another are called rearrangement ions. Rearrangement processes are common in unsaturated compounds and are favoured even at low electron voltage.

The most common type of rearrangement involves intramolecular migration of hydrogen in molecules containing heteroatom. The "McLafferty rearrangement" is a common example. It involves the migration of γ hydrogen followed by cleavage of β bond and leads to the elimination of a neutral molecule. Ketones, aldehydes, amines, substituted aromatic compounds, etc. show this type of Rearrangement, e.g. in case of carbonyl compound.

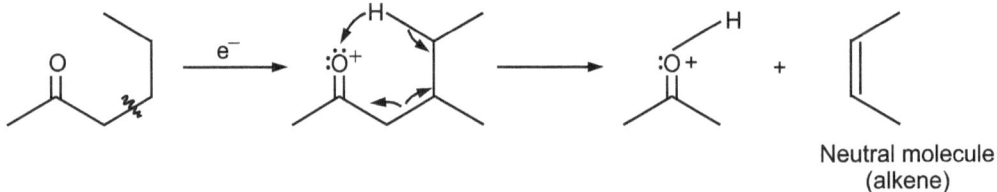

Neutral molecule
(alkene)

Fig. 26.10

3. Metastable ions:

Ions in mass spectrum usually produce sharp and well-defined peaks. However a mass spectrum occasionally shows some diffused, broad, low intensity peaks usually at non-integral masses. These peaks are due to metastable ions.

If the ion m, produced in the ion source is very stable, it remains undecomposed during its passage through the accelerator, deflector and to the detector. On the other hand, if m is very unstable, it immediately decomposes into smaller fragments in the ion source and each of the fragment ion is deflected and recorded separately according to its m/e ratio. However, when the ions of intermediate stability undergo fragmentation during or immediately after acceleration but prior to magnetic deflection, these ions will give rise to weak and diffused peaks at non-integral masses, called metastable peaks.

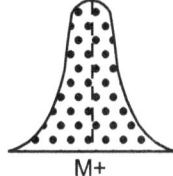 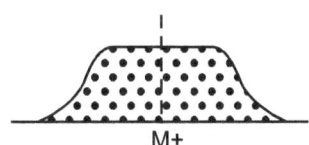 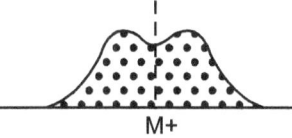

Fig. 26.11: Metastable peaks

A flat-top metastable peak shows that kinetic energy is released during the fragmentation process.

4. Multiple charged ions:

The removal of two or more electrons from a molecule without fragmentation is possible in case of organic compounds with aromatic rings and compounds containing conjugated systems. Thus, the ions may exist with two or three charges instead of the single charge. They are called double, triple or multicharged ions.

The double charged parent ions are formed by the loss of two electrons. They appear at half the mass of the molecular ion. A triple charged ion formed by the loss of three electrons from the neutral molecule and will occur at 1/3 of its actual mass since it carries three positive charges.

$$M + e^- \rightarrow M^{++} + 3e^-$$

$$M + e^- \rightarrow M^{+++} + 4e^-$$

Double charged ions are often helpful in confirming the molecular weight.

5. Isotope ions:

Most elements are mixture of two or more stable isotopes differing by one or two mass units. Chlorine and bromine have two isotopes (^{35}Cl, ^{37}Cl and ^{79}Br, ^{81}Br) in the ratios 3 : 1 and 1 : 1 respectively. Similarly elements like carbon, hydrogen, oxygen, sulphur, etc. have one major isotope which is more than 90 per cent abundant and a minor isotope. Fluorine, phosphorus and iodine are monoisotopic elements. The presence of these elements in a molecule is often recognised by the characteristic isotopic clusters observed in the spectrum. Thus in the spectrum of methyl bromide the molecular ion peak is a doublet consisting of two equally intense peaks one at m/e 94 ($CH_3\ ^{79}Br$) and the other at m/e 96 ($CH_3\ ^{81}Br$). These isotopic clusters are referred to as isotopic peaks. They are helpful in determining the presence of such elements in a molecule.

6. Negative ions:

Though in ionization process positive ions are produced, in few cases negative ions do get formed. This happens because of the capture of electron by a molecule during collision of molecules. These are not observed with the usual mass spectrometer unless some modifications are made. These are generally ignored during studies.

FRAGMENTATION PATTERNS

The molecular ion M^+ (usually highly unstable) unless stabilised by some structural features tends to fragment to produce an even-electron ion. Even electron ions are usually more stable than odd-electron ions because of the stabilising effect of electron pairing.

Generally, the molecular ion is represented with a delocalized charge. Dieresis's approach has been to localize the positive charge on either a π bond (except in conjugated system) or on a heteroatom, e.g. molecular ion produced from ketone.

$$R—\overset{\overset{\displaystyle O}{\|}}{C}—R' \quad \xrightarrow{e^-} \quad R—\overset{\overset{\displaystyle O^+}{\|}}{C}—R'$$

Molecular ion

A single-barbed fishhook (➡) designates the shift of a single electron. Cleavage of a bond requires the movement of two electrons. However, to prevent, clutter only one pair of fishhooks will be drawn. The probability of cleavage of a particular bond is related to the bond strength, to the possibility of low energy transitions and to the stability of the fragments both charged and uncharged formed in the fragmentation process. Knowledge of pyrolytic cleavage can be used, to some extent, to predict the likely modes of cleavage of molecular ion. Because of the extremely low vapour pressure in the mass spectrometer there are very few fragment collisions.

A number of general rules for predicting prominent peaks in electron impact spectra are recorded and can be summarized below:

1. Most compounds give molecular ion peak but a few do not. Existence of molecular ion peak in the spectrum is dependent on the stability of molecular ion. The order of decreasing stability of the molecular ions is: aromatic and heteroaromatic compounds > conjugated polyenes > alkenes > cycloalkanes > ketones > n-alkenes > ethers > esters > acids > alcohols > amines. Thus, molecular ions are usually very abundant in compounds that contain cyclic structures, double bonds and especially aromatic or heteroaromatic rings.

2. In case of alkanes, the relative intensity of the molecular ion peak is the greatest for the straight chain compounds but
   (a) The intensity decreases with increased degree of branching.
   (b) The intensity decreases with increasing molecular weight in a homologous series.

3. Cleavage is favoured at alkyl substituted carbons, the more substituted, the more likely is the cleavage. Hence, the tertiary carbonation is stabler than secondary, which in turn is stabler than primary. The cation stability order is $CH_3^+ < R–CH_2 < R_2\ CH^+ < R_3C^+$. Generally, the largest substituent at a branch is eliminated most readily as a radical, presumably because a long chain radical can achieve some stability by delocalization of the lone electrons.

$$R-\overset{|}{\underset{|}{C}}-\Big]^{+} \longrightarrow R^{\bullet} + -\overset{|}{\underset{|}{C}}-$$

4. In alkyl substituted ring compounds, cleavage is favoured at the bond β to the ring giving the resonance stabilized benzyl ion.

$m/e = 91$

5. Saturated rings containing side chain, lose the side chains at the α bond. The +ve charge tend to stay with ring fragment.

6. The cleavage of a C–X bond is more difficult than that of a C–C bond (X=O, N, S, F, Cl, etc). If occurred, the positive charge is carried by the carbon atom, and not to the heteroatom. The halogens having great electron affinity do not have tendency to carry the positive charge.

$$-\overset{|}{\underset{|}{C}}-\overset{|}{\underset{|}{C}}-X^{+} \longrightarrow -\overset{|}{\underset{|}{C}}-\overset{|}{\underset{|}{C}}{}^{+} + X^{\bullet}$$

e.g. $(R-CH_2-Br)^{+} \longrightarrow R-\overset{+}{C}H_2-Br^{\bullet}$

7. Double bonds favour allylic cleavage and give the resonance stabilized allylic carbonium ion.

e.g.

$$CH_2 \dagger : CH-CH_2-R \xrightarrow{-R'} \overset{+}{C}H_2-CH=CH_2$$

$$\overset{+}{C}H_2=CH=\overset{+}{C}H_2$$

8. Compounds containing a carbonyl group tend to break at this group with positive charge remaining with the carbonyl portion.

9. During fragmentation, small, stable neutral molecules, e.g. water, carbon monoxide, alcohol, ammonia, hydrogen sulphide, hydrogen cyanide, carbon dioxide, ethylene etc. are eliminated from appropriate ions.

e.g. $R-CH \overset{+}{\frown} CH_2 \longrightarrow R^{+} + CH_2=CH_2$

MCLAFFERTY REARRANGEMENT

This is the commonest type of rearrangement involving intramolecular rearrangement. A γ-hydrogen atom is transferred through six member transition state to an electron deficient centre followed by the cleavage of β-bond. The reaction results in the elimination of a neutral molecule. The charge is carried by the oxygen containing fragment unless additional substituents are present in the side chain which can stabilize the positive charge.

To undergo a McLafferty rearrangement, a molecule must possess:

1. A side chain containing at least three carbon atoms, the last bearing a γ-hydrogen atom and
2. An appropriately located heteroatom (e.g. O) and a π-system, usually a double bond which could be a carboxyl group or an olefinic double bond or an aromatic system.

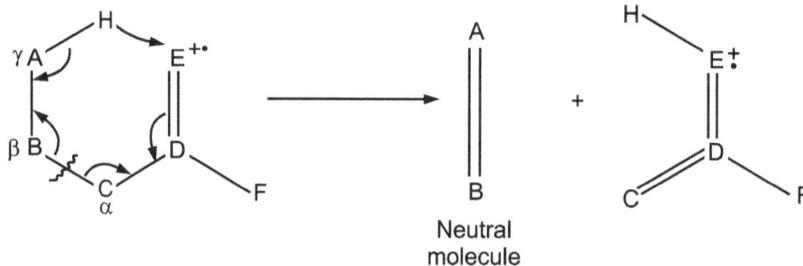

This type of fragmentation mode is exhibited in the case of carbonyl compounds (ketones), aldehydes, esters, amides, carboxylic acids, alkyl benzenes, phenyl ethanols etc.

INTERPRETATION OF MASS SPECTRA

The information needed is usually about the structure of the compound. Interpretation of mass spectra will provide a part of the information required. Following is a general approach.

1. Recognition of the molecular ion peak:

The mass spectrum should be first examined for the molecular ion peak wherefrom molecular weight and hence the molecular formula can be found. The abundance of the molecular ion peak indicates about its stability. The most stable molecular ions are those of purely aromatic systems.

2. Isotope effect:

Heavier isotopes give peaks at m + 1, m + 2, m + 4 etc. from the height of such peaks molecular weight can be determined. An increase in peak size relative to other peaks, as sample size is increased or the repelled voltage is decreased designates that peak as m + 1 and affords indirect identification of the molecular ion.

3. The "Nitrogen rule" is often useful in finding out molecular ions. It states that

(a) If the m/e is even for the parent ion; it contains even number (including zero) of nitrogen atoms. If m/e is odd, it contains odd number of nitrogen atoms.

(b) Fragmentation at a single bond gives an odd numbered fragment ion from an even numbered molecular ion and an even numbered ion fragment from an odd-numbered molecular ion.

Thus rule (a) gives number of nitrogen atoms present in the molecules and rule (b) gives number of nitrogen atoms present in different fragments.

4. Fragment ions

The various m/e values of various fragment ions are observed from graph and a tentative conclusion about the nature of fragment ion is made. Some examples are given below.

Peak at m/e value	Tentative fragment ion
29	CHO, C_2H_5
30	CH_2NH_2
31	CH_2OH, OCH_3
43	CH_3CO

5. Ring rule

This is used to calculate number of unsaturated centres. The number of unsaturated centres (R) is given by

$\quad$ R $=$ Number of rings + Number of double bonds + Twice the number of triple bonds

From above results, different molecular formulae are put forth and say X, Y, Z are three compounds having this molecular formula. Then using authentic samples of X, Y and Z their mass spectra are obtained and compared with the mass spectra of the sample under consideration and the final result about the given compound is drawn.

This is called as 'Finger print matching and is best done by computer matching of mass spectra of unknown with a spectrum from a library of known spectra.

APPLICATIONS OF MASS SPECTROMETRY

Mass spectrometry has several applications in analytical field. Some applications are given below:

1. Mass spectrum of a pure compound provides important information for identification by the help of molecular weight, molecular formula and by fragmentation pattern.

   Mass spectrometry is one of the best tools for the determination of molecular weight of a substance. When a substance is bombarded with moving electrons and its mass spectrum is recorded, the mass of the peak at the highest m/e reveals the molecular mass accurately. This helps in molecular weight determination. Similarly, one can find molecular formula of a compound.

2. Mass spectrometry is very useful for the preparation of pure isotopes, high polymers and natural products can be analysed by mass spectrometry.

3. Mass spectrometry can also be used to distinguish between cis and trans isomers. Since the stability of ions produced may differ for cis and trans ions significantly.

4. Mass spectrometry is also useful in study of free radicals, determination of bond strength, evaluation of heat of sublimation etc.

5. Mass spectrometry is extremely useful in analysis of closely related compounds like hydrocarbons, petroleum products, lubricating oils etc.

6. In inorganic trace analysis, mass spectrometry can be used for trace analysis of elements in alloys and minerals and in superconductors.

CHAPTER ... 27

SEPARATIONAL TECHNIQUES

INTRODUCTION

Importance of separational techniques has been recognised since the ancient times. Separation of active principle from a given material or a formulation received very much attention both from isolation and analysis point of view.

Ever since ancient times analyst or pharmacist have been confronted with a task of separation of a complex mixtures. The separation of active principles from the preparation like tinctures, extracts, pills or separation and isolation of vitamins, enzymes or hormones from their natural source had always been a tough task. Even now-a-days we find pharmaceutical preparations or formulations of very complex mixtures e.g. we find many formulations like tablets, capsules, other liquid oral preparations including parenteral preparations of multivitamins, antibiotic mixtures, analgesic-antipyretic formulations, hormonal preparations, expectorant-antitussives and many formulations containing more than one drug. Analysis of such preparations and detection of one constituent in presence of other may be easy in some cases but very difficult in other cases. There may be interference which might be competitive, partial or non-competitive nature.

It is thus necessary to separate the constituents of given mixture or formulation before an appropriate analytical method is applied. In order to achieve this one of the two methods are often adopted. These are (i) To remove interfering substance or (ii) To remove or isolate the active substance. Now depending upon the type of preparation, nature and amount of active material either of the above method is adopted e.g. in analysis of nicotinic acid tablets or tolbutamide tablets it is easier to remove the excepients by filtration from the tablet powder as impurity after dissolving the powder in appropriate solvent. In case of belladonna herb or extract it is easier to remove active substance (alkaloid) by isolation method.

In order to achieve separation, various methods are adopted depending upon the nature and amount of material. These methods are based on some principles of chemistry. Some simple methods used in separation are discussed below:

1. Crystallization:

If a given mixture is not of complex nature, then the material can be dissolved in suitable solvent, concentrated and left for crystallization. On cooling, crystals of single material or mixed crystals get separated out. This is filtered out. This method is only applicable when the solute is crystallizable. Further, other constituents and impurities should be as far as possible less in amount.

2. Filtration:

For simple formulations like tablets or capsules containing single active material, filtration method can be used as a separational method. The powder of tablet or from capsule can be dissolved for its active constituent in a suitable solvent either by shaking or warming and then the contents filtered through filtering media. The active material will pass into the filtrate and impurity will be left out on filtering media. This simple technique is routinely adopted in pharmaceutical analysis, e.g. assay of nicotine acid tablets or tolbutamide tablets etc.

3. Sublimation:

This separational method is adopted for those substances present in a mixture which can undergo sublimation. The preparations containing thymol, camphor, menthol or sulphur etc. can be subjected to sublimation for separation of these constituents. However, this method has limited applications as very few substances can undergo sublimation without decomposition.

4. Distillation:

This method is used in analytical chemistry for the separation of liquid from a given mixture. A liquid sample may be water miscible or immiscible, and having low or high boiling point. Depending upon the nature of liquid sample appropriate method of simple distillation or fractional distillation can be adopted. The analytical technique of the above distillation method is well illustrated and described in standard text books. This distillation method of separation is obviously possible only for the liquid type of constituent in a sample material.

5. Extraction:

Solubilizing the active constituent and removing it with a suitable extracting solvent is the most common technique followed in the field of analysis. The extraction method can be classified into two categories:

    (a) Solid-liquid extraction and

    (b) Liquid-liquid extraction.

In both the types, there are various methods and devices adopted for complete separation of one or more active constituents from a given mixture. These methods are of continuous or discontinuous or stepwise extraction type.

SOLID-LIQUID EXTRACTION

In solid-liquid extraction method, active constituent from solid material is extracted out by using suitable extracting solvent. Thus, this method is called solid-liquid extraction. For achieving extraction, different techniques are adopted such as maceration, percolation or a continuous extraction. These methods are mostly adopted for the isolation of active constituents from crude drugs. For continuous extraction, Soxhlet extraction apparatus is used (Fig. 27.1). It consists of three parts. A suitable size round bottom flask forms part A. Main body of the unit containing thimble for holding sample material is part B, while condenser forms part C. Solvent is placed in flask (A) and heated on water bath or hot plate. Vapours of solvent pass through side arm of the body to the condenser. On condensation, the droplets of solvent fall on the sample placed in thimble and extracts the constituents.

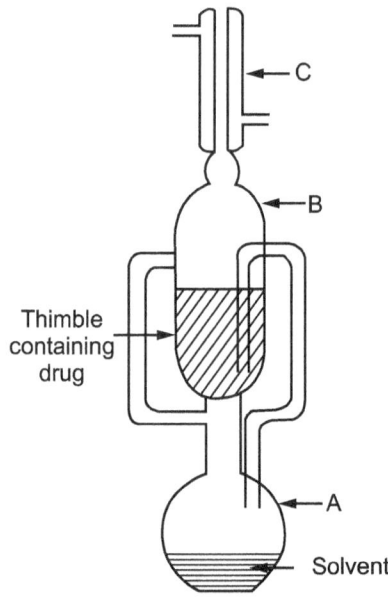

Fig. 27.1: Soxhlet apparatus

By siphon mechanism, the extracted material is passed to the flask. Thus, continuous extraction of material is accomplished using very less volume of extracting solvent.

LIQUID-LIQUID EXTRACTION

This is an important tool used in separation technique. It is based on Nernst law which states that "The ratio of activities of a solute species in pair of two immiscible liquids at an equilibrium is a constant".

According to law, if two immiscible solvents are in contact with each other and a solute or substance that is soluble in both solvents is added to it then the substance will distribute itself in both solvents in such a way that the ratio of concentration of two solutions is a constant. This phenomenon is referred as distribution coefficient or partition coefficient.

According to the law $\frac{C_u}{C_l}$ = K or K_d where 'C_u' refers to concentration in upper phase and 'C_l' as concentration in lower phase. K or K_d gives the ratio and is called distribution coefficient or partition coefficient.

In order to bring separation of solute using a pair of two immiscible liquids, a separating funnel is used (Fig 27.2). Two liquid phases (in equal amount) are placed in separating funnel and a solute whose partition coefficient is to be determined is added to it. The funnel is shaken to mix two phases intimately and then left on stand to separate the liquid phases. Since, the two liquids used are immiscible they separate on standing. In the process, extraction of solute is carried out. After removing the phases, content of solute in both phases is determined. The ratio of these gives distribution coefficient or partition coefficient.

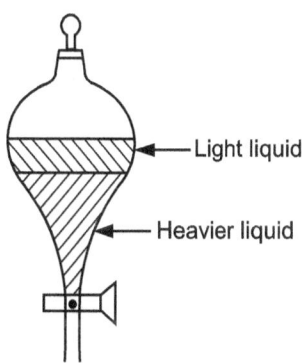

Fig. 27.2

If we consider 'p' as a fraction of solute in upper phase and 'q' as a fraction of solute in lower phase then the quantity 'p' is said to be as

$$p = \frac{\text{Amount of solute in upper phase}}{\text{Total amount of solute}}$$

Amount 'p' in upper phase can be calculated as p = $C_u \times V_u$ (where C_u is concentration in upper phase and V_u is volume in upper phase).

Total amount of solute = $C_u V_u + C_l V_l$. (where C_l is concentration in lower phase and V_l is volume in lower phase). If the ratio of volumes are designated as U = $\frac{V_u}{V_l}$.

Then fraction $$p = \frac{KU}{KU + 1}$$ Now since $p + q = 1$

The amount of $$q = \frac{1}{KU + 1}$$

In distribution coefficient or partition coefficient, the amount of volume of liquid phases used hold important factor. It is necessary either to use large volume of extracting solvent (for single extraction) or better to use small successive portions of extracting solvents to bring complete extraction. From the above it also makes clear that larger the partition coefficient, larger will be the solute found in upper phase (extracting solvent) after equilibrium.

The above discussion gives a mental picture that there is no molecular association, dissociation ionization, polymerization or any chemical reaction occurring between the solute and extracting solvents.

DISTRIBUTION RATIO

It is the ratio of concentration of all species of solute in each phase of solvent and it is denoted as D or K_d. This differs from distribution coefficient which gives ratio of undissociated or unionized solute in a pair of immiscible liquids. Many substances like weak acids get partially ionized in aqueous media. The pH of aqueous phase brings marked effect on the extraction of such acids.

Let us consider the distribution of benzoic acid (HB_z) between ether and water. As per distribution coefficient

$$K = \frac{[HB_z]_e}{[HB_z]_w}$$

Where the letter 'e' and 'w' as suffix refers to ether and water respectively. Now we know benzoic acid is poor water soluble solute but gets ionized in aqueous phase and $HB_z = H + B_z$.

Let K_a be the ionization constant, then as

$$K_a = \frac{[H]\,[B_z]}{[HB_z]}$$

The distribution ratio $$D \text{ or } K_d = \frac{[HB_z]_e}{[HB_z]_w + [B_z]_w}$$

The relationship with distribution coefficient K is given by

$$D \text{ or } K_d = \frac{K}{1 + Ka/[H]_w^+}$$

Thus, when $[H]_w^+ >> K_a$ then 'D' is equal to K or in other words if 'K' is large, more benzoic acid will be extracted into ether layer.

Furthermore, benzoic acid shows dimerization in benzene if it is used as extracting solvent. Benzoic acid forms dimmer through hydrogen bonding as

Or

$$2HB_z = HB_z \cdot HB_z$$

If we consider, b = benzene, w = water

Then $$K_d = \frac{[HB_z . HB_z]_b}{[HB_z]_w^2}$$

And $$\text{overall } D = \frac{[HB_z . HB_z]_b}{[HB_z]_w + [B_z]_w}$$

Thus, it becomes clear that distribution ratio D gives a ratio of total concentration of benzoic acid in organic layer to its concentration in aqueous layer.

For most practical considerations, distribution coefficient or partition coefficient is taken into account for separational purpose.

In the above discussion, we have considered distribution of a single solute in a pair of immiscible liquids. If more than one solute is present in a mixture, the distribution of both solutes in the same pair of liquid will follow the distribution law. Now the feasibility of their resolution or separation will be governed by "Separability factor β". This separation factor β is the ratio of K_1/K_2, where in K_1 refers to the distribution of solute 1 in a pair of equal volume of solvents, while K_2 refers to the distribution coefficient of solute 2 in the same pair of solvents. If the ratio turns into unity then the two substances cannot be separated out. Greater the deviation of β from unity, greater is the ease of separation.

Resolution of a mixture of solute containing more than two or three constituents will be possible only if the distribution coefficients of each constituent are distinctly different.

Factors influencing liquid-liquid extraction:

Number of factors affects the distribution coefficient of a solute. These can be utilized for affecting separation quantitatively and satisfactorily. Some factors having marked effect are as follows:

1. Choice of solvent:

Variety of solvents is available for extraction of a solute. These are *(a)* heavier or lighter than water *(b)* has high or low boiling point and *(c)* different vapour pressures. The choice of suitable solvent is governed by various factors. The extracting solvent should have

(i)   high distribution ratio for the solute,

(ii) low viscosity and sufficient density difference,

(iii) low toxicity and inflammability,

(iv) it should be cheap, easily available and should have easy recovery

Furthermore, distribution coefficient is greatly influenced by chemical nature of solute and other solvent. Thus, a solvent which gives highest partition coefficient should be preferred. Generally, solvent ether, chloroform, carbon tetrachloride, benzene, petroleum ether, ethylene dichloride etc. are used as extracting solvents in pharmaceutical analysis.

2. pH Effect:

This plays a very significant role in extraction process. In pharmaceutical field, it is generally observed that most drugs or substances are either weak acids or weak bases or their salts. Solubility characteristic of these substances largely depends upon their ionic form. It is known that neutral substances are soluble in non-polar solvents while ionized species are more soluble in polar solvents. These forms can be interchanged by adjusting pH of a medium. Utilizing this principle alkaloids from their preparation are isolated and extracted. After making the preparation alkaline, alkaloid from their salt form is converted into alkaloid base which is then extracted with organic solvent.

3. Salting effect:

In the extraction procedure, this phenomenon is widely adopted. If the salt concentration of aqueous phase is raised very high, then the solubility of non-electrolyte in aqueous phase will be reduced. This helps in having more effective extraction by organic solvent. The reduction of solubility by increasing the ionic strength is known as salting out effect.

In extraction of ephedrine from its salt the solution is made alkaline and then large quantity of sodium chloride is added to the aqueous phase. The ephedrine base is then extracted out using solvent ether.

TECHNIQUE FOR SOLVENT EXTRACTION

In industry and analytical field separation of constituents is carried out by employing solvent extraction techniques. The extraction may be accomplished by the following two processes:

1. Batch extraction:

This is a simple and widely used method. This method is applicable for a solute having large distribution ratio. In this method, solute is extracted from one layer of liquid by distributing it with a second immiscible liquid using separating funnel. For more effective and complete separation, many times extracting solvent is divided into portions and multiple extractions are carried out.

2. Continuous extraction:

This method of extraction is carried out when the distribution ratio is low. The method makes use of continuous flow of immiscible solvent through the solution to be extracted. Although distribution equilibrium is never reached during the time of contact, solute gets removed continuously by the passing or flowing solvent. For this method special type of continuous liquid-liquid extraction apparatus is used.

Continuous extraction apparatus are of two types:

(a) Extracting solvent lighter than sample solute

(b) Extracting solvent heavier than sample solution.

(a) Extraction of lighter type:

The apparatus employed is shown in Fig. 27.3. It consists of flask A, main body of the thimble B and condenser C. The size and dimensions of the apparatus vary depending upon the quantities to be used. A suitable extracting solvent (lighter than sample solution), i.e. ether is placed in flask A. It is connected to the body B which holds sample solution up to its half capacity. In this placed a glass tube having funnel shape opening at one end and a glass bulb with holes at other end. This body is then connected to the condenser. The solvent in flask is heated. Vapours of solvent pass into condenser, falling as droplets into the funnel type glass tube. The droplets escape through the bulb and being lighter passes through the sample solution. In the process, it extracts solute and gets accumulated on the top of sample solution. When sufficient quantity gets collected, it overflows back to the flask. This process is continued till complete extraction is effected.

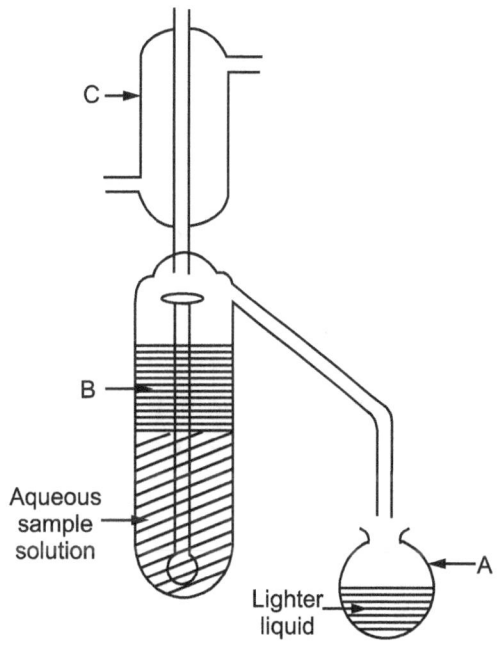

Fig. 27.3

(b) Extraction of heavier type:

This apparatus is similar to the former type but differs in design (Fig. 27.4). The extracting solvent (heavier than aqueous solution) is placed in flask A and heated. The vapours pass from side tube of the body of apparatus B to the condensers on cooling the droplets of solvent passed through sample solution and gets accumulated at the bottom of the body of the apparatus wherefrom it overflows into the flask. This achieves complete extraction.

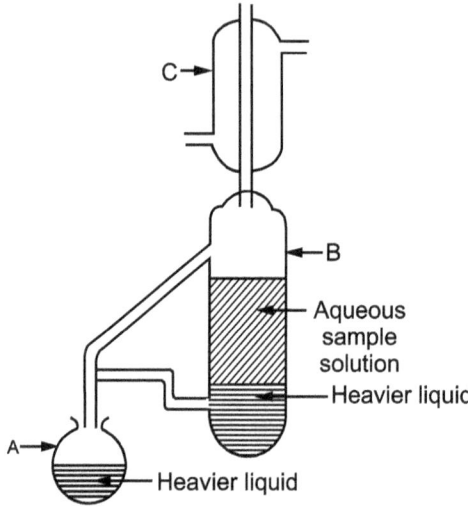

Fig. 27.4

COUNTER CURRENT DISTRIBUTION

Liquid-liquid extraction method is commonly used to separate constituents by employing separating funnels. If a mixture contains two or more substances having similar distribution coefficients then more extractions using large number of separating funnels will be required. This process is very inconvenient and modifications are needed for effective separation. One of such modified methods is a Counter Current Distribution (CCD).

It is a refinement of basic liquid-liquid extraction which permits separation of substances with very similar distribution behaviour effectively. The term counter current means that two phases move in opposite direction, i.e. in counter current fashion.

PRINCIPLE OF SEPARATION

For distribution of single solute between two immiscible liquids, the fraction 'p' getting transferred into upper phase is a function of partition coefficient 'K' and ratio 'U' of upper phase to lower phase as $p = \dfrac{KU}{KU + 1}$ and the fraction 'q' is given by

$$q = \frac{1}{KU + 1} \text{ as } p + q = 1$$

For effective separation, greater the value of K, the larger is the portion of p solute that will pass in the upper phase (i.e. extracting solvent).

Now in order to achieve multiple extractions simultaneously a special apparatus is used. Lyman Craig has developed a machine that performs multiple extraction of each phase by opposite phase semi-automatically. The apparatus is called as 'Craig apparatus' and that is the basic unit of counter current distribution technique.

Craig Apparatus

The apparatus consists of series of special type of separatory tube so connected that the outlet of one tube flows into the inlet of the next tube. The size and shape of the tubes vary depending upon the volume of liquid phases to be handled. The tube, known as upper and lower are identical in size and are so connected that they can hold liquid phases and allow transfer of lighter (upper) phase liquid to flow into the other tubes (Fig. 27.5).

In the operation sample is introduced in lower tube number one in fixed volume of lower phase liquid. Similarly, other lower tubes are charged with fixed same volume of lower phase liquid. Now upper tubes are also filled with equal volume of upper phase (extracting) liquid. The upper tubes are connected with next number of lower tubes and the assembly is rocked back and forth at an angle of $45°$ around pivot P. After equilibrium has been achieved the assembly is rotated at $90°$ and upper phase solvent is passed into next tubes holding lower phase liquid. Such shaking and equilibration is carried out many a time till separation is effected. Hundreds of such assemblies are mounted side by side and all rocked and rotated simultaneously by a motor timed to operate as directed.

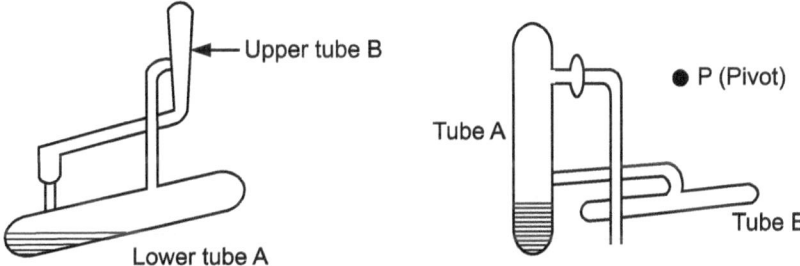

Fig. 27.5

Suppose, we want to distribute a solute with distribution coefficient K = 1 in equal volume of upper phase and lower phase. To start the operation, we introduce say 64 mg of the sample in the tube number 0 of lower tube. This tube is connected to tube number 1 of the upper holding extracting (upper phase) solvent. After equilibration (shaking and separating) one-half of the solute will be in upper phase and one half will remain in the lower phase. The upper phase of the tube 1 is transferred to tube 1 of lower and to the tube 0 a fresh change of upper phase liquid from tube 2 is added. After equilibration and transfer, the quantities get transferred as shown in Fig. 27.6.

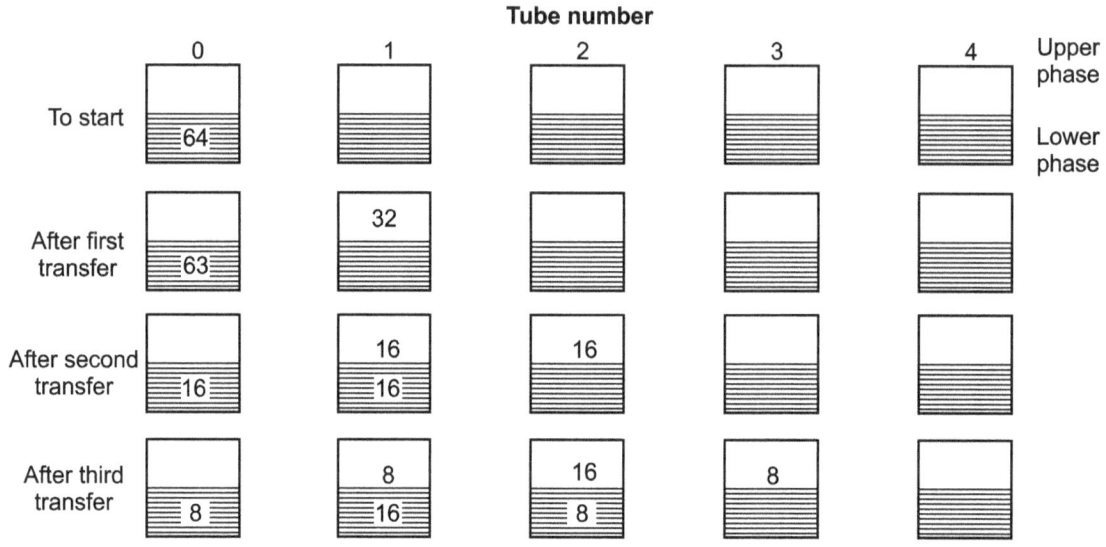

Fig. 27.6

The distribution of solute proceeds as shown above. The above pattern is a simplified process for a single solute. For a mixture containing two or more solutes with different distribution coefficients, separation proceeds on the similar lines and solutes having large partition (distribution) coefficient progress fast through the transfers. This process thus allows effective separation of a mixture.

✱✱✱

CHAPTER ... 28

THERMO-ANALYTICAL METHODS

INTRODUCTION

Amongst various analytical methods, which have gained importance, thermo-analytical methods occupy a prominent position. There are many analytical methods wherein use of thermal coefficient is involved. However, they do not provide analytical information. The thermo-analytical methods involve measurement of some property of the system as a function of temperature. There are various methods under this category like,

1. Thermo-Gravimetric Analysis (TGA)
2. Derivative thermo-gravimetric Analysis (DTG)
3. Differential Thermal Analysis (DTA) and
4. Thermometric Titrations (TT)

Table 28.1 gives the classification of Thermo-analytical methods.

Table 28.1: Classification of thermo-analytical methods

Name	Property measured	Apparatus involved
1. Thermo-gravimetric analysis	Change in weight	thermo-balance
2. Derivative thermo-gravimetric analysis	Rate of exchange of weight	thermo-balance
3. Differential thermal analysis	Heat absorbed or evolved	DTA apparatus
4. Thermometric titrations	Change in temperature	Titration colorimeter

In thermo-analytical methods the data is obtained in the form of continuously recorded curves, known as thermal data.

THERMO-GRAVIMETRIC ANALYSIS (TGA)

In gravimetric analysis, ignition or heating of a precipitate or residue is carried out on a burner or in an oven at a fixed temperature generally around 100–120°C. In this method, no cognizance is taken of the temperature of the flame. This method, though satisfactory in determining the final change at the highest temperature, does not give any idea of the intermediates formed or obtained at the varying temperature of flame. With the advancement in modern recording thermo-balance it is now possible to obtain records at varying temperature during heating. Thus, this technique is concerned with recording of change in weight of a sample or system with increasing change of temperature at a predetermined and linear rate. The thermo-gravimetric balances developed by P. Chevenard and Duval have been, now-a-days extensively used in thermo-gravimetric analysis.

Principle and the method

This can be illustrated by taking a hypothetical compound XCO_3 $2H_2O$ and heating it in a linearly programmed furnace and recording the loss in weight by thermo-balance. When the loss in weight versus increasing temperature is recorded, a graph is obtained as shown in Fig. 28.1.

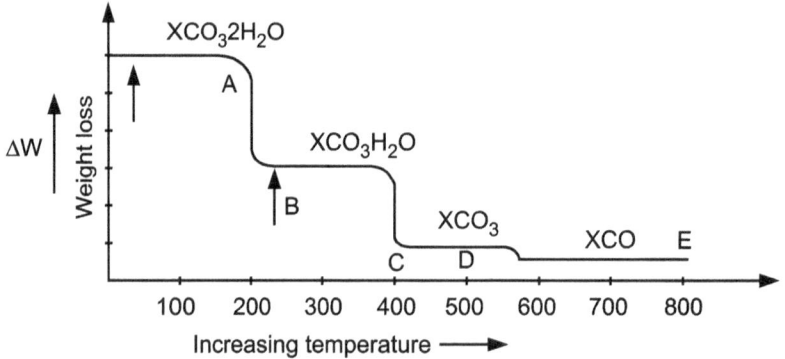

Fig. 28.1

From the graph it will be evident that at A one molecule of water is evolved out. A break will be obtained at B due to loss of another water molecule and reaching to constant weight at C that of anhydrous X CO_3. Weight loss is negligible during C–D as compound is in anhydrous carbonate form. At point D, the compound X CO_3 begins to decompose, giving out CO_2 and forming oxide XO. The D–E conversion of XCO_3 to X–O which remains constant till further decomposition of X–O into metallic X is obtained.

The thermal stabilities of the original sample, intermediate compounds as well as the final products can be known by the examination of the various regions in the graph. Quantitative analysis can be made to determine the stoichiometric of the compound at any assigned temperature.

In thermo-gravimetric curve, the plateau is indicative of constant weight, represent stable phase over the particular temperature interval. The sharp curve or inflection indicates the change occurring in compound by the temperature alteration. This may occur due to formation of intermediate compound or absorption or loss of some volatile matter from the solid phase.

In the thermo-gravimetric analysis the curve recorded or obtained depends upon the various factors such as (a) The rate of heating, (b) The nature or type of crucible or furnace, (c) The atmosphere, and (d) The nature of sample.

It has been observed that in some samples the extent of decomposition is greater at slow rate of heating than for similar sample at a faster rate. The nature and type of furnace or crucible may affect the rate of evolved volatile matter to escape at differently. The nature of reaction, depending upon whether exothermic or endothermic, also affects the rate and the nature of sample. Finely divided sample is preferable in analysis for satisfactory results.

Instrumentation:

In thermo-gravimetric analysis, the sample under study is continuously weighed during its heating programme, using a thermo-balance. The data is recorded either manually or better by using automatic recorder. Two techniques of analysis are generally adopted.

(i) **Dynamic TGA:** In this type the sample is subjected to a continuous increase in temperature linear with time.

(ii) **Isothermal TGA:** In this methodology, the sample is maintained at a constant temperature for a given time during which its weight is recorded. Temperature is increased, maintained for fixed time and sample weighed again.

The essential feature of instrumentation consists of the following components:

1. Thermo-balance
2. Sample holder
3. Furnace
4. Programmer device and
5. Recording device.

Thermo-balance: This is the most important part of the instrument. Accuracy, reproducibility, sensitivity, toughness, etc. are some important features of thermo-balance. Generally, balance should have the following characteristics:

1. It could cover wide range of temperature.
2. It should have high degree of mechanical rigidity and electronic stability.
3. Temperature recording should be within ± 1°C.
4. It should be capable of recording changes in weight rapidly, accurately and continuously as a function of temperature and time.
5. The heating rate should be linear in temperature range. A schematic line diagram of modern thermo-balance is shown in Fig. 28.2.

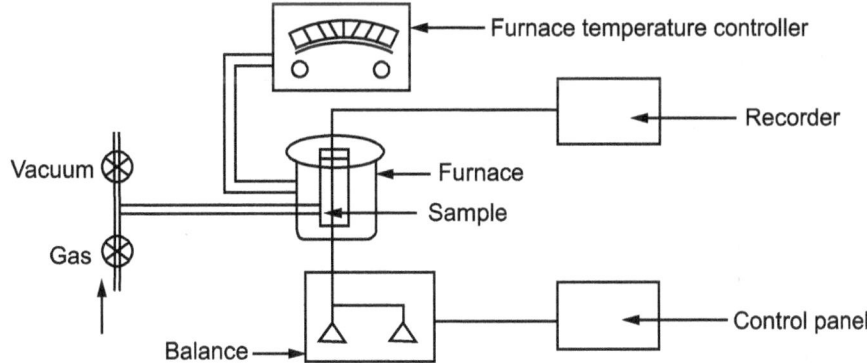

Fig. 28.2

(i) Recording thermo-balances are of:

1. Deflection type or
2. Null type.

In deflection type they are:

(a) Beam type: In which conversion of beam deflection is recorded as a signal on photographic recorder or measuring device.

(b) Helical type: These involve use of spring which contracts or elongates as a result of weight changes during heating.

The Null point balances are most common. In this, a sensor is employed to detect deviation of beam from a null point. Opposite force of electrical/mechanical is supplied to the balance beam to restore null position. The opposing force is calibrated to the weight change which is recorded directly.

(ii) Sample holders:

This is most important in accurate thermo-gravimetric analysis. Depending upon the nature of sample, its weight and quantity to be handled, crucibles of different size and shape are employed. These are constructed from various materials like glass, quartz, aluminium, stainless steel, platinum etc. These generally are of two types:

(a) Shallow pan for holding samples which eliminates gas, vapours or volatile matter by diffusion during heating or,

(b) Deep crucible for general purpose.

(iii) Furnace:

These are made from high quality metal and vary in shape and size. These are so made that sample can be easily introduced. Temperature of furnace is maintained between 1000°-2000°C by temperature control panel. Both linear and fixed temperature heatings are maintained by the use of thermocouples like chrome - alumel, copper - platinum, platinum - rhodium. For higher temperature tungsten or rhenium thermocouples are used.

(iv) Furnace temperature programmer:

These are the controllers which can provide gradual rise of temperature at a fixed rate. This device has a course and fine control knobs through which desired temperature with respect to rate/time can be obtained. This controlling is done by increasing voltage through the heated element by motor driven variable transformer or by different thermocouples.

(v) Recorder:

These are of common type having strip and pen mechanism. Electrical supply duly amplified is fed to recorder chart. The speed of recorder is variable and adjusted according to the use.

Factors Affecting Thermo-gravimetric Results:

The two important factors affecting the results are:

1. Instrumental factors and
2. Characteristics of sample.

1. Instrumental factors:

These include various aspects of instruments like furnace heating (its temperature and rate), recording of changes on chart (its speed), furnace atmosphere (its rate of cooling and maintaining temperature), sample holder and its geometry and the sensitivity of balance.

It is observed that if a substance is allowed to heat at fast heating rate the decomposition temperature will be higher than at slower heating rate. In case of heating of calcium carbonate the decomposition takes place at higher temperature if it is carried out in atmosphere of CO_2 than nitrogen. It is known that the temperature, rate of heating of furnace and furnace atmosphere affects results.

The geometry of sample holder i.e. flat disks or deep crucibles also affect results. A shallow dish gives rapid exchanges of gases and volatile matter from sample to surrounding atmosphere in furnace.

2. Characteristics of Sample:

The important factors about the sample are: (a) weight of sample, (b) particle size of sample (c) nature of evolved gas or volatile matter, (d) thermal conductivity of sample, and (e) the heat of decomposition of the reaction.

The method of preparation of sample and the sample packing in the sample holder also affects the TG curves. Thus, the thermo-gravimetric curve obtained for sample of magnesium hydroxide from natural source and from precipitation method shows different temperatures of decomposition.

DERIVATIVE THERMO-GRAVIMETRIC ANALYSIS

This is a thermo-analytical method (Gravimetric) which measures the rate of change of weight in thermo-balance with the temperature. This method has an advantage of being able to identify and analyse sample mixture. The commercial instruments record the curve to take derivative automatically.

Fig. 28.3 shows the TGA and DTG curves for the pyrolysis of mixture containing calcium and magnesium carbonates. This figure shows plateau in temperature at 700 but shoulder at about 850 in DTG graph. This method has advantage in (a) Testing purity of sample (b) Study of organic compounds, (c) Setting of suitable standards for compounds, and (d) Analysis of complex material etc.

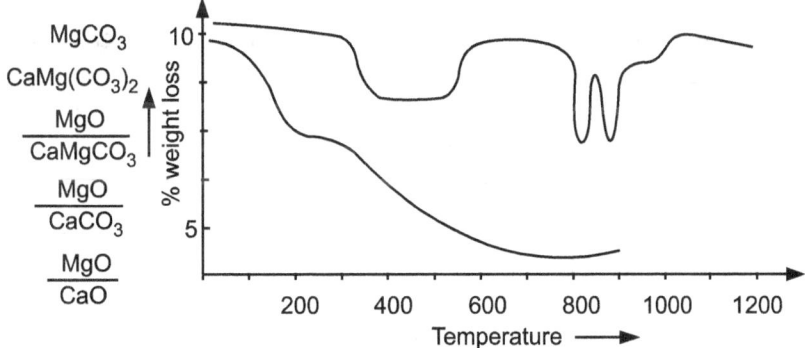

Fig. 28.3

DIFFERENTIAL THERMAL ANALYSIS (DTA)

This is a comparison method and is based upon the principle that the thermal effects associated with the physical and chemical changes are measured by differential method in which the heating temperature of sample is continuously compared with the temperature of inert (reference) standard. The difference in temperature (ΔT) is recorded as a function of reference material temperature or time.

This is illustrated in Fig. 28.4.

This is explained by taking example of sample material being heated in a furnace, the temperature of which is increased at linear rate. Simultaneously, a reference inert sample such as aluminium oxide is heated in the same furnace. The temperature difference between sample and reference material is continuously measured against furnace temperature.

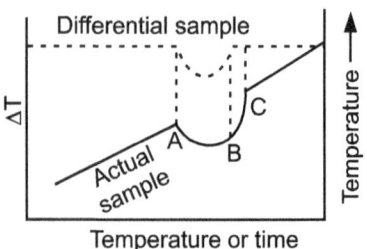

Fig. 28.4

The graph shows two lines of actual sample temperature (–) and differential temperature (- - -). In the graph of actual sample temperature at point 'A' the sample is assumed to undergo some endothermic reaction and does not show linearity with time (lag effect) to point 'B', after which sample temperature increases and becomes equal to the furnace temperature at C. Thus during heating, transition begins at 'A' both for sample and reference material and completes at 'C', the peak ABC is maximum at 'B' is obtained and is a differential temperature curve. Beyond 'B' curve returns to base line as AT = 0. For exothermic transition the curve will be in opposite inverted position.

This technique is useful in studying the thermal effects be endothermic or exothermic caused by physical phenomena such as fusion, crystal form, boiling; vaporization, sublimation, etc. and of chemical reactions involving dissociation, decomposition, oxidation, dehydration, displacement, etc. Chemical nature and identification of substance can be done by the information obtained from these studies.

THERMOMETRIC TITRATION

The thermometric titrations are also called enthalpy titrations. Many chemical reactions are accompanied by heat and if the course of a reaction is followed by observing heat changes during titrations, enthalpy titrations can be performed. Thus in thermometric titrations changes in heat of reaction are plotted by recording changes in solution temperature against the volume of titrant added.

In experiment, solution of sample material is placed in thermally insulated beaker and titrant is added continuously or in fixed increments from thermostated burette. Changes in temperature of sample are measured by accurately calibrated thermometer or thermocouple. A sharp break in the curve indicates the end point.

The thermometric titrations have successfully been applied to neutralization reactions of acid/base (like NaOH *vs*. HCl, phosphoric acid *vs*. NaOH, boric acid *vs*. NaOH etc.), Complexation like (Mg, Ca *vs*. EDTA), Redox (Ferrous *vs*. ceric, chromate, H_2O_2 *vs*. ceric, oxalic *vs*. permanganate) and precipitation (Ag *vs*. HCl, $CaCl_2$ *vs*. oxalate) titrations.

Thermometric titrations using various solvents like acetic acid, carbon tetrachloride, benzene, etc. have also been successfully carried out.

INDEX

***

www.ingramcontent.com/pod-product-compliance
Lightning Source LLC
Chambersburg PA
CBHW081145020726
47504CB00009B/2007